RELATIVE MALICE

MARLA MADISON

This novel in no way attempts to duplicate the police procedures or actual police departments in Eau Claire, Wisconsin or any other cities mentioned in the story. Any discrepancies in procedure, locations, or fact, may be attributed to the author's creativity.

Acknowledgments

I would like to thank the members of my writer's group whose support and instruction has been invaluable. Donna Glaser, Helen Block, Marjorie Doering, and Dave Tindell, you've helped me accomplish this second novel despite all the pitfalls along the way.

Thanks to Terry Lee, my significant other, for understanding the time it takes to write a novel, and supporting my efforts. A special thank you to my dear pets, Skygge and Poncho, for being faithful companions during the writing process.

Interested readers, please contact me at mam887@gmail.com or on my blog at marlamadison.blogspot.com. I would love to hear from you. All emails will be answered as soon as possible.

1

Friday, 11:45 pm

Wakened by strange noises, ten-month-old Philly Glausson raised her head of blonde curls. She rolled to a sitting position in her crib and wrinkled her small face, preparing for a howl. Distracted by sounds she didn't understand, the child pulled herself over the railing of the crib and slid easily to the floor as she'd done many times before to the dismay of her anxious mother. Crawling to a playhouse in the corner of the room, she took refuge inside its canvas walls and curled up with her favorite pink blanket pressed against her cheek.

Less than an hour from the first sounds of intrusion, the Glausson home was silent. A bitter draft of late November air from an open patio door chilled the rooms, congealing pools of blood on the polished wood floors.

The lifeless bodies of the family, Chelsea and Mark Glausson, their seventeen-year-old daughter Sienna, and three-year-old son Evan, lay like ragdolls tossed aside by a neglectful child. Their lifeless forms would remain in place, limbs stiffening, souls drifting to another plane of existence as their bodies awaited discovery.

The crib—and the playhouse—were empty.

Saturday, 10:00 am

Detectives Hank Whitehouse and Kendall Halsrud moved through the macabre scene in the kitchen of the Glausson house, where the bodies of an adult male and female lay on the floor, shot in the head. Whitehouse unpeeled a foil-wrapped candy and shoved it into his mouth, as he was prone to do when stressed, never mind the gore. A crime scene capable of stressing even the most seasoned law enforcement officer, CSU had already marked an area where one of the first responders had lost his breakfast.

Kendall moved away from her partner. She'd seen death many times during her career in law enforcement, but never anything like this. With a population of 100,000, Eau Claire, Wisconsin had its share of murders, although most of them tended to be drug-related or the result of domestic disturbances.

Her stomach tolerated the scene, but the extent of the violence made her want to cry out in anger. She left the carnage in the kitchen to look over the family photos adorning a wall of the family room that held the bodies of the two Glausson children, Sienna and Evan. The family looked happy in the pictures, smiling and loving, Mark Glausson's long arms embracing his attractive wife. He'd been a tall man with angular features, brown eyes, and a smile so warm it emanated out from the silver frame.

In another shot, surrounded by football players, the teenage daughter posed wearing a red-and-white cheerleader outfit; a beautiful girl with hair a cascade of silky auburn tresses. The image of a perfect teenage princess, Sienna Glausson was the adored and popular kind of girl that Kendall, with her tall, rangy body and dull, sandy hair, had envied in high school.

Kendall took a deep breath and turned back to the room, ready to examine the visage of death spread out before her. Sienna lay on the ginger brown carpet, her lovely hair stringy with gore, her penguin-trimmed flannel pants lying next to her naked lower body. A white lacy bra dangling from her shoulders had been sliced open at the front, as had the oversized T-shirt she'd been wearing. Brown eyes stared vacantly at the ceiling, her gamine features frozen in a mask of terror, a bullet hole on the left side of her forehead. Sienna's death, appearing to have been accompanied by sexual torture, had to be the worst of the four.

Across the room, her younger brother had been shot neatly in the forehead, like the bodies of the parents.

"Fucking nightmare," Whitehouse growled. "Who does this kind of shit?"

Kendall held her tongue; she'd learned to let her partner vent once he started swearing. More than twenty years her senior, he was within months of retirement. Her superiors told her she'd been partnered with Whitehouse so she could learn from his many years of experience, but realistically she knew he'd been the only one willing to work with a new woman. So far, their pairing was working. They'd established a cooperative, albeit temporary, bond.

"The daughter's the only one they messed with other than shooting them. Do you think it's possible she was the reason for all this?" she asked.

"Too soon to tell." Whitehouse pulled off his gloves and ran stubby fingers over his sparse, gray hair. "This is the worst break-in I've ever seen. Too bad it didn't happen six blocks over, in Chippewa's territory."

Kendall wouldn't admit to her partner she felt exhilarated to be a part of an investigation of such magnitude. The street, blocked off after the discovery, would soon fill with official vehicles from all branches of law enforcement. Media vans would fight their way in, reporters demanding a statement. A rookie detective of ten months, Kendall's excitement overrode her horror.

She nodded toward the fireplace, where a portrait of Chelsea Glausson smiled charmingly down on them, her glossy red hair fluffed like a fallen halo around her soft, ivory complexion. "Don't you think it's strange that the daughter was raped and not the mother? Mrs. Glausson was an attractive woman."

Whitehouse, typically a man of few words, shrugged his shoulders. "Looks like they came in through the back, found Mom and Dad in the kitchen, and hit them first. Had to silence them both fast, they didn't have time to rape her. Must have used some kind of silencer—it doesn't look like the kids tried to run out. They must have been in here watching TV."

A giant flat screen, still tuned to HBO, had the sound muted. The rooms weren't in serious disarray, but drawers and cupboards stood open. They'd have to establish what, if anything, had been taken.

Someone must have refastened the patio doors that had been standing open when they arrived. As the rooms warmed, the blood softened, and its coppery scent reached Kendall's nostrils. She bent over the boy, hesitant to touch his small body even with her gloved hands. It looked like his only injury was the bullet hole in his forehead, a tidy death compared to that of his sister.

Whitehouse asked, "Do we know if anything was taken?"

Kendall flipped open her notebook, where she'd jotted down the little information she'd received from the officers who'd found the bodies.

"Not yet. The nanny found them. The EMTs treated her for

shock and took her to the hospital. She'll be familiar with the house; she cleaned for them, too, and said she'd know if anything was missing. We'll take her through the house again later when the bodies are gone and she's had a chance to calm down. She did say the family didn't have a lot of relatives."

"What do we know about the family?"

"According to what they got from the nanny, they were close, didn't go out a lot, and didn't entertain. Mark Glausson, the husband, was a doctor at Luther-Midelfort and worked in the ER. Mrs. Glausson worked from home for a local furniture store. Just a normal family."

Whitehouse hmphed. "Like there is such a thing."

A short, bespectacled CSU tech swathed in white protective gear came down the steps from the upper floor and approached them. "Bad news. They had another kid—an infant. There's an empty crib upstairs, some blood on the floor, but no baby."

The senior detective's face reddened. "Jesus Christ! They killed a baby and took the body? How fucking sick is that?" He pulled out a freshly ironed handkerchief and wiped his brow before digging in his pocket for a lint-covered roll of candy.

"It might not be the baby's blood on the floor—maybe the child wasn't even here tonight," Kendall said. "She could be with a relative or a friend of the family." She hadn't noticed any typical baby paraphernalia or photos of the child around the house. Not impossible the baby might not have been in the house to begin with, but it could be wishful thinking.

"Sure. The kid was out with friends," Hank added snidely, as the tech turned to go back upstairs.

Kendall, used to her partner's sarcasm, ignored the jab. "You referred to the perp as 'they.' It could have been just one assailant."

Whitehouse hmphed again and left the room, headed for the upper level.

Was the baby dead? If so, where was its body? Did the killers take the child with them? The first responders said they'd searched the house when they came in, so it wasn't as if they might still find the baby—or its body—in the house. Kendall couldn't imagine perps sick enough to take a tiny child's body with them, much less voice it aloud.

She'd never seen or heard of a case this strange. Not in northwestern Wisconsin, anyway. She turned back to the photos, wondering once more why none of them featured the baby. In the early years, parents usually covered the house with baby pictures. But the baby would have been the Glaussons' third child. Photos diminished with subsequent children; maybe that was the easy answer.

Waiting for the medical examiner to arrive, they continued their search of the house. They avoided the baby's room with its blood evidence, leaving it as pristine as possible for the ME. In a room obviously used as an office by both adults, Kendall picked up another photo of Mark Glausson. His ruggedly handsome face appealed to her. Why didn't she ever meet anyone like him? She returned the photo to its spot on the desk, thinking that even if she did, he'd most likely be attracted to women like Mark Glausson's wife: perky, petite, and feminine. He wouldn't have given a second glance to a woman like Kendall, with her tall, rangy body, mousy hair, and tough demeanor.

The medical examiner came and went, adding nothing new to what they'd already gleaned from the scene. He speculated the time of death at sometime around midnight, a fact Whitehouse had guessed at long before the ME had arrived on the scene. Kendall knew it could be weeks before they got test results back from the state lab. They'd have a lot to do until then. First, they needed to establish whether the murders had been done by someone with an ax to grind with the family for some reason or if they were a random act by strangers. Less likely, but still necessary to consider, had Sienna Glausson been the primary target?

Kendall and Whitehouse planned their investigation schedule before leaving the house: the uniforms would do the door-to-door questioning; the techs would comb the woods behind the house. The two detectives would go back to the office to call the Glaussons' relatives and interview friends of the family. They planned to meet the nanny back at the house for a more detailed walk-through the next day. So far, cash and credit cards from purses and wallets were the only items obviously missing.

When the CSU techs were on their way out, the short one came over to them and placed a large, plastic container at their feet. "Present for you. Too bad it can't talk. You'll have to call Animal Control." He left the room before they could protest.

Hank picked up the carrier and looked inside its mesh door. "Crap. A cat. I hate cats. We won't get Animal Control out here this late on a Saturday afternoon." When Kendall didn't offer to deal with the animal, he dropped the carrier, letting it clatter to the floor. "I'll toss it in the river on my way home," he threatened

Kendall wouldn't put it past him. She squatted, peering into the carrier. A large, white cat with a round, gray spot centered between its eyes and nose cowered wide-eyed toward the back of the container. She didn't particularly like cats, either, but the sight of a life remaining amid all the carnage moved her.

"I'll deal with it," she said. "One of the relatives may want it. If not, I'll drop it off at the shelter on Monday."

Whitehouse snorted but said nothing and walked to his car. Kendall followed, the container with the orphaned cat banging against her leg, wondering how she managed to get herself into these things. She had enough complications in her life right now.

2

Ignoring questions shouted by the media, Kendall pushed her way through the crowd toward her five-year-old Highlander. She noticed a scuffle taking place at the end of the driveway as a couple of uniforms struggled with a young man fighting to make his way to the house.

She walked over to them. "Detective Halsrud," she announced. The three of them froze. "What's going on?"

The young man turned to her. He gasped for breath, the officers still restraining him. "I have to see Sienna!"

One of the officers said, "This guy's trying to get in the house. Says he's the girl's boyfriend."

The boy, about twenty, looked at Kendall, his dark blue eyes pleading. "Please, just tell me if Sienna's okay. No one will tell me anything."

"I'll handle this," she said, pissed that the guy hadn't been brought to their attention. Freeing him from their clutches, Kendall led him over to her car. She opened the back to put the cat carrier inside, forgetting the interior had already been packed to the rooftop with all her earthly belongings. Crap. She kept forgetting her residence problem.

"Hang on a minute." She walked around the car and set the

cat carrier on the passenger seat, where it perched precariously on a stack of old books.

Kendall returned to the boy and opened a small notebook. "Okay, name?"

"Jeremy Dahlgren." He frowned, looking toward the car. "That's Malkin, Sienna's cat," he whispered.

Kendall looked him over. Girls his age would describe Dahlgren as hot—tall, dark-haired, with a body the result of either a lot of time working out or playing sports. He and the Glausson daughter would have made a handsome pair.

"How long have you and Sienna been dating?"

"Almost two years. I'm going to UWEC now—she's still a senior in high school, but we're keeping it together, you know? Is she okay? They're saying everyone in there is dead." He choked out the last words.

She realized he must not have arrived until after the bodies had been removed from the house. Kendall dreaded what she had to tell him. "I'm sorry, Jeremy. It's true. I'm afraid that's all I can tell you." He turned away, his shoulders shaking as he succumbed to grief.

They'd gotten the media's attention; the vultures were moving in. She put an arm around his shoulder. "Jeremy, I don't want those reporters to glom onto you. I have to talk to you some more, but you shouldn't drive. Is there someone who can bring you to the station? If not, I'll have one of the guys give you a ride."

Feeling guilty that her car barely had room for a cat, much less a witness, Kendall figured that's what she got for procrastinating. She'd been essentially homeless for five days and had made little effort to find a place more permanent than the mom and pop motel where she'd been bunking.

Jeremy nodded toward a young woman who appeared at his side. "This is Ruby, a friend of mine from school. She can give me a ride."

Ruby, who looked enough like Chelsea Glausson to be related, nodded, a cloud of strawberry-blonde curls bobbing with the movement of her head. "Sure, I'll drive you." They walked to her car, a rusty old K-car, a model Kendall didn't remember seeing since the nineties. Watching them from a distance, she realized Ruby's resemblance to Mrs. Glausson was mostly due to the hair. An attractive girl, but her edges were sharp, nothing light or perky about her. Kendall made a mental note to question her; she might have known Sienna.

The cat complained when Kendall slid into the driver's seat. "Quit your bitching, cat. Things could be a lot worse; you could have gone home with my partner."

The cat began howling as the Highlander picked up speed, the force of the feline cries amazing Kendall with their sonorous volume. By the time she reached the station the howls had become infrequent, diminishing to a low, pathetic mewing.

"You must be running out of steam. Hope that's not catching." Kendall stepped out of the car. The animal would have to wait it out until she made arrangements for its board.

She found Jeremy Dahlgren in an interview room. When he accepted her offer of a soda, she took advantage of the time alone to take out her phone as she walked to the break room. There were at least five calls from her father. The man didn't know when to quit. A retired cop, he still had an ear to the force's grapevine. Since he'd found out about his daughter's living situation, he hadn't let up on insisting that she move in with him and his brother Al. The two men had been sharing her father's bi-level since her mother left more than four years ago.

Kendall entered the break room and punched in her father's number.

"Kenny, I saw you on the news."

"Dad, listen—we'll talk later. I have to ask you a favor. Will you keep a cat for me for a few days?"

"A cat? You don't even have a place to stay and you got a cat?"

"I didn't get a freaking cat, Dad."

He wouldn't stop talking at her, and Kendall had no time to assuage her father's concerns about her personal life. He should know how busy she'd be after a multiple homicide. The clock was ticking on the investigation. She might have to cut him off, find some other way to deal with the animal.

Finally, his relentless dialogue ended. "Oh. It's the family's cat."

"Right. You'll need to pick up cat food and a litter box." When he hesitated, she said, "I can't talk now. You want to help me out? Pick up the damn cat."

Kendall returned to find Jeremy Dahlgren with his elbows on the table, his head in his hands. She passed him a can of soda and sat across from him. "I'm sorry about Sienna, Jeremy. And her family."

"Thanks."

"Can you tell me where you were last night?"

He jerked up straight in the chair. "You don't think I did it?"

"Relax. It's a formality, but we have to eliminate you as a suspect. Then we can move on and find out who did this. Right now everyone's considered a person of interest."

"I was with my study group until about ten. Some of us

went out when we were done and had something to eat. I think I got home about midnight. My folks were still up, you can ask them."

She passed him a pad of lined paper. "I'll need the names and phone numbers of your friends. And your parents."

While he wrote, she asked, "Tell me about Sienna. Did she have any enemies, anyone she was having a problem with?"

He stopped writing. "This wasn't just about her, was it? Her whole family was murdered."

"Part of finding out who murdered the family is determining whether this was done by someone who had a problem with the Glaussons or even with a single family member. We need to know as much as possible about all of them." Kendall didn't mention the infant. They were keeping a lid on the baby situation, at least until they got the results of the analysis on the blood drops found in the baby's room. For now, there was no reason to let it be known the baby could still be alive.

"So, you've been dating Sienna for how long?" Kendall asked,.

"About a year and a half, two years."

"Is your relationship an exclusive one?"

Jeremy finished his list and passed it over to Kendall. "Yeah. For about a year now. Sienna didn't have any enemies. Everyone liked her. Her family kind of kept to themselves, you know? I don't know why anyone would have anything against them."

"Sienna was an extremely attractive girl. Maybe someone was jealous of her, or another guy resented that she only dated you—"

He stopped her. "No, there was nothing like that. She would have told me about it."

"How about girlfriends? Anyone she was close to?"

"Sienna had lots of friends. Probably Jennifer and Katelyn were the ones she spent the most time with."

Kendall turned the paper around and had him add the names of Sienna's friends and how to contact them. "Did the family have any relatives you know of?"

"Not that I heard about. And I never met any."

"What about the rest of the family? Are you aware of any problems?"

"No. I told you, they were all nice people."

Kendall remembered the cat. It might not be too late to intercept her father. "Would you like to take Sienna's cat?"

Jeremy's eyes filled with tears. "I can't; I'm allergic to cats. Will he be all right?"

"Don't worry. If we have to, we'll find a home for him." Kendall passed him one of her cards. "I'll have to talk to you again, Jeremy. If you think of anything before then, call me. Sometimes what seems like an unimportant detail could be vital information." As he rose to leave, she asked, "Will you send Ruby in now?"

Ruby Rindsig, her wild curls tamed with an elastic band, took the chair Jeremy vacated. She sat primly, her buttocks nearly on the edge of the seat.

"Why do you want to talk to me?"

Defensive, are we? "Were you with Jeremy's study group last night?" A question Kendall already knew the answer to; her name had been on Jeremy's list.

"I was. We were at one of the guys' apartment until about ten."

"Did Jeremy leave at the same time you did?"

Ruby wrinkled her patrician nose. "You don't think Jeremy could have done this, do you? He loved Sienna. He was like—part of their family."

"Please. Just answer the question."

"Yes, Jeremy was with us. Five of us went out for a pizza at the Pizza Hut over by the university. We were all there until close to eleven."

"Did you know the Glaussons, Ruby?"

"I knew Sienna from school, but not real well. She was a year behind me."

Kendall explained once more how important it was for them to rule out the possibility that the murders were personal. "Is there anything you can think of that might explain their deaths?"

"No. Like I said, I didn't really know them."

Kendall concluded the interview. She didn't care for Ruby Rindsig. Dahlgren might not be aware of it yet, but she had a feeling the girl wanted to take Sienna's place with him. In Kendall's opinion, a woman who moved in on a man right after his girlfriend was murdered couldn't be trusted.

Whitehouse motioned Kendall to his desk as she came out of the interview room. "Get anything?"

"No. He seems like a good kid. The girl not so much, but she didn't really know the family. She went to the same school as Sienna, but said she didn't know her."

Whitehouse reached in a pocket and frowned at the empty candy wrapper in his hand. "I talked to Mark Glausson's brother, Graham. He'll be in tomorrow. Said he and his brother have been 'on bad terms' for some time. Wonder what that's all about. He's a bigwig at one of the paper mills, lives on Lake Wissota. He didn't seem too concerned about his brother, but sounded pretty broken up when I told him about the rest of the family. When he comes in, we'll take him to make the formal IDs; then we can interview him."

Thinking about the ID process sent a shiver up Kendall's spine. Definitely not something she looked forward to, but she'd have Whitehouse with her.

"No other relatives?"

"None. The brother said their folks passed about six years ago. Glausson's wife grew up in the system—parents killed in a car accident when she was six."

"Any close friends?"

Hank referred to a rumpled notebook. "Yeah, got one name. Betty Ruffalo. A neighbor said she was tight with Mrs. Glausson. Ruffalo runs a pizza joint called Emilio's on the north side of town. She sounded pretty shaken up. She couldn't leave yet because one of the employees called in sick tonight. She'll be free about eleven when things slow down at the restaurant. I told her I'd send you over."

At the words "pizza joint," Kendall's mouth watered. She'd had nothing but coffee all day. She didn't ask why her partner wouldn't be accompanying her; it had been a long day, and she'd welcome some time alone. "Sure. I'll stop over there when I leave."

"Monson and Burnham were over at St. Luke's talking to some coworkers of Doctor Glausson. They did an inventory on his floor—no drugs missing and no incidents of missing pharm since Glausson started. Hopefully, that eliminates the doctor/drug angle. Far as the hospital goes, anyway. Everyone liked him, no obvious grudges, yada, yada. Looking more like a random hit."

"How about a disgruntled patient?"

"No hint of that so far, but they'll be going back to the hospital tomorrow to question the day crew."

"Any word from the field?"

"They're still searching all the areas around the house. Nothing so far and nada from the neighbors. The houses are all pretty far apart in that subdivision, and everyone minds their own business." Whitehouse rubbed his eyes. "I'm gonna take off pretty soon. Not much more we can do tonight."

What was Whitehouse thinking? A case like this could keep them going all night. It wasn't like him to ditch a case, but he'd been openly unenthusiastic about this one. Kendall's mind crawled with copious lists of things that still needed to be done. For starters, they would have to interview Chelsea Glausson's coworkers, even though she worked from home. There was an FBI agent who kept calling, someone would have to talk to him, and they needed to have a group meeting. "Before you leave, we should probably get everyone together, go over what we have so far and give out assignments for tomorrow."

"I've already set it up. Tomorrow morning, eight o'clock."

It irritated Kendall she hadn't been consulted before he set the meeting. The others assigned to the case would want to hear from them tonight. She realized there was nothing stopping her from interacting with them herself—have a pre-meeting, which could get things organized for the next day. But Kendall would have plenty to do to fill in the time until she went to talk to Chelsea Glausson's friend.

Ed Lipske called over to her. "Hey, Kenny. Someone's looking for you."

Her father stood at the front desk, dressed like he had a

date. He usually did. Ignoring a barrage of his questions, she hurried him out to her car and handed him the cat carrier. "He's all yours."

"It's a boy?"

"What? I don't know what it is. I felt sorry for it, okay? Poor creature, his whole family's dead."

"Kenny, I'll take care of the cat. But what about you? You can't stay at that Bates Motel forever."

"It isn't a Bates Motel, Dad. The place is clean and the owners are fine. It's temporary. I'll figure things out."

"I told you not to move in with that dyke."

"That's enough, Dad. I'm an adult. Who I live with or don't live with is none of your business. I don't have time for this." She turned to go back into the station.

"Kenny, wait. Al knows this guy, Morrie Wychen. He owns a bar near and has some apartments upstairs. One of them is empty. He'd love to have a cop living in the place." He held out a piece of paper. "Here's the address. At least give it a look-see."

She took the note, glancing at the address and the name of the bar. Catering to the over-sixty crowd, The Rat Pak was an old-fashioned tavern featuring an antique jukebox that cranked out the music of Sammy Davis Jr., Dean Martin, Tony Bennett and other crooners of the '40s and '50s. Not the kind of place the police got called in to break up bar fights; the clients didn't have the strength or the energy.

She gritted her teeth. "Thanks, Dad. I'll check it out."

3

After leaving her father, Kendall started putting all the information from the case on a whiteboard. Since she couldn't very well do an end-run around Whitehouse's plan to put off a meeting until the next day, she talked to the other officers and added everything they had accumulated. It wasn't much, but it would keep things organized and would look like progress to the lieutenant.

When her phone rang, she saw the call was from her uncle. She opened it, certain more pressure to move into the apartment above The Rat Pak was imminent.

"Kenny, I know your dad told you about the apartment. Listen, Morrie is a good guy, and he's real fussy about who he rents to. A cop living there would be cheaper than an alarm system for him. I think he'd give you a break on the rent."

She acquiesced. "I'll take a look at it when I have a chance."

"Your Dad and I are going to our Sons of Norway meeting tonight. We can stop in there when we get done. Maybe I'll see you there later?"

"Don't plan on it. I have to talk to a witness at eleven."

"Morrie said he'd be around till closing."

"All right. I'll stop in if I'm done before then."

Kendall closed the phone and saw Gene Tarkowski, an FBI agent out of Milwaukee who covered northwestern Wisconsin, walking toward her. Would the FBI try to muscle in on them?

"Hi, Kendall. Whitehouse around?"

Kenny wondered how long it would be before she'd be respected as half of an equal partnership. "No, he left for the night."

The agent walked over to the board she'd filled in. He studied it for a minute. "Don't have much, do you?"

"It's a start. Nothing links the crime to anything personal with the family yet." She resisted asking him the purpose of his visit.

Tarkowski's bushy, gray-threaded eyebrows met over narrowed eyes. "What do you think?"

Asking her opinion. That was a start. "My gut says personal, but I couldn't give you a concrete reason why. The girl, I suppose. The perps—or perp—spent a lot of time on her. It was ugly, with a lot of damage done to her face. She appeared to have been fiercely raped in every possible orifice."

He studied the photos of Sienna. "Without anything else to go on, I'd have to agree with you. Have you looked into similar invasions?"

"We're short-staffed—haven't had a chance. The chief called a couple guys back in from vacation—deer hunters. They'll be here in the morning, kicking and screaming."

Tarkowski chuckled. "We're in Wisconsin and it is November, isn't it?" He took a seat in the chair next to Kendall's desk. "There were some break-ins over the past twelve months or so that are similar to this one. The first was in Green Bay, the other one happened over in Stillwater last March. We got involved on the second one because it crossed the state line. I wasn't on the case, so I don't know any details off the top of my head."

"I remember those. Were they the same doers?"

"There's a possibility the Green Bay attack was drug related. There were never any strong leads on either one, but there were similarities. The same gun was used in both of them, which makes it pretty certain there's a connection.

"I'm on my way up to the casino in Hayward to take some statements on an illegal gambling situation. I'll see what I can get for you on the other invasions and stop back in tomorrow on my way home."

The attitude among most of Kendall's coworkers was not positive when it came to the FBI wedging themselves into one of their cases. But considering her partner's abrupt dismissal of the case, Kendall figured they'd need any help they could get. She'd never heard anything negative about Tarkowski himself.

She watched him walk out, his stride long and purposeful, his reddish hair graying, his tall body still fit. Although younger than Whitehouse, probably in his early fifties, Tarkowski was just as close to retirement.

Kendall noticed the lieutenant moving in her direction; she thought he'd left for the night. Things just kept getting better and better.

Lieutenant Ray Schoenfuss ushered Kendall into his office and shut the door behind them. He faced her without taking a chair or offering her one. "Kendall, Hank just had a heart attack."

"What?" That was the last thing she'd been expecting.

"Diane just called me. He's going to be okay, but they're doing a bypass on him tomorrow."

Kendall felt shallow realizing she wanted to ask Schoenfuss how Hank being gone would affect *her*. "That explains why he was in such a hurry to leave; he wasn't feeling well. I'll go see him. Which hospital is he in?"

"Diane said they didn't want him to have visitors tonight. Not until after the surgery."

Kendall didn't know what to say. Was he going to make her ask him what he planned to do about Hank's absence from the case? "We have a meeting set for tomorrow morning. I have everything outlined on the whiteboard, and I'm going to interview a friend of Chelsea Glausson's tonight."

"Good. Hank would want you to keep everything going as if he were still here. He won't be back for some time, of course, and I've decided to let you take the lead until then."

Elated, Kendall's tightened diaphragm relaxed. "Thank you. I won't let you down."

"You can't work it alone, so I'm assigning you a new partner. Ross Alverson. He's been around for a while and he'll be an asset with this kind of thing. This case will be everyone's top priority. Keep me in the loop, and remember I'm here if you need anything."

Ross Alverson. Fighting for control, Kendall excused herself and went back to her desk. Alverson was a scene-stealing, limelight-seeking, pain-in-the-ass womanizer. Kendall despised the man, but if she played her cards right, she'd be able to stay as independent of the slimy bastard as possible. She figured the one advantage of being a woman less than jaw dropping in the looks department was she didn't have to worry about the Ross Alversons of the world hitting on her. She missed Hank already.

Her reports were finished forty-five minutes before her appointment with Chelsea Glausson's friend, Betty Ruffalo. She wouldn't have to deal with Alverson until the next day; he was one of the detectives who'd been called in from deer hunting. She'd have just enough time to hit a drive-through and eat a burger on her way to the interview.

"Detective Hall-shrood," a voice said behind her, dragging out the pronunciation of her name. "I hear rumors it's going to be the Ross and Kenny show from now on."

Kendall's nerve centers knotted. Alverson—back already. Dealing with him in her present state of mind wouldn't be easy. Difficult to be diplomatic when you've been working for more than fifteen hours. "That's Kendall to you, Detective." At least she'd been able to control herself enough to add "Detective" rather than "asshole."

"I hear we have an interview at eleven. Ready to go? I'll drive."

"Just so we're on the same page, Alverson, *we* don't have an appointment—I do. If you're interested in what we have so far, I've outlined it all on the whiteboard. Acquaint yourself with the case. We're having a joint meeting in the morning. I'll talk to you then."

Still wearing a camouflage suit with an orange vest on his tall, spare frame, Alverson held out his hands as if to ward off blows. "No prob. I'll get right on it, sir." He turned away, but she could swear he muttered something that rhymed with witch.

Kendall felt like she'd hit a brick wall as she drove to her appointment with Betty Ruffalo. Food would have to wait; by the time she left the station, there'd been no time for a drive-through. Her black suit felt like it was decaying on her body, and her feet were as numb as her overworked brain.

She hoped Alverson had gotten the message she was top dog in the investigation. He wasn't a bad cop, really, just someone she didn't like to be around. The dirtbag had even managed a lecherous eyebrow wiggle in her direction before she'd finished her speech.

Emilio's Pizzeria sat on a side street near the University of Wisconsin-Eau Claire campus south of downtown. Unable to forget her hunger, Kendall recalled the fare was especially good.

A few diners lingered in the small dining room that featured the ubiquitous red-checkered tablecloths and wine bottles topped with melted candles. The inviting scent of baking dough and tomato sauce trumped the cloying odor of hot candle wax. The background music sounded like the Three Tenors.

A teenage boy with spiked hair and dark circles under his eyes worked the register. He must have been looking for Kendall; he directed her to a back office where Betty Ruffalo, in a rumpled, tomato-stained white apron, sat behind a desk piled with papers and pizza boxes. Her face was tear-stained, and her makeup looked like the morning after a bender. She stood and offered her hand to Kendall.

"I'm sorry for your loss," Kendall said.

Nearly as tall as Kendall, Ruffalo looked to be in her late forties. Her grip was warm and strong. She returned her generous body to the chair behind the desk and gestured for Kendall to take a seat across from her. "I can't believe this is happening. I just saw Chels yesterday."

Kendall had her notebook out. "And where was that?"

Betty raked her fingers through a head of thick, dark-brown hair a shade removed from black. It fell in loose waves that brushed the top of her shoulders, with only a few gray strands glistening at her temples. "Mark wasn't working at the hospital last night. He offered to stay home with Evan so Chels and I could get together. She was housebound with her work, and with Evan, of course. We did a little shopping at the mall, then had dinner at Red Lobster." She sniffled and reached for a tissue. "Good Lord, I would never have imagined it would be our last time together."

Kendall waited while Betty wiped her eyes. "Ms. Ruffalo, can you think of any reason the family might have been at risk?"

"No, not at all. And call me Betty, please. I've been searching my memory all day. Chels didn't get out much because of her son. You know about Evan?"

"Yes. He was autistic."

"He was a handful, but Chels was devoted to him. She refused to consider institutionalizing him even when Mark tried to convince her it could make a big difference for the boy."

"What about the baby? How did she have time to take care of her?"

"Philly was a little angel. Never caused a bit of trouble, a real dream child, luckily, since Evan was so high maintenance." She dabbed at her eyes as she talked. "The only problem Chels ever had with Philly was her crawling out of bed at night. The little imp started doing it at nine months. I couldn't believe it when Chels first told me about it. She and Mark panicked the first time Philly got out of her crib during the night. When they looked for her in the morning, she wasn't in her bed or anywhere else in the house. They were afraid she'd been abducted, but she was asleep in Evan's playhouse. Well, it's not a house really. It's a canvas cover pulled over a card table. Evan spent hours in it every day. He's the one who found Philly, just when they were about to call the police."

Interesting about the baby, Kendall thought. Could she be hiding somewhere they hadn't looked?

"Detective Halsrud, I'm so sorry. I forgot to offer you something. Would you like a soda? Water? Something to eat?"

Kendall's taste buds had been on red alert since inhaling the tantalizing smells in Emilio's. But unlike many of her coworkers, she made it a practice not to indulge when offered a free meal. "I'll have a water, thank you."

Betty Ruffalo left the room. Kenny made a quick call to the officers on security at the Glausson house and asked them to go through the house once more, double-checking any place a small child might hide.

When Betty returned a minute later, she was carrying two bottles of water and a takeout box. "Are you hungry? I haven't been able to eat all day, but maybe with some company . . ."

She opened the box, releasing a scent so inviting, Kendall would have recognized it as a pizza from a ten-foot distance with her eyes closed. But she never ate with witnesses. Or in front of them. "Sorry, I can't. Thank you, though."

"It'll go to waste if we don't eat it. Someone ordered it and didn't pick it up. I just nuked it for us." She handed Kendall a napkin and a bottle of water.

Hell with it. Just this once. Kendall reached for a slice of the steaming pizza, thick with cheese and pepperoni. Neither of them spoke as they ate, giving Kendall time to think about what she still had to ask her witness. She'd wolfed down two pieces of the pie before realizing Betty hadn't finished even one.

"What can you tell me about their marriage?" Kendall asked. "Were they happy?"

"As happy as any, I imagine. Chels wasn't one to complain

26

about her husband like so many women do. I know they loved each other."

"So, nothing stands out that was problematic?"

"I met Chels when my granddaughter was in the pediatric ward at St. Luke's. She had lymphoma, but she's in remission now. Evan was there at the same time; he was only about three and had broken both his legs jumping off the roof of the garage. He was a difficult patient because of his autism. Chels never left his side. We spent a lot of time together.

"The only issue I know about happened before I met them; they lived in the Twin Cities at the time. Mark worked at the VA hospital. He got the notion that he needed to make a difference—he wanted to spend a year in Iraq. Chels opposed the idea, of course. Evan was a difficult child, and she was working full-time. They moved here, and Mark left for Iraq only a few weeks after they got settled. I think her agreeing to let him go to Iraq was a trade-off for his willingness to move the family here.

"Chels wanted to raise their children away from the Cities. She wanted a simpler life for her kids. Anyway, with Evan in the hospital, and Sienna in grade school, she had a tough time coping with it all. I'm not sure she ever forgave Mark for not being there for them."

"Why Eau Claire?" Kendall asked.

"I'm not really sure. She told me she'd done a lot of research before deciding. I suspected she hoped if they lived here, Mark would mend fences with his brother."

"Did she tell you why they were estranged?"

"She did—in confidence." Betty paused. "It doesn't matter anymore, I suppose. I'm sure you'll be talking to Gray soon if you haven't already. His name is Graham, but Chels said he prefers Gray. I don't know the details, but she told me there'd always been a rivalry between the brothers. After their mother gave birth to Graham, she was told she couldn't have any more children. So when Mark came along barely a year later, he was their miracle child. When Mark entered medical school he achieved sainthood in his parents' eyes. The real problem between them was because of money. The Glaussons paid a fortune to put Mark through medical school, and then when Graham got out of the Air Force and asked for a loan to start a business, they turned him down.

"That's more or less the gist of it."

Kendall felt her body aching for sleep as the heavy food hit her stomach. "Do you know if Dr. Glausson kept any drugs in the house?"

"I know Chelsea told him she didn't want any around. He kept a medical bag with a few emergency supplies in his car, but that was it as far as I know."

"How about money? Do you know if they kept much cash in the house?"

"I really don't know about that. Chelsea always used a credit card when I was with her."

Kendall closed her notebook. She'd talk to Betty Ruffalo again, but later, when she was more clear-headed and had different questions.

"I think that's all I need for tonight, Betty. Thanks for talking to me." She handed Betty one of her cards. "Please, call me if you think of anything that might be important."

The restaurant had the "closed" sign turned toward the street when Kendall left Betty's office, eager for the night air to sharpen her senses. The empty dining area had a TV mounted in the corner, set to a local station; breaking news showed a building in flames, surrounded by fire trucks.

Dear God, the setting looks familiar. It was the motel where Kendall had been staying.

4

The Rat Pak, situated in the middle of a string of five businesses, sat on a side street abutting a wooded bluff. It was located only a short distance from the Chippewa River, which divides downtown Eau Claire. The building, mostly dark brick and limestone block, looked like it had been ensconced at the foot of the bluff since the beginning of the previous century. A hair salon on one side and a dry cleaner on the other hugged the tavern. A bead shop and a check-cashing place followed from the salon toward the corner. There were no lights on in the aging homes on the other side of the street.

Kendall drove past, noticing only two cars parked in front of the tavern. She turned around where the street dead-ended at the edge of the bluff. An apartment recommended by her uncle wasn't high on her list of ideal residences, but with the motel closed, it wasn't like she had a lot of immediate choices. Determined to bring a quick resolution to her living situation, she parked and walked toward the bar.

A dark figure stepped out from an unlit doorway next to the tavern as Kendall approached the door; in a heartbeat, she whipped out her gun.

"Kenny, put the gun down—it's me!"

"What the fuck are you doing here?"

Kendall's former roommate stepped out of the shadows. "It's good to see you, too."

Linda Johnson, now known as Natalie Drake among the Chippewa Valley theatre set, stepped out of the shadows. Nat wore a dark leather jacket and a black knit cap pulled over her waist-length, ebony hair. Ghost white in the dim streetlight, her face still bore the heavy makeup she wore in *The Bride of Frankenstein*, her latest thespian project.

Kendall holstered her gun, thinking how on edge she must have been to react the way she had. "You scared the crap out of me. What do you want, anyway? I got your message, Nat, loud and clear. Stuffing all my things in the car while I was at work? Real mature."

"I'm sorry, Kenny. I shouldn't have done that."

That was an understatement. "How did you find me?

"I was coming home from the theater and saw your car drive by. I wanted to talk to you, so I followed you here. I want you to come back."

"Come back? You know it wouldn't work. We don't want the same thing."

"We could go back to how it was."

"I don't think that's possible, Nat."

Natalie took Kenny's hands in hers. "I am sorry. Promise me that you'll consider it, anyway. I hope you'll still think of me as a friend."

Kendall had known Nat was gay when she agreed to be her roommate. She'd liked Nat and convinced herself many people of the opposite sexual persuasion were successful roomies. It had worked well for a long time; Nat was gone most evenings and

Kendall days, so they seldom overlapped. Until the night Kendall went out with Nat and her theatre friends to celebrate the success of her latest play. In an alcoholic haze, Nat made a pass when they came home, and foolishly, Kendall spent the night in her bed. For Kendall it had been a spur of the moment, liquor-induced, sensual experiment, but Nat had perceived it as a beginning.

The next morning Kendall had to spell it out for her, and the message hadn't been well received. When she came out of work that afternoon, she found her car jammed with all her belongings.

Now Nat thought they could still be friends? Leery, Kendall said, "Sure. I'd like that."

Nat squeezed her hands and disappeared back into the night.

Kendall watched her leave. "I'm sorry, too," she whispered.

In the intensity of their exchange, neither of them had seen the slight figure huddled in the doorway of the hair salon.

Intrigued by the conversation she'd overheard, Brynn Zellman waited in the doorway until the tall woman who'd wielded the gun disappeared into the tavern. Her stance had been that of a cop, but why would a cop be visiting the bar? Nearly closing time, there wouldn't be more than a handful of the regulars still parked on the red-velvet bar stools.

Brynn unlocked the door leading to the floor above the storefronts, recalling as she scaled the stairway to her apartment, the only unfamiliar car out front had been a dark blue SUV. It was packed to the gills with things that even in the dim lighting looked like personal belongings. It seemed unlikely a cop would be here to look at the empty apartment so late on a Saturday night.

Brynn had been bugging Morrie to rent it out. It felt kind of creepy to have a vacant apartment right across the hall. She kept imagining sounds coming from the place late at night. It would be a relief to have someone living there again—even a cop.

The only patrons remaining in the bar were a heavy man in a dark suit sitting at one end of the bar, and at the other end, a couple that seemed to be avoiding each other's eyes. A frowsy-haired woman in a red sweater and a white apron stood behind the bar, polishing glasses. Strains of Dean Martin singing *Return to Me* flowed from an old-fashioned jukebox with glass columns of rotating colors running up each side. When Kendall asked for Morrie, the tightly permed bartender gestured toward the back room. "In there."

Morrie looked like an aging hippie in beads and silver earrings. He didn't seem to go with the Rat Pak motif of the bar, but at least he wasn't wearing tie-dye. He stood and held out his hand. "You must be Kenny."

Kendall cringed. Would she ever get rid of the name Kenny? Although it was the obvious diminutive of Kendall, the name always brought up her mother's disappointment at Kendall's lack of femininity and her father's anxious attempts to turn her into the boy he'd always wanted.

She shook Morrie's hand, noticing a narrow strip of brown leather held back his salt and pepper hair in a short tail. "Detective Halsrud." She didn't add, "to you," although at times when people insisted on calling her Kenny, she was tempted.

Morrie accepted the stiff greeting with a smile. "Let me show you the place." He picked up a set of keys and led her though a door opening into a back hallway. "There are two ways to get upstairs. The doorway in front is always locked. The door to the parking lot in the back is open unless the bar is closed."

At the top of the steps, on the side facing the bluff, a hallway ran toward the south. A short corridor branched off in front of them, on either side a door to an apartment. The upper half of each door had a windowpane of textured glass. Lettered with names of businesses, they'd obviously been in place since the '30s or '40s. The one on the right was made up of colored, leaded glass like that in a church window and in its center, a beveled crystal circle about ten inches in diameter. From the circle, chips of color radiated out, creating a brilliant kaleidoscope effect. Black lettering along a bottom panel spelled out, "Fortune-teller." Backlit by light from inside the apartment, small shapes of colored light decorated the hallway.

"That's been here forever and a day," Morrie offered. "When I bought the place I found out a widow lady had it put in. She was a tenant for at least a hundred and ten years. Told fortunes for a living. Her sign's still downstairs over the front door to the apartments—Madam Vadoma."

Kendall raised her eyebrows.

"Seriously, she had to be more than ninety when she passed a couple years ago. Some of her clients kept coming even after she was gone. The new renter decided to follow in her footsteps. She's been playing the suckers since she's been here."

"She tells fortunes?"

"Calls herself a psychic reader or some horseshit like that. I think she needed the dough, you know? She won't bother you; she's shy, keeps to herself unless she needs something."

Morrie inserted a key into the door across from the psychic. Stenciled on its textured, glass window was PHILLIP J. PARKINS, PRIVATE INVESTIGATIONS. "See? The place was made for you."

Having a firm resistance to planting roots, Kendall wasn't so sure. Before moving in with Nat, she'd spent nearly two years renting the lower level of a house belonging to a divorced salesman who travelled more than he was ever at home. Before then, it had been studio apartments in buildings that guaranteed anonymity.

The door opened into a narrow living room with two tall windows looking out toward the tree-covered bluff. A short utility bar sided by two rickety stools divided the room from the small kitchen area. The carpeting was a worn, institutional gray-green, and the walls were seriously yellowed. Not inviting. But painting supplies and carpeting samples were sitting on the counter; evidently Morrie planned to fix the place up.

"I'm putting in new carpeting and painting the whole place. Tell you what—stay for a week—on me. Then if you make it permanent, I'll decorate however you want. You can pick the colors."

Kendall moved to look at the other rooms. The bathroom had just had a makeover and still smelled of caulk. The larger bedroom faced the bluff and had a decent-sized window; the other was windowless but had a small skylight.

Morrie added, "The place comes partially furnished. But look at that bed—it's brand new."

The bed looked like the only piece of furniture not dating back to the Depression era. Right now it looked enticing. The mattresses at the motel left a lot to be desired—not that that particular motel was even an option any longer.

Kendall decided it wouldn't hurt to take the guy up on his offer and stay for a week. When she said she'd try it out, he asked if he could help her bring some of her things up, making Kendall wonder if Uncle Al had ratted her out to the guy by telling him much more about her situation than she would have liked.

Morrie followed her to her car and helped carry up what she'd need for a temporary stay.

5

Kendall stretched out on the bed fully dressed and immediately drifted off. It felt like only minutes had passed when she was jerked awake by a dream—a dream starring a curly-haired baby and a young boy. Kendall shuddered, trying to shake off images of the Glausson family. Serious sleep didn't seem like a possibility.

She changed clothes and went back out into the night. The Glaussons' neighborhood bordered the Chippewa River north of Eau Claire; the street the house was on ended at a cul-de-sac that met the edge of a wooded area staked off for development. The Glausson house, whose lot bordered the river, sat lit up like a party was in progress. A black-and-white was visible at the curb and an unmarked parked in the driveway. She'd have company—one of the other detectives must not have been able to sleep either.

An officer she used to work with sat inside the door working a sudoku when she entered the house. "Hey, Halsrud. You caught a big one. Bet you're missing Hank."

News travelled fast in the department. She nodded toward the interior of the house. "Who's here?"

He turned toward the back. "Alverson. I think he's upstairs."

At least the creep was showing an interest. Kendall mounted the stairs and found Ross Alverson in the baby's room. He'd changed out of his hunting attire, wearing jeans with a sport coat too short for his tall body. He stood holding a digital photo frame, handing it to her as she approached. Inside the frame, pictures of Philly Glausson flipped through at two-second intervals. All that innocence—snuffed out as quickly as a candle on a birthday cake. Refusing to get emotional in front of Alverson, she returned the frame to its place on the dresser.

"Sucks, doesn't it?" he asked.

"She could still be alive."

"What about the blood stains?" He pointed to the markers on the floor that outlined where the techs had found the blood.

"We don't know it's hers."

"Right. Not yet."

Kendall bit her tongue rather than argue. Was she the only one who believed the child was still alive? Remembering what Betty Ruffalo had told her about the little girl, she walked to the playhouse. Kendall lifted the flap and looked under the table. It was empty inside except for a brown teddy bear and a crumpled, pink blanket, both of them probably Philly's. They bagged them and moved downstairs.

They stopped in the kitchen, Alverson's height somehow incongruous against the cabinets with their telltale blood spatters.

"Do we know if anything's missing?" he asked.

"Just cash and credit cards, so far. According to a friend of Chelsea Glausson, the doctor didn't keep drugs at home. There's nothing to indicate they'd come in here looking for anything in particular. With no survivors it's hard to know what might be missing. The nanny's going to go through here again in the morning; she may be able to tell us more."

After they'd gone through the stacks of mail, letters, and notes on Chelsea Glausson's desk, Kendall decided to call it a night. "It's nearly three a.m. Let's wrap it up for now. I'm going to get a few hours sleep before tomorrow's meeting."

Alverson held up a business card. "What about this?"

Kendall moved closer to read its face. "Callandra – Psychic Interpretations" was printed in the center of the card with a local phone number underneath. Another fortune-teller mention in one day—what were the chances?

"What do you think?" she asked. "Worth looking into?"

"Nah, probably not. I dated a chick that called those nine-hundred numbers and paid big bucks to psychics—it's all a scam."

"I suppose." Kendall tucked the card into an evidence bag and jotted the information into her notebook.

She walked out into the night, Alverson trailing behind her. "You know, you're looking good, Kenny."

The bullet Kendall had taken to the abdomen right after she'd made detective had left her thirty pounds lighter. Though at 5'11" she hadn't been grossly overweight, she had discovered she felt better without the added pounds and was managing to keep them off. But a compliment from a sleazeball like Alverson didn't feel like praise.

She stopped and faced him. "Let's get something straight. I told you once tonight, my name is Kendall. Use it. And any discussion of my personal life, including my appearance, is off-limits. You got that?"

He backed off, muttering, "Just making conversation."

———————

Kendall climbed the stairs to the apartment, wondering if Chelsea Glausson's "Callandra" could be living right across the hall. A faint glow from behind her neighbor's window scattered bright prisms of light onto the opposite wall. Inserting her key in the lock, she heard a door open behind her. A tiny woman in a white chenille bathrobe stood just inside the open door. She held a miniature silver tray with a teacup balanced in its center.

"I'm Brynn. I saw you on the news. I thought you might need this." She offered Kendall the tray. The delicate china teacup, painted with purple pansies, held a silver filigreed ball. A tiny chain connected to it draped over the side of the cup. Kendall didn't remember what the gadget was called, but her mother had been a tea drinker; she knew it held tea.

"I'm Detective Halsrud. Kendall."

When Kendall didn't reach for the tray, Brynn explained, "It's a tea ball filled with a special blend of tea—it'll help you sleep. Don't worry, it's made with all natural ingredients."

She accepted the tray, noticing that although the woman handing it to her had a face unlined by time, her hair was pure white and as feathery as a duckling's coat. Except for the colorless hair, she could be fourteen.

"Thanks. I'll try it."

Her neighbor turned back to her doorway. "All right, then," she said, disappearing behind the glass-paned door.

She'd seen her on the news? How had she known the person she'd seen on the news resided across the hall? Morrie must have told her, but that would mean an awfully late communication. Odd. But it didn't matter; Kendall only planned to stay in the apartment for a week. She could tolerate odd for that long. Her new neighbor certainly wasn't talkative, so she wouldn't take up Kendall's time or try to be best friends. Kendall set the tea aside, not ready to accept offerings from a stranger.

Her bathroom, newly remodeled, still smelled of fresh wood and caulk. A mirror ran the length of the vanity, appreciably high enough for Kendall to see even the top of her head.

Alverson had said she looked good, not that a compliment from him meant a whole lot. She let her hair down and ran a brush through it. Just plain brown. With a positive spin, sandy. Nat had always encouraged her to put highlights in it, but she'd never gotten around to it, just like she'd never taken time to buy clothes to complement her new figure. She supposed the weight loss flattered her face, exposing her high cheekbones. And her eyes weren't bad, a rich amber brown. Her nose, though, couldn't be helped. It had a bend at the top that reminded her of a boxer who'd spend too much time in the ring. She hated it, although no one else had ever commented on it.

She stepped into the shower, hoping it would calm her frazzled nerves. Standing under the steamy water, she realized her neighbor must be an albino; it would explain the white hair. Kendall hadn't gotten a good look at her eyes, but expected they would be very pale or colorless even, depending on the extent of her deformity—if albinism was considered a deformity. Kendall wasn't familiar with albinism or if there was a politically correct term for it.

Refreshed but wide-awake, she reviewed her notes in bed. She needed some sleep before facing another day like the one she'd had. Reassuring herself she had no reason not to drink the tea she'd been given, Kendall got up and added boiling water to the tiny cup.

It didn't taste half bad. Within minutes her nerves uncoiled as sleep washed over her. She drifted off thinking she'd need a massive supply of the stuff to get her through the Glausson case.

6

Sunday

Carrying a bag of bagels and an assortment of spreads, Kendall entered the meeting room well before eight; she'd learned preparation was the ultimate cure for pre-meeting nerves. The whiteboards were filled out, she had her list of the things they had yet to cover, and detailed assignment schedules were ready.

The chief was scheduled to do a press release at nine and wanted their input. She'd have to keep everyone on track in order to be done in time to meet with him before his speech.

When everyone was in place, Kendall announced, "Diane Whitehouse called to tell us the doctors are operating on Hank this morning. He's having a bypass that's considered routine surgery. They don't expect any complications, but he won't be able to have visitors for a few days. His secretary is taking up a collection for flowers, so anyone who wants to chip in, see Joanne."

The first order of business was to review everything they already had, including the little they'd gotten back from forensics. When they concluded, Alverson spoke out. "How long are we going to concentrate on the Glaussons? Seems to me this was a stranger invasion. They took cash and credit cards. We need to be working it from that angle—looking for the perps."

"Gene Tarkowski from the FBI stopped in last night," Kendall responded. There was no need for body language training to read the negativity in the room at the mention of the FBI. "Tarkowski said the FBI believes our murders are related to two other home invasions in Green Bay and Stillwater. You probably all remember the one in Stillwater last winter. The one in Green Bay was about a year and a half ago. The FBI got involved because the second one was Stillwater, Minnesota, which crosses state lines. Tarkowski's going to be here sometime today with more information. If our invasion is related to the others, his input will save us a lot of preliminary work, so let's hold off on going in the direction that these murders were a one-time stranger thing. I'll get back to you with whatever he has by the end of the day. We'll regroup later today and see where we are."

Joe Monson stood. "We're still going to be searching the woods behind the house again today, but what about the river? Their house is right on it."

Alverson took the question. "We know all about the Chippewa, Joe. Bodies get carried downstream—fast. The riverbanks near the house were searched yesterday. If the kid ended up in the river, she would be a long way downstate by now. If we get lucky, someone finds the body along the way."

They were dehumanizing the child, as if it were a given she was dead. Kendall stepped forward, her hands on her hips. "The baby's name is Phyllis and the family called her Philly. Let's quit referring to her as 'the kid' and stop assuming she's dead."

When the room went quiet, Alverson said, "In case Philly Glausson *is* dead, we've put a notice out to departments south of here to be on the watch for her body. Meanwhile, I think the search teams should move south along the river in case her body ended up on a riverbank somewhere south of here."

From the back of the room, "What's the chief going to say to the press about the baby?"

"I don't have any details, but I'd expect him to say something like 'We're cautiously optimistic the baby is still alive.'"

"Have we put out an Amber Alert?"

Kendall wasn't happy with the answer to the question. "Not yet. We're short in criteria—we have no description of an abductor or his vehicle. The baby's face will be all over the news; for now that'll have to be enough."

The discussion continued. When they were winding down, the subject of the Glausson baby came up again.

After stuffing half of a cream-cheese covered bagel in his mouth, Alverson stood and approached the whiteboards. "I think we're wasting our time looking for the baby. We need to be looking for the perps." He pointed to facts on the whiteboards. "First, we found the baby's blood on the floor. Why would they hurt the baby if they were going to take it with them? It's not like the kid could have been resisting. And if someone just wanted to take the kid, why knock off the whole family? There'd be easier ways to get their hands on it. The baby's dead, nothing else makes sense."

Patience, Kendall cautioned herself. "You're probably right, Ross. But if there's even the smallest chance Philly Glausson *is* alive, we have to keep searching for her." Kendall knew she should add "or for her body" but wanted everyone to maintain enthusiasm for the search. It would wane quickly if they didn't find her soon.

Kendall went over the assignments for the day, then wrapped things up by saying, "We have to make sure we've done everything possible to rule out a family connection. If there is one, the most likely intended victim was the girl, since she's the only one they abused. Ross, when you and Joe interview her friends, get names of anyone else in her social circle or at school we need to talk to. Schoenfuss said overtime won't be an issue for now, so let's meet back here at five."

An hour later, Kendall looked up from her desk as a tall, well-dressed man approached. She did a double take. From the few photos she'd seen of Mark Glausson, it was obvious Graham Glausson looked enough like his brother to be a twin.

He stopped at her desk. "I'm Graham Glausson. Where can I find Detective Whitehouse?" The request sounded like a command; Glausson was a man used to giving orders. He eased off a pair of deerskin gloves, stuffing them into the pocket of a full-length, black leather coat.

"Unfortunately, Detective Whitehouse is in the hospital." She stood, offering her hand. "I'm Detective Halsrud—I'm in charge of your family's case."

He ignored the offered hand, making no effort to hide his displeasure. Apparently the man disapproved of a woman handling a murder case. Kendall immediately dropped him into her "arrogant prick" file. Still, the man had just a lost a brother.

"Mr. Glausson, I'm sorry about your brother and his family. I assure you we're doing everything possible to find out who's responsible. Our entire force is working on it, in addition to the county sheriffs, the FBI, and the state police."

Glausson's expression didn't change. His face, a shade away from handsome, retained its lines of resentment. "What do you need from me?"

"I'll have to get a statement from you, but we can do that later. If you're up for it, we need someone to make a formal identification of the victims."

"I'll do anything I can to help."

Relieved that was settled, Kendall wished she hadn't sent Alverson out with Monson. His male presence would have reassured Glausson. Ironic.

Franklyn Teed, the county medical examiner, ushered Kendall and Graham Glausson into a room where four bodies covered with pale blue sheeting lay on gurneys. Teed offered his condolences and asked if Glausson was ready to view his brother.

Glausson's lips stiffened. "Go ahead."

Teed pulled back the sheet covering the first body, exposing Mark Glausson's face, his features remarkably similar to those of Graham's. Except for the neat bullet hole in his forehead, he appeared at peace; he could have been enjoying a quiet nap.

Glausson exhaled pent-up breath. "That's my brother Mark."

The ME quickly lowered the sheet and moved on to the others. Glausson contained himself well; he might have been observing strangers. Until finally Chelsea Glausson, his brother's wife was exposed. His face crumpled. Kendall nodded to Teed and led Graham out into the waiting area, where they took a seat on a seasoned, red-leather couch.

"I'm sorry we had to put you through this," she said.

He stood abruptly. "It had to be done." He wiped his face with a handkerchief. "But where's Philly?"

Crap. Whitehouse talked to him the night before. Hadn't he told Glausson about the baby?

"I thought you knew. We haven't found her body. A team has been searching for her since yesterday afternoon."

"I've been avoiding the news, Detective. I assumed they all died the same way." As he choked back a sob, Kendall stood and reached to console him. Unexpectedly, he clung to her, his large hands tight on her back. His body against hers felt warm, solid with maleness. She berated herself for enjoying the feel of him at a time like this. Her dalliance with Nat must have stoked her sensuality. He released her a moment later.

"My apologies—I don't usually fall apart."

"Anyone would under the circumstances," she said. "Let's get out of here. We can stop for some decent coffee on our way back to the station."

Sunglasses covering her eyes and a hood over her white hair, Brynn stepped out into the hallway carrying a bag of trash. An animal carrier sat in front of the door across from hers, the garbage bag beside it filled to capacity. She noticed a note taped to the top of the carrier.

When she came back up the steps after her trip to the dumpster, she couldn't resist reading the note.

> *Kenny,*
>
> *I've been trying to call you all morning. I can't keep the cat—turns out I'm allergic. Hope you can find it a good home. If you want, let me know and I'll take it to the shelter for you.*
>
> *Love, Dad*

The cat mewed softly when Brynn looked through the latticed door of the box. Her mother had never allowed pets. "Too messy," she'd always said. Brynn opened the door and scooped out the big white cat, which began a fierce purring when she cradled it in her arms.

"What's your name, kitty-cat?" She turned over the animal's tag. Malkin. *A malkin was a witch's familiar.* Brynn was a card reader. It was fate—this cat was meant to be hers.

Kendall and Graham Glausson sat across from each other in an interview room. She began, "Detective Whitehouse told me you were at a meeting Friday night?" He hadn't really, but he'd left his notebook.

"Yes. Our plant in Wausau is negotiating with the union. I'm spokesperson for the company. I told the other detective that we didn't break up until sometime after one. My team went out for breakfast, so I wasn't home until about four a.m."

Graham Glausson was VP of a paper company with locations scattered about the state. "We'll need verification of that. Names and phone numbers." She passed him a notepad.

"You don't think I had something to do with this?"

"No, but it's part of the process—we have to rule you out."

"I'd have no reason to do such a thing—nothing to gain. Mark and I didn't get along, but our differences were nothing that would provoke either of us to murder." Glausson started writing.

Kendall wondered if there was something he wasn't telling her. She waited a bit, then asked, "Can you think of any reason someone would have a grudge against your brother or a member of his family?"

He pushed the tablet back to Kendall, his eyes a deep shade

of blue-gray. He had a prominent nose, but it fit well with his features. Like his brother, his hair was thick, pecan brown. "Not that I'm aware of. But I didn't know them very well. I helped Chelsea out a few years ago when Mark was overseas and she needed a hand when Evan broke his legs."

"Any drug use in their background?"

"Not that I know of. Chelsea had a tough life as a kid, but she never said anything about using drugs. And my brother wasn't the type. Mark believed addictions were a weakness, not a disease. A surprising attitude really, since he was a doctor."

Kendall heard his cell phone vibrate, but he ignored it. She handed him one of her cards. "That'll do it for now, Mr. Glausson, but I'll be talking to you again. Call me if you have questions or think of anything else. I'll keep in touch, let you know whatever I can about how things are going."

She caught a glimpse of him through the window as he walked to his car, phone to his ear, deep in conversation. Work? Or a woman?

7

Alverson gave Kendall the name of a therapist who came into the Glausson home two afternoons a week to work with Chelsea Glausson's son. Kendall decided to talk to the woman herself. Having spent time with Chelsea, Rachel Jennings could be an excellent source of information.

Jennings' address wasn't far from The Rat Pak, so she'd be able to make a quick trip to the apartment first, drop off her dry cleaning and more of her clothes. She arrived to find the cat carrier, along with a bag of cat paraphernalia, parked in front of her door, a note from her father taped to the top of the carrier. She'd forgotten about the cat. Shit, what was she going to do with an animal when she was gone sixteen hours a day? She'd forgotten to ask Glausson if he wanted it.

After tossing an armful of dry cleaning on the kitchen counter, she went to get the cat and read the note from her father. The carrier was empty. Kendall turned to see Brynn standing in the doorway behind her, the white cat cradled in her arms, purring loudly. "He was lonesome."

Despite the dark glasses she wore, Kendall could see Brynn was barely out of her teens, if that. "No problem."

"Morrie charges more rent for pets."

Not my concern. A week and I'm out of here. "He's not mine; I'm only going to be keeping him temporarily."

"Are you taking him to the shelter? I'm sorry, I read your note."

I don't have time for this—the cat or this conversation. "I'm not sure yet."

Brynn held the cat closer. "I'll keep him."

Glausson might take the cat, but somehow she didn't see him as a cat person.

Before Kendall could respond, Brynn asked, "Did he belong to those people who were murdered?"

No reason to hide the obvious. "He did. I'm not sure yet if anyone from the family wants him. If you're sure you want him, I could find out and let you know." It was hard to judge the girl's emotions behind the dark glasses, but Kendall thought her face brightened.

"Can he stay with me for now?"

Kendall would be happy to see the orphan get a good home, not to mention she wouldn't have to be the ogre responsible for taking it to the shelter. "Uh—sure. That would be good, I'm not around very much."

"All right, then." Brynn picked up the bag of cat supplies and moved toward her door.

Odd little duck. Kendall put the carrier inside Brynn's door. "Don't forget this."

She wanted to ask Brynn about the card they'd found at the Glausson house, find out if Brynn was Callandra, but it would have to wait.

———————

Rachel Jennings' house was in a neighborhood of single-family homes whose origin probably dated back to the '70s. Sided in a soft yellow, Jennings' small bungalow had what looked like the tail end of a rummage sale going on in the detached garage. A sign, "Everything 50% off," was posted in front of the door.

A tall, gray-haired man wearing a red and white Wisconsin Badgers sweatshirt stood at one of the tables, deep in conversation with a woman deliberating over the purchase of a set of dishes.

"Excuse me." Kendall flashed her ID. "I'm Detective Halsrud. I'm looking for Rachel Jennings."

"That's my wife. She's in the house." He pointed to a side entry. "She's pretty shaken up," he warned.

In answer to Kendall's knock, a blonde woman in jeans and a bright orange sweater came to the door. Her eyes were rimmed with red and her hair hastily tied back into a short ponytail. Kendall produced her ID and introduced herself.

Rachel Jennings opened the door. "Come in. I've been expecting someone from the police department. You'll have to excuse the mess. There are some things you can't give away."

The kitchen, although clean, was stacked with boxes and every surface covered with family treasures. Rachel took Kendall into the living room, where they sat across from each other on matching, blue-plaid sofas.

"I know this may be difficult for you, Mrs. Jennings, but I have to talk to you about the Glaussons. Not many people seem to have known them very well."

Rachel wiped her eyes. "That's true. The family didn't have

time to socialize much, I suppose. Mrs. Glausson, Chelsea, was devoted to Evan. She rarely left him. And Dr. Glausson worked long hours at the hospital."

"Do you know where the Glaussons were going yesterday, why a nanny was coming?"

"Priscilla Olson? She babysat occasionally, but she wasn't a full-time nanny. Chelsea told me she got along beautifully with Evan. I believe they were going to Sienna's cheerleading competition in Chippewa Falls."

"Did Mrs. Glausson confide in you?"

"She seemed to enjoy having someone to talk to, so I stayed late when I could. I wouldn't really say she confided in me."

"Did she ever tell you anything indicating she might have reason to be afraid? Maybe someone bothering her or her daughter?"

Rachel blinked back tears. "No. Nothing like that."

"What did the two of you talk about?"

"She didn't talk about anything very personal. We discussed Evan mostly, then subjects like current events, books, even politics."

Discouraged, Kendall struggled for more pertinent questions. "Did she ever talk about her marriage—how she and her husband got along?"

"I know she would have liked him to be home more, but she said that's the kind of man he was, dedicated to his work. She never complained about him."

"What about their daughter? Did you get to know her at all?"

Rachel smiled sadly. "Sienna was a popular girl. Chelsea said she had activities every day of the week and still pulled good grades. I didn't see her very often, and when I did, she'd come in, grab a snack and head for her room. Your typical teenager."

"And the boyfriend, Jeremy, did you see him there?"

"Once or twice, but I never talked to him. I know Chelsea and Mark liked him, approved of the relationship."

"Did Chelsea ever mention Mark's brother Graham?"

"Yes. I met him after Mark left for Iraq; he helped out when Evan broke his legs. He was around quite a bit at the time. She didn't say much about him other than she hoped he and Mark would mend their fences."

Maybe Alverson was right—the break-in had nothing to do with the family. She'd forgotten to ask Graham why he and Mark were on the outs; all she had was Betty Ruffalo's hearsay from Chelsea. His alibi checked out, so maybe the issues between the brothers weren't important. But she'd have to ask, get his spin on it. She couldn't believe she'd overlooked it. Stress and lack of sleep were taking their toll.

"I noticed they didn't keep photos of the baby around the house. Do you know why?"

Rachel frowned. "No. I never thought about it. Now that you mention it, that is unusual, isn't it? She showed me the digital photo frame she kept in Philly's room, though. Philly was such a beautiful child. And so good-natured."

"One more thing—we found a business card from a psychic on Chelsea's bulletin board." Kendall glanced at her notes. "Callandra. Was Chelsea seeing her?"

"I forgot about that." She sat up with a look of surprised remembrance. "Callandra warned her—she told Chelsea and Sienna to be careful, but Chels didn't take it seriously. I didn't either when she told me about it." Rachel covered her face with her hands. "God, why didn't she listen?"

Kendall gave her a minute to blow her nose. "Did she see her often?"

"No. Just the one time. Sienna and her friends were into the whole occult thing—you know, with all the vampire stuff so popular with the kids, that was the next step for them, especially the girls. She wanted to go to the psychic fair that was in town last spring, but Chels wouldn't let her go. Chels finally broke down and went with her. Sienna had a reading, then insisted Chels have one, too."

"And Mrs. Glausson didn't take the warning seriously?"

"No. But her daughter did. Chels told me Sienna was afraid to be in a car after the reading and constantly bugged her about keeping the doors locked."

"Were they in the habit of leaving the doors unlocked?"

"Always. But to pacify Sienna, Chelsea started locking them when she was home alone with Evan and Philly."

Was this a bizarre coincidence? Could Callandra have known about the murders by some method other than psychic foreshadowing? If Brynn were Callandra, she hardly seemed like the type who would have any connection to the kind of monsters who would execute an entire family. But you never knew. Kendall had to talk to her.

8

The five o'clock meeting went much like the one earlier: there was nothing new in the search for the baby; Sienna's coworkers reported she'd had no enemies; everyone loved her; and nothing conclusive had come back from the ME. The baby sitter's second trip to the house revealed nothing missing other than what they'd known the night before; cash, credit cards, and a few pieces of jewelry were all that had been taken.

Alverson strolled in as the meeting wound down, with FBI agent Gene Tarkowski on his heels. After her brief allusion to the FBI's interest in the case at the morning gathering, Kendall felt it appropriate to give Tarkowski the floor. At least that was her plan until Alverson took over the meeting.

"I've got something that might be important." He read from a small leather notebook. "A high school girl told us about an email that went around about six months ago. It was advertising for virgins, offering them top dollar for their—and I quote—introduction to womanhood. She didn't know how many of the girls in her class got the emails, but she thought quite a few had, including Sienna Glausson."

Lipske asked, "What's that got to do with a whole damn family getting murdered?"

"Maybe nothing, but it needs checking out even if it isn't related."

Getting paid for your virginity? What next? Kendall wondered why this was the first they were hearing of it and if the email had been serious. Alverson was right; someone had to look into it even if it wasn't related to the Glausson murders. And they'd have to question Sienna's close friends and the boyfriend again.

After Alverson's updates, Kendall introduced Tarkowski.

He took the podium. "All of you are probably aware that there have been two other home invasions similar to this one. The first one was in Green Bay a little more than a year ago, and the most recent, which you'll probably remember, happened last March in Stillwater. The Green Bay incident didn't get much press because there was a possible drug tie-in that made it look like the murders might have been related to a buy."

Discussions broke out around the room.

Tarkowski held up his hands. "I know, I know—seems like it had to be one or the other—a home invasion or drug incident. But you know how it is. The simplest solution always seems like the best, especially with everyone short-staffed. In light of what's happened here, we're going to add manpower to both cases. I've given Detective Halsrud copies of the files on the other two incidents. We lifted some prints in Green Bay but got no hits from them, and we weren't even sure they belonged to the doers. But we've got them for comparison if you get another print."

"Is there anything that proves it's the same guys here?"

"We're pretty sure the other two invasions were done by the same unsubs, since the bullets matched in both cases. Here, there are similarities, but also some differences. We're waiting for ballistics to confirm whether the same gun was used here. Detective Halsrud will share the details with you after she's gone through the files. For now, I'd advise you to keep looking at the family, find out if there are any connections there."

"Were there kids in the other ones?"

"Not in Green Bay. But in Stillwater, the family had a thirteen-year-old girl and a ten-year-old boy. None of them survived."

"Was the girl raped?"

"No."

Kendall added, "We haven't gotten much back from forensics yet. Since most of our evidence gets sent out, it's going to take a while. They did find a partial print on the daughter's wrist; we're waiting to see if that turns out to be enough for a match. If not for an ID, possibly a match to one from Green Bay. And they didn't find any semen, no hairs, nothing. Our killers were careful."

Alverson snorted. "Or just damn lucky."

Kendall arrived at the apartment after ten, bone tired. The painters had been in, the living room walls freshly painted a nondescript shade of off-white. She hadn't gotten back to Morrie with a color preference. It hadn't mattered since she didn't plan on staying. But the walls looked clean and fresh, the paint covering the ugly, aged surface.

After she'd changed into jeans and a sweatshirt, she remembered Callandra. Could Brynn be Chelsea Glausson's fortune-teller? It hardly seemed likely the teenager with albinism, living right across the hall, could be Callandra. There was only one way to find out, and if she were going to do it tonight, she had to do it now before fatigue overcame her.

The colored glass panes in her neighbor's door were lit from behind—Brynn must still be awake. Kendall knocked softly.

Brynn opened the door dressed in a charcoal gray sweat suit and track shoes, dark glasses still perched on her slightly hooked nose.

"Sorry to come by so late."

"It's okay. I'm a night person."

"I'd like to talk to you for a minute."

Opening the door wider, Brynn motioned her inside. Even with her undeveloped appreciation for décor, Kendall liked the cozy interior. Furnished with antiques and old-fashioned memorabilia, the effect was warm and inviting.

"Actually, this is an official visit," Kendall added, following Brynn into the small living room. A latticed teak screen carved out an alcove in the back of the room where a small, round table with two chairs on either side sat in front of two tall, narrow windows.

The white cat, comfortable in his new surroundings, perched on the table and gazed out the window while the soothing notes of a harp flowed from an iPod system on a nearby shelf.

Kendall took a seat on a sofa that had to be more than seventy-five years old, upholstered in deep maroon velvet. "Do you go by the name Callandra when you do your readings?"

"Yes."

The ambiance in the apartment was muted, supplied by candles and mood lighting. Nothing you could read a book by, much less a face. It was hard to tell what Brynn was thinking behind the dark glasses. Kendall thought about asking her to remove them but thought better of it. This was a preliminary interview, and Brynn wasn't a suspect.

"Do you remember doing a reading for Chelsea Glausson?"

In nearly a whisper, Brynn said, "I was going to talk to you about that."

"When did you see her?"

"June seventeenth. I had a booth at the psychic fair."

Kendall remembered being invited to attend when she was still living with Nat. Way too "woo-woo" for her taste, she'd begged off. "And she came in to see you?"

"Yes."

Kendall sighed. She was finding Brynn's reluctant conversational style annoying. "And then what happened?"

"I was only doing one-question readings."

"I'm going to need more than that." Damn, she needed to see the girl's eyes.

"I'm not sure I should tell you."

"I don't believe a psychic interpreter can claim privilege."

"She was with her daughter. I saw the daughter first, then she made her mother come in."

Finally used to the dim lighting, Kendall could see Brynn's hands twisting in her lap. Kendall's questions were upsetting her. "What happened during your readings?"

"The girl wanted to know about her boyfriend—she asked me if they would get married someday. But I saw something different in the cards . . . something she didn't ask me about. Death."

Naturally, Brynn didn't expound. "Then what?"

"I had her reshuffle the cards and we did another spread. It didn't change. I don't like to tell people bad things, so I just answered the boyfriend question."

She saw death in the cards. Right. Kendall had never been a believer in the occult. "Go on."

The cat appeared next to Brynn, rubbing against her leg. She scooped him up and held him tightly against her chest before settling him on her lap. "Malkin. Do you know what that name means?"

"Not a clue."

"Malkin is a cat that's a witch's familiar. Like in that movie—*Bell, Book and Candle.*"

Kendall still had no clue.

"It's an old movie from the '50s. With Kim Novak. That's how I knew Malkin and I were destined to be together." As if knowing he was being talked about, the big cat mewed softly and rolled over, seeking attention. Brynn rubbed his belly. "I thought Morrie told you about me."

"He didn't say you were a witch."

Kendall saw her smile. Fleeting, but definitely there. A first.

"That's funny. No, I'm not a witch. I just started doing this for the money."

That *was* what Morrie had told her. "So, getting back to the Glaussons . . ."

"The mother told me she wanted to know what the future held for her. Her cards were nearly the same as her daughter's. They showed death. Violent death. I didn't know what to say. Nothing like that ever happened before. It scared me."

Relieved Brynn had finally loosened up, Kendall had to admit the girl's story was getting interesting. "So how did you handle it?"

"I made up some things about her future, and told her she might want to be careful; there was a possibility of danger in their lives."

"How did she react to that?"

"She laughed."

"So she didn't take it seriously."

"She promised not to walk under any ladders or let a black cat cross her path, but I knew she was kidding around. I was frightened for them. They seemed like really nice people, so I told her a ten-minute reading wasn't very accurate and offered to have her come here for a complete session, free of charge. That's when I gave her the card. She never called."

Kendall shivered. In light of what she'd seen at the Glausson house, Brynn's interpretation of the cards was eerie. "The cards didn't tell you what was going to happen?"

"No. But telling someone when he or she is going to die? That's kind of . . . my specialty."

9

There were nearly a dozen private detective agencies listed in the yellow pages, but the few that Gray Glausson had been able to get through to on Sunday night either sounded like idiots or were overeager, making him suspect money as their only motivation. He didn't pretend to know a lot about police work, but he knew the first few days in an investigation were critical.

He paced the length of his office. A solution would come to him, but he kept seeing Chelsea's face and feeling he'd let her down. Finding her little girl was all he could do for her.

Adam Nashlund, grateful for an excuse to leave the house, showed his ID to the night guard at Chippewa Paper Products. The dark-skinned guard handed it back.

"Sorry, Mr. Nashlund. Didn't recognize you."

Why would he? As head of security, Nash spent most of his time traveling to CPP's other locations in the state. "No problem."

The VP's message had been to come to his office ASAP—he'd added no details. Nash had heard about what happened to the Glausson family. Under the circumstances, he wondered what

Graham Glausson was doing at the plant and on a Sunday night to boot. He found him standing in front of the floor-to-ceiling windows in his spacious corner office, hands laced together behind his head.

Nash tapped on the door as he entered.

Glausson turned and came over to greet him. He held out his hand. "Gray Glausson. Adam, thanks for coming. I hope I didn't take you away from anything."

"No problem. Call me Nash, everyone else does." If they were going to be on a first name basis, it meant only one thing—Glausson wanted something. Nash had only met Glausson once, right after he'd been hired and was introduced to all the big muckety-mucks. "I heard about your family. I'm sorry."

"That's why I wanted to see you. You were a police detective in Eau Claire before you came to work for us, isn't that right?"

"I was."

Glausson wiped his face with his hands. "Okay, here's the thing. I need some advice. I'm not very confident about the police in Eau Claire. I made some calls, checked into detective agencies, and so far, I have to tell you they didn't sound any more promising."

"Who's handling the case?"

"A Detective Whitehouse at first. But when I was there today, they told me he was in the hospital. His partner, a woman, is in charge now." He handed Nash a business card. "Do you know anything about her?"

Kendall Halsrud. "Never worked with her. But I still see some of the guys. If there were anything bad to know about Halsrud, it would have been discussed."

Glausson leaned forward. "That's reassuring, but I'd like to hire you. You were highly recommended when we brought you on board for your security position, and I'd be more comfortable if someone I trusted was working on this. I want you to find my niece."

It occurred to Nash that "someone he trusted" more likely meant someone he could control. "I'm not a detective anymore."

"But you'd have insights no one else would have."

"I can give you some names. A lot of the PIs in this area are retired cops—they know the ropes."

"I'll pay you a hundred dollars an hour for the time you put into it—on top of your regular pay."

A hundred an hour. Glausson was speaking his language. But there were things to negotiate. "What about my job?"

"I'll personally see to it that most of it is delegated to others. You can attend to whatever you have time for, but the murder of my family and finding their baby takes top priority."

Getting involved seemed a little crazy, but the Glausson home invasion was big. He would be back doing—well, sort of doing—the work he loved. His wife wouldn't be happy about it, but he'd worry about that later. "One more thing. The extra money you pay me? I want it in cash."

"That can be arranged."

"And just so you know, I won't be doing any end runs around the cops. I'll get as much as I can from them, try to find out if they're doing everything they should be. I'll do my own thing. Anything I find I'll have to turn over to them." Kendall Halsrud could be a problem, but not one Glausson needed to know about.

Glausson offered his hand to confirm their deal. "I understand. I'll feel better knowing you're on it. You'll have to keep me abreast of what you're doing, of course."

"Sure, no problem." Now he had to hope that the Halsrud woman would be open to working with him. And if not *with* him, then staying the hell out of his way.

Kendall wasn't sure she'd heard right. Death was Brynn's specialty? "What does that mean?"

Brynn stood and moved toward the adjoining kitchen. "Let's have some tea."

Were they back to that again—avoidance? Perhaps Brynn was just being sociable, but Kendall doubted it. She may need to be reminded that Kendall came over here officially and she *had* to answer her questions. She followed Brynn into the small kitchen, a mirror image of the one across the hall, except this one was painted a soft aqua with one wall covered in sepia photos from what looked like the turn of the previous century.

"Tell me, how is death your specialty?"

Brynn had her back to Kendall, busy preparing tea. "It was Madam Vadoma's specialty. Her real name was Ethel Weissbrodt."

That had to be the old fortune-teller whose name was still on a sign outside the building, the one Morrie told Kendall about. "Wasn't she dead by the time you moved in?"

"Morrie put a For Rent sign in the window right after she died."

Brynn *was* back to avoidance. Kendall wanted to shake her. "So, if you never met her, how did you start telling fortunes?"

"Morrie had a hard time renting the apartment because all

of her things were still in it and he didn't have time to get rid of them. I rented it as it was."

Kendall gritted her teeth. "Please. Answer the question."

"I didn't exactly start." She served Kendall a cup of fragrant tea in a paper-thin, white china cup and saucer.

Kendall could have used something stronger than tea to help her through the exasperating conversation. "What does that mean?"

Brynn sipped her tea. "The day I moved in, an old lady came to the door. I guess she didn't see very well because she thought I was Vadoma. I explained who I was, but her hearing wasn't too good, either. She begged me to do a reading for her. She wanted to know when she was going to 'pass' and told me that was what Vadoma did for people."

A fortune-telling death-predictor? Too weird. "How did you know what to do?"

"I told her I didn't know how, but she started crying, so I brought her inside and made her tea. She told me she needed to know when she was going to die because she wanted to plan her funeral and get her will in order."

Intrigued with the story, Kendall realized it had taken the fortune-telling experience to get Brynn talking. "Then what happened?"

"I told her again I wasn't a card reader, but she said it didn't matter, because the cards read themselves. She said Vadoma's spirit was still here and would help us. She told me how to shuffle and spread the cards."

"Did you have a Tarot deck?"

"No. Vadoma didn't use a Tarot deck. I used a deck of cards I found in the secretary desk."

"But how did you interpret the cards?"

"I didn't. I just told her the cards didn't say exactly when it would happen,

but they said she should be prepared."

Kendall was impressed by Brynn's compassion for the woman. "You told her what she wanted to hear. She was okay with that?"

"That made her happy. She made me take fifty dollars."

"So that's how death became *your* specialty?

"Yes. I needed the money, so when other people came by, I told them I was taking Vadoma's place. They mostly asked questions about death. And Vadoma, Ethel, had a journal with notes about the cards. It was easy."

Brynn quickly picked up their cups without offering a refill. Apparently, she'd reached her limit of extended conversation. She edged toward the door, sending Kendall the message it was time to leave. Though wanting to hear more about Brynn's transformation into Madam Vadoma's replacement, Kendall figured that could wait. In the meantime, she'd run a background on the younger woman.

Brynn flipped up the hood of her sweatshirt, covering her white hair. "I have to go for my walk now."

A walk this late at night? Kendall stepped into the hall, holding back a police officer's caution about walking alone after dark.

"Morrie has dollar-burgers on Monday nights. Until ten," Brynn said.

A bit of information she hadn't even asked for. "Good to know."

Kendall entered her apartment thinking there really wasn't much she could do with Brynn's story. But she would have to find out how Brynn knew something was going to happen to the Glaussons before the murders took place. She was pretty sure Madam Vadoma hadn't told her.

When Brynn left the building, the temperature had dropped. She felt the chill through her sweat suit and picked up her pace. She hated leaving Malkin alone so soon after bringing him into a strange home, but he seemed content.

She welcomed the darkness; daylight bothered her weakly pigmented eyes. Her vision wasn't 20-20, but she didn't need to wear prescription glasses. Nighttime was her friend. She blended in after sundown when no one noticed her unorthodox appearance.

Kendall seemed nice, but she asked too many questions. Brynn wasn't used to people asking personal questions—it made her nervous.

Kendall's cell phone buzzed as she was about to take a shower. She didn't recognize the number. "Halsrud."

"It's me, Hank."

"You shouldn't be on the phone.; you just had surgery."

"I snagged the wife's cell phone—I can't talk long."

"How are you doing?"

"Just peachy. I've got a zipper in my chest and a tube up my dick, how do you think I'm doing? Tell me about the case, but keep it short."

"Tarkowski thinks it might be the same perps here that did

the invasions in Green Bay and Stillwater. The Feds are working that angle now, so we've been focusing on the Glaussons until we hear more from them. We haven't found much, and, so far, forensics is a bust, except the blood we found in the baby's room has been identified as Philly Glausson's. The search teams haven't turned up any sign of her. And one rather bizarre thing—Chelsea Glausson saw a psychic six months ago who told Chelsea and her daughter they were in danger."

"Fuck me! That fortune-teller—a little white ghost, about five-three, nineteen or so?"

Kendall dropped onto a chair. "You met her?"

"She came in to warn us that two women were going to meet with violent deaths."

"And?"

"I blew her off, what do you think I did?"

"You didn't ask their names or file a report?"

Before he could answer, she heard an exchange of voices that didn't sound pleasant. A feminine voice spoke. "Kenny?"

It was Hank's wife. That was the end of the shoptalk. "Yes, Diane, it's me. Sorry about that."

"It's not your fault, dear. I know how he can be."

"So everything went well?"

"It did. They're going to put him in a regular room soon. I'll let you know when he can have visitors."

Kendall couldn't believe it. Hank Whitehouse hadn't filed a report. That had to be a first. But she knew how he felt about psychics assisting the police; apparently his cynicism extended to all forms of the occult. Brynn hadn't mentioned going to the police, although Brynn rarely said anything she didn't have to.

Before she closed the phone, she saw she had a message. It was from Betty Ruffalo, asking Kendall to call her. Good, she wanted to ask Betty about Brynn. She connected to the number.

"Oh. Detective Halsrud. I didn't expect to hear from you so soon. You told me to call you if I thought of anything else."

"Sure. Any time."

"I just remembered something. It probably doesn't mean anything, but a few months ago, Chels and Sienna had psychic readings done. The psychic warned them they might be in danger."

Kendall decided not to share the fact that she already knew about it. "How did she handle that?"

"She only told me about it after she realized it bothered her daughter. Sienna had just gotten her driver's license and loved driving, and after the warning she was afraid to get in a car. And when Mark and Chels told her they couldn't afford a security system, she wanted them to put deadbolt locks on all the doors."

"And did they?"

Betty started to choke up. "No, but Chels started keeping the doors locked when she was home alone with the kids."

"Thank you for letting me know, Betty. I'll look into it."

Betty's voice trembled. "The last time I was at the house Sienna said something to Chels about the patio doors being unlocked when she came home. Chels said, 'It's been months, Sienna. I told you it was all nonsense.'"

10

Monday

The first call from Adam Nashlund came in before nine. Kendall didn't take it. After the first one, his calls were scattered throughout her day, all ignored. She'd never really met the man, but considered him responsible for her brush with death when she was shot as the result of a drug event he'd put in motion. Working undercover at the time, if he'd followed proper procedure on the sting, she wouldn't have been shot. He wasn't a cop anymore; she had nothing to say to him.

Alverson and fellow detective Joe Monson came back in at noon after interviewing girls at the high school about the virgin emails.

"Did you get anything?" Kendall asked.

"Supposedly only about six girls got the emails. That we found out about, anyway." He held up a metallic-red laptop. "We got this from Hayley Frank, one of the Glausson girl's BFFs. It still has the email on it. I thought we could have it traced. Another girl who got one is dropping hers off later."

Kendall sighed. Computer analysis was limited in their station, and the officer who did it wasn't available. Maybe she'd pass it on to Tarkowski, let the FBI experts examine it.

"Did you talk to Ruby Rindsig?"

"I don't think that name was on my list. She one of the high school chicks?"

"No, but she would have still been in school when the emails went around. I must have forgotten to add her." Kendall had no real reason to interview Rindsig again, just that there had been something about her. "Call Tarkowski about the computers; see if they'll do the trace on the emails. I'll talk to the Rindsig girl myself."

It was after two o'clock when Kendall finally finished the mountain of paperwork related to the case. She pulled her coat on and went for her car; she needed a break from the monotony of the written word.

Ruby Rindsig's address turned out to be in a trailer court on the northwest side of the city, not all that far from the Glausson house and across the Chippewa River from the mini-mansions in its elite subdivision. The trailer with the number she'd written down sat at the far end of the park, long and weather-beaten, decades past its prime.

The man who answered the door leaned heavily on a walker, its legs ending in fluorescent green tennis balls. His odor wafted out into the cool air, contaminating it with a sour, acrid stench. Kendall showed him her ID. "Detective Kendall Halsrud. Is Ruby Rindsig here?"

He examined the ID. "Nah. She ain't here much. What's she done?"

"You're her father?"

"That's me. Girl spends all her time at school—hasn't got no time for her old man."

Kendall felt a flash of sympathy for the girl; the father was her only relative on record. She handed him one of her cards and told him to have Ruby call her. She'd find the girl at school if she didn't hear from her.

It was after nine p.m. by the time Kendall headed for the apartment. She didn't realize she'd forgotten to eat until she entered the back hall and inhaled the enticing scent of fried food coming from the bar's kitchen. What the hell, she had to eat. She took a seat at the bar in front of the redheaded bartender she'd met the first night she came in. After ordering a beer and a burger basket, she noticed Brynn duck furtively into a booth toward the back of the room.

A man who'd been sitting at the front of the bar walked over and stopped beside Kendall. He had collar-length, dark hair, and walked with a swagger that announced he was full of himself. She disliked him at first sight.

He leaned on the bar at her side. "The elusive Detective Halsrud—the woman who doesn't take calls."

Adam Nashlund. She should have recognized him. He looked just like she remembered him—wearing an Army Surplus store, khaki jacket, torn jeans, and an arrogant grin. Kendall raised her beer to her lips.

He offered his hand. "Adam Nashlund. You can call me Nash."

Kendall remained facing the bar.

He climbed on the stool next to her. "Hey. I don't bite."

"Your fuck-ups get people shot."

"Ouch." He kept studying her. "You've been around long enough to know there's always more to a story than what trickles down."

He had a point, but Kendall wasn't ready to concede it.

He kept pushing. "Can we forget ancient history? I need to talk to you about the Glausson murders."

"Why? You're not a cop."

"Gray Glausson hired me. He wants to find the baby, and he's worried the kid isn't your top priority. Well, not you personally, but the morons in ECPD."

Was one of the "morons" close to the investigation talking to him? Someone who'd been at the meeting and knew there were opposing factions on whether the Glausson baby was still alive? Not that she'd ever prove it, but it pissed her off.

"So what, you're a PI now?"

"No, just doing a favor for Glausson. He's my boss. I work security at CPP."

She snorted. "How nice for you."

He ignored the dig. "Hey, it could be worse. Glausson was going to hire Maggie Cottingham."

Kendall rolled her eyes. Maggie Cottingham was notorious—a dark-rooted, blowzy blonde, ambulance-chasing attorney who fancied herself an investigator. How the woman ever passed the bar, no one knew. Her presence at the station usually managed to clear it of all personnel with an excuse to vacate the premises. Nashlund wasn't Cottingham, but she didn't want him anywhere near her case. Or her.

When her food was placed in front of her, Kendall stood and picked it up. She turned to him for the first time. "Sorry, I'm eating with a friend."

Brynn looked surprised when Kendall slid into the booth across from her. Or as surprised as someone wearing dark glasses in a dimly lit bar could look. Kendall chewed a bite of her burger. "You were right. Good burgers."

Brynn picked up a fry, daintily dipping it into a side plate nearly filled to capacity with a giant puddle of catsup. "I like the fries best."

"How's the cat doing?"

"He's fine."

"I haven't found out yet if the relatives want him." Graham Glausson would be the first call on Kendall's to-do list, but after meeting Nashlund, the cat wouldn't be the immediate topic of conversation.

Kendall wondered why Brynn needed dark glasses in the bar, recalling she'd also been wearing them when she visited Brynn's apartment. She suspected at times they were a shield rather than a necessity. Kendall was ready to ask her about it when Nashlund, carrying a basket of food, slid into the booth next to Brynn.

Kendall bristled. "Don't you ever wait for an invite?"

"Hey, a guy can only wait so long before he has to take matters into his own hands." He picked up his burger and took a bite nearly big enough to halve it. He turned to Brynn and nodded toward Kendall. "She should work with me, don't you think?"

Brynn shrugged and licked catsup off her fingers. "I don't know."

One thing about Brynn—Kendall would never have to worry about her talking too much.

The greasy food suddenly wound through Kendall's intestines like copper tubing; she should have expected as much after her hit-and-miss meals of the last few days. She bolted for the ladies room. With any luck, Nashlund would be gone when she got back.

After Kendall left, Nash turned to Brynn. "So. How long

have you and Kendall been best buds?"

Brynn stuck another fry into her mouth.

"Tell me, how do I win her over?"

She tapped the corners of her mouth with a napkin. "I don't think I should talk about her."

"Why not?"

"I don't think she'd like it."

Nash leaned nearer to Brynn until his face was inches from hers. He reached up and gently slid off her dark glasses. Brynn's ice-blue eyes, shining like faceted mirrors, were turned ever so slightly toward each other.

"Yowza! You could kill a guy with those eyes." He raised his eyebrows, meeting her frigid stare. "Sexy, very sexy."

Nash slid the glasses back into place. "Thanks for the peek."

When Kendall came back to the booth, Nashlund wore an idiotic grin, and Brynn's body language said she wanted to crawl under the table. She sat down to finish her burger when her cell went off. It was Alverson.

"Newsflash. One of the search teams found a baby blanket stuck to a dead tree along the river."

Kendall's heart sank. "Where are you now?"

"I'm on my way over there. They're on the east side of the river about a quarter of a mile south of Clairemont. They're going over the area to see if there's anything else."

"I'll meet you there in fifteen."

Kendall wrapped up her burger, ignoring Nashlund's inquisitive look.

He narrowed his eyes. "Not gonna share?"

When she didn't answer, he stood and handed her his business card. "In case you change your mind—I'm available." He walked toward the door.

Kendall watched his departing back. "Asshole."

Brynn followed her gaze. "I thought he was nice."

Kendall arrived on the scene, the riverbank lit up like a baseball diamond. An area about twenty yards wide was taped off along a section of the riverbank thick with shrubs and clumped winter grass. Kendall could see her breath in the frigid night air. Fortunately there hadn't been much snow yet—nothing that stuck to the ground, anyway. If there were anything to be found, at least it would be visible.

The techs, spread out along the edge of the river, sifted through dead leaves, sticks, and assorted debris, looking for anything that could possibly be evidence.

Alverson stood nearby, talking to a sixteen-year-old boy wearing what looked like an advanced Boy Scout uniform.

"Detective Halsrud," Alverson said, "this is George Cline. He's the one who found the blanket. He's with a group of Explorer Scouts."

The boy stood at attention, and for a moment Kendall thought Cline was going to salute. She was about to ask what an Explorer Scout was and then decided it didn't matter.

"George, tell me what you saw when you found the blanket."

"We were walking the riverbank with lanterns and noticed something pink caught on a dead tree. When we got closer, we could see it was a baby blanket because it had little panda pictures on it."

"Did you notice anything else?"

"No. We followed orders and called in right away, then waited here. We didn't touch it and tried not to move around a lot."

They dismissed the Explorers from the immediate area. The techs bagged the blanket and various detritus, but other than the blanket, none of it seemed relevant to their case. Now they'd have to wait for forensics to do their thing. Meanwhile, she'd have to call anyone who might remember if that particular blanket had belonged to the Glausson baby.

By the time she and Alverson headed for their cars, her fingers felt nearly frostbitten. She couldn't wait to be in her car with the heater cranked up, but there was something that couldn't wait.

"Hey, Ross, I need to talk to you." He stopped walking and faced her.

"Do you still see Adam Nashlund?" Kendall asked.

Alverson hadn't been Kendall's chief suspect as the one blabbing to Nashlund, but his slow reaction to her question gave him away. He'd deny it, even though his tells were obvious. She didn't give him a chance.

"From now on, I'd appreciate it if you didn't share anything about this case or any other police business with anyone except your fellow officers. Am I clear on that?"

His face screwed up, ready to protest, before expelling a long breath of air that raised a white, frosty barrier between them.

"Okay, I had a beer with the guy. Is that a crime?"

"No, but discussing this case or anything involving police matters isn't professional and could lead to a reprimand. Keep your yap shut from now on."

"He's not a bad guy, you know."

Kendall resisted the urge to slug him. Adam Nashlund could go to hell and Ross Alverson could accompany him on the trip.

11

Kendall spent the morning working on reports and wondering where to go next with the investigation. The discovery of the baby blanket had turned out to be a bust; neither Betty Ruffalo, Evan's therapist, or the baby-sitter recognized it, although that didn't guarantee the blanket wasn't Philly Glausson's. The initial exam done by the ME showed no evidence of blood on the cloth or anything else that could identify its owner.

There was a camping area not far from where the blanket turned up; it could easily have drifted down from there. But there hadn't been camping weather for weeks and the blanket looked too new to have been out in the elements that long. Too new to have been along the river for even the four days since the murders. It was up to forensics now to see if there was any trace on it. Meanwhile, Kendall had detectives checking area stores in an effort to find out where it had been sold and hopefully, who'd bought it.

Kendall rose from her chair for a second cup of coffee just as a woman came rushing toward her desk. Walking masterfully in a pair of outrageously high stiletto-heeled pumps was one of the most beautiful women Kendall had ever seen. Nearly eye-level with Kendall, she'd have been average height without the shoes.

"I'm Graham Glausson's fiancée." She shoved a piece of paper at Kendall. "This was on Gray's windshield this morning, Detective."

Kendall took the sheet of loose-leaf paper. Scrawled across it was, *"If you don't want to end up like your brother, back off."*

A nasty tingle travelled Kendall's spine. "And your name is?"

"England Duran." She rested her finely manicured hands on Kendall's desk. "I'm a model."

How nice.

Kendall ushered her into a conference room, much to the disappointment of the male onlookers. Her beauty out of place in the well-used room, England Duran would have been at home on a throne, smothered in queenly robes while being fawned over by adoring slaves. *At least she's not perky.* Her luxurious, black hair fell in a silky stream to the middle of her back, and except for a slight overbite and fashionably inflated lips, Kendall thought she bore a resemblance to Morticia Adams.

"Why isn't Mr. Glausson with you?"

The woman slapped a diamond-decorated hand on the table. "What are you going to do about this?"

Kendall would have made book on Glausson having no idea his woman was here reporting the note. "The note will be sent for fingerprinting. We'll have to take your prints too if you've handled it without gloves." Glausson's prints were already on record, along with the DNA he'd willingly submitted.

"That's it? You aren't going to protect him?"

"I can't order protection on the basis of a threatening note. This could be from a crank. A crime as sensational as the Glausson murders brings out all the crazies."

Duran sniffed. "I should have known it wouldn't do any good to come here with this. You can't do anything until something happens to him, right?"

Kendall felt light-headed from the shallow breaths she took to avoid inhaling Morticia's cloying perfume—maybe it was laced with formaldehyde.

"If anything else happens, let us know."

England Duran fixed a narrow gaze on Kendall as she rose to leave. "I'll have Gray call you."

Call me, my ass. Glausson was probably making a beeline for his minion, Adam Nashlund. *Let him pay Nash to watch over his royal behind.*

Early that afternoon Ed Lipske came to Kendall's desk. "I ran that woman you asked me about. Brynn Zellman."

"And?"

"Turns out she has a sheet, but its sealed—Juvie. I asked Schoenfuss to see if he could unearth it. He said FYI, but not for public knowledge, she's a hacker, on probation as we speak."

A hacker? Everything about the girl was unexpected. Or weird. "Do you have the name of her probation officer?"

"Yeah. Linda Fournier." He handed Kendall a small sheet of paper with the officer's name and number on it.

"Thanks. You wouldn't know if she's in?"

"Yup. She can see you if you get there between two and three today."

Later, Kendall left the station and crossed the river to the courthouse where the parole offices were located. In her office,

Linda Fournier stood on her tiptoes watering a giant spider plant suspended from the ceiling in an old-fashioned macramé holder. Fournier had to be in her fifties, her tightly curled hair dyed a flat, shoe polish black, and her clothes, librarian-conservative. She saw Kendall walk in.

"Detective Halsrud. Please, have a seat."

The only seat in the tiny office sat beneath the spider plant. Kendall's height permitted the lowest spiders to graze her hair. She brushed them aside, wondering if they unnerved the parolees who sat across from Fournier.

"I'm here about Brynn Zellman."

"Oh, dear. Is Brynn in trouble?" The woman even talked like a librarian. "I'm working on the Glausson murders. Right now she's a person of interest, like everyone else we talk to."

Fournier took a seat behind her desk. "Good. The poor thing is really trying to make a nice life for herself."

"How did she end up on parole?"

"I suppose you could call what Brynn did cyber-vandalism. Brynn is talented with computers. Her hacking wasn't really malicious; she used her skills to pay back people who had made fun of her. People can be cruel when a person looks different. Brynn was picked on everywhere she turned and never developed the assertiveness to deal with it."

Kendall made a mental note not to anger the girl. "How long has she been on parole?"

"Since she turned seventeen. About a year and a half now. She only has six months left."

"Probation lasting this long seems a little extreme for the offense."

"It's lengthy, yes, but she was spared community service. She might never have been caught, but her mother came into her room one day and saw what she was up to."

"Her own mother turned her in?"

"It is surprising, except her mother was one of the people Brynn was driving crazy. Mrs. Zellman is one of those anal types who balance their checkbook to the penny every month. Brynn started making sure the numbers in her mother's account were off, causing her mother and the bank many hours of work trying to find the errors. Her mother was furious." Fournier adjusted her glasses. "Her mother is obsessively controlling and treated Brynn like a hothouse flower. According to Brynn, she couldn't even breathe without her mother's permission. Now the girl is determined to remain independent."

Kendall could sympathize. Her relationship with her own mother had never been greeting-card perfect. "If she was seventeen, why has she been allowed to live on her own?"

"An uncle who died a few years ago left Brynn a considerable amount of money. Her mother controlled it, although he hadn't specified when or in what manner she was to receive it. Brynn went to court in order to get the money transferred to her own account. She asked for it in monthly installments, and at the same time she applied to be an emancipated minor."

Surprising. "I didn't think that was easy to do."

Fournier sighed. "No, not usually. Her mother was livid. I testified on Brynn's behalf, Detective. I believed that Brynn would do better on her own by learning how to deal with the world. She sees me every week now, and a social worker drops in regularly."

"Do you know if Brynn has friends that could be a bad influence on her?"

"I don't think she has *any* friends, much less unsavory types. Detective, I must say, I can't imagine Brynn had anything to do with the Glausson murders. I'm sure you can tell I have a soft spot for the girl—she's quite unlike most of my parolees."

"How did you feel about the psychic readings?"

"I approved it, although I suppose the IRS might be another matter. Her trust fund check isn't very large, and that's what she lives on, so she needs the extra money. She says she's going to quit doing it when she gets off probation and can get a real job working with computers."

"Do you think Brynn believes she has psychic abilities?"

"No. She thinks the old fortune-teller did and is somehow guiding her readings."

That fit with what Brynn had told her. Fournier excused herself to take a call, speaking in a tone of voice and using vocabulary that definitely weren't library lingo. Kendall tried not to smile.

"Sorry about that, Detective. Parolees enjoy testing their limits."

Kendall glanced at her notes. "Brynn's a person of interest because last spring, she did readings for Sienna Glausson and her mother, Chelsea Glausson. According to Brynn, the cards foresaw violent death for them. In the aftermath of what happened, her prediction, if that's what you'd even call it, is suspect. You know the police aren't big on coincidence. Or psychics."

The probation officer gripped her hands together. "Brynn did tell me about the incident, but didn't mention their names. She was very upset after it happened and talked about giving up her readings. I was the one who insisted she go to the police. Not that I had any illusions they would act on it, but I thought

Brynn might feel better if she did something about it."

Kendall stood to leave. "Have you ever been curious about her readings—curious enough to have her do one for you?"

"Yes. I did. Her reading was uncannily accurate. She told me someone close to me would die soon."

"And someone did?"

"Yes. My mother. She'd been in a nursing home for years, and she passed about a week after Brynn told me about it. It was a blessing, really. My mother didn't enjoy life anymore."

Propped in his hospital bed, Hank Whitehouse looked as pasty as a prisoner on release day. At least he appeared to be tubeless. Kendall took a chair next to his bed.

"About time you show your face," he growled.

"Uh, I've been a little busy?"

"I want every detail."

"You've probably heard most of it."

"Not from you."

"I heard from Tarkowski on the way over here; the FBI might have a lead in the Stillwater case, but I haven't gotten any details yet. I've got to admit that being in charge of a big case isn't all it's cracked up to be—seems like all I do is keep up with reports."

Whitehouse adjusted his bed, moving up to eye level with Kendall. "Comes with the territory. Quit griping."

"Glausson's fiancée came in this morning. Someone put a threatening note on his car during the night, telling him to back off or he'd end up like his brother."

"Back off of what?"

"He's trying to find his niece. It sounds to me like someone's warning him off of searching for the baby."

"Possible. But it could be someone with a bug up his butt about the guy for some other reason, nothing to do with the murders. Glausson may have no idea she brought the note in."

"I think you're right about that, but it's strange he didn't let us know about it himself. I'm on my way to see him when I leave here. The fiancée is quite the looker—must be a replacement wife."

"Nah. I know a little about the guy. Never been married. He's been too busy climbing the corporate ladder at the ass-wipe company."

Kendall chuckled. "The girlfriend is up in arms because we aren't putting a cop on him. I told her the note wasn't enough and he should keep an eye out, let us know if anything else suspicious happens."

"All you can do."

The way Hank's eyelids were drooping, she wouldn't have time to give him all the details he'd asked for. She'd have to get what she came for before he drifted off.

"How well do you know Adam Nashlund?"

"Nashlund? Why?"

"I thought you probably heard about it. He's been working at CPP since he left the force; he's head of security there. Glausson has him working the case for him, trying to find the little girl. Nashlund came to see me last night. He had the nerve to tell me he thinks we should collaborate."

"You could do worse. Guy was a good cop.

What? "That so-called 'good cop' got me shot."

Kendall would have expanded on the subject, but a nurse in

a bright green smock and white pants a size too small for her full figure pushed her way between Kendall and the bed. The nurse passed Hank a small pill container and a cup of water, watching him closely while he swallowed the pills. After she left the room, Hank pressed a button, lowering the head of his bed back to where it had been.

"I need to get some sleep."

Kendall hadn't expected Hank to drop the subject of the shooting so easily; she'd always refused to discuss it with him.

"Just one more thing," Kendall said. "Back in the day, who did Nash hang with?"

"Your buddy, Alverson." His eyes closed, signaling the conversation was over.

12

Before she drove out of the hospital parking lot, Kendall's phone buzzed.

"We have a suspect in the home invasions," said the FBI agent, Gene Tarkowski.

"How did you find him?"

"The old story—he was picked up in Minnesota for speeding, mouthed off enough to get cuffed and the car searched. They found a gun in the trunk, a .38, same kind used in the invasions. He was carrying an amount of cash similar to what was missing in your case."

"Sounds kind of light."

"Yeah, but they have a rush on ballistics. They're holding him in St. Paul on a concealed weapons charge."

"Where will he be taken for questioning?"

"Stillwater. Since his crimes cover two states, we'll be running the show. One of our agents will do the interview. I wanted to give you a heads-up right away."

Kendall was steamed, but she knew they wouldn't be having this conversation unless the powers that be had already approved the takeover by the Feds. Trying to fight it would be senseless.

Tarkowski continued, "His name is Travis Jordan. He lives

in Minneapolis and works construction."

Kendall struggled for words. She should be grateful they might have found the perp responsible for the murders, but knowing she wasn't involved in the arrest really grated.

"Does this Jordan have a sheet?"

"No. He's stayed under the radar, although he travels in questionable circles."

"What can you tell me about him?"

"Not much. He's twenty-five years old, African-American with green eyes."

Kendall had to keep reminding herself that it was the result that mattered—putting him behind bars where he couldn't kill any more innocent people—if they even had the right guy.

When the call ended, she punched in Alverson's number. "What are you doing?"

"We're at the high school, talking to girls about Sienna and the virgin emails again."

"Wrap it up. I'm headed to CPP to talk to Glausson. Meet me in their parking lot when I'm done, about half an hour from now. We're going on a road trip, but keep it to yourself."

She'd worry about repercussions later.

Graham Glausson's secretary ushered Kendall into her boss's empty office, gesturing to one of two chairs facing a long mahogany desk before leaving to get Kendall a cup of coffee. Too wired to sit, Kendall toured the photos and awards adorning his walls. She saw a few family shots: a photo of the Glausson boys looking younger and happier, one of the parents, and a few of the family in various poses in a wood-paneled speedboat. A glamorous, professional portrait of England centered a shelf whose only other addition was a photo of the couple in formal wear talking to the governor.

Graham Glausson entered the room, tall and imposing in an expensive heather brown suit.

"Detective Halsrud. Do you have news for me about my niece?"

"No, nothing about Philly. I wanted to discuss the note you received."

"Note?"

"Yes, Mr. Glausson, the threatening note you found on your car this morning."

Glausson sank heavily into one of the chairs in a conversation area at the back of the room. "You can call me Gray, Detective. England brought it to you, right?"

"Yes."

"I told her not to, but she can be rather headstrong. I know what the note is about; it has nothing to do with what happened to my brother's family. CPP is still in contract negotiations at the Wausau plant, and things aren't going well. There'll probably be a strike come the expiration date of the contract. The situation is heating up, and I have no doubt the note has something to do with it—there've been other incidents."

Kendall studied him. He looked tired, his eyes lifeless, his hair looking like he'd run his fingers through it more than once that day. His explanation about the note made sense. "Let me know if anything else happens. If you have a problem in Wausau, call the WPD. It's best to be cautious."

Gray wiped his face with his big hands. "I heard you talked

to Nash."

Her intention to complain about his hiring Nashlund had lessened in priority since the call from Tarkowski. "I wanted to talk to you about that. He asked me to let him work the case with me. I can't do that. He's interfering in a police investigation."

He crossed his arms over his chest. "I have to do anything I can, Detective. My niece may be out there somewhere, in God only knows what conditions."

Kendall had been eager to talk to him more about Nash, but she had to get on the road for Stillwater before she was ordered to stay put. She turned to leave, then stopped.

"Oh, I keep forgetting—I have to do something with the cat we found at the Glausson home; it belonged to Sienna. Would you like to have it?"

"I can't, England's allergic. Will you have to take it to a shelter?"

"A neighbor of mine has been taking care of it. She's willing to keep it if you can't."

"Good. I'll contribute to its care if necessary. If it doesn't work out, let me know. I'll find it a home."

Kendall thanked him and hurried to the car.

With the Highlander pointed toward Stillwater, Kendall fought to keep the car within ten miles of the speed limit on I-94 while she listened to Alverson bitch.

"The Fibbies are taking over the whole fuckin' thing? Even the search? Makes us look like a pile of dog crap."

Even though she'd had similar thoughts, Kendall was sick of hearing him grouse before they'd gotten ten miles out of Eau Claire, and having second and third thoughts about her decision to include him.

"Ross, there's nothing we can do about it. We aren't even authorized to be making this trip; Schoenfuss could call us in any minute now."

He pulled out his phone and made a show of pressing the off button. "Then tough shit. I'm unavailable."

Kendall picked up speed. Travis Jordan may not be in Stillwater yet, but she'd damn well be there when they brought him in.

They pulled into the Stillwater police station an hour later. As they walked in Kendall said, "Remember, Tarkowski said the agent doing the interview is trying to make himself look like the big dog here. So pucker up, we may have to kiss his ass to get anything out of him."

Ross sneered. "Yeah, right. Then I'll go toss my lunch."

A detective wearing a Stillwater ID and a sour expression greeted them. Detective Sheila Olson stood about three inches shorter than Kendall and wore a bright red blazer over a pair of neatly pressed khakis. Her perfectly bobbed hair swung about her face with her least movement.

"Agent Kahn is interviewing the suspect. You can wait in here." She led them into a room lined with shelving and stocked with coffee makers, newspapers, and a ratty leather sofa, apparently their break room.

Kendall stopped Olson before she rushed out. "Do you know how it's going?"

Olson looked like she was trying to decide how much to tell

them. "You had a similar invasion in Eau Claire, didn't you?"

So we have to find common ground. "Yes, just a few days ago. And we haven't found out anything about the baby. That's why we're here. If you get anything from Jordan about the child, we want to be able to jump on it immediately."

Olson nodded, her hair bouncing. "I understand, but you may have made this trip for nothing. Jordan asked for an attorney as soon as he got here. No one knows how he managed it, but a criminal defense attorney from the Cities showed up only minutes after they brought him in. Lucille Bellamy. Ever heard of her?"

Kendall frowned. "She's good. Kahn won't get anything from him if she stays on the case."

Alverson opened his mouth as if to add a gripe, when a man obviously an FBI agent entered the room, his ramrod-straight posture hinting of a long-term military background. His age didn't fit with long-term, however; he had to be in his early thirties.

Detective Olson made the introductions.

Agent Gerald Kahn stood about an inch under six feet and had a long, narrow nose, its profile as triangulated as a wedge of gouda cheese, above a pair of nearly nonexistent, colorless lips. "Detectives. What can I do for you?"

Kendall reminded herself of her own advice to remain subservient. "We're here to help in any way we can. Our priority is to find out what happened to the Glausson baby. Can you tell us what you've gotten from the suspect?"

Kahn ran one hand over a bristly buzz cut. "I can't help you, Detective. Jordan didn't tell us anything before or after he lawyered up, and now Bellamy's monitoring our questions. If we're going to pin him to these murders, we'll need solid evidence because we aren't going to get a confession anytime soon."

He stopped talking when a woman wearing a fitted, navy blue suit entered the room. Kendall recognized Lucille Bellamy from a news clip on a Minneapolis TV station several months ago. In her fifties, the woman was distinguished by an asymmetric face whose muscles on one side appeared to have been destroyed by a stroke, although the deformity was reported to be the result of an unusually severe attack of Bell's palsy. The left side of her face sagged, the eyelid nearly covering one blue eye. When she spoke, only one side of her mouth moved.

"Am I missing a meeting of the minds?"

No one in the room spoke. Lucille Bellamy, despite her odd appearance, exuded authority and intelligence. Kendall wondered how Bellamy ended up in Stillwater representing Travis Jordan.

Kahn introduced her to Kendall and Alverson.

Bellamy faced Agent Kahn head on. "If you're finished questioning my client, Agent, I've got better things to do than wait for moss to grow on my ass here in Stillwater. Arrest him or cut him loose."

Kahn's thin lips flattened into a straight line. "Sorry, Counselor. We're holding him until ballistics on his *illegal, concealed* weapon is completed. If you prefer, we'll book him on a weapons charge for the time being. Your client broke the law. He's not going anywhere."

Kendall was beginning to enjoy their barbed repartee when Kahn's cell phone buzzed. He excused himself and left the room.

She turned to Bellamy. "I'd like to question your client, Ms. Bellamy. One of the crimes he's suspected of took place in Eau

Claire. It's imperative that we find the missing baby, a girl not even a year old."

Bellamy's mismatched eyes followed the direction Kahn had gone with his phone. The functioning corner of her mouth raised in amusement. Clearly, she was aware Kendall would be going in without Kahn's approval.

"All right, Detective, come with me."

Travis Jordan looked younger than his twenty-five years. His aqua-green eyes, high cheekbones, and mocha complexion hinted of a mixed ethnicity and lent his face a unique handsomeness. It always surprised Kendall when a perp turned out to be attractive, rather than some kind of horned monster.

"Travis," Bellamy said sweetly, as if she were talking to the boy delivering her groceries, "these are Detectives Halsrud and Alverson from Eau Claire. They would like to ask you some questions."

Jordan could well remain mute as he'd done for Kahn, but this would be Kendall's only chance to confront him. She didn't have time for preliminaries. She identified herself and Alverson for the record, then reached into her briefcase and pulled out photos of the Glaussons. She spread the death photos on the table, facing Jordan.

Her voice was cold, her words sharp as razor-blades. "I'm sure you recognize the Glausson family. Their home was invaded last Friday night." She waved a hand over the photos. "This is what's left of them."

Under a neatly trimmed Afro, Travis Jordan's blue-green eyes remained emotionless as they scanned the photos. Centered above his left ear was a rectangular area of shaved scalp, tattooed inside it in Gothic letters, "TRAVIS."

Alverson broke the silence and snarled, "Where's the baby?"

Kendall knew Alverson had been ready to burst and touched his arm to quiet him.

"We need your help, Mr. Jordan," she said. "The baby's missing, and her remaining family needs to know where she is. We have to find her before any harm comes to her."

Bellamy leaned toward her client and whispered in his ear. His sullen gaze remained unchanged.

Kendall brought out a photo of Philly Glausson and laid it on top of the others. "This innocent child deserves to be with family."

Jordan's eyes slid to the child. He sneered. "I'm not telling you jack. Take your pictures and shove 'em up your ass."

Alverson pushed across the table in Jordan's direction. Kendall grabbed his arm and brought him back to a sitting position just as the door opened and Kahn walked in.

"This interview is concluded." He motioned for Kendall and Alverson to follow him from the room.

The two men left the room ahead of her while Kendall returned the photos to her briefcase. Jordan's gaze remained focused on her. In a loud, nearly singsong whisper, he said, "Fuckin' baby's dead, bitch."

Kendall froze. "What did you say?"

Bellamy attempted to restrain her client as he spun out of control, grabbing the edge of the table and screaming, "You heard me—the baby's dead! Dead! I fucked the piece of shit and it's dead! Then I threw its bloody carcass in the woods for the animals."

Kahn pulled Kendall out of the room and went in to confront Jordan. As the door closed behind her, Kendall could still hear Jordan yelling, along with Bellamy's voice telling him to shut the fuck up. Kendall was nauseous remembering his words, grateful to be away from them.

She expected to be chastised for her impromptu interview with Travis Jordan, but a few moments later Kahn joined them, his face surprisingly devoid of animosity. "I'm going to let this pass, Detective. Anything Jordan says can be added to the evidence that's already been acquired. Convicting him won't be difficult with what we have on him."

The phone call must have been his source of this new evidence. "And that is?"

Apparently too exhilarated about his evidence to contain it, Kahn said, "The ballistic report came in—the same gun was used in all three invasions—his. It was hidden in the trunk of his car and his fingerprints are all over it."

"What about the partial we found on one of our victims? And the one in Green Bay? Do they match Jordan?" Kendall asked.

"We have the weapon, what more do you want?"

Was it possible all Kahn cared about was having enough evidence to make his arrest stick? "If the partial isn't a match, Jordan might have had an accomplice who took the child."

"An interesting suggestion, Detective. But it sounded to me like Jordan just admitted killing the child. I believe your chief told you we've taken over the case; let us follow up on anything that could lead to the child or indicate whether there was another unsub. We'll find the baby. And in case you aren't aware of it, a partial won't hold up in court unless it has a decent point match-up."

Kahn couldn't care less about Philly Glausson. It was time

to back off. Kendall followed Alverson out the front door and handed him the car keys. "I think you'd better drive."

"You okay?"

"I will be if I don't puke. That fucker's rant was hard to take."

"Yeah, but at least we know what happened to the kid."

Too upset to argue with Alverson, she knew Jordan's disgusting words could have been nothing more than payback for being taken into custody or for being confronted with the Glausson photos. She hoped so. The alternative was too ghastly to contemplate, even for a cop.

13

Wednesday

When Kendall came to work early the next morning, Shchoenfuss paced in front of her desk.

"Halsrud and Alverson—in my office."

They seated themselves across from the lieutenant, who'd taken the chair behind his anally neat desk.

"Halsrud, care to explain why you two went to Stillwater without my okay?"

Kendall said quickly, "It was my idea, sir. And I never told Ross we didn't have your permission."

"That doesn't sound like an explanation." He addressed Ross Alverson. "Is that true?"

Alverson hesitated. "Partially."

"Partially?"

"She didn't tell me, and I didn't ask. I figured we were on our own. I wanted to go. You know it's hard to give up an important case."

Schoenfuss rocked back in his chair, tenting his fingers. "I understand that. Which is why just this once I'm going to overlook it. Keep in mind it's no longer our case. Unless we're asked to assist, we're out of it. That's a direct order."

"But Kahn's ignoring the fact that the baby could still be out there somewhere," Kendall protested. "He's only searching for her body. And there might have been an accomplice. He's not pursuing that, either."

"Halsrud, you've done a good job on this case, but your involvement is over. If the child is alive, the Feds will find her; they're still searching. They have more funds and manpower than we do. If there was an accomplice, it's their problem, not ours. And there are still groups here searching for the baby."

He raised his hand to Kendall's objection. "No arguments. Ross, your partner is back tomorrow, and you can return to what you were working on before this hit the fan. Halsrud, you'll be on your own until Hank either comes back or gives his retirement notice. I'll have new assignments on your desk before noon. Are we clear on all that?"

"No, sir, we aren't," Kendall said. "I want to keep looking for the baby."

Schoenfuss clenched his teeth. "Which part of a direct order don't you understand?"

"It's just that I hate giving up on the child. The media will be asking about her, and we'll look bad if we aren't doing anything."

Kendall knew she'd gotten to him. He sighed. "All right, but it's secondary to your other assignments. And don't piss off the Feds."

As they walked out of the office, Alverson said, "You're a glutton for punishment, Kenny."

Kenny. Kendall, relieved by the reprieve from Schoenfuss, let it go.

Kendall's new assignments sucked. The first one, a rape case, possibly a serial, wasn't even in their jurisdiction. But Chippewa Falls PD was asking for help; they believed the rapist might reside in Eau Claire. The other case was a follow up on the virgin emails. Kendall had no idea what she'd do with that one. Even the Feds hadn't been able to trace the website advertising for virgins.

Two sex crimes. Alverson would be the first to label her the Panty Police, a term passed around to any detective who happened to be working on a sexually motivated crime. Kendall hated to complain about it since that was the area she wanted to work someday, in a bigger city as part of a special victims unit.

The phone on her desk rang. It was the front desk. "Halsrud, there's someone here to see you. I'll send her up."

Kendall watched Ruby Rindsig walk toward her. In jeans and a navy blue peacoat, a red backpack slung over one shoulder, Rindsig had the whole student look going. Contrary to the popular flat-ironed hair trend, she wore her fiery curls in a red mane that tumbled over her thin shoulders. Pink-cheeked from the cold, her face was bright with unexplored youth, causing Kendall to wonder if she, herself, had ever had anything remotely resembling that quality.

"I heard you were looking for me," Rindsig said.

"That's right. I'd like to talk to you about something."

She took Ruby into the small conference room and offered her coffee. When they were seated across from each other, Kendall asked, "Are you aware that a while back, emails went out to high school girls offering them money in exchange for their virginity?"

The girl didn't bat an eyelash. "Sure, I knew about it."

"You received one?"

Rindsig's hesitation gave away her first sign of uncertainty. The girl would be smart enough to know they might find out if she lied about it.

"Yeah. I got one."

"Do you have any idea who was sending them?"

She wrinkled her nose. "No. I thought it was gross. I deleted it right away."

Kendall studied her for a moment, wondering what it was about the girl that kept bugging her. She remembered feeling Ruby was trying to move in on Jeremy Dahlgren, Sienna's boyfriend. "Have you seen Jeremy lately?

"Sure. I see him at school; we're in a lot of the same classes. We belong to the same study group. We told you about that."

That didn't give away much, although Kendall hadn't missed the fact she'd said "we."

"How's he doing?"

"Pretty good, I think."

"You haven't asked him?"

"No. I guess if he wants to talk, he will."

"Have you thought of anything else about Sienna that might help us?"

Rindsig shook her head.

Kendall had the feeling the girl knew more than she was telling but didn't think it was the time to press her. "That's all for now, Ruby. We may need your computer. In case you find that email on it somewhere, don't delete it again."

The computer comment broke through Rindsig's posturing.

Her green eyes shifted nervously as she stood to leave.

Kendall wanted that computer. "You could just leave it now. We'll check if the message is still there."

"Sorry. I have a paper due tomorrow, and everything I need is on it. I'll drop it off some other time."

Just then Joe Monson called over to Kendall as they left the conference room. "Kendall, the medical examiner called. He wants to talk to you. Something about the Glausson baby."

"Thanks, I'll be right on it."

Ruby asked, "The baby? They said on the news the baby's dead."

"They say a lot of things on the news." Kendall had been afraid once a public announcement revealed the baby had also been murdered, public interest would wane, making it harder for her to convince the lieutenant to keep the case open.

Kendall gowned up and entered the autopsy suite. Franklin Teed was dissecting the body of an elderly man while Zydeco music played happily in the background. Maybe that's what it took for Teed to set aside the morbidity of his work—the upbeat music and years of working at the autopsy table.

He looked up from the open chest cavity. "Detective Halsrud. I left a message for you, but I didn't expect a house call."

Kendall wondered how he'd recognized her when only her eyes were visible over the mask and gown she wore. "I needed to get out."

He reached over to a Bose sound system on the shelf behind him and turned off the music. "I finished my report on the

Glausson infant's blood. I wanted to talk to you before I turned it in. I hear the baby is dead?"

Kendall sighed under the mask. "That's the general opinion."

"You aren't convinced?"

"No, but that might be wishful thinking on my part."

"I'm almost done here. I have an intern who'll finish up for me, then we can talk."

Teed's office, a genuine hole-in-the-wall, was packed with folders, professional magazines, and glass jars, the contents of which Kendall didn't want to speculate on. He cleared off the solo guest chair and offered her a cup of coffee. She declined.

"I'm afraid what I have to tell you won't give you any additional hope for the child. The DNA results on the blood from the child's room confirms the initial report; the blood belonged to the Glausson baby."

Did Travis Jordan's rant in Stillwater tell the real story? Or was it still possible there was another explanation?

"There wasn't a lot of blood in the child's room," Kendall said. "Travis Jordan claimed he raped and killed the child. Wouldn't you expect there to be more blood if that were true?"

"Possibly. However, if such a young child were raped by an adult male, most of the blood would have been on his clothing."

Kendall felt nauseous. Again. The sight of the autopsy she'd just seen was nothing compared to the mental snapshot of an adult male raping a baby.

"I'm sorry," Teed said, softly. "I know this discussion doesn't make your day any easier."

Kendall picked up the offered report and stood to leave. "No, it doesn't." Schoenfuss would see the report and be even more determined to close the case. As she walked to her car a thought occurred to her; —what if someone *wanted* them to think the baby was murdered? A stretch, of course, but not impossible. Maybe she'd have to consider the murders were all about the baby.

14

Kendall moved a few boxes stacked in the second bedroom, looking for her running shoes, hoping some exercise would relieve her frustration at having to turn over the case. She couldn't help thinking Travis Jordan's outburst had been a spiteful retaliation at being arrested. She still believed there was a good chance Jordan hadn't acted alone. If the man had an accomplice, Kendall was determined to find him; he could be the key to finding Philly.

She left at a slow jog, running along the street parallel to the river, and as she ran, planned her solo investigation. Since her time would be limited, she'd have to use it wisely. The image of Philly Glausson's bright little face kept her thoughts on the case she'd been told to restrict to secondary status.

Kendall moved north and then looped around after about thirty minutes, heading back to the apartment when the first snowflakes speckled her face. A car slowed down next to her as she passed the hospital complex on Belvedere.

The driver called out to her. "Detective! Kind of cold for a run, isn't it?"

She recognized the voice. Nashlund. His car crept along at the side of the road, window down, annoying the traffic behind him. "Take a break, I'll buy you a cup of coffee."

Kendall raised a middle finger, pointing it toward his car.

He chuckled. "I want to talk to you."

Not stopping, she yelled, "Bite me!"

He must have found out about Jordan. She wondered who told him, but the media had likely broken the story by now. Ignoring Nashlund, Kendall picked up her pace cautiously as the snow glazed the sidewalks just enough to make them slippery. Eventually, his car gained speed and vanished from her line of vision.

When she got back to the Rat Pak's parking area, he was standing under the small overhang above the back entrance, leaning against the building.

"I heard about the arrest. Good news, right?"

Kendall couldn't tell if he was being sarcastic. "Get lost."

He blocked her entry. "It's over, then. They got the perp. Finite."

She knew he was baiting her, but said, "It's over for ECPD, anyway."

"FBI taking over the whole thing now?"

"Yeah. I have permission to work it in my downtime, as long as I don't ruffle any Fed feathers." Kendall couldn't believe she was whining to Nashlund—a new low on an already sucky day.

"Maybe now I can convince you to join forces so we can find out what happened to the Glausson baby."

Kendall could use an ally, but Adam Nashlund? "I'll think about it."

"Could you think any faster if I told you what I found?"

"What?"

He grinned. "I haven't got squat."

She kept a straight face. "That's what I thought."

He stepped closer. "Here's what I'm thinking. There were no traces of the kid found anywhere but in the house. No blood, no body, no clothing. Well, the blanket, but that wasn't anything, right?"

Admitting it gave up nothing. The blanket held no trace elements and was sold in every discount store in the city. "Right."

"If she's still alive, why? Did they sell her? Give her to a pedophile? If they sold her and she was illegally adopted, it'd be difficult, but we could try to find out where and when. If there's a perv angle, baby-pervs are a minority in the short-eyes community, so there wouldn't be that many to check out. We'd have to get names of known ones in the area and find out if one of them has the kid before he destroys her."

Kendall winced, still having a hard time dealing with the thought of a pedophile who preferred babies. She wasn't ready to share Jordan's admission with Nashlund. "Those would be two angles to work," she admitted. "I've been thinking it's possible the whole thing was about the baby."

"See? All the more reason to go after it on that assumption and try to find the kid. One problem, though."

She suspected his arrogance assured him that she'd agree to work with him. "What's that?"

"Access. We'd need computer access, someone who knows how to pull a needle out of a cyber haystack. Especially on the adoption theory."

"I can try tomorrow." *Crap, am I agreeing to work with him?* At ECPD they only did the basics; anything complex and they had to go begging to a larger department for help. Those were usually backed up, creating an ongoing dilemma.

He must have taken her answer as agreement. "I had a friend who could find anything you wanted. Not necessarily legally, though. Too bad he's not around anymore."

Kendall hadn't realized how badly she wanted the Glausson murders solved, not just handed over. And more importantly, Philly Glausson found alive. But did she want those things badly enough to risk her career by cooperating with Nashlund?

Eerie in the hush of the snowfall, his cell phone sounded the theme song from *Dragnet*. He explained, "My son put that on my phone," and pushed the power button. He listened for a few seconds, had a brief exchange with the caller, then said, "I'll be right there."

"It's Glausson. Someone took a shot at him." Nashlund hurried toward his car, then turned back to her. "Coming with me?"

Kendall had a nanosecond's hesitation. He wasn't being a smartass tonight; maybe she'd seen his irritating side first. Or he could be making an effort because he wanted something from her. But they both wanted to find the child—it was all that mattered. She climbed into his car. He pulled out like a shot, but grabbed her wrist when she took out her phone to call it in.

"If you're coming with me, you're unofficial."

Gray Glausson's lake house faced the east side of Lake Wissota, a few miles northeast of Eau Claire. His place, the last house on a small, side street perpendicular to the lake, was a rambling, log and stone one-story that looked like it had been added onto many times over the years. The other houses on the street were dark, possibly owned by residents who'd left for the winter.

A black SUV sat in the street in front of the house and Glausson's Escalade was parked in the driveway, the window on the passenger side framed with shattered glass. A dusting of snow lined the seat.

The front door opened as Kendall and Nashlund walked up to the house. Gray Glausson filled the doorway, backlit by flickering light from a fireplace.

"Detective Halsrud. I didn't expect to see you here." He turned to Nashlund.

"Long story, chief. She's here unofficially."

Glausson stepped aside for them to enter a large room casually decorated in leather furniture, warm pine paneling, and rough, wood-hewn floors strewn with carefully placed forest green throw rugs.

A man stood in front of the fireplace holding a brandy snifter. Fifty or so, he was dressed in a corduroy sport jacket over a pair of well-pressed jeans.

Gray said, "This is William Hinz. He's our union's national bargaining representative from New York. He's in town until our contract expires in Wausau."

Hinz stood a few inches shorter than Kendall, but she felt his strength when he took her hand. He had a stocky build, but not an ounce of fat lapped over his tooled leather belt. After the introductions, he retreated to a chair next to the fire.

Kendall wondered what a union bigwig was doing at the home of the company's VP. "You think this shot at you resulted from another contract negotiations problem?"

Before Glausson could answer her snide question, Kendall moved toward the door. "I'm going to take a look outside."

Nashlund trailed behind her, then reached in his car and

tossed her a heavy, hooded sweatshirt. "Kind of abrupt with him, weren't you?"

Shivering in the damp cold, she pulled the sweatshirt over her nylon running clothes and walked over to the Escalade. "I didn't have anything to say to him." She hesitated. "We should have him come out here, though and show us where he was standing when the bullet hit the car."

"Nah. He said on the phone he'd just gotten out of the car when it happened. You could cut him a little slack; he just wants to find his niece." Nashlund stood at the driver's side with the door open, mimicking the stance of a person exiting the car.

"It didn't hit Gray, so where's the bullet?" he asked.

He sat in the driver's seat, his dark hair dusted with snow and highlighted by the interior light. "Asked and answered. Here it is." He pointed a small flashlight at the dashboard, where a ragged opening centered the screen of the navigation system.

Kendall looked around at the deserted neighborhood. "Let's try to get a bead on the angle. Maybe we'll be able to tell where the shooter was standing."

Nash slid a pencil into the hole. "The bullet's in there pretty far. We'll need a mechanic to get it out for us." He angled the pencil in an effort to trace the trajectory of the bullet. "What do you think?"

Kendall estimated the line of the pencil and walked toward the street. "The first driveway on the left. The shooter parked there."

"Let's take a look. Not that we'll find anything in this snow."

"He could have parked somewhere else and just stood over there."

"I don't think so. Do you?"

Kendall tried to put it all together. Glausson believed both incidents, the note and now the shot, were an outcome of difficult negotiations with the union. It seemed awfully extreme that they'd try to kill the man, or even risk firing a warning shot in his direction.

"Go ask him if either of them noticed any strange cars around. They might have; all these houses look like they're empty for the winter."

"He already told me that when he called me. He was talking to Hinz on his cell when he got here tonight; he didn't see anything. Hinz came over from his hotel after it happened."

Kendall wished she hadn't agreed to keep the incident quiet. "I'm not convinced this has anything to do with union stuff, are you? And if Hinz is the union honcho, why are he and Glausson so damn cozy if they're on opposite sides?"

"Guess you don't know anything about union negotiations. A lot of contract deals are wired. The big dogs reach a private agreement, and then try to manipulate the negations toward the deal. Private sector bargaining is nothing like the cops' negotiations."

He was right. She didn't know much about it. The cops in Eau Claire had a union contract, but it settled amicably every year.

"If the shooter was standing in that driveway, he wasn't a very good shot, was he?" she asked.

"The guy wasn't trying to hit him. It was a warning move like the note. Supports the union contract motive."

"But it also fits if someone's warning him off his search for Philly."

"I don't think this has anything to do with the murders,"

Nashlund said. "The guy responsible for killing Glausson's family is in jail." He looked at her through hooded eyes. "Unless there's something you aren't telling me."

After informing Glausson of their differing opinions regarding the note and the shooting incident, Kendall and Nash drove back in silence. There hadn't been much conversation on the way over, either. Since she obviously found him irritating, Nash had decided to let her take the lead on any conversation. She'd let her guard down tonight and come with him, probably because she wanted to be on the inside of whatever was happening with Glausson.

He'd use whatever worked to gain her trust. Everything he'd heard about her told him she was a good cop. Even Alverson thought so, but Alverson wanted to get in her pants. But that guy wanted in every woman's drawers except the real dogs. Kendall offered an offbeat type of attraction. He hadn't remembered her much from his time on the force. Now, he admired her tall, confident posture, competent but womanly; she'd shed a few pounds since the shooting. She'd pulled her hair band off tonight after her hair had gotten wet, and her long, sand-colored hair softened her features and highlighted her eyes, the color of his favorite brandy. Not that her looks mattered to him. Nash had a rare quality for a cop—he never cheated.

Before they turned onto her street, he took a call from someone Kendall assumed was his wife, apparently asking him where he was and when he'd be home. She hadn't pictured him with a wife, and marveled at his subservient responses.

"Yes. I'm taking tomorrow and Friday off. I'll have plenty of time to pick them up, don't worry about it."

It sounded like relatives were arriving at the airport. Kendall suddenly remembered why; tomorrow was Thanksgiving. That explained all the voice mail messages—messages she hadn't answered—from her father and her uncle. She was responsible for contributing wine and pies for the holiday feast. With everything that had been happening in the last few days, that chore had been last thing on her mind.

Jolted from her thoughts as they turned into the parking area behind the bar, Kendall saw two black-and-whites with lights flashing, parked in front of the rear entrance. A uniform stood at the door next to a small, shivering form. Brynn.

She approached them and held up her ID in case the guy didn't recognize her. "Detective Halsrud. What's happened here?"

"A break-in. Someone tossed her apartment." The officer, tall and imposing, nodded toward Brynn, standing dwarfed at his side.

Kendall turned to Brynn. "Are you all right?"

Stupid question. Brynn looked nearly in shock, quivering with cold. The snow had stopped after a one-inch accumulation, but the temperature had fallen. Like Kendall before her run, Brynn must have left for her walk before it dropped; she was only dressed in a gray sweat suit.

Nash covered her with his jacket, buttoning it up for her as if she were a child. Her voice diminutive, she said, "I'm okay. But will you please find out about Malkin? They won't let me go back up there."

"Sure, I'll do that right now." Kendall started to ask Nash to stay with Brynn, but he had his arm protectively around the girl, sheltering her from the cold.

The beautiful glass panel on Brynn's apartment was shattered on the lower side above the doorknob. Bad enough someone had broken in, but a precious antique had been destroyed. The once cozy apartment was in total disarray, all Brynn's belongings tossed about the rooms. A patrol officer stood at the door, and EC's other female detective, Paula Burnham, watched as a tech dusted for prints.

"Hi, Kendall. I hear you live across the hall. Nice door."

"I'm staying here temporarily," Kendall corrected. "Anything taken?"

"I don't think so. The owner had her wallet with her and didn't think there was anything missing up here on her first go 'round."

"Have you found her cat?"

"No cat. Probably hiding somewhere, staying away from the fracas."

"She's pretty worried about it. Mind if I look around?"

"Be my guest. My partner's off tonight."

Kendall searched for the cat, finally finding him under Brynn's bed, squeezed back into the corner as far as possible. It took a lot of patient coaxing before Malkin got close enough to grab. She picked him up and joined Paula in the living room.

"We have to have the tech check him out. I think this guy has blood on one of his paws and I'm pretty sure it's not his." Kendall pointed to a brown stain on Malkin's right front paw.

Paula twisted her mouth in a grimace. "How would it pick up blood if it was hiding? Assuming there was any blood."

"Won't hurt to check it out."

"You know, we're only giving this so much time because an officer lives across the hall."

Bitch. Burnham's sour personality made her unpopular among the detectives and right now the woman's attitude was pissing Kendall off. Kendall knew she had nothing to gain by rising to the bait.

"I know. I appreciate it, Paula." Kendall hung on to the squirming cat as the tech took samples from its paw.

Morrie walked in carrying a large piece of plywood. "Kendall, glad you're here. Can't believe this happened. We didn't hear a dang thing downstairs. Guess your neighbor was on one of her night walks when it happened."

"Convenient for whoever broke in."

"I'm just going to nail this on the door for now." He put down the board. "Not sure she'll want to stay here tonight, though."

"She can stay with me." Did that come from her lips? Kendall was shocked at her offer; she'd never been much of a "girl-friend" person. A tomboy since adolescence, she'd clung to that role, stifling any scrap of developing femininity.

"You might want to think about a way to make the back entry to the apartments more secure," she suggested.

"You're right. I need to do that."

After the police presence left, Kendall watched as Morrie nailed the board in place. "Gotta be careful with this. I don't want to make the break worse. I'm hoping it can be repaired."

"It'll be pricey," Kendall said. "You'll need a stained glass expert—one that specializes in restorations."

"Cheaper to get a new door. Hate to change only one,

though, especially this one. I'll check around. This should tide her over for now." The board covered the bottom half of the stained glass window.

Morrie locked up behind them as they left.

Kendall found Nash and Brynn waiting for her in the hallway, Brynn still bundled up in his coat. She handed Malkin to Brynn and opened the door to her apartment, where Nash settled Brynn on the sofa with a down comforter wrapped around her thin body.

He took in the boxes stacked against the wall. "Moving in or out?"

"Not sure yet."

He nodded as if understanding her indecision.

"Maybe this break-in will convince you I'm right about the incidents with Gray," Kendall said. "They're all related and they aren't about union problems."

"You think someone was sending you a message by breaking in right across the hall? If that's the case, then why not your place?"

"I don't know. Maybe Brynn's door was too inviting to pass up." She threw her coat over the boxes. "It doesn't matter. I'm back to new assignments tomorrow, anyway."

"Keep an open mind. This could be a random break-in," he said.

Kendall doubted it, but didn't argue the point. "I don't know about you, Mr. Nashlund, but I never had supper. I'm ordering a pizza if you're interested."

"Mr. Nashlund? Shit, only my son's teachers call me that. Call me Nash."

She sighed. "Kendall."

By the time the pie arrived, Brynn, who'd insisted on mushrooms, was sleeping. Kendall and Nash tucked into the pizza. When they'd finished eating, Nash said, "I'd really appreciate it if you worked with me on this. I think we'll have a better chance of finding the Glausson baby if we work together."

His polite phrasing caught Kendall off guard. She agreed before her memories of the day she was shot, returned. "My time will be limited. I'm only supposed to be working the baby angle in my spare time."

"What's your next move?"

"I'm not sure. Known pedophiles? Baby brokers?"

"We need a good computer person."

"You know what I have to work with—and he's off this week. The Feds would be the best source for that."

"No way. We'll think of something." He stood and picked up his coat. "I better take off. Unless you need me for anything."

She pointed to Brynn. Nash carried her to the bed, where Kendall took off her shoes and hoodie, then covered her with the quilt.

He gave Kendall a quick two-fingered wave as he walked out the bedroom door. "I'll be in touch."

15

Brynn woke to find herself in a strange room. She looked out the window and saw the view hadn't changed; the same trees lined the bluff behind the building. She sat up in bed and remembered her beautiful apartment. The sanctuary she'd made for herself had been destroyed. But she'd fixed it up once; she could do it again.

A note propped on the bureau alerted Brynn that Kendall had gone out to buy pies and wine for her family's Thanksgiving dinner and would be back after she stopped at the station.

Brynn had somewhere to go for the holiday meal, but hadn't taken advantage of it since she left home. She had no desire to see her mother. One sumptuous dinner wasn't enough to entice her to visit her childhood home, even though her parole officer advised Brynn she should never burn all her bridges; she might need her mother someday.

Kendall's living room looked just like it had the night before, filled with packing boxes, a few items of clothing tossed about, and a pizza box on the counter next to her laptop. Brynn had been too tired and stressed to eat pizza with Kendall and Nash when it was fresh. She raised the lid of the pizza box and saw two pieces left in the box. Breakfast.

She sat at the counter eating the pizza and staring at the open laptop in front of her. She hadn't used a computer in a very long time. Being this close to one again made her palms itch. She placed a tentative finger on the touchpad; the screen lit up. Sliding her fingers across the surface of the keys, she thought of the massive world residing right there inside the computer's slick, metallic exterior. Last night after they thought she was asleep, she'd heard Kendall and Nash discussing what they needed. Brynn could help them find the baby.

Her moral dilemma tugged at her while she ate. If she helped Kendall, she'd be violating her parole. But she liked Kendall and Nash, and she wanted to help them find out who had the baby. She picked up the laptop and carried it to a small chair next to the window where she could keep an eye on the parking lot. Brynn flexed her fingers and began tapping the keys.

It was quiet in the station. This early on a holiday morning, the detectives' division was deserted. There had already been a shift change and apparently those on duty were out. Kendall finished some reports she'd been putting off and got up to leave when she noticed the two laptops on her desk, next to them a note from Joe. They belonged to two of Sienna Glausson's friends who'd admitted getting the virgin email ads. Not surprisingly, the department and the FBI had gotten nothing from them.

Kendall stared at the laptops, one a shiny metallic red, the other a somber, gunmetal gray. Bringing evidence home could result in discipline. But the laptops had already been searched. Technically, they weren't evidence at the moment. Kendall's eyes scanned the room before placing both laptops into her briefcase.

She walked out just as her father appeared at the top of the stairway.

"Figured I'd find you here. Don't you answer your phone anymore?"

"You know I've been busy." The downside of having a retired cop as a father, Jim Halsrud could walk in whenever he wanted, and he always knew every step of her career.

"How long does a call take?"

Kendall walked to her car, her father following at her side.

"You do know what day—"

She cut him off. "It's Thanksgiving, and yes, I bought the pies and the wine. The usual: one pumpkin, one apple, one bottle of white wine, and one of red."

"Are you coming to the house now?"

"Now?" He didn't usually push her like this. "It's only ten in the freakin' morning."

"I know, I know. It's just that there's someone coming today who I want you to meet, so I'd like you to be there before dinner."

"Your chick-of-the-month? Wouldn't miss it." Kendall opened the door of the car and carefully placed her heavy briefcase behind the seat.

"Kenny, come on. Quit busting my chops about the women I date. I'm having fun, which is something I didn't get much of when your mother was around."

Kendall felt her blood pressure rising. "No one asked you to stay married to her, Dad. You chose to put up with all her shit, so quit acting like a martyr."

Still talking, he backed away from the car as she started the engine. He raised his voice. "I can't change the past, Kenny. I'll see you later. We'll have dinner at about two."

Driving back to the apartment, Kendall cooled down. She hadn't had the worst childhood, hadn't been abused, locked in a closet, or gone without anything. But watching her father kiss her mother's lily white ass all those years had been hard to take. The two of them put so much into their relationship games, there'd been little left for Kendall.

Her mother, obsessed with appearances, had made life hell for her father until he'd bought the bi-level in Oak Ridge to make her happy—a house that on a cop's salary was a huge drain on the family finances. And worse, her mother never appreciated it; nothing ever satisfied her craving to move up in the world. Too bad that hadn't been her only craving. Her other vice had changed her daughter's life forever. The thing that happened when Kendall was a teenager? Unforgiveable.

Despite it all, her father stayed with her mother. Kendall had been long gone from home when her mother finally left her father. He'd been miserable afterward, but once he got over it, he acted like he couldn't get enough of dating as many women as possible. The man had gone from one extreme to another.

When she got back to the apartment, Brynn, along with two strangers Kendall later found out were maintenance workers sent up by Morrie, was hard at work putting her apartment back in order. She stayed for a while lending a hand, then left to get ready to leave for her father's.

Kendall didn't recognize the strange car parked in her father's driveway, a late-model Cadillac. The new woman must have a lucrative job, or be a well-alimonied divorcee. Kendall stepped into her father's kitchen: a woman stood in front of the stove next to Jim, who was stirring something in a large kettle.

Dressed for the holiday, she wore a long sweater covered with turkeys, cornucopias, and Pilgrims. The lower half of her generous body was wedged into a pair of black leggings. When they turned to her, Kendall was aghast to see the woman was Maggie Cottingham, attorney/investigator from hell. There was no doubt in her mind the witch had glommed onto her father for only one reason—to get closer to the Glausson investigation.

Her father made the introductions, oblivious to Kendall's negative body language. He had to have known this would piss her off.

After mulling over her options and deciding to contain her anger, Kendall said, "Nice to meet you." and left the room, looking for her Uncle Al. She found him in front of the TV set in the lower lever of the bi-level home, where he'd taken up residence with her father when his wife died. It had been a welcome relief to her father, who'd been having a hard time with the house payments since he retired.

Kendall took a seat next to her uncle on a huge, curved sofa, each section with its own cup-holder and easily sprung leg rest.

"Want a beer?" he asked.

"Got anything stronger?"

He chuckled. "I take it you met Maggie."

"She's why you're hiding out down here?"

"Nah, just taking in the game. I'll go up later."

Kendall and her uncle shared a passion for college football. They spent a few minutes discussing the Badgers' chances for the season, and then watched as the pro game began on the large-screen TV.

Kendall couldn't get her mind off her father and Cottingham. "Where did he meet her?"

"Didn't ask."

"You know she's only with him because of me."

"You? How do you figure?"

"She's been trying to wear two hats lately, attorney and investigator. She tried to muscle in when she found out Gray Glausson was going to hire a PI to find his niece. I heard it from the guy who got the job."

"If he didn't hire her, why would she care about it?"

"That bitch always cares—it's what she does—sticks her nose into everything, considers herself Eau Claire's Charlie's Angel. Good thing I haven't been talking to Dad about the case. She's sleazy enough to facilitate a little pillow-talk to pry information out of him."

Brynn's apartment was back in reasonable order by early afternoon. The glass items that had been smashed would have to be replaced, but she'd gotten them at garage sales and would find others to replace them. Morrie arranged for a leaded-glass expert, a woman named Francesca Main, to come over and look at Brynn's door. She'd called Brynn and made an appointment for the next day.

Feeling better now that her apartment had been restored to order, Brynn was hungry and dwelling on Thanksgiving dinners of the past, the kind with turkey and all the side dishes. She loved the stuffing. A great big helping of dressing along with some white meat, maybe a little gravy on top, and you could keep all the extras. She'd just have to decide if she wanted it bad enough to call her mother. No, probably not. Maybe Morrie would bring her some leftovers like he had last year.

Kendall's key burned in Brynn's pocket. She hadn't had much time with the laptop before she'd seen Kendall pull into the parking area.

She crossed the hall and let herself in, surprised to see two other laptops on the counter. They had to be related to the case. She took a seat in front of the three computers and massaged her fingers—she'd repay Kendall and Nash.

16

Nash left home after dinner on the pretext of dropping off his son at a friend's house, not intending to hurry back. His in-laws were decent people, but after listening to their idle chitchat all day, he needed a break.

The Glausson baby never left his mind. The first thread they had to unravel would be the child molesters—they had to find the baby pervs, disgusting as that would be. He had to rely on Kendall to find a way to track them down, since his contacts were long gone.

He dropped Ryan off at an address a few blocks away from the Rat Pak and took a chance that Kendall might be around. Her car was gone, but a light was on in Brynn's place. Funny she'd be home at this hour on the holiday. He decided to stop in, see if she knew when Kendall would be back, and maybe ask her if she needed a hand with anything.

Brynn answered the door, the white cat content in her arms. "Kendall's not here."

"Mind if I come in?" He thought she looked at him suspiciously, but she opened the door to let him pass. "The place looks good. Must have been a lot of work."

"I had help. They were here for three hours."

Nash wasn't sure why he wanted to talk to the girl. At first he'd been curious about her relationship to Kendall, but that question had been answered when he found out they lived across the hall from each other.

"They did a great job." She didn't ask him to stay. He noticed a small table across the room with a deck of cards on it. Must be where she did her thing.

"Thought I'd ask you to tell my fortune." He'd kill some time until Kendall showed up.

Her eyes narrowed. Or maybe he'd imagined it; she was wearing a lightly tinted pair of sunglasses. "I don't tell fortunes, I do readings."

"Whatever. I can pay you if you want."

She put the cat on the floor. "All right. Fifty dollars."

"Fifty? You don't come cheap." He opened his wallet and offered her the bills, certain she expected him to decline and leave.

After grabbing the money, she led him over to the table holding the cards and offered him a seat on a wire ice cream chair he hoped would accommodate his weight.

"I'll be right back."

When she came out, he had a hard time hiding his astonishment at her transformation. Brynn's short, white locks had been replaced by a hairpiece so natural, if he hadn't known it wasn't hers, he'd have never guessed. Glistening strands of silvery-blonde hair fell to below her narrow shoulders, and wispy bangs graced her forehead, nearly meeting the pale blonde eyebrows she'd penciled in. Her amazing eyes glittered in the candlelight. She looked like a magical nymph, a character straight from a fantasy film.

Silently, she took the chair across from him, the draped

white gown she wore nearly dusting the polished wood floor. Nash made an effort to keep from gaping, thinking the getup alone made the fifty worth it.

"How come you only look like this when you work?"

She shrugged. "People like it."

She handed him a deck of ordinary playing cards, their backs decorated with medieval peacocks. "Shuffle the cards, then place the deck in the center of the table. While you're shuffling, think about a question you want answered."

When he'd finished, she picked up the deck, holding it sandwiched between her palms. "What is your question?"

"The Glausson baby; is she alive?"

"The question has to be about you."

"Okay. Will I find her?"

Brynn gave him an exasperated look. "I'm not sure that'll work."

She turned over four rows of four cards each, face down. "The row closest to you represents your past, the next one, the present, then your future, and the row farthest from you will reveal the answer to your question.

"Now turn over the cards in the row closest to you."

After they were turned, she studied them. "You've had some trouble in your past. Danger, maybe failure, a lost job?" She looked at him for confirmation.

Nash remained stoic despite the accuracy of her words. She could have found out a lot about him from Kendall or online, but why? He didn't think Kendall would have discussed him with her. She couldn't have known he'd be here tonight, or that he'd ask her to do a reading. After he'd turned over the row representing the present, she said, "There's a woman in your life.

Things are difficult between you."

He tried to sit straight in the uncomfortable little chair, feeling like the temperature in the room had gone up ten degrees. Stone-faced, he turned over the third row.

"Your future." Brynn frowned. "Your relationship with the woman is going to change. She's leaving."

Nash cleared his throat. How had she managed to find his sore spot? Things weren't great with Shari since he'd announced he was going to work with the police to find Philly, but leave him? He didn't see it, although there had been a lot of things he hadn't seen until it had been too late. He'd talk to his wife when he had a chance to be alone with her. Then he caught himself—this was stupid—everyone knew these readers were phony.

"As you turn over the last row, think about your question."

Brynn studied the cards he overturned, her face expressionless.

Impatient, he asked, "Well, am I going to find the kid?"

"The cards aren't specific on something like this. Two of them represent danger, possibly failure, but the other two show success. They aren't speaking very clearly. I told you it might not work."

Nash shifted his weight; he was uncomfortable as hell and out fifty bucks. "Anything else?"

"Yes, one more thing. Your car is pulling out of the parking lot."

"My car? What's that got to do with—"

Suddenly he realized she was looking out the window.

He leapt up so fast, the small chair overturned, frightening the cat and sending it scurrying under the couch. He got to the window just in time to see his car turning into the street and remembered—he'd told Ryan where he'd be.

"That goddamned kid!"

When Nash arrived at home, Shari and her parents were play-ing Scrabble at the dining room table. Shari looked up from the game. "Where's Ryan? Is he spending the night with Todd?"

Nash nodded toward the kitchen.

She left the table and joined him at the granite island. "What's wrong? Is he all right?"

"He's fine. He *is* having an overnight—at the police station."

She paled. "What?"

"The good news is he won't be arrested for car theft, because it was our car he drove off in while I was talking to a witness. I had a cop I know pull him over. They're going to hold him over-night even though we won't be insisting on his arrest."

Nash stopped her when she opened her mouth to protest. "Don't look so outraged. If I didn't have contacts he would have been booked. He won't be put in with any other prisoners, so you can calm down. The kid needs to have some accountability, Shari. Crap, he took the damn car from right under my nose."

Her mouth formed an angry line. "*None* of this is good news, Adam. What was he thinking? I know he's angry because we took away his driving privileges, but this? I just don't know what to do anymore."

She called him Adam. Never a good sign, but he could see she was near tears and took her in his arms. "We're doing every-thing we can for him. Maybe he'll shape up when he graduates in June and has to make his way in the world by himself."

Shari felt good in his arms. He still loved her, but the gap between them he'd hoped would close when he'd left the force wasn't narrowing. They'd been through so much together that he'd assumed they were past the worst life had to throw their way. He felt her tears on his neck and became aware that while she wasn't pulling away, she wasn't sharing the embrace.

It was after eleven by the time Kendall had Ryan Nashlund situated in a holding cell and made sure everyone on duty understood the situation. Luckily, Schoenfuss was off for the weekend. Lipske was on desk duty and had agreed to look in on the boy at regular intervals.

The kid tried to act tough, but Kendall wasn't fooled by his cool act—his bobbing Adam's apple and flushed complexion gave him away. Ryan's bravado despite the situation he'd gotten himself into reminded her of his father. She wondered if Nash realized how much they were alike.

When she got back to the apartment, she knocked on Brynn's door. "It's Kendall."

Brynn opened the door, the white cat at her feet. "Morrie brought me some turkey. Do you want a sandwich?"

It was just like Brynn to begin a conversation far from the matter at hand. But it had been hours since Kendall's uncomfortable repast at her father's house. Luckily, her cousin and his wife had shown up with their new baby, whose happy jabbering had taken some of the tension from the air during the meal. She hadn't eaten since.

"Sure. Got some white meat?"

They ate sitting across from each other at the counter. "Morrie brought this?"

Brynn nodded. "He did last year, too."

"Didn't your mother ask you over for dinner?"

"She always asks—I don't go."

Kendall didn't pursue it. The girl would tell her about her mother when she was ready. "Your place looks great."

Brynn patted her lips with a napkin. "I had help." She reached to the side of the counter and handed Kendall a sheet of paper. Written in a perfectly executed cursive, were the names of three men and one woman. All of them had addresses and phone numbers below their names.

None of the names were familiar. "What is this?"

"I used your computer," Brynn admitted. "I wanted to help."

Damn. She should have asked Brynn for help before there was any chance of getting her in trouble. "Before you tell me anything about these names, is there any way your searches can be traced back to you? Or me, since it's my computer?" Kendall knew it was possible to do an anonymous trace; she just had no idea how difficult it was to accomplish.

"No. I did it so it can't be traced." Brynn stood up to clear the table. "It just takes longer that way."

"Okay, who are these people?"

"They're registered pedophiles that live within a two-hundred mile radius of Eau Claire, and they—" she hesitated before whispering her next words, "they all like babies."

Kendall folded the paper and stuffed it into her pocket. "You heard me talking to Nash last night."

Brynn nodded. "Am I in trouble now? It's all right if I am. I want you to find the baby."

"No, you aren't in trouble. That's what I wanted to talk to

you about. After you told me about meeting the Glausson women and predicting danger for them, I had to check you out. You understand that, don't you?"

Brynn shrank lower in her chair. "Yes."

"I talked to your parole officer, and we came to the conclusion that your only connection to the murders was your reading with Mrs. Glausson and her daughter." She saw Brynn's brow furrow. "I'm not going to debate your psychic abilities, or those of Vadoma. That topic isn't germane to this discussion.

"Officer Fournier gave me permission to have you do some computer research for me providing you're supervised. I agreed to the supervision part, so no more sneaking around, okay?"

Brynn reached into her pocket and slid the key to Kendall's apartment toward her.

Kendall handed it back. "Keep it for now. It would be easier for us if I could let you work when I wasn't home, but for now we'll follow procedure. I'll see what I can do to get you off probation, since you only have a few months left. If I can show the Parole Board you've helped out on a critical police matter, it will go a long way toward getting you off of it right away."

Kendall's cell chimed, and she stepped into the living room to talk to Nash.

"How did it go with Ryan?" he asked.

"He played Mr. Cool. Didn't want a soda or magazines. Lipske's keeping an eye on him tonight." She heard him expel a long breath.

"My life is so fucked up."

Surprised at the personal comment, Kendall didn't know what to say. "Sorry."

"You on duty tomorrow?"

"No. I have the day off. I'll come in early, though, and meet you when you pick up Ryan. We can talk then."

"Okay. Did you have a nice dinner with your family?"

She snorted. "My dad is dating Maggie Cottingham, and she was at dinner today."

"You kiddin' me?"

"Wish I was. But it gets better—she gave me a tip—actually something interesting."

"No way."

"Way. Turns out she'd been hired to find an eighteen-year-old girl who went missing right after that virgin email thing hit cyberspace."

"How come you guys didn't know about it?"

"Probably because the girl's disappearance coincided with her graduation and eighteenth birthday. And she had a history of running away."

"Right—and I suppose all her favorite things were missing with her."

"You got it. Cottingham hit a wall with it at about the same time the parents' funds ran out, but she swears she had nowhere else to go with it."

"Yeah, right. You think that email business could be tied to the Glaussons?"

"I don't know. I did for a while, but I don't think it's too likely anymore. If I can find the girl, it'll free up more of my time since that's one of two cases on my plate right now."

"I'm gonna let you go. Things are a little dicey here. I'll see you tomorrow."

Kendall walked back to Brynn. "How would you like to start tonight?"

17

Ryan Nashlund looked only a little less sullen when Kendall arrived at the station the next morning. Playing the injured party, he'd still refused food or drink during the night. After an unsuccessful attempt to engage him in conversation, Kendall went back to her desk.

Nash showed up minutes later.

"I'm not sure this experience has enlightened him," Kendall said. "He hasn't eaten or said a word since we brought him in."

"I'll deal with Ryan when I get him home. Thanks for going along with the tough-love plan."

"No problem. I found a computer person. I have names of four pedophiles in the vicinity, those who prefer babies."

"That was fast. Who did the work?"

"I'll have to tell you about that later. Turns out I'm driving to Milwaukee today." Kendall and Brynn had worked until one a.m. when a joyous Brynn announced she'd found the missing girl, Brittany Markowicz. Kendall had been impressed by the discovery; Markowicz had changed her name. She was living in an apartment in Milwaukee near Marquette University and was registered there as a first-year student under the name Georgia Hughes.

"I thought you were off today," Nash said.

"I was." She looked around to be sure no one was listening. "But I want to talk to that missing girl I told you about, the one who went missing shortly after the virgin emails hit cyberspace. My source located her for me; that's why I'm going to Milwaukee. If I can get the case put to bed, I'll have more time to work on finding the Glausson baby."

He didn't ask her for details. "Sounds like a plan. My wife's leaving to stay with her folks for a couple weeks and taking Ryan with her, so I'll be able to work with you this weekend. What do you think?"

Kendall still had serious doubts about working with Nashlund. "I don't know how much time I'm going to have. It's at least a four-hour drive to Milwaukee, and I might have to stay the night, depending on how it unfolds."

His face furrowed. "I have an idea. Let me make a call." He left the room with his cell phone tight to his ear.

When he returned, he was grinning. "Bingo! Booked you a roundtrip to Milwaukee and you'll be back in time for dinner."

"You have a flying carpet?"

"Better. Gray has a little Cessna. I'll give you directions to his hangar. He'll meet you there in an hour."

Kendall headed for the airport doubting the wisdom of letting Glausson take her to Milwaukee. He remained a person of interest even if he did have an alibi, but technically the Glausson case wasn't hers anymore. When she arrived at the hangar, Gray

Glausson, dressed in jeans and a blue denim shirt under a deer-skin jacket, was examining the plane with an attendant wearing blue coveralls.

"Detective. You're right on time."

"Thanks for the ride. Do you have business in Milwaukee?"

He handed a clipboard to the man in coveralls. "I do now. We have offices and warehouses there. I was due to go, anyway. And I'll do anything I can to help you to find my niece. Even if it means an unscheduled visit to Milwaukee."

He pulled over a wheeled staircase and adjusted it next to the plane. Self – conscious with him, she was glad she'd let her hair down and worn her one pair of pants that fit her tall frame. Kendall climbed up into the passenger seat, hoping her anxiety wasn't visible. She'd never ridden in a small plane.

As the Cessna ascended easily into the air, Kendall's stomach rose with it. When the plane leveled out, she realized being in a small aircraft felt like being separated from the world she knew, an experience unlike that of flying in a commercial jet. Glausson was so close she could smell his expensive cologne, and when his hand brushed her thigh to reach for a control, her anxiety spiked. But he handled the plane expertly, which shouldn't have surprised her; he'd had a seven-year stint in the Air Force.

When they landed, a company car met them at a small Milwaukee airport. Kendall had called ahead to the Milwaukee Police Department. Their computer crimes department hadn't heard about the emails, but they were sending an MPD detective to join her when she interviewed Brittany Markowicz.

Glausson dropped her off at the station, where she met a tall, dark-haired detective named Richard Conlin. He introduced himself as being from the homicide division.

Kendall asked, "Homicide? We may be looking at something like statutory rape or solicitation, Detective Conlin, but no homicide that I'm aware of."

"No worries. We're short staffed this time of the year like everyone else."

"And you got the short straw?"

"Something like that." He laughed, the lines at the corners of his eyes, next to the silver hair at his temples, giving away his age as somewhere around fifty. Taller than Kendall, he was well built, but not as tall or as magnetically handsome as Gray Glausson.

Brittany Markowicz's apartment just off Wisconsin Avenue was in an old brick building housing eight units. It looked rather elite for a college student's budget, but the girl could be sharing with other students.

Appearing little like her high school photo, the girl who answered their knock was nevertheless recognizable as the missing Brittany Markowicz from Eau Claire.

Conlin addressed her by the new name. "Georgia Hughes?"

"Yes?" She reached up and tucked her long blonde hair behind her ears.

He showed his ID and made the introductions. "Do you mind if we come in?"

If she was nervous about their visit, Brittany Markowicz hid it well. She gestured to a room adjoining a U-shaped kitchen area.

They took chairs around a glass-topped table, which along

with the other furnishings, weren't those typically found in a student's residence. The décor looked like it had been arranged with a one-day shopping trip to the nearest furniture store; too perfectly matched to have been developed over time. There were no signs anyone else shared the apartment.

Kendall began the questioning. "Georgia, we know you're Brittany Markowicz. Are you aware you're being sought as a missing person? Your parents are worried sick about you."

She shrugged. "They didn't give a crap about me when I was living there."

"They hired a private detective to find you. But changing your name, made it just about impossible."

"I had to change my name. I want to make something of myself."

"You couldn't do that as Brittany?"

"Not if I'd stayed at home. And not if they found me. They'd find a way to ruin everything."

Kendall suspected she knew what "everything" referred to. "Just what would they ruin for you, Brittany?"

She waved her hand, indicating the room. "This apartment. School. I'm in pre-law at Marquette and have a 3.8 GPA already. At home I'd be delivering pizzas and sharing a dumpy place with four other people while I went to UWEC. Or worse, I'd be living at home."

"We know what you had in your bank account when you left—three hundred dollars. How can you afford this apartment and Marquette tuition?" Kendall asked.

"I'm an adult now. I don't have to tell you anything."

Kendall pressed, "Maybe you can explain how you got accepted into Marquette with a fake name and no high school records."

"I had connections."

Conlin dropped the bomb. "We know about the emails. That's how we found you."

Her body, encased in designer clothes carefully crafted and layered to look carelessly casual, betrayed her first sign of nervousness. She began crossing and uncrossing her legs, repeatedly tucking the same strand of hair behind one ear.

He asked, "Who's paying for all this?" When she said nothing, he continued, "You may as well tell us; we can find out easily enough."

"Then I guess that's what you'll have to do."

Conlin and Kendall exchanged a look. Kendall said, "We'll arrest him, Brittany."

"You can't do that! I wasn't a minor. I was eighteen."

Conlin said, "He used the Internet to purchase sex—that's a crime regardless of age."

Kendall admired the ease with which Conlin exaggerated Brittany's benefactor's culpability, knowing how hard it would be to make a case against him.

Brittany sat back and crossed her arms, a determined pout on her glossy, pink-tinted lips. They got nothing more from her before leaving the apartment.

Kendall had gained little except the ability to assure Brittany's parents their daughter was alive and well; there'd be no need to tell them the girl's living arrangements. She'd give the Markowiczes the information on their daughter's whereabouts and let them find out the rest for themselves. Before they pulled out into traffic, she noticed Conlin busy on his Smartphone.

When he put it away, she asked, "What do you think? Any possibility of an arrest?"

"Probably not. I just got the guy's name from the apartment rental records. Tenzin Chopak. He's married, lives in town, and rents her place under the name of his business. It's supposedly a haven for out-of-town clients. I'll pay Mr. Chopak a visit; see if he'll cough up anything on who was behind the website. Want to come along?"

Kendall was torn. It was basically Milwaukee's problem now since that was where Chopak resided. "If you're all right with it, I'll let you take over."

"We'll have to find out if he was involved in the site itself or just a customer. We can't arrest him for solicitation without proof, and the girl seems happy with the arrangement. I'll see what our computer guys can do."

"I don't get it," Kendall said. "Is money enough to keep a pretty, intelligent young girl in a long-term affair with a married man twice her age?" Maybe she just couldn't fathom it because she'd never been able to pick and choose men at will. Her few relationships with men had been strictly chance affairs and always at their whim.

Conlin snickered. "He's a means to an end. The girl's ambitious; she'll drop him like a hot rock when she has what she wants."

"Or he'll move on to the next virgin and leave her high and dry," Kendall added.

"There's always that. But I have a feeling this one is shrewd enough to have a plan B ready for a rainy day." He looked at his watch. "I have to make a stop at home. Mind riding along? It's only a few minutes from here."

Gray's meeting wouldn't be over until two. "Sure. I'll have Mr. Glausson pick me up there, if that's all right."

They stopped in front of an old brick duplex north of the valley bisecting the City of Milwaukee. A tasteful brown sign with gold lettering hung from a post in the small yard. T & J Security. Kendall wondered how a cop could be involved in a business on the side.

He noticed her looking at the sign. "Not mine, although I'm getting a lot of pressure to join the staff. It's a security agency run by my girlfriend. She's a former cop."

The office must have been adapted from the front half of a first floor flat. Heavy, dark walnut woodwork prevailed in the floor, the doorways, and the built-in glass cabinets on the far wall. On the left was a waiting area furnished in mission-style chairs and tables, the shelves packed with books, many of them true crime and suspense fiction. The other side of the room had a large oak desk with a wall of matching file cabinets and two rust-colored leather barrel chairs in front of the desk. Both areas sported large, leafy fig trees in bronze containers and brightly printed area rugs.

A woman casually dressed in navy jeans, white turtleneck, and a short, blue corduroy jacket entered the room. A denim sling with a baby tucked inside hung from her neck. Her cobalt blue eyes sparkled. "Hey, you made it."

Conlin put his arm around them. "TJ, this is Kendall Halsrud, the detective from Eau Claire I told you about."

Kendall sat down next to TJ on one of the long leather sofas in the waiting area and watched her ease the baby out of the carrier. The child couldn't have been more than four months old.

"He's cute. A boy, right?" Kendall held one of the tiny pink feet, its little toes wriggling as the baby twitched his arms and legs and made soft baby noises.

"Yeah. This is RJ, for Richard Jeffrey."

TJ didn't mention the baby's last name, and Kendall wondered if Conlin was the daddy; neither he nor TJ wore wedding bands. "He looks brand new."

"Just popped out a couple months ago. Thought he was stayin' inside forever, for a while there. Wanna hold him?"

The child felt like it weighed no more than the white cat, so delicate Kendall could see his veins through the whisper-soft skin, like one of those science models that exposed the internal workings of man. When TJ jumped up to take a phone call, Kendall kissed the baby's soft cheek. He grunted and grabbed at a strand of her hair. When he started to make fussy noises, she stood up, walking him slowly around the room, enjoying the feel of him in her arms and his powdery baby smell.

TJ came back in a minute later. "He loves that. Could walk him all day and he wouldn't complain."

"How long have you had this business?"

"Not long. I'm doin' mostly security stuff right now, but I'll branch out when I get someone to work with me. Got a friend who comes in part-time, helpin' me get things set up."

Kendall couldn't help admiring TJ's looks. She managed to be enormously attractive with no signs of makeup. She had high cheekbones over a wide smile, framed by a smooth-as-caramels, mocha complexion.

"Detective Conlin said you used to be a cop."

"Ancient history. Seems like a lifetime ago."

Kendall was about to ask why she quit the force when her

cell phone buzzed. She transferred the baby back to his mother.

"Detective Halsrud."

"It's Gray. Are you still working?"

"No, we just wrapped it up."

"My meeting's over, but there's a storm going through Madison. It's moving northeast. I'd rather not fly through it, so why don't we have lunch somewhere before we leave?"

18

Nash didn't think he'd ever seen his wife get ready to leave as quickly as she had after he brought Ryan home. Granted, it had been a while since she'd visited her parents, but taking off like this in the middle of their visit made him nervous, even though she purported Ryan's latest brush with the law to be the reason for the sudden trip. He couldn't shake what Brynn had told him. Was Shari getting ready to leave?

After Nash left the force, he'd expected Shari to be content. She'd hated the hours he had to put in, and the long absences during his undercover work put a strain on family relations. If his career change made her happy, it hadn't been visible. Nash preferred to go with the flow of the relationship and not look for problems. If they weren't fighting, then everything was cool.

It hadn't taken long before he discovered the PI license wasn't going to enable him to support his wife and child. The job at CPP came along at the right time. In so many ways, it was a real gravy job—great hours, benefits, decent pay—but boring as hell.

The fortune-teller had probably been right. His marriage was in jeopardy, and until Shari and Ryan came home there wasn't a damn thing he could do about it.

Now he had the weekend off to dwell on it. At least if everything went as planned, he'd be working with Kendall on Saturday and Sunday. Remembering the list of names she'd shared with him, he wondered if she'd be pissed if he checked on one of them without her. But she was eager to get going and time was everything in cases like this.

An hour later, he was headed north on 53. One of the names on the list was in Cameron, a small town about an hour north of Eau Claire. As he drove, the radio announced a storm system headed for the area, but hopefully it wouldn't hit while he was on the road.

The guy's name was George Iseroth, and the address was a street name with one of those annoying fractions they used around the small county lakes in northwest Wisconsin, 26-7/8 Street. When he pulled off the highway and entered Cameron, Nash stopped at a convenience store to ask for directions since the address was off the radar of his GPS.

The residence was on the upper end of Prairie Lake, part of a chain of lakes bordering Chetek, a town right off of 53. After driving around on what seemed like every road touching the northern end of the lake, he spotted a mail carrier who quickly pointed out where he'd gone wrong. The address was that of a small cottage behind a lake home at the tip of a narrow peninsula. He'd probably driven past it three times.

He parked at the entrance to the short, wooded street leading up to the main house. Its owner, according to the mailman, was Viva Jennemen, an eccentric woman in her 60s with yellow hair and a habit of talking a person's ear off, given even the tiniest opening. Her property had two cabins in the back that used to be rented out to vacationers. One of them was currently rented long-term to George Iseroth. The carrier had never seen the man whose mailbox sat next to Jennemen's at the side of the road.

Nash opted to talk to the property owner first. If she lived up to her description, he might get all the information he needed without even talking to Mr. Iseroth and unnecessarily alerting him. She answered the door at his first knock. Her brassy, yellow hair had gray roots nearly an inch long, and her floral-patterned dress hung to within a few inches of her red and white Nikes.

"What?"

Her abrupt welcome hardly seemed like that of a woman who loved to talk. "Mrs. Jennemen, my name is Adam Nashlund." He pulled out his PI creds, glad he'd kept them up despite their non-use. "I'd like to ask you a few questions."

She wore a faded, black cord around her neck holding a pair of reading glasses. After perching them on her beak-like nose, she studied the card. "I guess this will get you in the door." She stood aside to let him enter.

He walked into an aged kitchen outfitted with harvest gold appliances and wrinkled wallpaper. It was open to a living area decorated in heavy Mediterranean-style furniture from the seventies. Although shag carpeting had made a comeback, the shabby, gold floor covering didn't look like it could be part of the new wave in home decor.

He turned down her offer of coffee and took a seat in the living room. "I'd like to talk to you about your renter, George Iseroth."

She screwed up her face. "Him? Don't know what you'd want with him, he never goes anywhere, an' never does nothin' but sit in that cottage and watch the TV."

Nash remembered Iseroth was in his fifties, rather young to be incapacitated, but who knew? "Is he handicapped?"

She chuckled, her heavy bosom bobbing. "Only in the head."

"Is Mr. Iseroth mentally challenged?" Nash asked, satisfied he'd remembered the politically correct term.

She waved a meaty hand. "Nah, just weird. Only goes out once a week. The bus that picks up the old folks from the rest home and takes 'em out shopping, picks him up, too. Don't know how he managed that."

"So he doesn't own a car?"

"Uh-uh. He lives on some sort of assistance; don't ask me what kind. Walks with a limp, but that's his only problem I can see. The man doesn't work, and us taxpayers are supporting him."

Nash had more important things on his mind than Iseroth's subsistence. "How long has he lived here?"

"About three years. Pays on time and lives quiet. Good renter."

Three years would coincide with his latest release from incarceration. Nash wondered if Jennemen was aware of it and decided against bringing it up unless he had to. "Does he have many visitors?"

"None that I've seen. What do you want to know about him for?"

"His name came up in an investigation. Nothing to worry about, he's not in any trouble." Nash wondered if he even needed to talk to the guy if he didn't own a car and never left the house. "What about your other cottage? Do you rent it out?"

"Nah. It needed too much work, so I shut it up. And the septic's old. If I do too much remodeling, the county will make me put in a new one. Costs an arm and a leg."

If the second cottage was empty . . .

"Mrs. Jennemen, does Mr. Iseroth use the other cottage for

storage?"

"No way. He doesn't pay me enough as it is. I keep it locked up tighter'n a drum."

"Do you check on it now and then?"

"I check on both my places regular-like."

Nash could picture her dropping into Iseroth's place every week after the bus picked him up. "So you'd know if anything funny was going on?"

She twisted her mouth to the side. "An owner has to be sure a renter is keeping up the place, doesn't she?" She didn't wait for an answer. "Keeps the place neat as a pin, if you must know."

"Does he own a computer?"

"Not that I've seen."

"And do you own one?" He hadn't seen one when he'd walked in, but there were two bedrooms and the door to one of them was closed.

She laughed. "Me? No way. We had one when the mister was alive. Until I caught him looking at naked ladies on the damn thing. The next time he left for work I took it out and threw it in the landfill."

Nash nodded agreeably, but thought that without a computer and married to Viva, the poor guy must have passed shortly after.

It wouldn't be impossible for Iseroth to have a computer. Jennemen had a large TV set in the living room. There'd have to be a cable hookup of some kind, since Nash hadn't seen a dish on the property. They'd have to check utility records. Nash stood. "Thank you for talking to me. I'd better drop in on Mr. Iseroth now."

She walked him to the door. "He hasn't done nothin' has he?

I'm all alone here. Winters we're the only ones left on this end of the lake."

He said wryly, "I'm sure you're safe, Mrs. Jennemen." He didn't add that she was too old by many decades to be of interest to Iseroth, whose preferences involved babies.

The back of Iseroth's cottage sat only a few feet from the lake, which by today's tougher DNR regulations, wouldn't be approved. Nash never had understood the endless "grandfathering in" process of things that didn't meet code.

He tapped on the door and practically had to stick his foot inside to keep it from being slammed in his face. Iseroth muttered a quick "Go away!" as soon as he saw Nash standing on the stoop.

"I'm not a cop. I just want to ask you a few questions."

Iseroth opened the door only enough to see the card Nash held out. "Ask."

"Can I come in to talk to you? Kind of cold out here."

"No."

It probably didn't matter. If he'd had any signs of a baby around, Jennemen would have commented on it. The cottage was much too small for anything to remain hidden. Nash figured he could see at least half of the place from where he stood once Iseroth opened the door. Nothing looked remotely suspicious.

"Mr. Iseroth, I'm working for Gray Glausson. I'm trying to locate his niece. She disappeared after the Glausson home invasion in Eau Claire." The guy had to have heard about if he was a TV addict.

"Fuck you!" Iseroth slammed the door. Nash heard a bolt snap into place behind it.

Nash walked back to his car. Some cop habits never die; he

added a few notes on Iseroth to those he'd collected while talking to Jennemen. Reading them back, he wondered if he'd missed anything. He made a note to look into Iseroth's finances and do a background on Jennemen. Short that, the only other thing to do would be to come back on Monday while the guy was on his weekly, golden-agers bus excursion.

Back on the highway, the wind had picked up, the sky dark and threatening as the first of the snow began to whiten the asphalt. He thought about Kendall and Gray flying back from Milwaukee in a small plane and made a quick Sign of the Cross.

19

Kendall and Gray ate in a booth at the back of a famous steak and rib house on State Street, not far from where Conlin lived with TJ. The food had been fantastic.

Kendall noticed Gray assessing her. "What?"

"It's been a long time since I had a meal with a woman who really enjoyed it."

"It was wonderful. I suppose your fiancé has to live on carrot sticks and lettuce." She hoped it didn't sound like she was fishing for personal information. Or being catty.

He grinned. "Yes, just like a rabbit. When she does order a steak or prime rib, she eats two bites and pushes it away. Men hate that, you know."

"I love to eat. Although I can't eat like I used to."

"Why's that?"

Kendall wished she hadn't brought it up. "I took a bullet in the abdomen about a year ago. It takes a long time for your system to get back to normal."

She was relieved he didn't ask for more detail.

"Does your boss know I flew you here?" he asked.

"No, he's off this weekend. Accepting the ride wouldn't be that bad except you're still officially a person of interest."

"I am? You know where I was that night." He accepted the bill from the waitress, and waved away Kendall's offer of money. "Do you think I might have paid someone to do the deed?"

"You wouldn't be the first one."

"I suppose not. And it's no secret how I felt about my brother. I'll clear it up for you, Detective. Before Mark and Chelsea moved to Eau Claire, she tried to get us together, played mediator for at least a year before she gave up. In all honesty, my grudge had been more with my parents than Mark. I was ready to let it go after they both passed. Chelsea had me convinced it was the right thing for both of us."

"Then your brother was the one who didn't want to patch things up?"

"I'm not sure he didn't want to, but he didn't have time to make it happen. My brother's always been too busy trying to save the world, to 'make a difference,' as he put it. Chelsea agreed to his tour in the Mideast, although I've never understood why."

Kendal wondered if Gray wasn't aware of the quid pro quo that had taken place between his brother and Chelsea because of it, that her agreeing to his tour was the reason Mark had been willing to relocate his family to Eau Claire.

"Do you mind if I ask you a personal question?"

He frowned. "Not as long as it won't require the presence of an attorney."

"No, nothing like that. I was just wondering what you'll do when we find your niece."

He placed a credit card on top of the bill without scrutinizing it. "I'm glad you said when and not if, Detective, but I'm not sure what you're asking."

He probably had no idea how much a small child would

change his lifestyle. "I meant how would you take care of her? You have a demanding career. Is your fiancé willing to be a stay-at-home mom?"

"England wants children, just not in the near future. I'd have to hire a nanny, I suppose, and spend less time on the job. I could do more from home if I had to."

"I'm glad you're giving it some thought." She wanted to tell him how hard it is on a kid without a mom who is interested in her. But she'd done enough delving into the man's personal life and didn't want to reveal any details of her own.

The trip back to Eau Claire felt like it took days rather than hours. Kendall white-knuckled it all the way as they followed the tail end of the storm. When the small plane lurched and tossed about, Glausson acted like it was business as usual while Kendall fought to retain the lunch she'd eaten in Milwaukee.

They arrived back in the hangar just after nightfall although it was barely five in the afternoon. Gray swung his tall frame out of the plane, making the long drop to the floor as if he practiced it daily. Kendall wasn't even sure she'd be able to navigate the portable stairs, which, unfortunately, didn't seem to be anywhere nearby. She opened the door, expecting to see that he'd pulled them over to aid her descent. Instead he stood below the plane and beckoned to her to jump.

"Reach over to the left and grab that handle. Swing down and I'll help you." He raised his arms.

Too proud to beg for the stairs, she did as ordered. She swung out and felt his body against hers as she slid down the length of him until her feet touched the cement floor. She didn't think he'd planned it, but as their eyes met, he leaned in and kissed her. The jolt that ran through her at the touch of his lips wiped out all thoughts of how inappropriate the kiss was on so many different levels.

"We made it!" He broke away, grinning, and walked over to check on the plane. Dazed, Kendall stood in place, willing her legs to support her. When she returned from a unisex restroom she'd spotted in the back of the hangar, he offered her a disposable cup and a bottle of Jim Beam. "You look like you could use this."

She poured an ounce of the liquor and downed it. "Just enough to get me home."

Kendall drove home feeling like she'd accomplished something by just getting back in one piece. The virgin email case was wrapped up on her end; Conlin would take over where Eau Claire left off. It would be up to Milwaukee's computer crime experts to put a stop to the website that had been procuring teenage virgins to sell their wares. Her cell phone buzzed as she pulled onto the street in front of the apartment. It was Nash.

"You made it back; what did you find out?"

"The Markowicz girl is alive and well. She's living in an apartment in Milwaukee and going to law school, all on the dime of the guy who paid to be her 'first.'"

"Interesting. What are you going to tell her parents?"

"Nothing, she's eighteen. I'll tell them how to contact her. Obviously, she isn't going to press charges or give up the guy who's supporting her."

"Great, you have one of your cases wrapped up."

"Yeah, and one to go. The other one shouldn't take me more than a few days."

"We need to talk."

"Sure. Give me an hour to get my land legs back. I'll meet you in the bar downstairs at six-thirty."

In her apartment, Kendall stood under a hot shower, warming her strained muscles and remembering how exciting Glausson's body had felt against hers. His kiss had been a momentary thing, an isn't-it-good-to-be-alive gesture. She'd be fooling herself if she imagined it meant anything more.

Nash entered the Rat Pak looking for Kendall and saw Brynn walking out the back carrying a bag of takeout food. The air was thick with the smell of hot oil. As he walked the length of the bar, he heard a comment by a heavy-set man to an even more portly crony on his right. "Hey, did you see that—the white-witch. I think I'll have her sit on my face and tell my fortune."

His pals guffawed at the lewd comment.

Nash hesitated, then stopped and tapped the guy on the shoulder. "Watch your mouth, asshole."

From under a greasy baseball cap, his pig-like eyes turned to Nash. "Who the fuck are you?"

"I'm the new bouncer. You're outta here." Nash motioned toward the door.

The guy started to take a swing at Nash, who dodged the blow just as an arm reached between them displaying a detective's badge.

"Detective Halsrud." Kendall slipped the badge back in her pocket. "Is there a problem here?"

Pig-eyes whined, "I didn't do nothin'."

Kendall grabbed the guy's arm. "The owner of this establishment would like you to leave."

The guy looked toward Morrie, who stood at the back of the bar, ignoring the scene unfolding six stools down. When he realized Morrie wasn't going to come to his aid, the big man sucked down the rest of his beer and slid off the barstool. He missed the nod of approval Morrie made in Kendall's direction.

"Okay, but I'm taking my buddies with me." He raised his voice. "And we won't be back."

After he'd moved ten feet toward the door, he turned around. None of his friends followed him; instead they stared into their beers while two couples further down clapped in approval at the eviction.

With a last sneer toward Kendall, he muttered, "Fuckin' lezzie," and continued toward the door.

Nash rushed out after the departing jerk with Kendall at his heels. By the time she stepped out the door, he had the man pushed up against the building.

"Enough," she yelled. "Let him go, Nash, he's not worth the effort."

Nash wanted to do the guy some serious damage, but eased up. "Don't show your ugly face around here again."

Pig-eyes waddled away.

Kendall faced Nash. "Looks like you have a few anger-management issues."

"What's with you? I try to nail the guy for you and you tell me I have *issues?*"

"I don't need you to run interference for me."

"I'll keep that in mind."

"Well," she offered, "I think Brynn will be grateful. I'm sure it'll get back that you defended her."

Nash never had understood women, and Kendall was no exception. He let it go. "How was the trip? Heard the weather got pretty hairy between here and Milwaukee."

Kendall rolled her eyes. "Hairy doesn't begin to describe it."

"At least you made it home, safely. Back to the matter at hand, I looked in on one of the baby-pervs while you were gone."

"I want to hear all about it. Let's go back in and get some food. I think my stomach's finally returned to earth."

They took a booth in the back, where they filled up on fried fish and coleslaw before discussing the case. Kendall told him what happened with Brittany Markowicz.

"Nice to pawn one off."

"I didn't. Milwaukee's on it because Markowicz and the guy who bought and paid for her live there. MPD's computer-crimes division has a lot more resources than ours, anyway. I'm hoping they can find the source of the original emails. Conlin will let me know if they trace it back to our area."

"Hey, I was just yanking your chain. I'm glad you got one of those cases off your plate so we can focus on finding the kid." He relayed the details of his trip to Cameron to check out Iseroth.

"You think that one's a dead end?"

"Maybe. It seems like it would be impossible for Iseroth to have pulled a covert baby-napping without the old lady seeing anything. He had no idea I would show up at his doorstep. His place is awfully small to hide a baby. And the guy doesn't seem to have any money. We could have your source run his financials and take a look at the woman just to cover all the bases. By the way, who is this super geek that got the names for you?"

"Do you have a nickname or a slur for everyone?"

"Not you."

She sighed. "Not yet, anyway. And you did go after that jerk for me."

He grinned.

"I'm not a lesbian, you know. But I've never denied it to my fellow officers since they're convinced of it, anyway."

"I knew that."

"You *knew*? You think you have some kind of gay-dar for women?"

"Nah. I just know people. I noticed how you eyeball Gray."

Kendall opened her mouth to protest.

Nash interjected, "Hey, he's a good-looking guy. Nothing to be ashamed of."

She quickly diverted the Gray Glausson discussion. "I'll tell you who's doing the computer work for us, but you have to agree to keep it under wraps."

His raised his heavy eyebrows. "You're doing something off the books? I'm all ears and locked lips. Spill."

She explained about Brynn's history with computers. "It isn't really off the books. Schoenfuss just doesn't know about it yet."

"She getting paid?"

Kendall looked down, stabbing at the last piece of fish on her plate.

"You're paying her out of your own pocket, aren't you?" he asked.

"No," Kendall said, "she's working on it as a favor. I'm going to try to get her paid as a civilian consultant, although if I have to I will pay her myself."

"I'll mention it to Gray. He'll pick up the tab."

"You know I can't accept money from Gray. But I'm wondering if we're going at this the wrong way by spending time on the pedophiles. What if the baby was sold to a baby broker for adoption? They command ridiculously high fees. "

"If that's the case," he argued, "she isn't in any immediate danger. And why the blood on the floor of the nursery?"

Kendall sighed. "It's a mystery, all right. Maybe we should be concentrating on a possible accomplice. If we find him, it could save us a lot of time."

Nash called the waitress over for another beer. "Run it by me; what do you have that makes you think Jordan had a sidekick?"

"For one thing, Sienna Glausson was violently raped. In the Stillwater case, there was a teenage daughter and she wasn't touched."

"What did the Stillwater girl look like?"

"What did she look like? Are you saying they would have raped her if she'd been a cute little cheerleader like Sienna? That's sick."

"You know it works that way. Maybe he only went for brunettes."

"The girl in Stillwater *was* a brunette," Kendall added.

"And once more, what did she look like?"

The girl hadn't been particularly attractive. Kendall ignored the question. "They found a partial on Sienna's wrist. It didn't match Jordan."

"How about the boyfriend?" he asked.

"No match with him either."

"Finding an accomplice would be the way to go if we had something concrete. Since we don't, I say we keep looking at the pervs."

Kendall agreed. "It's just not happening fast enough. Tomorrow we can visit the others on our list. I'd better go now; I still have to drop in on my partner tonight at the hospital and then go over some of this with Brynn. "

"I'll come with you to visit Hank."

"Sure. Let's go."

In the hallway to Hank Whitehouse's room, they passed dozens of visitors straggling out. Visiting hours were over, but Kendall's badge bought them extended time.

Hank's back was to them, an IV stand on wheels clutched in his hand as he navigated himself back into the hospital bed. Kendall turned her head to avoid a display of his butt, visible between the flaps of a blue hospital gown as he backed into the covers.

He eased into the pillows, modestly covering himself as he saw them enter the room. He snorted. "The streets should be safe now that you two are pairing up. You working the Glausson case?"

Kendall grinned. "Why else would I be hanging around with this loser?"

Nash chuckled. "She loves me, just won't admit it."

Whitehouse seemed to weigh their banter. "Enough with the quibbling. I've been watching the news—they got the perp but not the baby. Said the Fibbies are taking over, that true?"

Kendall thought the grapevine must be slowing down if he only knew what he'd seen on the news. "Yeah. Schoenfuss gave me the okay to keep working the case, but only when my regular caseload allows time for it. He dumped two sex crimes on me. It doesn't leave me much time; that's why I hooked up with Nash.

"Travis Jordan confessed to killing Philly Glausson, but I'm not sure I'm buying it. I suspect Jordan had an accomplice; at least I think he did with the Glausson family."

"An accomplice? What've you got to go on?" Hank asked.

"Not much." She told him what little she had.

He grunted. "Hard to run with that. You're still looking for the kid, right?"

"Yeah. A few drops of blood were found on the floor of the baby's room. Just enough to identify it as Philly's. We're checking out baby-pervs."

Hank's face twisted with disgust. "Son of a bitch."

"Jordan himself doesn't fit the profile of a pedophile. He has no history with kids. They interviewed a long list of women he's been with and none of them said a thing about him having unusual sexual proclivities."

"If you're right about an accomplice, maybe it's *his* thing."

"That's what I'm thinking. We've got a list of four offenders that prefer babies and live in the area. Nash already talked to one of them. So far, it doesn't appear he's involved. I have the weekend off, so we'll be interviewing the others tomorrow and Sunday."

She looked toward Nash, who'd been staring at a TV set mounted on the wall opposite the bed. He turned. "So Hank, when are they going to spring you from this spa?"

"Not soon enough for me," he grumbled. "I'm sick of being poked and prodded, but at least they took the tube out of my dick."

Nash winced.

Hank said, "They must be really short-handed if they have Kenny working alone. I need to get back to work and keep her out of trouble. Word of advice? Don't overlook the baby-brokers. It's a thriving business. Young girls don't believe in abortion anymore—they keep the kid and then wake up to how hard it is to raise it alone. They sell to the highest bidder for up to a mil."

"We're starting with the pedophiles because her life is in jeopardy if she's with one of them," Nash explained. "If a broker sold her, chances are she's safe until we find her."

Hank humphed. "Just saying—keep an open mind, check out everything."

20

Saturday

Kendall and Nash drove south from Eau Claire until they pulled onto a street of typical Midwest homes. Modest, wood-framed, two-story bungalows, well-kept and graced with mature oak and pine trees. She'd called ahead to the local police department in Greenfield, Minnesota, a small town north of Rochester, to notify them she'd be in town to question John Traynor, the next sex offender on their list. They gave her the go-ahead without insisting on joining them when they questioned Traynor.

Nash, driving his wife's beige Malibu because it was less conspicuous than his or Kendall's car, stopped two doors down from Traynor's address. "You sure that's the right place? There's two kids in the front yard."

Kendall wanted to believe it was a mistake, but the house number was the one printed on their list. "It's a holiday weekend, maybe the kids are just visiting."

"What's wrong with our freakin' system? These offenders can't live within a thousand feet of a school or a playground, but if they move in with someone with kids, then that's okay?" Nash spouted.

She opened the car door. "Let's not pre-judge. Those kids might live next door." They didn't have time for debating the inadequacies of the system. "Come on. We'll surprise him."

The children, a boy about ten and a girl who looked two years younger, were riding away from the house on their bikes when Kendall and Nash reached the porch. A woman barely over five feet tall answered the door wearing faded jeans and a man's flannel shirt hanging to her knees. She had a fat-cheeked baby balanced on one hip, a baby with black hair bearing no resemblance to Philly Glausson.

"Does John Traynor live here?" Kendall asked.

The woman's eyes shifted from Kendall to Nash.

"I'm Detective Kendall Halsrud from Eau Claire, Wisconsin, and this is Adam Nashlund. We need to speak to Mr. Traynor."

The woman kept staring. Kendall wondered if there was something wrong with her when a man's voice called out from the rear of the house. "Who's at the goddamn door?" When he appeared behind the woman seconds later, Kendall held out her badge.

"What the fuck? Can't you people let me live my life? That arrest was nothing but a mistake. Just ask my wife, here. Mary Ellen, tell them." But when his wife opened her mouth to speak, he stopped her with a harsh glare. "I got a job and pay my taxes like everyone else around here. Don't need you cops busting my chops every time a kid goes missing."

Kendall stepped forward. "Who said anything about a missing child?"

"That's what it always is." Traynor whispered something to his wife. She left with the baby, who'd started crying when Traynor raised his voice. Stepping to the side, he opened the door all the way.

"Go ahead. Look the place over. I got nothin' to hide. The only baby here is my kid, and I can show you her papers."

Her papers. Dogs have papers. Is that how this piece of shit thinks of his child? Kendall wanted to toss him in a cell and throw away the key.

They toured the house as quickly as possible, noting baby things in most of the rooms. Kendall's skin crawled as Traynor followed her, his marble-hard, dark eyes on her every move. What were the chances he wasn't abusing his baby? She wondered if it were possible for a monster like him to love his daughter enough to protect her from his own disgusting urges.

Two of the upstairs bedrooms obviously had occupants under the age of twelve. Nash had been right. The kids they'd seen in the yard lived there. She kept combing the house, going over and over every nook and cranny until Nash pulled her out of Traynor's range of hearing.

"She's not here."

"We might have missed something," Kendall insisted.

"We haven't missed anything. Come on. We have other stops to make."

She hated leaving the creep with three children. In a voice loud enough for Traynor to hear, she said, "I want to stop at the Greenfield station and see if they're aware of the living situation here."

Nash looked at her with resignation. "Let's do it."

Kirk DeForrest, a professor in the economics department at the UW campus in Madison, was the third name on Kendall's list.

Another atrocity, but at least he wasn't working with young kids. He'd never been convicted of molestation thanks to a loophole in the law; DeForrest, who wore a hearing aid, had claimed his device wasn't working on the day of his arrest. A tenacious attorney successfully argued the police should have given him the opportunity to get the device repaired before reading him his Miranda rights. What a crock. Kendall had to admire Brynn's search skills in finding DeForrest without a conviction.

He lived in a rural area northwest of Madison. Kendall called the county sheriff's department to notify them of her impending visit. The deputy who answered sounded put out at the interruption and with a minimal amount of conversation, gave them the go-ahead to visit DeForrest.

She frowned. "He hadn't heard of the incident with DeForrest, said it was before his time."

"So? Things will go smoother for us without the locals butting in."

"I know, but you'd think they'd at least pretend to be interested."

"You already forgot about Greenfield? They're gonna bust Traynor for having his wife's kids living with them."

"I know, but there's the baby. She's the one most at risk, and there's nothing they can do about that."

The GPS took them to a two-story brick home, set into a hillside adjoining a neat farm whose buildings were well-kept and freshly painted. Outlined with white fencing, a pasture between the house and the outbuildings held a group of American Saddlebred horses huddled together against the wind.

"They must be paying academics well these days," said Kendall, looking over the grounds. "I think I'm in the wrong line of work."

Nash pulled into a long, curved drive leading to the house. "Hey, you're doing what you love and the bennies are good. Who needs all this?"

"Might be nice to have a place to hang my hat." Would it? She was still wrestling with whether to stay in the apartment. Something about signing a lease made her nervous, and her one-week trial ended today. The reasons for her resistance to a permanent residence were complicated, but she'd have to give Morrie an answer soon.

DeForrest came to the door neatly dressed in khakis and a maroon crew neck over a white, button-down collar shirt.

Kendall introduced herself and Nash and explained why they were there, expecting to get the door slammed in their faces. Like Traynor, DeForrest surprised her by inviting them in. "I have nothing to hide. The incident I'm sure brought you here was a long time ago. It was an unfortunate miscarriage of justice."

It was a miscarriage of justice all right—for the people. Stepping into a wide foyer decorated in startling black and white, Kendall bit back what she wanted to say, words that would have gotten them thrown out.

"I understand you feel that way, but you need to understand we have a job to do. There is a baby missing, and we have to find her."

"You won't find the child here." He waved his hand toward the interior of the house. "Be my guest. Look around."

They didn't wait for DeForrest to change his mind, and moved through the rooms quickly. The black and white theme dominated the interior of the house, accessorized with brilliant touches of red. The master bedroom, done entirely in white on white, was decorated with Asian style furniture, lacquered in shiny ebony black.

"This guy must come from money," Nash muttered.

Kendall looked in the closets. "He's anal as hell. I've never seen a closet this perfect, have you?"

"Not mine."

The house had no sign of a child having been there. She hadn't expected they would find anything, but the neatness glared.

They returned to the living room, where DeForrest waited, a smug smile on his face. "Satisfied?"

"The outbuildings. Are they yours?" Kendall asked.

"Yes. I rent them out."

"All of them?"

He smirked. "Yes. All the buildings are being used by other parties."

After they took their leave of DeForrest, Kendall got in the car, irritated. "What a prick."

"He let us in, didn't he?"

"The guy gave me the creeps. It's like he was waiting for us and had everything set up."

"I don't see how he could have known we were coming. The sheriff's office wouldn't have tipped him off."

"Something was off," she said. "Did you notice he didn't have any computer equipment?"

"I saw a laptop."

"Yeah. On a built-in desk where he puts his mail into neat little keyholes and pays his bills."

"What did you expect?"

He wasn't getting her point. "Here's the thing. Assuming his arrest was spot-on and the guy's a pedophile, he's been off the grid for what? Four years?" She checked the sheet from Brynn. "Yeah, four years. So what's he doing for kicks? He's not married. There were no signs of a woman in that house except maybe a cleaning lady. How's he getting his jollies?"

"If you're thinking it has to be through the Internet, it doesn't take fancy equipment for that."

"I know. But a guy with that much money? It doesn't play."

"Maybe he has an elaborate system at work."

"Sure, but he wouldn't dare use it for *that.* "

Nash grunted assent. "I think I saw a diner in that small town we passed through on the way here. Let's get something to eat. I think better on a full stomach."

21

Brynn spent the day visiting chat rooms and coming up with nothing, her search limited by the capacity of Kendall's laptop. She needed more power and a second machine, a system like the ones at the college.

Sneaking into a few classes had been easy for her until the instructor caught up to her in the hall one day and suggested she sign up to audit the course. She'd broken away from him as quickly as possible and never gone back. Observing the computer class had been the closest she'd come to violating her probation, but she'd wanted to keep up with the latest technology.

It was Saturday of a holiday weekend. If the lab was open, how many people would even be around? She packed up a few things, including Kendall's laptop, and left the apartment.

There were two students in the computer lab, totally absorbed in what they were doing. Neither looked up as she quietly took a place in a workstation at the back of the room. Her fingers raced across the keyboard. In seconds Brynn had logged in as a student.

In their last conversation, Kendall told her they hadn't found any phone communication between the freaks on the list Brynn had given them. If they were staying in touch with each other, it had to be online. The darker sites changed URLs often enough to make monitoring them nearly impossible, but those would be the ones they'd gravitate toward. Using two computers, she searched the chat rooms where pedophiles hung out; it took her nearly an hour to zone in on two sites she thought might be productive.

Next, she had to trace whether the pedophiles on their list were using one of the sites to communicate with each other; unfortunately, finding them while they were active would require constant surveillance. And it would only be possible after she'd identified at least one of their usernames. Brynn was up for it, but after a few hours, she needed a break. And food.

She left the computer lab feeling an odd sense of accomplishment, even though all the ground she'd covered hadn't borne fruit. It didn't matter. The elation she felt working with computers again made it worth every minute she searched.

As Brynn moved toward the exit, she noticed a student bulletin board packed with flyers. One of them caught her eye. It advertised an after-hours night walk for anyone interested in winter constellations. Participants were encouraged to bring portable astronomy gear. She'd been on these excursions before, not as a stargazer, but to have company on her evening strolls. This one started at nine that night, which would give her time to eat dinner and begin her surveillance of the websites before she left.

Better equipment would make the job a lot easier. Kendall had offered only her laptop. Brynn couldn't afford to buy herself a new system; she barely met her expenses from month to month. She could ask her mother to fund it, but that would cost her; the last thing she wanted was to become indebted to the woman.

Funny her mother hadn't contacted Brynn about her possible early release from parole. Maybe she was out of town on one of her bridge cruises. Now there was a trip for the idle widows. Her mother, in Brynn's opinion, was the epitome of the Jewish princess made famous by one-liners spewed out by stand-up comedians. Her obsession with the game of bridge spiked when Brynn's father died suddenly of a stroke five years ago. Strangely, the game hadn't replaced her obsession with her daughter.

Brynn knew how to play her mother; she couldn't just ask when she wanted something from her. The next time Monica Zellman came lurking around, as she would sooner or later, Brynn would find a way to slyly encourage the gift of a new computer. Or not, if the woman still carried a grudge.

The stargazers were bused from a pickup spot downtown to a county park north of Eau Claire. In Brynn's experience, walks like these were usually made up of retirees who'd discovered the art of astronomy as a late-life hobby. Apparently all of them didn't just sit on their fannies around bridge tables. When she arrived she was dismayed to find in addition to the usual attendees, a group of giggling teenage girls huddled together, most of them clutching their phones, madly texting while they waited. Judging by their level of enthusiasm, the astronomy walk fulfilled a class requirement. Brynn considered leaving, but she rarely spent much time with the rest of the group on these excursions, anyway.

The walk itself covered a distance of about a mile, winding through the park following an asphalt trail before moving into an elevated meadow to observe the heavens. It was a cold, moonless evening, perfect for picking out constellations in the star-filled sky. There was snow on the ground, but not enough to deter the walkers.

When they were all gathered in the center of the meadow, a few of the serious gazers mounted telescopes on tripods. Brynn kept walking, careful to stay in view of the others. The area was too formidably dark to wander out of calling distance, even for Brynn, who was used to walking alone at night.

A half hour passed. From a distance, Brynn noticed the group getting ready to leave, the group leader flashing his light her way, signaling her to join them. She started to move toward the center of the meadow, when she heard a noise behind her that sounded like someone moaning. She stopped and turned her flashlight in the direction of the sound. No mistake—someone was in trouble not far from where Brynn stood. She followed the voice to a stand of pine trees and discovered a young woman lying inside, only partially dressed. She edged close enough to see a knife protruding from the girl's abdomen. Making an effort not to panic, she remembered taking out the knife could be dangerous.

The girl spoke in a thready voice. "Help me."

Brynn knelt next to her and took her hand. "I'll get help."

"No, don't leave me. He's still here."

Whoever hurt her was still around? Fear nearly overcame her, but Brynn had to get help. "I won't go far. Just far enough so they'll see my light."

Brynn took a few steps out of the trees and began to wave her light in circles, screaming, "Over here."

She saw an answering light. "Call 911!"

22

The diner, decorated in typical red-checked tablecloth style, had a few patrons sitting at a counter lining the side of the room. The rest of the place was taken up with tables for four, most of them unoccupied. Kendall hadn't realized she was hungry until she took in the scent of baking meatloaf, a favorite meal when she was growing up. Prepared by her father, of course, since cooking hadn't been one of her mother's favorite pastimes.

Kendall and Nash took a table at the window, and over the special of the night, meat loaf and baked potatoes, they discussed the stops they'd made.

"Those pervs—they're disgusting," Kendall commented.

"They are. But our goal is to find Philly Glausson, not to get these mopes behind bars, much as we might want that outcome."

The meatloaf had been divine, but Kendall hoped she wouldn't have to pay the price of the heavy meal on her sensitive digestive system. Since taking the bullet, her traumatized stomach often objected to heavy meals.

"They had to be in touch with each other,' she said. "How else would the two we talked to today have known we were coming?"

"Just because they let us look around, it doesn't prove they knew we would be there—it just tells us they're careful. Traynor's wife may not have a clue who he really is. He would have denied the charges against him and kept anything incriminating well hidden. In a surface search like we did at his place, it doesn't surprise me we didn't come across anything; the same goes for DeForrest. The guy's a professor. He wouldn't risk having anything suspicious in plain sight."

Kendall started to protest when, as she'd feared, her abdomen began to object. She excused herself and quickly left the table.

When she came back, Nash asked, "Post-GSW problems?"

He was the last person she wanted to discuss it with; she still blamed him for what went down the night she got shot. She turned an acid look in his direction. "Maybe I have my period. Ever think of that?"

Instead of being embarrassed at her comment, Nash reached across the table and grabbed her hand. Quickly conscious it was the same size as his, she pulled away.

"I didn't think of that," he said, "because I know a stomach shot can leave you with problems. It's time we cleared this up. I was in charge that night, but the truth is, the sting went south because of the drug runners, not anything we did. We plan busts as tightly as possible, but we can't always control everything. Shit happens."

Shit happens? Kendall hated the phrase. Like that covered anything that went wrong in the world. "What kind of shit was that, your incompetence?"

Nash sat back and shook his head. "I felt terrible about it—still do—that clusterfuck is why I left the force. And don't forget, I took a bullet, too."

Kendall sensed his sincerity. But why hadn't she been told what happened? It seemed odd at the time that the other detectives were kept from the truth. There was something Nash wasn't telling her. It was possible he was protecting someone. Maybe one of his people screwed up when the scenario changed unexpectedly.

"My partner lost his life because of that screw-up. You and I are still around to bitch about our wounds," she reminded him.

"You think his death has been easy for me to live with?" he asked. "I looked in on you a few times when we were both in the hospital, you know."

Remembering the night she was shot, Kendall felt the onset of tears stinging her eyes as her throat tightened. Her partner, Tom Kaiser, hadn't been her favorite person, but as officers, they'd complemented each other. She'd taken his death hard. In her nightmares, it had been Kendall lying in the casket.

Nash leaned forward. "I'm sorry it happened. For all of us. You can believe me or not, but I hope you will because I think we work well together and I respect you."

Kendall wasn't ready to let it go, but not wanting to discuss it further at the moment, she changed the subject. She opened her notebook.

"One more of them to see tonight, Patricia Clemmons. She's in the Waukesha area. I have an idea that might save us a trip. How about I get in touch with Detective Conlin from Milwaukee and ask him if he can make a call for us?"

An anonymous tip had come in, informing the Milwaukee police that the Bradley Center, where the Bucks were scheduled to play basketball Saturday night, had an explosive device waiting for a crowd of nineteen thousand. As a result, the bomb squad, along with all available law-enforcement personnel, was called in Saturday afternoon to search the enormous arena and contain the surrounding area, located in downtown Milwaukee. Detective Richard Conlin, one of the detectives called in to duty, left home at three p.m.

TJ sat at her desk working on her quarterly income tax reports, something she described as shit-work. The baby was visiting his grandparents, so when the dreaded chore was completed, she planned to change into something fleecy, order a movie, and pop some corn.

The ring of the landline phone was a welcome distraction.

She snatched it up. "T & J Security."

"TJ, hi, this is Detective Halsrud from Eau Claire. Is Detective Conlin in?"

"He won't be available for a while. Can I help you with somethin'?"

"I'm working that case I told you about yesterday—looking for a missing child. We're talking to baby-pervs in our area. We had four on our list, and we've met with three of them. So far, I haven't had a problem with any of the local cops, they've been more than happy to let us do our thing, but we've been in rural areas. The last one is in Waukesha, which might be more complicated. I was hoping Detective Conlin would make a call for us. He isn't answering his cell."

TJ took it in. It wasn't much, but it would break the monotony. "Don't know when you'll be able to talk to him, but give me the info and I'll see what I can do."

"Her name is Patricia Clemmons. The address is 4851 Brighton, Waukesha."

TJ recoiled. "A woman?"

"Yeah, I know. It's revolting. They all are."

Fucking baby-pervs made TJ's skin crawl. "I'll make some calls."

After she hung up, TJ looked up the name of the detective who'd helped with the case against James Wilson the year before. Tom Zabel had seemed like a good guy.

He picked up on the first ring. "Zabel."

"Hey. TJ Peacock. Are you on tonight?"

"No, and this better not be a crisis because I have tenth row center tickets for the Bucks game—they're playing Chicago tonight."

She couldn't imagine how he hadn't heard about the bomb, but didn't want to burst his bubble by telling him there might not be a game. If the arena weren't cleared in time, it would be cancelled. She explained why she was calling, told him what Halsrud needed.

"Okay. I'll pave the way for your friend from the North Country."

"Uh, thinkin' about goin' out there myself. Save her a trip."

"I'll get it set up for you. If it goes south, don't call me. I'll be drinking beer and cheering for the good guys."

After notifying Kendall she'd be checking Clemmons out for her, TJ fled Milwaukee, headed for the Waukesha address Kendall had given her. It felt good doing something of substance. The security gigs she'd been working since RJ was born paid the bills, but they were as exciting as a Tupperware party on a Friday night.

The address, a dead-end street on the east side of Waukesha, was a dark brick, aging duplex. No lights were on and the driveway was empty. She pulled the Mini into the driveway and approached the front door. A duplicate door to the right led to the upper flat.

She tried both bells and knocked repeatedly on each door with no response.

Determined to get something, she walked to the neighboring house, which was the last one on the street, and rang the bell.

A dark-haired woman answered the door. "Yes?"

TJ flashed her PI credentials. Something about the woman struck her as familiar. "I'm looking for a woman named Patricia Clemmons. I was given the address next door. Any chance you know her?"

The woman opened the door to TJ after introducing herself as Tanya Porter.

The inside of the house belied the shabbiness of the aged exterior. Shiny hardwood floors gleamed under carefully placed, bright-colored throw rugs, the furniture a tasteful mix of antiques and modern. TJ followed her into a kitchen done in white enamel with silver appliances and the same hardwood flooring. A large pot simmered on the stove. It smelled like chicken soup.

Porter offered, "Would you like some coffee? I just put it on."

TJ figured the woman had something to tell her and accepted her offer, watching as Porter got up and walked to a wheat-colored, granite countertop to pour. Suddenly, TJ recalled how she knew her—her walk gave her away.

The chick had been a hooker, back when TJ worked vice. It was years ago. No wonder she didn't recognize her. Gone were the striped stockings, miniskirt, and low-cut, sequined tank tops she'd favored. She was simply dressed in jeans and a crisp, white blouse, sans makeup, with her thick hair pulled back into a ponytail tied with a bright red scarf.

After she'd poured the coffee, she sat across from TJ at a low counter. "You remember me, don't you?"

TJ smiled. "Yeah. Took me a while. You look different."

"My street name was Mia, but I go by real name now, Tanya Porter. It took me a long time to stash enough money to quit the life. It was a real bitch, hiding the cash, staying clean. But I'd had enough: too many STDs, cut lips, all-nighters. Bought this place, then bought the place next door a year later. I've got a decent job in town selling fancy bedding. How ironic is that?"

Porter owned the building Clemmons had lived in. Now she was getting somewhere. "That's great. Not many women pull that off. So, you must know Clemmons."

"Yeah. I rented to her for about a year, but she's been gone for months. I'm getting the place fixed up before I rent it again."

Shit. This is going to be a dead end. "Any chance she left a forwarding address?"

"Sorry. She didn't want to leave one. She wanted me to do a walk through the day she moved out so she could get her security deposit back. She asked for cash since that's how she always paid me. I checked the place out and gave her the money."

"Didn't you think it was strange? Paying you with cash?"

Porter folded her arms across her chest. "Two important things I've learned in life are to always cover my ass and to ask as few questions as possible. I hire ex-cons to do my remodeling, and pay them in cash, too. Keeps things simple."

"Mind if I look around the place?"

"Why are you looking for her?"

184

TJ wondered if she should tell her about Clemmons. The woman would have been on the perv registry; it would have been no secret. "You aware she was on the Sexual Offenders List?"

"Yeah. She told me up front. This neighborhood is mostly old folks, so since there's no kids around, I figured it wouldn't be a problem. I agreed to rent to her and she agreed to a three-month security deposit. She didn't cause any problems for me, and the neighbors never bitched about it."

Tanya handed TJ the key. "I'm leaving soon, so just drop the key in my mailbox when you're finished."

23

Kendall and Nash were on the road back to Eau Claire when TJ called. Kendall was driving and handed her phone to Nash.

"Adam Nashlund here. I'm with Detective Halsrud. "

If TJ was surprised Kendall had a partner, she kept it to herself. "I took a drive out to Waukesha myself. Your lady chickenhawk flew the coop about six months ago. I'm in her place now, lower flat in a duplex. The landlady let me in. It hasn't been rented yet, so thought I'd take a look around. Place is spotless, an' she didn't' leave no forwarding address. Sorry I couldn't get more for you."

"That's too bad, but thanks, you've saved us another four hours on the road."

"Went through the brother's place, too. Nothing there, either."

Nash straightened in his seat. "Her brother?"

"Landlady forgot to mention him. I talked to a neighbor on my way out and she told me about him. He lived in the upper. Said she thought he was handicapped, hardly ever left the house an' never talked to anyone."

When Nash started swearing, Kendall asked, "What?" He raised a hand to quiet her.

"TJ, can you get a description of this pair and call me back?"

"I'm on it."

Muttering to himself, he closed the phone.

"What's happening?" Kendall asked.

He repeated what TJ had told him. "I have a bad feeling this Clemmons and her so-called 'brother' might be Jennemen and Iseroth, the old bat I talked to in Cameron and her renter. It's not unusual for these sickos to move around like nomads, trying to escape the registry."

TJ called back minutes later.

After he closed the phone, he slammed a hand on the dashboard. "Fuck!"

"Tell me."

"I should have figured it out. The descriptions fit. Jennemen must have been claiming Iseroth as her brother when she lived in Waukesha as Clemmons. She totally duped me. Did a great job of acting like a wacky old lady."

Kendall felt her intestines roiling again. She didn't ask if he was sure; it made an ugly kind of sense. "We can be in Cameron by nine."

"It'll be too fucking late. They'll be gone."

"Quit beating up on yourself. You couldn't have known."

"Damn. I should have asked the mail guy how long they'd been there. We can't have them picked up without solid evidence. We're screwed."

"But you said their places were too small to hide a baby," Kendall said.

"I know. But there's a vacant cottage next to Iseroth. Like a moron, I didn't ask her to show it to me."

"Maybe we can get enough on this group to interest the Feds," she said. "With Traynor in Minnesota, our pervs are in two states—it does become their jurisdiction."

"I hate giving the fucking Feds anything."

Kendall called the Cameron police. The officer on duty agreed to cover Jennemen's place until they got there.

They stopped at Kendall's apartment for coffee on their way to Cameron. Kendall found a note from Brynn next to her computer.

"It says she went on a group astronomy walk and won't be back until about eleven. And she needs a better computer." Kendall snorted. "I knew that was coming."

Nash settled on the couch. "So, what have we got? Traynor and DeForrest seemed suspiciously prepared for our visit. Are they all in touch with each other? Some of them could be, and it's possible they all are. If we're right, Iseroth and his so-called sister have been alerted by now. I'm not sure about calling the Feds, although Tarkowski's pretty trustworthy. You might want to ask him if they're looking at any of them right now."

Kendall felt weariness overcome her. "I still want to go to Cameron and see the setup they have. Maybe we can get into that outbuilding."

"Maybe we should wait and get a warrant."

"Assuming we could get one. You know what they say—it's easier to apologize than ask for permission. I'll take my chances. Let's go to Cameron." She yawned. "Although, I'd rather stay here, take a hot shower and a get good night's sleep for a change."

"Sounds good to me. Call me when the shower's hot."

Kendall chuckled. "You're starting to sound like Alverson."

"You think? Nah, he'd probably run the other way if you took him up on one of his suggestions."

And you wouldn't? She thought better of asking him. It had been an offhand comment. Men didn't invite her into the shower with them. Instead, she said, "I'll make us a thermos of coffee to take along."

Attorney Lucille Bellamy entered her townhome bone tired but smug with satisfaction. One of her researchers had discovered the search of Travis Jordan's car hadn't been exactly kosher, and Lucille had been all over it in a heartbeat. She'd waited until late Friday to file the Motion to Suppress, thinking that with the holiday weekend beginning, the reaction wouldn't hit the fan until Monday morning. Everyone would come in to work on Monday bloated and weary from the weekend, and it would hit them in the face like a whipped cream pie.

Travis Jordan could be back on the street in a matter of days. Any regrets Lucille had about her hand in his release were outweighed by her belief that the cops had to hold up their end of the system with a clean arrest. They should have known better than to give her an edge. What was nagging at her, though, was what Jordan let slip when she'd gone to the jail to give him the good news.

She decided her conscience wasn't going to keep her from preparing the chicken breast she had marinating or cooking some pasta to go with it. A glass of wine would be called for, too, although she wasn't supposed to be drinking anything alcoholic because of the anti-viral meds she still took. The doctor had advised her it was unlikely they would help at this stage of her palsy, but she'd insisted. She was too damn young to keep walking around looking like a stroke victim lolling in a wheelchair along the hallway of a nursing home. Lucille's strong sense of self wouldn't let her give up—the meds gave her hope.

Sitting in her formal dining room accompanied by her favorite music, a light piece by Mozart, she enjoyed her dinner, complete with two glasses of the forbidden wine. The buffet next to the table, covered by a lacy scarf under dozens of framed photos, supported a pink enameled frame holding a photo of her new granddaughter. The happy, youthful face pricked at Lucille's conscience; little Amy was about the same age as Philly Glausson.

Nash and Kendall were ten miles south of Cameron when Kendall's phone buzzed.

She opened it, expecting it to be Brynn. The number was blocked.

"Halsrud."

"I have some information for you."

Kendall didn't recognize the woman's voice. "Who is this?"

"I'm only going to say this once—Travis Jordan didn't kill the Glausson baby."

24

While they waited for the paramedics, Carlee Somerfelt clung to Brynn's hand with what little strength she had left. Brynn whispered to the girl to hang on; everything would be okay as soon as they got her to the hospital. Tears streaming down her face, Brynn prayed for the girl's life while speaking assuring words she feared were meaningless. Her face drained of color, the girl looked like she was dying.

When the paramedics arrived, they quickly sized up the situation, commending Brynn on refusing to let anyone remove the knife from Carlee's abdomen. The girl was quiet except for a moaned, "No," when they tried to remove Brynn's hand from hers. One of the paramedics, a woman who didn't look a lot older than Brynn, bent over and promised the girl they'd let Brynn come with them, but first they had to get Carlee on the gurney for transport to the hospital.

Brynn followed them to the ambulance, where she was allowed to take a spot close to Carlee. The female paramedic added notes to a chart while her partner hooked Carlee up to an IV and took her vitals. When he finished, she said to Brynn, "Okay, take her hand again. Talk to her like you were before and we'll see if she responds."

The girl's hand felt cold. Brynn's tears resumed their embarrassing progress down her face. "Carlee, it's me. Brynn. I'm right here with you. Can you hear me?"

Carlee moaned.

"Don't try to talk. You have to rest. We'll be at the hospital in a minute. The doctors will fix you up." Her grip tightened on Brynn's hand.

The lights were on in Viva Jennemen's small house and in Iseroth's cottage. Jennemen's old van sat in front of the garage. Nash parked two doors down from Jennemen's place, relieving the Cameron cop.

Kendall yawned. "It looks like they're still here."

"I figured they'd have taken off."

"Maybe we're wrong about all of them being in touch with each other."

Nash grunted. "Maybe. Try Brynn again. Can she pull phone records?"

"I can get those from someone at the station."

"Right now?"

"Probably not. I'll keep trying Brynn."

"I'm going to try to get close enough to see what those two are up to," Nash said. "I don't think there's anyone else in residence on this street right now; everyone's gone for the winter. Turn your flashlight on to signal me if you see someone coming."

Glad he was dressed in dark clothing, Nash crept through the trees, making his way to the house. He could see through a side window that Jennemen was sitting in a mustard yellow recliner in front of a large TV, an open beer and a bag of corn chips next to her on a side table. She'd drifted off.

He crept around the house, careful to stay hidden by the shrubbery in case Iseroth poked his nose out. The other rooms looked normal, her bedroom door open, admitting enough light to make the room visible from the window. No sign of any baby stuff.

At Iseroth's cottage, a TV was on in the living room, but Iseroth wasn't in sight. There were two tiny rooms off the living room, one a bedroom that barely had enough space for a bed, a dresser, and a nightstand. The other room was even smaller. A fifties-style, floor-to-ceiling pole lamp gave the room a soft glow. Iseroth sat at a desk, engrossed by something on a computer screen.

Nash crept back to the car. "They don't look rattled; looks like they're settled in for the night. Jennemen's snoozing in a recliner. She has a computer in the second bedroom, but it's ancient. Iseroth's using a laptop as we speak."

"Could you see inside the empty cottage?"

"Yeah. If it's being used for storage, there's not much there and everything's out of sight. No baby."

Kendall's phone buzzed just as they were deciding whether to go back to Eau Claire.

"Alverson here. What are you up to?"

"None of your business. I'm off this weekend."

"I know. A little white-haired chick asked me to call you. She's in the ICU at St. Luke's. I'm calling from the lobby."

Kendall's stomach pitched. "What happened to her?"

"Her? Nothing. She's waiting for our vic to come out of surgery. Says she promised to stay with her until the parents come."

"What vic?"

When Kendall and Nash arrived at the hospital, the only two people in the ICU waiting area were asleep in front of a muted TV. Kendall flashed her ID at the desk and asked the nurse where she could find Brynn.

The bright-eyed, young nurse explained that Brynn was in the recovery room with Carlee Somerfelt. "You can't go in there, but I'll tell her you're here."

"Is Detective Alverson here?"

"Is he the tall one?" When Kendall nodded, she said, "His partner left and he said he'd wait here until you arrived. He must have gone down for coffee."

They found Alverson in front of a coffee machine on the first floor.

"How is Brynn involved in this?" Kendall asked.

Alverson took in Nash standing at Kendall's side. "What are you two doing together?"

Kendall grabbed Alverson's arm, leading him across the room where they could talk without Nash overhearing. "I asked you a question."

"Take it easy. It's like I told you; a teenage girl was raped and stabbed in the county park north of town. She was with some kind of group on a walking tour looking at stars. Your friend was with the group. The vic and some of her gal pals from college were there on a field trip. When they were getting ready to leave the park, and found that Carlee Somerfelt was missing, your gal found her. The vic won't let her out of her sight."

"How bad is Somerfelt hurt?"

"She's one lucky lady. The knife missed her vitals, but she lost a lot of blood."

"She'll make a full recovery?"

"That's what the doc said."

"Do you have any leads on her attacker?"

"Not yet. They did some fingernail scrapings. Teed thought he got enough to be usable, but that'll take some time to ID."

"So you have nothing."

"That's about it. Until she talks, we don't have squat. The parents were at a wedding in Madison. Had their cell phones turned off for a while, but they're on their way. Boss said this one is all yours, could be related to those rapes." He turned back to the machine to retrieve his coffee.

Kendall and Nash went to find Brynn.

Nash, Brynn and Kendall sat in Kendall's living room, empty fast food wrappers on the coffee table in front of them. Kendall and Nash had waited with Brynn until the Somerfelts arrived at the hospital. When Brynn turned down Kendall's offer to spend the night, Nash walked across the hall with her and inspected each room before returning.

He closed the door behind him. "Think she's okay?"

"She felt good about being there for Carlee, and she's going back tomorrow to see her, which may be therapeutic for Brynn. She witnessed a scene that would make a cop squeamish. They checked her out at the hospital; she wasn't in shock."

"Tougher than she looks. Do you think this is the same rapist Chippewa's been looking for?"

"Carlee Somerfelt fits the profile of the victims, so Schoenfuss assigned me to start working it. One of the women who was raped said the guy smelled like he'd been working on cars. That was really the only thing they had to go on. Other than that, it was the usual; the guy was average build and height, face covered by a ski mask. I plan on making the rounds of garages, see if anyone gets skittish."

"That's about all you can do unless Somerfelt has something else to add." He yawned. "Don't you think it's strange that Brynn happened to be there when this guy struck again?"

"It had to be a coincidence."

Their eyes met. Kendall knew he was implying Brynn might have been the intended victim. But it made no sense. "I'm not a big fan of coincidence either, but what else could it be? We were the only ones who knew Brynn was going on that walk."

He stood and stretched. "I'm just saying there've been too many coincidences for me, starting with the threats to Gray. And someone broke into Brynn's place."

"Those could be explained; you thought Gray's threats were related to his union problems and the break-in, random."

"I'm not so sure, anymore. There could be a connection here somewhere. Maybe someone's trying to scare us off."

"But why go after Brynn? Not many people know she's been helping us. No one I'd suspect of this." Kendall's mind spun with possibilities. "There's not much we can do about it except keep her covered."

Nash frowned. "I've been thinking about Jennemen again. The old bat lied about everything, even about having a computer. We didn't run a background on her, and it bit us in the ass. So what's your game plan for tomorrow? Want to go back to Cameron?"

"I suppose we should keep watching them. I have to talk to Carlee first thing in the morning, providing she's conscious. You go ahead, and I'll drive up as soon as I can."

"Works for me. We need enough to get warrants on those freaks. Maybe Tarkowski can help us out."

"Yeah, I'll try him tomorrow." Kendall picked up their empty glasses and carried them to the counter.

Nash walked toward the door. "We'd better have a talk with Brynn tomorrow and ask her to quit her lone night walks. Tell her to buy a treadmill."

25

The guys started calling him Sharky when his second set of teeth came in as far apart as slats on a picket fence. He was watching a rerun of *Jaws* with his buddies when they came up with it. His teeth—added to his long, flaring nose and widely set eyes—did give Gerald Fostvedt a shark-like appearance. Jerry, as his mother called him, didn't object to the nickname. It could have been a lot worse.

He dropped out of high school in the middle of his junior year when he discovered that his hobby, working on cars, could get him a job at the car repair shop down the street. He made good money, enough for a decent car and a fake ID to get him into the bars on weekends. He didn't give a shit about things the other kids went gaga over: sports, dances, pep-rallies, and after-school clubs. It was all a load of crap, strictly for the favored few and the nerds.

He wanted to save enough money to get his own place. His mother was never around, and most of the time his two stepsisters acted like he didn't exist, running around the trailer half-naked. But the bitches had smokin' hot bodies. Hot bodies the sluts let him use when they wanted something from him, money or a freebie repair when their car broke down.

After watching them get ready for a night out, he'd jerk off while his rap music cranked in the background; then he'd go out searching. It was easy to find a girl stupid enough, or wasted enough, to trip out to her car on spiky high heels.

Then one hot, humid summer evening, *she* strolled out of a club after midnight. Unlike the usual airheads, she scoured the lot as she walked, one of her hands hidden in a jacket pocket. Clutching a knife? Pepper spray?

He'd known he should let her pass. She looked like trouble, but she also looked like the hottest thing he'd ever seen on two legs. She passed the opening between two SUV's, where he'd been crouched awaiting his next prey. He saw her face as a pair of headlights from a retreating car highlighted it.

It couldn't fucking be!

Who the hell did she think she was, all got up like a whore? He stepped out of the shadows.

26

With Brynn next to her in the Highlander, Kendall left for the hospital before nine. She and Nash had agreed not to let Brynn go anywhere alone.

Carlee's mother sat at her bedside and rushed out to greet them when she saw Kendall and Brynn nearing the open door. She smiled at Brynn. "Thank you for coming. She's been asking for you."

Awkwardly, Brynn introduced Kendall. "This is my friend, Detective Halsrud."

"Mrs. Somerfelt, I'm sorry about what happened to your daughter. You understand, we have to talk to her. I know you wouldn't want her assailant to go unpunished."

"Do we have to do it now? She's so upset . . . She could have died last night."

"If too much time passes, she'll tuck any memories of the attack into her subconscious and it'll be too late to get any useful feedback. I think whoever did this to her may be responsible for a series of rapes in our area. What he did to Carlee tells us he's escalating; the next girl may not survive."

Lois Somerfelt took them into Carlee's room. The girl's eyes were closed as Kendall and Brynn took up positions beside the bed. Kendall spoke softly. "Carlee? I'm Detective Halsrud. I'm with the Eau Claire Police."

The girl didn't stir.

"I have Brynn with me. You remember Brynn, she was with you last night.

She's very worried about you."

Carlee opened her eyes and looked at Brynn. "You came."

Brynn took her hand. "Kendall needs to talk to you, Carlee. She said I can stay with you if you want me to."

The girl whispered a weak assent.

"I know this is hard for you, Carlee," Kendall began. "But I need you to tell me everything you can remember about the man who did this to you. Do you think you can do that?"

Carlee's eyes glistened. She tightened her grip on Brynn's hand.

"Let's try this," Kendall said, her voice low. "Close your eyes and pretend you're watching a movie of what happened last night." Carlee shut her eyes. "Take some deep breaths. Then picture yourself in the park last night with your friends. Remember, he can't hurt you anymore. You're safe here in the hospital. Tell me what you see."

A moment passed. Kendall wondered how safe Carlee really was in the hospital and considered putting a uniform at her door. She'd run it by the boss later.

"There were seven of us from school," Carlee finally whispered. "The astronomy walk was on a list of things we could do for extra credit. When we got to the meadow, one of the men let me look in his telescope; it was so cool. I never saw stars that way before. Then I went to find my friends; they'd walked over toward the trees. I heard their voices, and started to go over to toward them."

She stopped talking. A lone tear slid from her closed eyes. "It happened so fast. I was between some trees and he grabbed me from behind. He shoved me down on the ground. Then he held my arms and pulled my jeans down. And he did it . . . He raped me." She choked up.

"Take some more deep breaths, Carlee," Kendall said, giving the girl a minute to compose herself. "Now describe how he looked, smelled, dressed, anything you can remember about him. If he said something to you, tell me what he said and what his voice sounded like."

After a short pause, she answered, "I didn't see much. He had on a leather jacket. And he was wearing a ski mask, so I couldn't see his face. It was dark."

Kendall hated to push the girl, but she had to have something—anything—to go on if they were to catch the animal that assaulted her. "Are you sure you don't remember anything else, Carlee? I know it's painful for you to play it back in your mind, but even the smallest thing could help us find him."

Carlee still had her eyelids squeezed shut, her breathing rapid. "He called me a bitch and told me to keep my mouth shut or he'd kill me. I did what he said, I never said a word . . . But he stabbed me anyway."

Kendall couldn't ask specifically about the man's scent. "Think hard, Carlee. Did he have an accent? Could you tell if he was Caucasian? Did he wear cologne?"

She sniffed and Brynn handed her a tissue. "He sounded young, but like a tough guy. You know, maybe about my age, but like he was trying to be a real badass. He didn't talk like a black guy, and I don't remember any accent." She wiped her face. "His smell. You said cologne. There was something . . . Yeah. He was wearing gloves, and when he had his hand over my mouth, it smelled like gasoline."

As soon as she got back home, Brynn opened the chat room of the site she'd decided was most likely to attract the pedophiles. If she only had another computer, she could be working on tracking their usernames at the same time she monitored the chat room.

Edgy, she flinched when she heard a knock at the door. Kendall had told her not to open the door to anyone she didn't know, and she didn't have a reading scheduled. When the knock repeated, she peered out into the parking area behind the building. A black Lexus like her mother's was parked in front of the door.

Monica Zellman entered the apartment when Brynn opened the door. Neither greeted the other. Her mother's gaze immediately assessed everything in the room, and Brynn reminded herself to be braced for a cutting comment on the décor. Monica's taste ran to Country French, brocade, and crystal lamps dripping with prisms.

She settled on the sofa. "You've fixed the place nicely." She stroked the ornate, oak secretary that had been Vadoma's. "This secretary is a gorgeous antique."

It had to be killing her mother not to ask how she managed to afford it. Brynn's parole officer must have counseled Monica to remain positive with her daughter if she wanted to renew a relationship with her.

"The woman who lived here before me left all her things behind. I kept most of it," Brynn explained. No need to tell her about Vadoma. Without the window in the entry door, she'd have no clue about Brynn's sideline. Except that Fournier had probably filled her in.

"I've missed you, Brynn."

She was amazed her mother's words weren't followed by a plea for her to come home. Good thing. If she and her mother were ever going to reconnect, Monica would have to accept Brynn's need for independence.

"I know you felt like I was overprotective, but I just wanted to keep you safe."

Brynn's bitterness spilled out. "Is that why you wouldn't let me learn to drive?" Driving had been a large bone of contention between mother and daughter.

Monica's eyes widened. "But darling, what if you had an accident?"

"I'm an albino Mother, not a hemophiliac." She should have bitten her tongue. At the moment she wanted something from her mother. But then Monica gave Brynn the perfect opening. "I see you have a computer already."

"I'm doing some work for a detective; that's her computer. Didn't Officer Fournier tell you about it?" She should have added that she could barely afford food, much less a computer.

Monica squirmed in her seat. Brynn knew her mother couldn't offer to return her old computer; her mother had dropped it off at a resale shop the day she'd found out about the hacking. "Well, darling," her mother said through tightened lips, "you've earned the right to own a computer again, I suppose. Why don't you let me buy you one?"

27

Kendall spent some time at the station writing up her report on the interview with Carlee Somerfelt and arranged for an officer to cover the girl's room. She talked to the Chippewa cop who'd been working the rape cases and he agreed last night's rapist sounded like it could be his guy. Tomorrow she'd make the rounds of auto repair shops.

Nash called just as she stood to leave. He'd been in Cameron all morning watching Jennemen and Iseroth.

"Anything happening?" Kendall asked.

"Nah. I'm thinking about calling it a day. What's new on your end?"

"I talked to the Somerfelt girl. She remembered her attacker smelled like gasoline, so he could be Chippewa's rapist."

"Or he stopped for gas on his way to the park."

"Cynic."

"Comes from years of following crappy leads. Did you call Tarkowski?"

"I did. I gave him the names of our baby pervs. He just called me back; they aren't looking at any of them right now. But he said if we get anything at all linking them to the Glausson baby, to let them know."

Nash chortled. "Yeah, right. Hand it over after we've done all the work."

"What crawled up your butt?" He'd been the one to suggest calling Tarkowski.

"I hate stake-outs. Too much time to think about my fucked-up life."

Kendall headed back to the apartment, trying to decide what to do next. She'd check in with Brynn, see if she had anything to report.

Brooding about the anonymous call she'd gotten the day before, Kendall still suspected it had to have been from Lucille Bellamy, Jordan's attorney. The call had stoked Kendall's determination to find Philly Glausson, but with the rape case and the attempted murder of Somerfelt on her plate, Schoenfuss wasn't going to be very receptive to her pursuing it. She'd tackle that problem tomorrow.

Brynn opened the door with a rather shit-eating grin on her face, the cat purring at her ankles. "I have to show you something."

Kendall followed her into the small second bedroom. Three computers and a printer were spread out on a long library table. One of the computers was a brand new iMac, whose giant screen took up a third of the table. The other, a laptop sitting next to Kendall's, was a Macbook Pro and connected to a laser printer. "Where did all this come from?"

Brynn answered, "Monica Zellman."

"Your mother." Interesting. That explained the smell of food in the apartment; mom must have cooked for her. Something had changed. Brynn never had a good word to say about the woman, but the gift couldn't have been timelier.

Kendall fumbled for her phone when it interrupted a brief nap.

"Kendall, it's Franklyn Teed."

"On Sunday?" Teed, the medical examiner, never called outside of work hours.

"I know, rather unusual. My wife's sister is here for the weekend and I needed to get out of the house."

"I've been meaning to call and ask you if you have anything on the break-in in my building."

"Right. Let's see; the stain on the cat's paw wasn't blood; it was something with spices and a tomato base. My guess would be spaghetti sauce. And there were no matches in the database for any of the prints except the resident of the apartment.

"I've been finishing up my final report on the Glausson autopsies. We'll release the bodies to the family early this week."

Kendall hadn't seen or talked to Gray since their flight to Milwaukee; this would give her an excuse to touch base with him. "I'll let the brother know."

"Getting to the reason I called; I had some time to kill, so I went over everything one more time before finalizing my report. I was looking at the DNA results, and I found something in the family that might interest you."

Kendall sat up, her pulse quickening. "They did DNA on the whole family?"

"That's standard practice in a case like this. As I was saying, I've examined the DNA results again. It seems Mark Glausson may not be Philly's father."

"And you're just finding this out now?" That could be huge. If Mark Glausson wasn't Philly's father, they would have another suspect—and another place to look for the child.

"Actually, my oversight is quite understandable under the circumstances."

Kendall didn't want to play guessing games. "Could you be more specific?"

"Family members have similar DNA patterns, so matches among the victims would be expected. But after examining the results more closely, it's apparent Gray Glausson is more likely the child's father. I hadn't examined his DNA before today, since there was no reason to. We'd need to run more sophisticated tests to be a hundred percent certain, but that would only be necessary if you needed legal confirmation. There's no doubt in my mind—Gray Glausson is Philly Glausson's biological father."

Steaming by the time Nash walked into the Rat Pak later that day, Kendall resolved to contain her fury. If she blew up, she wouldn't be able to read him, and she wanted to be able to tell if he'd known about Philly's paternity.

They took a booth near the back of the bar and faced each other across the table over glasses of beer.

Nash gulped his drink. "That hits the spot. Nothing new from Cameron, but I think I want to go back tomorrow morning when Iseroth's gone so I can get into his place and that other cottage. Anything new since I talked to you?"

"Brynn has two new computers. Top end, I might add."

"Who popped for that?"

"Her mother. Brynn hasn't spoken to the woman in almost two years. I got the feeling Brynn only caved because she wanted something from her."

"Good for her. Didn't think she had it in her." When Kendall raised her eyebrows, he added, "You know what I mean . . . Be a little manipulative to get what she wants."

She gave him a piercing stare. "Right. If you want something bad enough, you lower your standards."

He grinned. "Are you insinuating that you lowered your standards to work with *moi*?"

She'd wipe that grin off his face. "Apparently lower than I thought. You've been holding out on me."

"Holding out on you?"

Kendall figured she'd get the best read on him by putting it right out there. "Mark Glausson isn't Philly's father."

His face froze.

"As it turns out, Gray Glausson is the sperm donor."

Nash sat back, his wry humor replaced by anger. "That's news to me. Glausson's been holding out on both of us."

Kendall and Nash rode in silence. She knew he was stewing about being left out of Glausson's confidence regarding Philly's paternity. It seemed rather sophomoric of him; he was being well paid to do the man's bidding. When they arrived at Gray Glausson's lake home, the door was opened by a woman Kendall didn't recognize until she spoke.

England Durand said, "Come in."

Wearing glasses, no makeup, her long hair tied back in a

loose braid, England was hardly recognizable as the model-like apparition who had invaded Kendall's office the week before. She invited them into the living room where a fire crackled invitingly.

Gray entered the room. "Glad to see you two. I hope you have something to tell me."

"We were hoping you had something to tell us," Kendall said.

"I do. We settled our union contract over the weekend. As always, there's some disgruntlement with the details, but not enough to provoke any more incidents."

"That's not why we're here."

Glausson appeared genuinely puzzled.

England rose from her chair. "Can I get you two something to drink? Coffee? Something stronger?"

Gray touched her arm. "No, stay here. Anything they have to say you need to hear, too."

Kendall wasn't so sure of that, but it was his call. "Why didn't you tell us you're Philly Glausson's biological father?"

Gray and England exchanged a look. He'd obviously told her before today. "Because I didn't know for sure, Detective. I suspected I might be because of the timing of Philly's birth, but when I asked her, Chelsea insisted it was impossible. That's why I didn't say anything to you. I didn't believe it was relevant even if Chelsea lied about it. Whether Philly is my niece or my daughter, we have to find her."

"You could at least have given *me* a head's up," Nash grumbled.

Gray's eyes hardened. "As I said, it makes no difference."

"You're wrong. It makes a big difference," Kendall added.

"It does if you think it makes me a suspect," Gray argued. "Or I should say, more of a suspect. You already have someone in custody for the murders, Detective, although I'm sure you're thinking I knew the man and paid him to do it. But go ahead and check my phone records and my finances—I never met the man or had any contact with him."

"I'll do that." Kendall stood and turned to Nash. "Let's get out of here."

Gray rose. "I told you once, I had no reason to kill them. Why would I? If Philly is my child, she had a good home and doting parents. My brother had no idea what happened between Chels and me."

Kendall wouldn't back off. "Are you sure about that? Funny thing is, the first floor of their house didn't have even one picture of Philly, or any of her things scattered about. I couldn't figure it out before; Chelsea must have kept her away from your brother to insulate him from his feelings about raising another man's child." This was only speculation on Kendall's part. The simple answer was probably that Chelsea had a preference for the convenience of digital photography.

"You're making that outrageous supposition based on pictures? You're wrong, Detective. Chels told me my brother adored Philly." Gray scowled. "How many times do I have to say it? I had no reason to have them murdered. My brother, sure. You could make a case that I had a motive to kill him. But the others? Think about it. It makes no sense."

Kendall didn't think it did either. But she didn't trust Gray Glausson. What else wasn't he telling them?

28

On the drive back, neither of them spoke until Nash pulled up behind the building. "I have an idea."

"I hope it's a short one. I need some sleep."

"Hey, don't be pissed at *me*. If I'd known Gray was the kid's father, I'd have told you."

"I don't know about that, but I believe you didn't know. So what's the bright idea?"

"We don't know squat; you only have the word of your mystery caller that Jordan didn't off the kid. We're forgetting about Brynn's other talent. I think we should have her do a reading for you."

"That's a bright idea? I thought you said she couldn't tell you anything about the baby when she did your reading."

"She couldn't, but I have all this other shit going on. With you she could focus on the kid."

"Are you insinuating I don't have a life?" She caught herself. "Don't answer that."

"I'm just saying—it can't hurt. I know you're in a knot about Philly, just thought it might help. Not saying I believe in it."

"It's ludicrous."

As Kendall stepped out of the car, another car pulled in—a

long, black Cadillac—Morrie's car with Brynn in the passenger seat.

Kendall watched as Brynn stepped out of the car. "I need to talk to you," she called to Kendall.

Kendall and Nash followed Brynn up to her apartment where she proudly showed Nash her new computers.

"Quite the setup. Have you found our baby-lovers?" he asked.

Brynn winced at the term. "I'm going to work on it tonight. But Kendall, Carlee remembered something. She told me to tell you about it." She looked at Nash. "I have to talk to Kendall alone."

Kendall handed him her keys. "Better make us some coffee."

When he left, Brynn began, "Carlee called and said she needed to see me. It sounded important, so I asked Morrie for a ride to the hospital."

"That was nice of him. I'm glad you didn't go out alone."

"He waited for me, too. They have a policeman outside of her room. His name's Jeff."

Apparently, there was something vital Brynn had to tell Kendall, but she was having a hard time getting it out. She steered her to the point. "Brynn, what did Carlee tell you?"

"It's kind of embarrassing." Brynn looked away.

"He tried to kill her, Brynn. Nothing about that counts as embarrassing."

Kendall waited. Was she going to have to pull it out of her?

Brynn had the cat in her lap, slowly stroking his long fur. "After he pushed Carlee down, he pulled her pants off and got on top of her. He made her take it in her hand . . . You know." Her face reddened.

"She had to guide his penis in for him," Kendall clarified. Carlee had evidently remembered another detail.

"Right. She said there was something on it . . . like an earring." She wrinkled her nose. "It was pierced."

Kendall let out her breath. Now she could find the animal without crawling through every car repair hole in town. There couldn't be that many pierced peckers in Eau Claire, Wisconsin.

After talking to Brynn, Kendall joined Nash in her apartment. He flinched when she told him how they'd be able to track Carlee's rapist.

"You men are so damn sensitive about your plumbing," She mumbled.

"That's rich. Imagine being nailed because a of dick dangle."

"A 'dick dangle?' You're kidding, right?"

"Yeah. I just made that up. Ironic, though. Guys' dicks get them in trouble all the time, but that's a new one, isn't it?"

Kendall turned to get coffee.

"Seriously," he said. "I think I can help you out here. There's a place in La Crosse that does all kinds of piercings. They specialize in exotics."

"And you know this, because?"

"You hear a lot of shit undercover."

Kendall contacted the station, gave them the name of the tattoo parlor in La Crosse and had the detectives put together a list of likely places in the immediate area for acquiring such an intimate piercing.

She put down the phone. "It could have been a home job."

"Right. Like any man would take a chance like that."

"It's something to consider. There's no shortage of morons

out there." Time to change the subject. "What do you think? Was Gray being honest with us about not knowing he's Philly's biological father?"

"The guy can be hard to read, but I think he's being up-front on this one. Pissed me off that he didn't tell me, though. If he weren't my boss, I'd tell him where to put it. But I'm into it now. We have to find the kid."

They'd finished their coffee when Kendall got a call from Morrie. "I almost forgot to tell you. Someone named Nat stopped in, told me to tell you she had something to tell you about your case."

Nat. Kendall hadn't returned the calls she'd received from her ex-roommate. Did she want to deal with Nat in front of Adam Nashlund? *What the hell.* He'd probably heard all about her eviction from Alverson. There'd been a crowd gathered around the Highlander the day she walked out of the station and found her car crammed with all her belongings.

In the downtown area just off the river, the theater was only a short drive from the Rat Pak. A few cars still dotted the parking area when Kendall and Nash arrived.

Nat waited for them on center stage; the actors she'd been surrounded by drifted toward the exits. Nat always presented as a treat for the eye, and tonight was no exception. Her dark hair, gleaming like polished teak, hung nearly to her waist, and her flawless complexion glowed under the softened stage lighting.

Nash took Nat's hand as they were introduced. "You probably don't remember me. I met you going through the reception line after *Strangers on a Train.* You were great."

Eyeing him up, Nat's lush lashes fluttered at the compliment. Kendall knew Nat was evaluating what her relationship was to Nash.

An outfit few women could pull off, Nat wore black tights under a long charcoal-gray sweater belted at the waist with a chain of silver hoops, her taut figure displayed to its best advantage. Her sweater ended just below her curved backside, her feet encased in a pair of high-heeled boots adorned with silvery fur from ankle to knee. She looked like something out of a fashion magazine, and on Nat it worked. Kendall could tell Nash was fascinated; he hadn't taken his gaze from Nat since they walked into the theater.

"You told Morrie you had something for us," she said.

Nat's amber eyes moved to Nash.

"He's working with us on this; Gray Glausson hired him."

Nat looked Nash over once more, admiration evident in her eyes. Kendall had known Nat to have an occasional fling with a member of the opposite sex.

"You're a PI?" Nat asked.

"For the moment."

"So what do you have for us?" Kendall looked around the empty theater. "Are we alone?"

"Yes, the others left for the night."

Nat took a seat in one of a group of director's chairs, done in brilliant, primary colors, her pose seductive, and her elegant dancer's legs crossed. Whether she'd posed for Kendall's or Nash's benefit, Kendall couldn't be sure.

Nat began, "A few years ago, I found myself in this situation. I was pregnant. My lifestyle, as you know, isn't suited to raising a child, so I took some time to explore my options. I was working on the acquisition of the theater at the time, and the attorney helping me set it up was a friend of mine. She knew I was pouring my entire savings into the endeavor and told me she knew someone who could find the child an excellent home if I was considering having the baby and giving it up for adoption. It would put enough money in my pocket to put me back in financial solvency. I took her advice."

Is this for real? "You never told me any of this," Kendall said.

"It never came up. It happened years before you moved in."

"Why didn't you come forward with it before now?"

"Back then selling my baby only ranked higher on my morality scale than killing it by having an abortion. It wasn't my proudest moment."

"Did your attorney give you the name of the person who paid for your child?"

She sighed. "That's one reason I didn't call you. The name had escaped my memory. But I was cleaning out some old files today and found her note stuck between some papers." She handed Kendall a folded sheet of yellow memo paper.

Kendall opened the paper and read the name printed across it. Written in a bold feminine hand was the name—the shifty lawyer, now her father's latest squeeze—Margaret Cottingham.

When Nash dropped her off at the apartment, a light still glowed from Morrie's office. Kendall stepped in. "You're working late."

He looked up from his computer screen. "You here about the apartment?"

"I thought I'd ask you if there was anyone else that wanted

the place."

"Anyone else?"

When Kendall didn't answer, he said, "You're making this difficult for me, Kenny. Tell you what. If you want to give me a month's rent, I'll let you stay on a month-to-month basis. Since you're a cop, I won't even ask for security. And I'll put in that new carpeting in for you. Pick out one of those samples I left."

"Whatever." She was taking the apartment; she'd worry about what it looked like later. Kendall wrote him a check before she could talk herself out of it or think about why putting down roots made her so uneasy.

Upstairs, she glanced at the stack of mail Nat had handed her when they left the theater. Yet another thing she had to do, file her change of address with the post office. Standing over the wastebasket, she dropped the junk mail in without opening it. Her heart stopped at the last piece of mail—the annual photo. She ripped it open and took out a picture of a young woman posed next to a fence surrounded by a beautiful autumn scene. *Beth.* She'd be eighteen soon. Would she want to meet her biological mother?

Maybe not. She looked happy. Happy, intelligent, and wearing a smile of anticipation for a life yet to be lived. Kendall wouldn't blame her if she didn't want to look backward. She added the photo to a stack she kept hidden in an old stationary box, trying to put it out of her mind like she did every year at this time.

Lying in bed later, details of the two investigations crowded her thoughts; it was becoming increasingly difficult to juggle them.

Finally, she drifted off amid thoughts of computers, abandoned babies, and Adam Nashlund.

29

Sharky had watched Carlee Somerfelt since the night she and her friends snuck into a club using fake ID's. He eyed her all evening when she wasn't looking, but when she left she'd been surrounded by a group of girls. It had been sheer luck he found out about the stargazing trip. She'd fallen right into his waiting arms. He'd stolen her virginity and her life. Or so he'd thought until the morning papers announced the girl survived the encounter. She wouldn't be able to identify him, though. The cops didn't have shit.

He'd worn a mask, gloves, and used a condom. The knife was sold in every sporting goods store in town.

The demand to meet tonight had to be fallout from what he'd done the night before. He'd been ordered to keep his nose clean, but it would be hard to deny he was the one who'd done the deed on Somerfelt. Too fucking bad if it hadn't gone over. He was through being a patsy. It was worth whatever happened as a result.

He hated waiting, but as ordered, he sat in his car in the dark parking lot at the designated time. *Crap, this place is colder than a witch's tit.* Damn heater sucked and he was freezing. He got treated like crap, especially when he asked to be called "the Shark" instead of that baby name, Sharky. He was done being the puppet and would announce it tonight. If he was going to be reamed out for what happened, then that was it. Didn't matter that he'd done it. It wasn't anyone else's business.

Monday

Kendall stayed behind while Alverson and his partner visited the local tattoo and piercing parlors She managed to avoid Schoenfuss, who after being gone for five days, had been locked in his office all morning, relieving her of having a conversation with him anytime soon.

She left the station early to visit the local car repair shops. With the little she had to go on—the gasoline smell on the rapist and the vague description—it wouldn't take more than the morning. Driving to the first auto repair shop, she mulled over her goal of working in a special victim's unit. It would mean relocating to a larger city. Would she have the stomach for it in the long haul? She wondered. The baby pervs had given her serious doubts.

Carlee had described her attacker as young, not too tall or heavy, wearing a leather jacket and a tough-guy attitude, which sounded to Kendall more like someone who'd be employed in a neighborhood shop. The mechanics at the dealership she frequented were older, late twenties and up. Before she left the office, Kendall eliminated the new car dealerships with a few calls confirming their mechanics were all older than 25—the jobs must pay well. She'd focus on the small independents first. There was so damn little to go on it was hard to know what to ask them. A young mechanic, not too tall or heavy, Caucasian, wore a leather jacket. Vague. Add to it, he liked to rape women and had a pierced cock.

She spent a minimal amount of time in the first few places and wondered if she was spinning her wheels. About to stop for lunch, she spotted an old-fashioned gas station that had two stalls for repairs. Not on her list, it looked like just the kind of place a young mechanic might get his first job. She parked and entered the station, walking into the first bay where an old van was on a hoist and a man in greasy coveralls swore into the phone he was holding.

"Fuck that, Arlie! Threaten me all you want, but it won't get your truck fixed any faster. The more time I spend talking to you, the longer it'll take."

The caller apparently didn't let up.

"How many ways do I have to tell you? Sharky didn't show up—I have cars backed up to my asshole—I'll let you know when I get to it. That's the best I can do." After a few seconds, he said, "Fine. Come and pick it up. I don't give a crap."

He threw the phone aside and saw Kendall.

"If you're looking for a car, get in line," he grumbled.

She held up her ID and introduced herself. "No, I'm looking for a man."

"Me too," he snarled. "Asshole mechanic didn't show up."

"I'm looking for a young man, probably late teens to early twenties. He's Caucasian and wears a leather jacket." She didn't add that he had a pierced penis; she didn't think men exchanged that kind of detail with each other and she doubted an establishment like this had community showers.

"That could be a lot of guys."

"We think he's a mechanic," she said.

"You think. Don't know much, do you?" He grimaced. "Sorry, I'm having a shitty morning here. My mechanic didn't show. Hell, he could fit a description like that. What do you want the guy for?"

Kendall was getting a buzz—this could be the lucky break she needed. "I can't reveal anything about an ongoing investigation. Tell me about this Sharky. He have a name?"

"I think its Gerald. Gerald Fostvedt."

"Is that how you make out his payroll checks?"

Kendall noticed the hesitation, guessing he didn't pay employee withholding taxes.

"I pay him cash. The kid's usually dependable."

"Kid? How old is this Sharky?"

"Seventeen. But he's a terrific wrench; knows his cars."

"What does he look like?"

"Shit, I dunno."

"Try."

"Well, he's skinny—about a half a head shorter than me, so about 5'8", I guess. Has dark hair, kinda long. He wears it oily and slicked back. Told me they call him Sharky cause that's what he looks like."

Kendall couldn't resist. "He has fins?"

"Funny. Nah, he has a long, thin face, and a big mouth. His teeth have spaces—like a shark."

"Do you have a phone number for him?"

"I do, but I can tell you he's not picking up."

"It's a cell phone?"

"Yeah." He edged closer to the van he'd been working on. "Are we about done here? I got work waiting for me."

"Do you have an address for him?"

He described an old motel, recently converted to studio apartments. "I think he said he rented the last one they had. Said it was his lucky number—three."

"What kind of car does he drive?"

"An old Camaro. Dark blue and beat up. He's gonna restore it."

Kendall left with directions to Sharky's apartment and the cell number he wasn't answering.

Sharky. He could be her guy. Rape and attempted murder on Saturday and on Monday a no-show at work. It fit.

There were two cars parked in front of the units where he lived, an old pickup and an ancient Honda four-door. She couldn't find a manager on the premises and no one answered at number three.

She left, drove a few blocks, and turned into the lot of a convenience store that sold deli sandwiches. Wolfing down a sub, a diet Pepsi, and a bag of chips without leaving the parking lot, she updated her notes, trying to decide what to do next. The garage owner hadn't known the names of any of Fostvedt's friends and except for mentioning that a girl called him from time to time, had been no further help. She'd cruise by Sharky's apartment once more since she was still in his neighborhood and search the area for a blue Camaro.

When there was still no answer at #3, Kendall checked for an arrest record on Fostvedt—he was clean except for a speeding ticket—and got the license number of the Camaro. Then she scoped out the neighborhood, paying close attention to parking lots of apartment buildings in case he was staying with a girlfriend who lived in the area. That and driving by his place got her nothing. Then she got lucky. An aging park nearby had been used to build a new baseball diamond for the local softball teams. The county had spared no expense; the stadium housing the ballpark had been done well, comfortably seating hundreds of fans. What little remained of the original park framed the baseball field on the back three sides and had never been renovated or kept up.

She turned into a deserted remnant of the park whose seedy parking areas served as meeting rooms for the non-discriminating. As she passed through the first one, she noticed a car parked in another space about a hundred yards over. What little she could see of the car was blue.

Kendall drove to the other lot. A blue Camaro parked there fit the description given by the garage owner and appeared to be empty. Looking around, she saw there wasn't much nearby except an old shelter that at one time housed restrooms. Surrounded by remnants of summer weeds and old shrubbery, it was plastered with graffiti and sat about twenty yards from the deserted car.

She left her car and circled the Camaro, seeing nothing remarkable. The plate matched Fostvedt's car. Glancing toward the shelter, she debated the wisdom of entering it without calling for backup, then decided against calling. Nothing indicated a crime had been committed. Fostvedt had likely met someone in the parking area and left in another other vehicle. If he was her perp, he might have abandoned the telltale car and taken off for parts unknown rather than face arrest.

The shelter, just large enough to house two small restrooms, had two doors into it, now only rectangular openings in the cement blocks; the actual doors long gone. As she approached, she feared what she would find—the smell of dying vegetation couldn't mask the scent of death.

Kendall unholstered her gun and called for backup before slowly turning into the shelter. A body lay on the filthy cement floor in a pool of congealed blood. Kendall backed away, careful not to disturb anything. If the body was Fostvedt and he turned out to be Carlee Somerfelt's attacker, it was possible someone had found out and decided to override the system.

She had little doubt what notable peculiarity the medical examiner would find when he had Sharky undressed on the table.

Maggie Cottingham's law office was in the middle of an aging strip mall on a frontage road parallel to 53. Flanked by a discount carpeting store and a battery shop, the glass front was discreetly covered by beige, vertical blinds. A sign painted in the lower right corner of the window read "M. L. Cottingham, Attorney at Law."

An empty reception desk sat in the waiting area. Kendall walked into the main office, where Maggie Cottingham sat slouched behind a desk fronted by two rattan chairs. She straightened. "Kendall. This is a nice surprise."

"It's Detective Halsrud. This isn't a social call."

Cottingham pulled off a pair of tortoise-shell readers. "Have a seat, Detective. I heard you found the Markowicz girl. That was good work; her parents are very relieved."

"Nice try, Maggie, but the virgin email case is over, and it's not going to do you any good to suck up." Kendall wouldn't dance around what she'd found out. "You know we're still looking for Philly Glausson. One of my sources told me you're in the baby brokering business."

The color drained from Cottingham's heavily made-up face.

Kendall had no sympathy for her. "You can talk to me here or we can go down to the station."

She nearly went for her gun when Cottingham reached into a lower desk drawer, relaxing as she saw her take out a bottle of Scotch and two crystal tumblers.

"I'll talk to you, but I'm going to need some moral support. Care to join me?"

Technically, Kendall was off the clock, but she didn't want to act too chummy. "No thanks."

Maggie took a healthy swallow of the liquor. "You can't prove anything, you know."

"Are you sure about that?"

Cottingham didn't look sure at all. "I am. And as an attorney who knows my rights, I could ask you to leave. But because of my relationship with your father, I'll talk to you without my own attorney. One caveat, however. This little talk is off the record. You want more than that, we go formal. Agreed?"

"Fine." Kendall wanted to hear what Cottingham had to say. That Cottingham and her father had an actual relationship was news to her. Knowing her father's history with women, she'd been hoping he'd follow pattern and have already moved on to the next one.

"Put your cell phone on the table. And recording device if you're carrying one."

Kendall stood and emptied her pockets. Cottingham checked Kendall's phone and digital recorder. "All right. I'll tell you about it." She took another gulp of whiskey.

"First of all, I no longer handle adoptions of any kind. My adoption service goes back more than 18 years to when I first got out of law school. I couldn't find a job and was forced to hang out my shingle. Things were tough—I couldn't support myself and my dog, much less pay off my student loans. I wasn't planning to do adoptions; I did the first one for a friend of mine. It was an old story; she'd put her longtime boyfriend through school, and when she got pregnant, he dumped her.

"She came to me and said she wanted to give the child up for adoption. She'd heard that people pay big money to adopt a Caucasian baby if an attorney brokers the deal instead of an agency. Like me, she needed money desperately. She begged me to find a couple who had money and would make good parents. She was willing to split the fee, so I did it for her. You'd be amazed at how easy it was to find people willing to pay a fortune for a baby."

Kendall didn't doubt it. "That was it? The one time?"

Cottingham swirled the liquor left in her glass. "I wish I could tell you it was. I got greedy, I suppose. But I really needed the money. After my practice got going, I quit."

"So how many adoptions did you handle?"

"Seven, over a period of eight years. And just so you know, I researched the couples completely. As well as any regular agency would. It was all legit and the babies went to great homes."

"You're out of it for ten years now? My source was more recent."

"I've had some calls since then, and I turned them all down. And before you ask, nothing recent. And also before you ask, I don't know of any baby brokers in the area."

———————

Kendall left Cottingham, satisfied the woman had been up-front; Cottingham's facts could be checked. Another dead end.

She tried Teed as soon as she got home. The medical examiner, sounding annoyed at the interruption, answering after five rings.

"Did you get a positive ID on Fostvedt?"

"Yes, his parents were here earlier."

"Sorry to hound you about this already, but I need whatever you have on him."

"I'm working on him now, Kendall. He died of a bullet wound to the chest at close range. You need details, you'll have to wait."

She didn't want to lead him. "I'm looking for something in particular. If it's there you would have noticed."

Teed humphed. "You know about his piercing."

"The vic said it felt like a small hoop earring."

"That's it. Gold, 14k, a half-inch in diameter."

"He's probably Carlee Somerfelt's rapist, unless penis piercings are becoming the new fashion statement for idiots."

Teed didn't laugh. "Anything else?"

"Yeah, I'd like his prints run against the partial from the Glausson case."

"Interesting. I'll get one of the techs on it right away."

"It's probably a long shot, but the rapes have similarities."

Frustrated, Kendall drove back to the office. The Cottingham adoptions checked out. She called Nash and filled him in on what happened with Fostvedt and Cottingham. For once, he had nothing to add. His lack of interest didn't improve her mood.

30

Kendall stopped for groceries, intending to cook her first meal in the apartment now that it was going to be hers for at least the next thirty days. It felt good to have her own place; it had been a long time. And since Alverson and his partner were working Fostvedt's murder, she'd be able to spend time on the Glausson case.

She checked in with Brynn, who was glued to the huge screen of the new iMac. Apparently at a critical point, Brynn waved her away.

Kendall made herself a quick grilled cheese and heated a can of tomato soup. Not much for a housewarming meal, but quick and comforting. When she finished, she fried another sandwich and took it over to Brynn, who grabbed it like it was a lifesaver.

"Have you even taken a break today?"

"No. Thanks for the sandwich. I forgot to eat."

"Any breakthroughs?"

Brynn's pale eyes sparkled. "I'm pretty sure I've found the right chat room. One of them got sloppy and I was able to track her username. She's the woman from Cameron, that Jennemen. I can't tell who the others are, but there are four of them that meet in a private chat room."

Four accounted for those they'd talked to, Jennemen, Iseroth, Traynor and DeForrest. "Can you tell what's going on?"

"They're talking about a package they're going to pass around. It couldn't be the baby, could it? Would they do something like that?"

"Hard telling what monsters like them are capable of."

The cheese sandwich Kendall had eaten turned leaden in her stomach. What had they stepped into? It was possible they were talking about photos or videos, which would be most likely. But passing a baby around? It didn't get worse than that.

Later, deep in much-needed sleep, Kendall woke with a start. Through slitted eyes she saw a figure standing next to her bed.

"Kendall! You have to wake up. There's another one talking to them; I think she's the one getting the package. She calls herself Mia."

Kendall slowly grasped what was happening. Brynn had found something important and let herself into the apartment. She had to get her key back from that girl. Brynn was shivering despite the heavy bathrobe covering her thin body.

"You didn't answer your phone, and I knew you'd want to know."

Kendall had forgotten to charge her phone. As soon as her muddled thoughts registered the enormity of the news, she crawled out of bed. Mia. Where had she heard that name recently? She had to make coffee and clear her head.

She read the chats and had a cup of coffee before it hit her—the name Mia—TJ, Conlin's girlfriend, had mentioned it to Nash. Something about the landlady in Waukesha. Crap, the landlady. Why hadn't she put it together? Especially after the

Jennemen-Iseroth connection to Waukesha. She plugged in her phone to call TJ.

It was nearly one when Kendall got off the phone. She'd been in touch with the Waukesha police through TJ and Detective Conlin. WPD had started a stakeout on "Mia," aka Tanya Porter, the former prostitute. They'd quickly pinpointed her as a member of the predator ring, possibly its ringleader. The Cameron police were watching Jennemen and Iseroth, and the county sheriffs had a bead on DeForrest. In Minnesota, the Greenfield police had called in the state BCA to watch Traynor. If the chatter was what it appeared to be and the members of the ring were going to share a purchased child, the pedophiles were all covered in order to save the child.

Kendall wanted to leave for Waukesha. She needed to be part of the takedown and be there when they got Philly out of the hands of those animals.

Schoenfuss had no idea any of this was going down and wouldn't look kindly on being left out of the loop. Should she call her boss and piss him off by interrupting his sleep, or suffer his wrath the next day? A successful outcome could nix any penalty, however. Since she didn't have any new cases, and with the Somerfelt and virgin email cases wrapped up, she opted for putting it off until the next day. She'd call him from Waukesha.

She looked over at Brynn, who was still glued to her computer screen. "I'm going to Waukesha."

"Aren't you going to call Nash?"

Brynn was right to remind her—Nash should know she was going and what was happening. She went back to her apartment and took out her phone.

He answered as if he'd been waiting for a call. "What's happening?"

She brought him up to speed on the pedophile ring.

"Damn! We should have figured it out."

"Guess we weren't able to sink to their level. Don't forget, you suspected they were in touch with each other," Kendall said.

He grunted. "At least now they won't get their slimy hands on the kid."

"I'm going to Waukesha."

"Don't the locals have it covered?"

"They do, but I want to be part of it."

"So do I," Nash said, "but I have no business being there. You don't, either."

"I couldn't sleep now, anyway. I may as well go."

"Your boss doesn't know any of this, does he?"

Kendall's excitement vanished. "No, he doesn't know yet."

"You'll get your ass in a sling if you go. I'll make you a deal—stay put and I'll go. I'll give you regular reports of what's going on. They can't do anything to me for showing up."

He was right. It didn't matter if she and Nash were the ones who'd uncovered the pedophile ring. Schoenfuss would still be angry and even more so if she didn't show up for work the next morning. And if she were being honest with herself, there wasn't anything she could bring to the bust except her ego.

TJ made it possible for Nash to be in touch with the team surrounding Tanya Porter's house. He spoke with Detective Tom

Zabel of the WPD. Zabel, along with three other officers, was stationed in an old motor home parked in a driveway three doors down from Porter's place.

The efficiency of Waukesha's placement was impressive. Zabel and his crew masqueraded as visitors to an elderly woman who lived in a neighboring home. Determining Tanya Porter was not in her residence, they'd furtively surrounded the house after getting the news via the chat room that the *package* would be changing hands late that night and would be picked up by Tanya Porter.

The local forensic units replaced Brynn's duties as cyber lookout, and were searching for a money trail that would confirm Tanya Porter as the ringleader. The others, Jennemen, Iseroth, DeForrest and Traynor, remained under digital and physical surveillance. The goal? To take the rest of the pedophile ring into custody at the same time they intercepted Porter with the baby. If the Feds found a money trail among the freaks, along with the chat records, it would put them all behind bars for a long time.

Nash parked in the lot of a local motel as close to Tanya's house as prudent considering the surveillance. At five a.m., he got the call from Zabel; they'd picked up Tanya after she'd entered the house with the baby. It was over.

I'm coming over there to pick up the kid," Nash said. "I have permission from her uncle, Gray Glausson." Not really true since he'd opted to hold off on contacting Gray until he knew something certain, but worth a try.

"Sorry, man. You know I can't let you do that. The baby has to go with family services first. It's protocol, my hands are tied."

He knew Zabel was right, but sometimes protocol sucked. "After all that kid's been through?"

"Hang on. They're bringing the baby out."

An endless minute passed while Nash waited for word that Philly was unharmed.

"I'm afraid I have some bad news," Zabel said."

Were they too late? "What did they do to her?"

"Nothing. The child looks fine, but it's not the Glausson baby. This kid is Asian."

31

Tuesday

Schoenfuss called Kendall to his office. He met her with his arms akimbo, his face red.

"What were you thinking?"

He didn't let her answer. "I told you to work on your other cases and leave this the hell alone, didn't I?"

Kendall fought to keep her next words non-confrontational. "You did, but you also said I could work the Glausson case in my spare time. Every hour I put in was on my own time. The other cases you gave me are put to bed."

"That might be impressive if you hadn't had help. Civilian help, I might add, and you know that's not acceptable."

"I had to use whatever means I could to find Philly Glausson. I told you I had a strong gut feeling she's alive. I still do."

"Right. That and five bucks will get you lunch at McDonald's."

"With Adam Nashlund's help I saved a child's life and exposed a pedophile ring. Those animals will be put away for the rest of their lives *because* I went out on a limb."

Her boss's expression hardened. It was time to shut up and

let him do the talking.

"I got a call from Agent Kahn. I thought I also told you to stay away from him."

Technically she had stayed away; they'd communicated by text message. "I haven't talked to Agent Kahn since the day I went to Stillwater." *Was texting talking?*

Schoenfuss took a deep breath. "He commended your work, actually. He called right after the Chief did the press conference."

Kendall knew he was getting around to dropping the other shoe. How much trouble could she be in, for God's sake? She'd staked her hopes on her "commendable" solve-rate outweighing the problem of Nash's involvement. "Channel 17 called. They've been doing a series on women in law enforcement and want to interview you about the pedophile-ring case. The Chief accepted for you."

Kendall's face burned. She hated media attention and he knew it. "Can't someone else do it?" *Someone who loves the limelight?*

He glared at her. "Don't let the door hit you on the way out."

Deflated when the FBI took over monitoring the pedophile ring, Brynn switched to searching through adoption ads. It was a time-consuming chore.

When she heard a knock on her door, it was a welcome distraction. She'd been given the green light on safety measures once Kendall found Fostvedt and identified him as Carlee's rapist.

A teenage boy stood at her door. "Hi. I'm looking for my dad."

She would have asked who his dad was if he hadn't borne an amazing resemblance to Adam Nashlund. Except for nearly a head's difference in height, and his auburn hair, he was a replica of his father.

He grinned. "I know you know him. Adam Nashlund."

"He's not here."

"I got back early, and I don't have my key to the house, just the car key."

What did he want from her? "Did you call him?"

"Don't have a cell phone."

She remembered the day he took off with his father's car. "Are you supposed to be driving?"

"I have a license," he said, ignoring the implication of her question. "Hey, it's cold out here. Can I come in for a minute?"

Kendall was about to leave the office when she got a call from Gene Tarkowski. "Nice work on the Porter case," the agent said.

"The Porter case?"

"Tanya Porter, the pedophile ring."

"Right. I'd forgotten her name. Did you get all of them?"

"We did. It's going well, too. They're pointing fingers at each other."

"That's great, although it isn't helping me find the Glausson child. Did you find the parents of the baby you rescued?"

"Not yet. There haven't been any reports of a baby missing in the area. If the parents sold their baby, they might not want to be found. But about Philly. Kendall, our people went over the entire area again, re-interviewed neighbors, and friends of the

Glausson's. There's nothing else there."

She groaned. "Pretty soon I'll be the only one who believes she's still alive."

"I understand. I've had a few of those cases myself, the ones you can't get out of your head. But that isn't why I called. I wanted to give you a heads up on this before it hits the news. Travis Jordan's attorney filed a motion to suppress the gun from evidence. She's claiming the search of his car was illegal. It's on the docket in Stillwater tomorrow morning."

An ice-cold wave of dread swept through her. "Is there a chance it'll stand up?"

"Hard to say, Kendall. You know how these things go. In a court of law, there are never any sure things.

Fighting discouragement, Kendall went to see Alverson and his partner, who were working Fostvedt's murder and talking to Chippewa in an effort to identify him as their rapist.

"While you're at it, would you look for anything connecting him to the Glaussons or to Travis Jordan?" she asked.

She stopped Alverson's protest with a raised hand. "I know we don't have enough evidence to support a connection, but the techs are comparing his prints with the partial we found on the Glausson girl. The results of a partial match may not hold up as evidence in a trial, but if Fostvedt was an accomplice, it could help us find Philly Glausson. The invasion here was the only one where there was a rape, and what Fostvedt did to Carlee was similar to what was done to Sienna Glausson.

"And remember to check him with Sienna Glausson and see if there's any connection there. You'll have to question her friends again."

Ignoring their unenthusiastic expressions, Kendall left the station. She wished she knew for sure if Philly Glausson was alive, not decomposing in a wooded area or being sold to an unidentified pedophile. And there was the possibility Travis Jordan could be released. What else could go wrong?

She drove home feeling like she must have missed something. They'd interviewed everyone who'd known or worked with Mark Glausson. And everyone related to or acquainted with Sienna had been interviewed more than once because of the virgin email case. What little they knew about Chelsea Glausson had come from her friend Betty and her son Evan's therapist.

The only things taken in the home invasions had been cash and credit cards. The money from the Glausson home had totaled a meager $580. What had Jordan been after? Was Gerald Fostvedt his accomplice? At least in the Glausson invasion? There were just too damn many questions and no answers.

Secrets. They had a way of coming around to haunt you. Was there something in the Glaussons' background she'd missed? Something that had made them a target for Travis Jordan? Neither the locals nor the Feds had found anything connecting the families in the three invasions.

Chelsea's friend, Betty Ruffalo. She'd try talking to her again. Before starting the car, Kendall punched in her number.

"Betty, this is Detective Halsrud. I'd like to talk to you again."

"Sure, Detective. I'm at my daughter's right now. Do you want to come here or would you like me to meet you at the station?"

Kendall got the address and minutes later pulled up in front of a modest ranch-style home bright with Christmas decorations. Christmas. It was hard to believe the holiday season had arrived while the rest of her world went to hell. Betty opened the door and led her into a small living room furnished in the early American style popular in the sixties. Rag rugs were scattered on the wood floor, and the walls were covered with artwork ala garage sale. The air smelled of lemon furniture polish and freshly baked cookies. They sat across from each other on matching upholstered rockers.

Kendall skipped any idle chitchat. "Betty, did you know that Philly was Graham Glausson's child?"

"I knew it was a possibility. And believe me, Detective, I wrestled with telling you about it. I didn't think it could be relevant, because no one knew."

"Anything could be relevant in an investigation of this magnitude."

"I'm sorry. It was bad judgment on my part not to tell you."

"Is there anything else you didn't think was important?"

Betty shifted her position in the rocker. "Is there something in particular you're looking for?"

"There wasn't much taken in any of the invasions," said Kendall. "I'm still thinking there has to be a personal link somewhere that precipitated all of them, but we haven't found anything connecting the three families."

"If I knew of anything, I'd tell you. Maybe your link lies with the other families."

There had to be something. "I don't think so. The ones in Green Bay and Stillwater have been examined for nearly a year, both by the local police departments and the FBI."

Betty Ruffalo's daughter, a tall, svelte version of her mother, entered the room to serve coffee and set a plate of Christmas cookies in front of them. Kendall realized she hadn't eaten since the stale doughnut she'd practically swallowed whole at the station that morning. Eager for a sugar rush, she quickly bit into a cookie, savoring its sweetness.

"Betty, can you think of anyone else who might have known Chelsea well enough to be of help?"

"No. Like I told you, she and I only met because of her son Evan and my granddaughter being in the hospital at the same time. She didn't have much time for herself."

"That's right. How is your granddaughter?"

Betty's face brightened. "She's wonderful. Still in remission and the doctors say there's no reason to think it won't be permanent. I'd show her off to you now, but she's at a play date with a little friend."

Kendall munched another cookie, realizing this was the second time she'd broken her rule about eating with a witness. Maybe cookies didn't count.

"What about Chelsea's past?" Kendall asked. "You said the Twin Cities had bad memories for her."

"That's right. Chelsea's parents died in a car crash when she was about six. There were no relatives to take Chels, and the family hadn't left any money that could help her out. She ended up in and out of foster homes."

"Did she tell you if any of them were abusive?"

"Chels didn't like to talk about them, but I think the last one was. She ran away when she was sixteen."

"How did she support herself?"

Ruffalo hesitated. Kendall could tell they were getting into territory about her friend that Betty didn't want to explore with the police. "Betty, you have to tell me anything you know about her past. Did she start hooking?" A question Kendall knew the answer to, but maybe it would get Betty to open up.

She exhaled as if she'd been holding her breath. "Not at first. She got a job busing tables at a Greek restaurant. She finally got to be a waitress, but they went out of business. She couldn't find anything else. When her money ran out, she ended up on the streets."

"Did she start using drugs?"

"Heroin," Betty whispered.

"Why don't you just tell me everything she told you about that time?"

"She was at a party the first time she tried the heroin. Chels was one of those people who got hooked with just one use. About a year later, a friend helped her kick the habit. She got work finally and then got her GED. She put herself through school. All of that took a lot of courage."

Could Chelsea Glausson's drug use so long ago be connected to the present? It didn't seem possible. "Do you know if she stayed in touch with anyone from back then?"

"If she did, she didn't tell me about it. Chels wanted to forget about her past."

A vision of Philly filled Kendall's mind, quickly overlaid with the shadow of another little girl. Kendall's eyes misted. The memory of the other child prompted Kendall's next question.

"Betty, was Chelsea ever pregnant during those years?"

Betty's face saddened. "Detective, why would it matter now?"

Kendall could feel it, Chelsea Glausson's past would be the key to opening the case. "She was, wasn't she? Something from her past could be connected to the present, especially if it involves a child. Tell me what you know about it, Betty."

32

Kendall rushed home after talking to Betty and found Brynn in front of the iMac, searching through adoption ads. Kendall had to give her credit; she was desperately trying to be helpful, despite having no guarantee she'd be paid for any of her work.

Kendall paced.

Brynn didn't look away from the screen. "What's wrong?"

"I might have a lead, but it raises even more questions. I wish I knew for sure the baby was still alive; if not, we're running in circles."

"Well, we could try doing a reading," Brynn suggested.

Kendall remembered Nash's suggestion. "It didn't help when you did Nash's reading. He said he asked about the baby."

"I know. But you said you're desperate."

Kendall had more respect for Brynn's computer skills than her supposedly paranormal ones. But she *was* desperate. "What the hell. Let's try it."

Brynn, ethereal in her white wig and other card-reading apparel, had candles burning on the sideboard next to her small table. In the midst of the candles, sat an aged photo in a gilded frame of a woman with brown, finger-waved hair.

"Thought I'd set the mood," Brynn said.

Kendall took a seat across from her, and they began the ritual shuffling and card placement. Brynn reached across the table and joined hands with Kendall. She addressed the old fortune-teller, her voice barely above a whisper.

"Vadoma, this is Brynn. I hope you don't mind that I've been continuing your work. I'm taking care of your things for you, too. They're going to repair the door soon.

"My friend Kendall needs your help. She wants to find a little girl named Philly. The police can't find her, and Kendall wants to know if she's still alive. If you can hear me, please give the cards your blessing."

Brynn released her hands from Kendall's. "I'm going to have you turn twelve cards over right away. I don't usually do it that way, but I want to get an overall feeling for what they'll be telling us."

Caught up in the moment, Kendall turned over twelve cards in rows of four. Brynn sucked in a breath as she looked over the exposed cards.

"The cards say the baby is still alive."

Kendall felt the hair on her arms tingle. It was the answer she'd wanted,

but did she dare give it any credence?

"This is weird, though," Brynn whispered.

"What?"

"There's a baby in the cards twice. The lower cards, two's and threes, represent children. A baby would be a two. See, you have a two of hearts and a two of diamonds right next to each other.

246

They're red suits, so that would mean girls."

More than one baby. *Had* Chelsea Glausson given birth all those years ago? Kendall felt foolish for seeking answers in the cards. Even more foolish for her fleeting thought the second baby might refer to her own child. Brynn had said they were both girls. But Betty Ruffalo had told her Chelsea might have been pregnant, although she said that Chelsea had been rather cryptic about it. For all she knew, Chelsea could have had an abortion. There was only one avenue Kendall could think of; she'd go to the Cities and try to find out how long Chelsea had been in the system after her parents died. And hope the case-worker who'd worked with Chelsea was still around.

After Kendall left, Brynn pulled off the white wig. She ran her fingers through her short, white hair and sat on the sofa with Malkin on her lap. She hadn't had a chance to tell Kendall about Ryan Nashlund. It was just as well. He'd asked her not to repeat what he'd said about his parents. He'd told her he and his mother came back early from his grandparents' house because his mother had decided to get a divorce.

Nash was a nice person. Brynn wondered why his wife wanted to divorce him. Kendall? No, there wasn't any funny business going on between him and Kendall; Brynn would have known.

Kendall went back to her apartment after the reading. Conflicted, she hadn't wanted to share her anguish with the girl. She'd done what she believed to be the right thing for her own daughter all those years ago, but there were times, like tonight, when she wished she were the one keeping her safe. There was no reason to doubt Beth had a wonderful family, but Kendall longed to be part of her life.

Her thoughts changed course abruptly when something she heard on the news caught her attention; a snowstorm predicted to unload more than a foot of snow was headed for the upper Midwest. *Damn.* She had to be in Stillwater tomorrow for the motion to suppress hearing.

It was hard to believe Jordan could be released, especially after his rant about the baby, but it wasn't unusual for a defense attorney to attempt to get evidence suppressed. And as confessions went, Jordan's—if they even considered his rant about the baby a confession—left a lot to be desired. Without the gun, there was little guarantee he could be convicted.

If Travis Jordan had a chance of walking, Kendall had to interview him while he was still in custody. The only way she could do that without begging for pre-approval from Schoenfuss, would be to leave now, then call in for time off in the morning. She had plenty of unused time to burn, and she couldn't risk being stranded in Eau Claire in the morning or having her boss tell her she couldn't go. She had to leave tonight. She'd just gotten dressed again when Nash called.

"Hey, looks like everything with the pedophile ring is wrapped up. We did good, didn't we?"

"I guess."

"What's wrong?"

"It's Travis Jordan. Bellamy filed a motion to suppress the gun from evidence. He might walk tomorrow. I have to talk to him again, ask him about Gerald Fostvedt."

"Have you found anything connecting them?"

"Alverson's working on it." She didn't share her suspicions about Chelsea's past, even though it was something else she wanted to hit Jordan with. Her suspicion had no shape yet; she feared talking about it might make it go away.

"You going to Stillwater tomorrow for the hearing?"

She should have known he'd ask. "No. I'm leaving now."

"Tonight? Why"

"There's a huge snowstorm headed this way. I can't risk not being there tomorrow."

"I'd go with you, but I have to deal with some things here. I'll meet you there in the morning."

Kendall had been on the road to Stillwater for nearly an hour when the first pain hit, a sharp one leaving her breathless when it subsided. The infection from the gunshot wound had to be back, what else could it be? Maybe adhesions. They'd warned her about them, but never said they would be so intense. An ER would be her only option if the pain continued. She wouldn't reach her own doctor at this hour.

She had to find out if the threat of Travis Jordan back on the streets was real. Agent Kahn had agreed to talk to her and she met him in a coffee shop close to the Stillwater station. Kahn sat at a table toward the back, one of few patrons out on a night threatening to burst with snow showers. He stood when she approached.

"Detective Halsrud. I have to commend you for a job well done by tracking down that pedophile ring. Good work. Now, what's so important that you had to see me tonight?"

"I want to talk to Travis Jordan."

His steely eyes studied her. "He's admitted killing the

Glausson child. What more can he tell you?"

"I'm still not convinced she's dead. You shouldn't be, either." She had no intention of telling him about the anonymous call she'd received.

"I'm not heartless, Detective. I've had the bureau's full manpower hunting for the child, and they've come up with nothing."

"But you've been looking for a body."

"I see no reason not to be."

"Why aren't you putting your resources into tracking down known or suspected child brokers?"

Kahn folded his arms across his chest. "You mean now that you've tied up the pedophile angle? Not going to happen, Detective, along with you interviewing Jordan again."

Kendall bristled, but didn't dare piss him off when she had one more thing to ask him. "The hearing tomorrow—how's it going to go?"

"You know there's no way to predict it."

"Are you familiar with the judge who's handling the hearing?"

"He's fair, not a bleeding heart, but not a vigilante, either. It could go either way. Right now, we're just trying to keep Jordan locked up."

He paused and pulled out his phone. "As long as you're here, I need a woman's opinion on something. What do you think of this?" He leaned over, holding out the screen of his phone. On it was a full set of glittering, glass dinnerware, etched crystal with a floral design and most likely accompanied by a big price tag.

"Christmas is coming and my bride loves antiques. I found this in one of the shops here and I'm thinking about buying it for her."

Strange man. Kendall couldn't believe he'd changed the subject to something so personal. He was the last person she'd have expected to take advantage of Stillwater's many antique shops. Having little interest in frivolous things herself, the set reminded her of her mother's expensive taste.

"For what that would set you back," Kendall advised, "I think you'd impress her more by getting her one kick-ass piece."

He frowned and returned the phone to his pocket. "You wasted a trip coming here, Detective. Go back to Eau Claire while the roads are still passable."

So much for the personal touch. Outside the window, huge flakes of snow had begun their dance to earth, already covering it with a white dusting.

Kendall wasn't going back.

The pains hit again shortly after she checked into the nearest hotel, stabbing at her like thrusts of a sword. With the snow accumulating so quickly, Kendall knew she had to get to the nearest ER while her car could still get her there. The Highlander's tires weren't the best; she'd neglected to put new snow tires on it. She looked up the address of the nearest hospital and walked back out into the storm.

33

Nash arrived home from Waukesha, surprised to find his wife waiting for him in the living room. When she'd left with Ryan on Friday, their return had been open-ended.

"Hey," he said, "I wasn't expecting you for a few days."

"Where've you been?" She wasn't smiling.

He explained he'd been in Waukesha and how he and Kendall had exposed a pedophile ring whose members were now in custody.

"That's it then, the case is over?"

"We haven't found the kid yet."

"The child everyone else believes is dead?"

He knew her thoughtless question had nothing to do with Philly Glausson. He'd quit the force to save his marriage and his going back to investigating—with the crazy hours that came with it—had to be the hair up her butt.

"Shari, this is *one* case. I'm doing it as a favor for Graham Glausson. You know the kind of money I'm getting for it."

"You're full of it, Nash. This has nothing to do with money. Admit it, you can't live without the drama of police work."

Before he could respond, his phone buzzed. Without thinking, he pulled it out to see who was calling. Brynn's name appeared on the screen.

Shari's lips formed a narrow line. "Go ahead, you might as well answer it."

He raised the phone to his ear.

"I'm worried about Kendall," Brynn said.

"She told me she was going to Stillwater. What's wrong?"

"She just called me from there to ask about my research. She said she might go to the hospital because she was having bad stomach pains. She told me not to call her father or her uncle."

Fuck. Kendall needed him. But Shari was already pissed. If he left . . .

He closed the phone.

"I know you want to leave, Adam," she hissed. "It's what you always do."

"Shari, we're looking for a baby, for Christ's sake."

She swallowed. "This isn't working for me, Nash. I'm filing for a divorce."

Shivering in only a hospital gown, Kendall sat on the edge of an examining table, waiting to see a doctor. The nurses had already done an ultrasound and drawn her blood. There was something they weren't telling her; she knew the signs. Her white count must be up, the damn infection back. But the pain didn't feel like last time. Maybe she needed a different antibiotic, or a couple hours with an IV line in before they'd release her. She had to get out of the hospital before morning. While she was in Stillwater, she hoped to find out more about Chelsea Glausson's early years in the Cities. Then there was Jordan's hearing tomorrow.

She couldn't miss it.

She shouldn't have come to the hospital; the pains were gone.

Suddenly they started again, doubling her over. Her hands gripped the edges of the table so tightly that when the pain subsided, they were cramped and sore. Her hands—ugly suckers that seemed bigger than her size ten feet. Man hands. It would never matter how much weight she lost, makeup she applied, or what she did with her hair, the freaking hands would never change.

A gut wrenching twist of pain sliced through her just as the doctor entered the room.

It was nearly ten by the time Nash pulled into the Stillwater hospital parking lot in a four-wheel-drive vehicle he'd picked up at the CPP plant. Kendall hadn't been at her hotel and wasn't answering her phone, so he'd driven to the only hospital in the area. He'd fought his way through the accumulating snow easily enough in the Land Rover, but avoiding other driver's mishaps had tested all his driving skills.

He showed the nurses his PI license and explained his relationship to Kendall. They insisted they couldn't tell him anything because of patient confidentiality. After a lengthy debate, they contacted the Eau Claire PD before finally telling him she'd had surgery and brought him to a waiting area near the recovery room.

An hour later, a doctor came in wearing a lab coat over a set of stained scrubs.

"Mr. Nashlund?"

Nash stood, a knot tightening in his stomach as the doctor

took time to introduce himself and shake his hand.

He put Nash at ease. "She's fine."

"What happened," Nash asked, "did the infection from her bullet wound come back?"

The doctor shook his head. "No, that appears to be healed. Her pain was the result of a bad case of gallstones. She's rather young for them, and that's most likely why they weren't diagnosed when she was hospitalized for the gunshot wound. We were able to use laser surgery, so she can leave in a few hours providing her vitals are all right and she has someone to watch her for the rest of the night. Otherwise, she'll have to stay here for twenty-four hours."

Kendall would demand to leave the hospital as soon as possible. He'd have to get her back home where Brynn could stay with her for the rest of the night.

"Can she travel?"

"Only as far as the hotel she's staying in. I wouldn't advise anything longer." The doctor turned to leave. "A nurse will let you know when you can see her. It'll be an hour or more."

He'd have to stay with her. All he had with him was a gym bag with a pair of sweats and clean underwear; he hadn't planned ahead in his rush to get to Stillwater. The gift shop off the lobby had closed for the night. He'd have to find the nearest Walmart for a few essentials, and hope it hadn't closed because of the weather.

He didn't know what to expect, but when they finally took him into the recovery room, Kendall lay pale, but lucid in a bed with its side rails raised.

"Get me out of here," she begged as soon as she saw him.

That he *had* expected. "What? You cant' say you're glad to see me, or nice of you to be here for me, Nash?'"

A brief smile crossed her lips. "I'd apologize, but I just had surgery. I get a pass."

"They won't let you go tonight unless someone stays with you. That would be me, so be nice. And I have to be here when the doctor talks to you, in case you don't remember your instructions. And before you ask, they won't include letting you work the Glausson case tomorrow."

"But the hearing . . ."

"I'll go and report back to you."

Nash left the room when the nurse came in to take Kendall's vital signs and give her a pain pill. When he went back in he was surprised to see her looking glassy-eyed and giggling like a kid on a snow day. She'd been alert the first time he'd been in the room. He went to find a nurse.

Kendall insisted on being discharged—laughing all the while—even though the doctor explained to them she'd had a reaction to the pain medication she'd been given. Unusual, but it happens. They made her sign yet another form, gave Nash three pills to give her when she needed them, and told him to watch her during the night.

Nash brought the car around while an attendant waited at the front entrance with a woozy Kendall sitting in a wheelchair. He thought it amazing that after such a serious surgery, she'd be released in only a few hours. Seemed like it was more complicated to have teeth pulled these days than have laser surgery on internal organs. He tossed the package with the things he'd bought at Walmart into the back seat and drove around to the front of the hospital.

Cold and messy, the hotel room revealed Kendall's state when she'd left. One arm supporting her, Nash turned up the heat, then helped her over to one of the beds, relieved she had a two-bed room; he wouldn't have to sleep on the floor. She stood next to the bed and dumped her things out of a plastic bag bearing the hospital logo: her underwear, and a pair of those ground-gripping socks they hand out to patients and probably charge fifty bucks for.

As if she'd forgotten his presence, Kendall began to undress. Nash, unsuccessfully trying to avert his eyes from her breasts, scrambled for the nightshirt he'd bought for her on his shopping trip. He held it out to her.

Still groggy, she touched the lettering on the red nightshirt. "Naughty or Nice? Guess I'll be naughty." Her pants slid to her ankles. Oblivious to her nudity, she pointed to the small bandages on her chest and abdomen. "See, hardly anything there. Teensy, little scars."

She ran her fingers over the gunshot wound below her navel. "Except for this ugly thing."

It *was* ugly. Nash felt a renewed twinge of responsibility for what had happened to her and to his fellow officers the night a stray bullet hit Kendall. His guilt faded at the sight of Kendall's body, statuesque and glowing in the soft light, replacing all thought with a sudden yearning to touch her. He sat on the bed, put his arms around her and gently kissed her scar, her skin cool and smooth under his fingers. She surprised him by clutching his face to her belly, her hands twined in his hair. He stood, his lips traveling up her body, grazing one erect nipple, but resisting a nearly overwhelming desire to linger on her lovely breasts.

He had to remind himself this wasn't the time or place for

what he wanted. And under the influence of the drug reaction, what Kendall wanted couldn't be trusted. She needed to rest.

He slipped the nightshirt over her head. "It looks good on you," he said. Then, in an effort to lighten the mood, "Hey, how many guys would buy a girl a fancy nightgown?"

She giggled. "Black lace would have been nice."

He didn't want to give up the feel of her body against his. *This is Kendall—get a grip.*

She clung to him when he started to back away, and in a heartbeat they were kissing, deep, hungry kisses that told him they'd both wanted this moment. When he lowered her to the bed, she whispered, "Don't leave me."

Nash couldn't remember when he'd wanted a woman as badly as he wanted Kendall at that moment. "I'm not going anywhere."

Kendall's eyes closed. She'd fallen asleep the moment she'd hit the bed. He slid her jeans off her feet and covered her as he would a child. After a quick shower, he set the alarm and fell into the adjoining bed.

She'd be furious if they missed the motion to suppress hearing.

Wednesday

The snow hadn't stopped falling until a fourteen-inch blanket muffled any sound from the sparse traffic outside the hotel.

Kendall woke slowly, trying to piece together where she was. Her gut ached when she rolled over on her back. It was coming to her, the trip to the hospital the night before, the doctor telling her she needed surgery. After that, everything was blank.

She heard steady breathing nearby. The room, still dark, didn't reveal who it was. Nash? It had to be, but why? He hadn't come with her to Stillwater. A hazy memory came back to her, kissing him, wanting him to make love to her. It had to be a dream or the result of the anesthetic they'd given her. It couldn't be real; she'd apparently just had surgery and still carried a huge grudge against the man.

She started to get up to go to the bathroom and winced with pain. Her movements would have to be slow. Gall bladder surgery, that's what it was. She remembered they were going to take out her gall bladder along with the dozens of stones it held.

The bright red numbers on the clock radio read 6:00 a.m. Kendall had things to do: find Chelsea Glausson's social worker and get to the Stillwater courthouse for the hearing. She rose slowly to a standing position, steadying herself with the wall next to the bed and followed it into the bathroom. A haggard woman looked back at her from the mirror, her hair falling below her shoulders in clumps. Her mouth felt like a Monday-morning hangover. And the nightshirt—where had that come from? Bright red, on its front was an oversized Santa face with "Are You Naughty or Nice?" printed below it.

She carefully lowered herself to the toilet to pee, grateful for the handicapped height of the hotel stool. When she'd finished, getting up became an insurmountable task. Before she managed to accomplish it, there was a gentle knock on the door.

"Kenny. You okay in there?"

Nash. He'd heard her get up. What was he doing here? "Yeah. I'll be out in a minute." A sharp pain prevented her from standing. "No, better make that five minutes." She broke out in a cold sweat as she made another unsteady attempt to stand. A sudden memory of the sensuous dream she'd remembered nearly made her laugh—what could be less sexy than asking a man to help you off the toilet?

"On second thought, I may need a hand," she called to him.

The red nightshirt afforded some semblance of modesty as Nash lifted her to a standing position. He walked her back into the room where she insisted on sitting in a chair rather than get back in bed.

"How did you know where to find me?" she asked.

"Brynn told me you talked about going to an ER. When you didn't answer your phone and weren't in the hotel, I went to the Stillwater hospital. They wouldn't tell me anything, so I had Alverson call them. After that, I was able to get the skinny on what was happening. They wouldn't release you unless you had someone to stay with you after the surgery. Don't you remember any of this?"

"It's all pretty surreal," Kendall said. "I remember the snow getting harder to get through. How did you get past all the accidents?"

"No problem. I've got CPP's Land Rover; it'll get through anything."

His dark hair was tousled from sleep. She recalled the feel of its coarse thickness between her fingers, or was that part of the dream? It must have been quite the dream, or an amazingly erotic moment for her to be feeling remnants of its sensuality despite her condition.

"Did they give me anything for pain?"

He held out a small, brown prescription bottle. "Just three pills. You had a bad reaction to the first pain meds, so they gave you these to try if you need them." He handed her the container and a bottle of water, which she used to take one of the pills. He said, "You were pretty out of it last night. Fell asleep before you needed them."

She was afraid to ask for the details. "My mid-section feels like a truck hit me. These pills better do the trick; I have a lot to do today."

He started to protest.

"Don't tell me I have to rest. I can do that tomorrow. I need to find Chelsea Glausson's caseworker when she was a teenager. And I have to be at the courthouse for the hearing."

He nodded toward the window. "There's more than a foot of snow out there. There won't be any government offices open this morning, and the hearing will be postponed. You may as well get some rest."

When he left to get them some coffee, Kendall washed up and did what she could with her hair. She looked like shit. Remembering she had her gym bag along, she took out the cosmetics kit Nat had given her when she was in the hospital with the gunshot wound, a double-edged gift since her roommate knew Kendall never wore makeup and Nat always encouraged her to use it. She'd stuck it in the gym bag and forgotten about it. Maybe today it would do its magic and help her look like she hadn't just had surgery the night before.

Kendall was dressed and ready to face the world by the time Nash came back to the room carrying a tray of breakfast selections from the hotel's buffet

"Hey. Where's that tired-looking chick I came in with?"

She scrunched up her face. "Don't make me laugh; it hurts!"

"Sorry. You look great."

He'd noticed the makeup. "How bad are the roads?" she asked.

"Depends where you're going. The interstate's plowed and in decent shape. Back roads are a different story. The courthouse is snowed in and they're working on the downtown streets. I haven't gotten through to anyone in the courthouse yet, but it's still early. I've been meaning to ask you; why the big rush to talk to the case worker?"

Kendall picked up a coffee and bagel. "I felt like there was something I was missing. The only Glausson we didn't know everything about was Chelsea. I talked to her friend Betty Ruffalo again. It turns out there was a lot more in Chelsea's past than anyone had told us. Her parents were killed in a car accident when she was six, and after that she was in and out of fosters. The last one might have been abusive, and she turned to the streets. Ended up hooking and on heroin."

He frowned. "Awfully long ago for there to be a tie to the murders. There weren't any drug connections with the family, right?"

How could she explain her intuition about this? She couldn't reveal her own closet of skeletons. "I don't think there's a drug connection. The tox screens were negative on all of the Glaussons. I think Chelsea had a baby when she was a teenager, one she didn't tell anyone about. Her friend Betty Ruffalo told me Chelsea had hinted about it."

"How could that be connected?"

"I'm not sure yet. But think about it—she gave up a child—now someone's taken hers. Seems like quite the coincidence, doesn't it? I took your suggestion and had Brynn do a reading. She said there were strong indications that Philly was alive.

There were cards that represented two different babies. I thought it could have meant Philly and the baby Chelsea had when she was sixteen." She didn't add that Brynn had said both babies were girls.

"Now you're believing in all that hoo-ha?" he asked.

"Not really, but it got me thinking. What if she had a baby back then and sold it to a broker?"

"How would that get her and her whole family killed?"

She had to run it by him. "What if Travis Jordan is the baby Chelsea gave up?"

"I think the anesthetic muddled your brain."

Kendall wanted to pursue the discussion, but realized he had a point about the anesthetic. She was having a hard time concentrating. And if the memories she was having weren't part of a dream, then whatever happened the night before had put her into erotic overload—with the man who got her shot.

Nash stood and took out his phone. "I'm not letting you go off on a wild goose chase in your condition. I read your instructions from the hospital—you can't drive for twenty-four hours. Let's see how things go with the hearing. If it's cancelled, and you're still up for it later, we'll visit DHHS."

34

When Nash left for the courthouse to find out if there was any news of the hearing, Kendall collapsed onto the bed, waiting for a second pain pill to revive her. When she closed her eyes, a scene ran through her mind, she and Nash, kissing like there was no tomorrow. It couldn't have been a damn dream; she would have forgotten it by now. Suddenly, it all came back to her, as vivid as a soap opera. She couldn't even blame him for taking advantage of her condition; she'd been the one throwing herself at him. At least he hadn't laughed and pushed her away. But the guy was married. And she didn't even like him. Or did she? Obviously, she'd liked him well enough last night.

It seemed like she'd barely drifted off when she heard Nash come back in.

"How are you feeling?"

"I've been better, but the nap helped." She started to get up.

"Stay where you are. The judge assigned to Jordan's hearing can't get out of his condo complex. It might not be a go today. I'm going to call the courthouse again at one and see what they have to say."

Kendall couldn't shake the sexual tension she felt. She watched Nash take off his jacket and boots, then put his gun on the bureau, admiring his wide back and tight butt. A ravenous monster named Libido sat in the corner of the room, beckoning to her.

Nash, however, didn't appear unsettled. He flopped down on the other bed and picked up the remote. After a minute or two of channel surfing, he turned it off.

"You awake?" he asked.

"Yes. Just resting."

"You want to talk about last night?"

Her heart started pounding. "No."

"Maybe you don't remember anything." He turned toward her. "I think you do; something's weird today. And I don't mean anything to do with the case."

Kendall kept her eyes closed. She'd thought she wanted him to bring it up, but now that he had, she didn't feel ready to face it. She whispered, "I remember most of it."

He came over to her and sat on the side of her bed. "I'm sorry. I feel like I took advantage of you while you were still under the influence of the drug reaction." He kissed her cheek. "You were so darn cute, though."

Was he making fun of her? No one could describe her as cute. And her behavior the night before had to have been from those pain pills. What was that stuff?

"Hey, look at me."

She opened her eyes. "Apology accepted. Now you can forget it happened." She turned away from him.

"Did I say I wanted to forget about it?"

Kendall reminded herself this was the man she'd despised for the past year. "Why wouldn't you? You're married, and I'm not your type." Crap. She sounded like a whiny teenager.

He gently turned her toward him. "Type? Are you crazy?" He stood up and started pacing, his dark eyes troubled. "I guess I'd better tell you this. Shari's filing for a divorce. She's not happy about me doing cop work again. When I left the job I thought it would make things better between us. I did it to protect my marriage, and I let everyone at work have a field day speculating why I quit. I told you my life was fucked up."

That explained it—Nash wasn't really attracted to her—he'd been reacting to his wife leaving him. Kendall didn't know what to say. Her pulse still racing, she said, "I'm sorry about your marriage." Feeble, but she had little experience with relationships and wasn't all that sure she was sorry.

"I feel like an asshole for dragging you into my messed-up life," he said.

Sitting on her bed again, he reached for her hands and took them in his. She snatched them away.

"What? Did I hurt you?" he asked.

"No. It's just . . . I hate my hands. They're like . . . cowboy hands or something."

She felt like an idiot. He was trying to have a serious discussion, and she was acting like a girl about the size of her hands.

His face screwed up. "You're kidding, right? You have a *hand* thing?" He took her hands in his again, studied them, and kissed each palm. "The first time I noticed your hands, you know what I thought?"

When she didn't answer, he said, "I thought, wow! I'd love to have those hands grabbing my ass while I—"

Kendall pulled a hand away and covered his mouth, fighting not to laugh.

"What's the matter, can't take a compliment?"

266

"Compliment? That was a porn comment."

"Come on," he said. "You know there's a buzz between us."

Her sudden need for him hurt as much as the post-surgical pain, frightening her with its intensity. He bent down to kiss her. His kiss was gentle, nothing like the night before. Kendall felt herself losing control, she wanted to drown in him, pull him close to her and never let him go.

When the kissing became urgent, he backed away and grinned. "See? It wasn't just the happy juice."

After a short nap, Kendall insisted she had to get up and make some calls, but Nash grabbed her phone. "I'll make them for you and tell everyone what happened. You need more rest before we go to the courthouse. Make me a list."

Later, Kendall wakened and looked at the clock. It was after one. She got out of bed, feeling a lot better. Nearly able to stand straight, she definitely felt steadier than she'd been earlier. When she came out of the bathroom, Nash had returned.

"You're looking better."

"Yeah, I feel better. Tell me what you found out."

"Brynn said she'd start looking for dirt on Jordan right away. And speaking of Brynn, did you know Ryan met her?"

"No, she didn't say anything about it."

"Shari told me he went there looking for me yesterday afternoon after they got back. Seems like he's fascinated with her computer searches. Supposedly they hit it off, and if you can believe this, she helped him with his homework.

"You don't sound particularly happy about it," Kendall said. "I don't think Brynn would be a bad influence, do you?"

He snorted. "You've got it wrong. Guess I never told you about Ryan. He's my son, but he has his shortcomings. I'm more worried about him corrupting her."

"Why?"

"The kid's a babe hound. I give him the talk now and then and make sure he has a supply of condoms. He's incorrigibly promiscuous; never has a girlfriend, just wants to lay the entire female half of the senior class. And maybe a teacher, too."

"Well," Kendall said, "Brynn's over eighteen and she told me she's never had a boyfriend. I can't see her jumping into anything."

"Maybe you should talk to her. I'd hate to think his sudden interest in computer forensics is a ploy to get in her pants."

"Sure, I can talk to her. Who else did you get in touch with?"

"I talked to Agent Kahn. You're right, he sounds like a real dirtbag, but he said he'd send your medical examiner a copy of Jordan's DNA report, ASAP. That was after he subtly insisted you were tilting at windmills. Guess I'd have to agree with him on that one.

"Then I talked to Schoenfuss, told him about your surgery and said to put you on sick leave. No problem there. He didn't even ask about the case or why we were in Stillwater.

"Alverson and his partner haven't found a damn thing connecting Gerald Fostvedt to the murders or to Travis Jordan. They never found Fostvedt's phone, but they're still working on it. I checked with the courthouse. The judge still isn't able to get in, and it looks like all his cases might be put off until tomorrow.

"I brought you this." He handed her a bag that smelled suspiciously like a burger. "Thought you'd need some sustenance, but no grease. One char-grilled burger from the restaurant, with a side of cottage cheese. Eat up and we'll take a ride to the courthouse if you can handle it."

Kendall grabbed the bag of food. She was starving.

The activity at the Stillwater courthouse had nothing to do with snow removal, the parking lot crammed with police cars, an ambulance, and a few media vans. More than one reporter stood in front of a camera, mouth pantomiming.

Nash parked as close as possible to the scene. "Fuck. This has to be bad news." He turned to Kendall. "Stay here, I'll find out what's going on."

Despite the effort it took to follow him, Kendall got out of the car and hurried to catch up. He might need her badge to cut through the crowd. She hadn't made much progress when she saw him turning back. He stopped her and took her arm.

"What is it?"

He kept walking. "In the car. I'm too pissed to talk about it in front of a crowd." He helped her back into the Land Rover.

"The judge called and arranged the hearing for one, then called back and cancelled again. In the meantime, some mental midget from the jail brought Jordan to the courtroom early. Don't ask me what happened. They don't broadcast the details of their fuck-ups."

Kendall nearly screamed. "He got away?"

"Fucker's in the wind. Your buddy Kahn's over there trying to spin it for the media. Asshole."

She took a deep breath. It wouldn't help to bitch about it. It was done.

"Did anyone see Jordan leave?"

"His buddies must have been here waiting for the hearing,

and when Jordan had a chance to walk, they all took off in a dark-blue Silverado. Any idea where they would go?"

Kendall tried to think rationally. "I still have the address of the place he was sharing with two other guys. It's in St. Paul."

"No, they can't go there now; it's the first place the cops will look for them. They'll have to find somewhere to hole up for a while, someplace the cops don't know about. Or ditch Jordan somewhere before they go back."

"I'll call Brynn and Alverson. See if they've come up with anything new on Jordan." Kendall took out her phone.

The call to Alverson turned out to be pointless; a multiple-car pileup on 53 had everyone covering it.

Brynn answered the phone breathlessly, as if she'd been laughing when the phone rang. "Hi, Kendall."

"Brynn, I need your help right away. Travis Jordan escaped before the hearing even took place. Have you gotten anything on him that might help us find him?"

"I don't think so. He got arrested for a couple misdemeanors; the latest was a bar fight, but you probably knew that already. That's about it."

"I want you to keep looking. We have to find him." She started to hang up, but thought of something else. "Wait, one more question. The bar fight. Do you have the name of the bar?"

"Hang on." Kendall heard keys tapping.

"It was in a roadhouse about ten miles north of Stillwater, right on the St. Croix. It's called The Wheelhouse."

Kendall and Nash left Stillwater heading north. When they were well out of town, Nash asked, "How are you doing?"

"I'm good."

"Do you need another pill? There's some bottled water in

the back."

"I'll take one if I need to, Mom."

He reached over and grabbed her knee. "Just checking. You'll have to be alert if we find this mope."

"I don't get it. Why would he run now, when the hearing could have set him free?"

"Because he's guilty and knows it would only be a matter of time before they get enough evidence to nail him."

"I suppose. I wanted to see how he would react to Gerald Fostvedt's photo. And I'd like to know if he's Chelsea's son. That would give him a motive."

Nash didn't comment. Kendall knew what he thought of her theory that Jordan could be Chelsea's son.

"I think we're getting close to this place. I'm going to drive past it, scope out the parking lot."

The Wheelhouse came into sight. It was a dark brown, weather-beaten structure, one story high and only about a hundred yards off the river. Parking ran across the front and one side of the building. Nash drove by. There were two vehicles in the front lot, a red Malibu and an old Chevy Trailblazer.

"Wait," Kendall said. "It looks like there's parking around the back." Nash turned the car around.

Kendall's pulse started to race. "There's a blue truck in back."

Nash pulled into the front lot next to the Trailblazer. "Wait here. I'll check out the back lot first, find out if the truck is a Silverado. If it is, I'll go in and see if Jordan's in there. If I spot him, I come back out and we call the Feds. Okay?" Not waiting for an objection, he stepped out of the car.

Kendall waited impatiently, wishing she weren't handicapped. Nash returned minutes later. "It's a Silverado. I'm going in. Call Kahn."

Kendall grabbed his arm. "No, let me go in. You cover the back. He can freak all he wants. He's a fugitive and I want to take him in. We can't call Kahn until we know for sure Jordan's in there."

"Kenny, you're in no shape for that. You can barely walk, let alone handle a punk like Jordan right now. If he's here, I say we call Kahn for backup right away."

He was right; it would be the best way to handle it, but it sucked. "Then what, we sit here with our fingers up our ass waiting for the Feds to show?"

"Use your head. Once the Feds get here," he reasoned, "where are Jordan and his boys going? There's only one way out and I don't see any boats lined up waiting to take them away."

Her temper flared. "Use my head? Who do you think you're talking to? Don't forget I'm the detective."

He gripped the steering wheel. "I know you're mad because you can't operate like you normally do. I get that. But if we try to take him, he could run again and I know you don't want that. I'll set my phone so I can call you if he's there without taking it out and tipping them off. I won't be able to talk, so just go ahead and call Kahn if your phone rings."

She nodded her assent, frustrated with her limitations.

Nash entered the bar chewing on a toothpick, hair slightly disheveled, and his shirttail hanging out under his battered jacket.

Waiting turned out to be impossible. Kendall pulled herself out of the car and moved toward the back entrance, her hand hovering over her gun. She could walk, but that was about it. She hated to imagine what a struggle would do to her stressed insides. It was a cold day, but sweat formed on her skin under her heavy clothing. She wanted to be between Jordan and the getaway truck in case he and his buddies got suspicious and tried to take off.

She made it to the back entrance trying to think of a way to disable the truck when she felt the vibration of her phone against her hip. Nash had recognized Jordan. Fighting to control her breathing, she backed further away from the door to make the call to Kahn.

Kahn picked up on the first ring. "This better be good. I'm up to my ass here. What do you want, Halsrud?"

"We found Jordan."

"You what!"

Kendall told him where they were and described the truck. She read off the plate number. "We'll keep them covered until you get here."

"Don't try to be heroes. The guys he's with are felons and probably armed."

"Fine."

Kendall knew Nash had been up against men like these before, but she'd be little help to him if things went south. They'd agreed to stay in place, Nash in the bar and Kendall in the Land Rover, until Kahn and his men arrived. She hated to think about the alternative: if the trio left the bar and she and Nash had to detain them.

She turned to go back to the car when she heard the sounds of a scuffle from inside the tavern. It was show time whether she wanted it or not. She froze in place, gun drawn, heart beating wildly. A minute later the door flew open. Two men ran out and jumped into the high cab of the truck. She watched helplessly as the truck squealed out of the lot. Nash must be taking on Jordan if his friends were so eager to desert him. What could have gone wrong?

When the door burst open a second time, Nash and Jordan stumbled out, clinched together. Jordan had a gun in his hand, and Nash was gripping his wrist. Kendall wanted to get off a shot at Jordan, but didn't dare without taking a chance of hitting Nash. She followed their progress into the lot, keeping her gun trained on them, waiting for an opportunity. Before she got one, Jordan's gun went off, leaving Nash on the ground, gripping his leg. Jordan took off running. Kendall fired at him as he disappeared around the corner of the building.

She ran to Nash and knelt next to him, fearful the bullet had hit his femoral artery.

"I can take care of this," he cried. "Go!"

Jordan had run toward the street. She hated to leave Nash, but Jordan was the only one left who could tell her what had happened to Philly.

"Kenny, stop him," Nash yelled.

She couldn't run, and it felt like she was moving in slow motion. Her abdomen hurt and her pulse raced. Staggering after Jordan, she knew her only hope was to get off an accurate shot. When she reached the front lot, he was running along the side of the highway, headed toward an area thick with woods. He left the road, lurching through the heavy snow. Kendall leaned on the hood of the Malibu and took a well-placed shot. Jordan went down.

She hadn't killed him; he was pulling himself up off the snow-covered ground. Two hasty shots buzzed near her and she slid to the ground for cover. By the time he managed to stumble nearer the woods, sirens were screaming in the distance. Wounded, he wouldn't get far; his blood would map his progress through the woods. Kahn would have to handle it from here.

Kendall hurried back to Nash.

35

Kendall and Nash were transported to the Stillwater hospital. An ER doctor checked her over, changed the bandages on her abdomen, and sent her away with a warning to get some rest. Despite her constant inquiries, they hadn't told her a thing about Nash, and all she'd heard about Jordan was that he was still alive.

Kahn had to be in the building somewhere. She found him in the ICU waiting room. "Detective Halsrud. I see you're all in one piece."

"Where's Nash?"

"He's in surgery. The bullet missed the artery. The doctor said he'll be fine, but there may be some question about a full recovery for his leg. You know how doctors are, they can't tell you anything for sure, but recovery from these things usually comes down to how hard you work with physical therapy. The waiting area for surgical patients is on the second floor, north wing."

When she said nothing, he added, "You never told me how you found Jordan."

"Is he alive?"

Kahn nodded toward the glass-enclosed room on their right. A cop in a blue uniform sat in front of it. "He needs surgery, but they have to stabilize him first. Don't get your hopes up; we won't be able to talk to him for some time—maybe days.

"I called your boss. Thought he should know about the fine work you did, you and Nashlund."

She didn't enlighten him about Brynn, who'd been a key player in locating Jordan. She swallowed hard, hating what she had to do. "Did someone let Nash's wife know he's here?"

"Schoenfuss said they'd take care of it."

"I'm going to go check on him." She felt her face growing hot and turned away form him before he noticed, grateful she hadn't had to be the one to call Shari Nashlund.

"I'll keep you updated on Jordan," he called after her.

A concession on Kahn's part, but Kendall had no time for gratitude. She hurried to the surgical floor, flashing her badge at the first nurse she found in the area. "Adam Nashlund. What can you tell me about him?"

"He's in surgery. The waiting area is over there." She pointed to a room off the main corridor. Kendall was happy to see a coffee and beverage station next to a full-length couch. She found a cup of orange juice, downed it, and lay down on the sofa.

She dropped off the minute she lowered her head. When she woke, the clock on the wall said she'd been asleep for nearly two hours. Someone had covered her with hospital blankets and snuck a pillow under her head. A nurse walking by saw her sitting up and rushed into the room.

"Detective, we didn't know about your surgery. I'm sorry I didn't offer to make you more comfortable while you waited." She turned to leave the room. "I'll be back in a minute."

A petite woman with short, auburn hair in a crisp, fashionable cut entered the room. She might've been in her late thirties but could have passed for a teenager in the right light. She had a small nose, bright blue eyes, and a reassuring smile.

"You're awake. Good. I'm Shari Nashlund." She held out her hand to Kendall, who wanted to sink back into the couch. She took the woman's hand, painfully aware Shari's hand looked like a child's inside her own.

"Kendall, I hope you don't mind, but I told the nurses you'd just had surgery. They brought me a pillow and some blankets for you. I'm glad you were able to get some rest. They said Nash's surgery went well. He's in recovery now. We'll be able to see him soon."

"That's wonderful." It was a relief that Nash would be all right, but meeting his wife, who'd turned out to be the kind of woman she'd always envied, made her want to bolt from the room. Visions of the previous evening with Shari's husband kept popping up in her mind like ducks in a shooting gallery.

"You need to rest," Shari said kindly. "Would you like me to drive you back to your hotel?"

Kendall studied her for signs of cattiness, but all she saw on Shari's face was concern. "Thank you, but I'll go back after Nash is awake. I need to tell him what's happening."

Shari took a seat across from her. "Sure. We can wait together."

Nash, his usual swarthy complexion pale, laid flat with his head on a pillow, his left leg propped up and swathed in bandages. Kendall stopped at the foot of the bed. She wanted to tell him how worried she'd been, how much it mattered to her that he recover. But with Shari out in the waiting room, everything had changed.

"You got Jordan, right?" he asked.

"Yeah, he'll need surgery when he's stable. He might not

make it."

"Has anyone questioned him?"

"No, he never regained consciousness after they found him."

He held up a hand. "Come here."

When she stood next to him, he took her hand. "I was scared shitless when you went after Jordan. I heard the shots and I was afraid it was you that went down."

"I came back to you after I shot him; you were passed out."

"Yeah. I think I gave it up once I saw you on your feet."

"What went wrong in there, anyway? Did Jordan make you?" she asked.

"No. I sat close enough to hear them talking. I was right about his friends; they'd been at the courthouse all morning waiting to pick him up after the hearing. Some court moron left Jordan alone, and he took advantage of it and walked. When he came out of the courthouse, his buddies assumed he'd been released and Jordan didn't set them straight.

"So, I'm sitting at the bar when guess what comes on as breaking news? Jordan's escape. They turned on him and told him he was on his own, they couldn't afford to get involved in a jailbreak. I was afraid they'd change their minds about leaving him there and tried to stop Jordan when he started to follow them out. That's when things got out of control. Sorry everything ended up on you."

"I'm just glad you're going to be okay." Kendall wanted to shed a few tears of joy, and tell him how much she cared about him, but this wasn't the time or place. There might never be one. She fought to hide her feelings, which she feared surrounded her like a brightly painted sandwich sign.

"I'm glad your surgery went well," she said. That sounded so freaking formal, but what could she say? *It was fun, but I see your wife is back in the picture and she can take over now?*

His dark eyes met hers. "Thanks for being here. But you should go back and get some rest."

Was he dismissing her? "Yeah," she said, easing her hands from his. "I should go."

"We still have to find the kid."

He'd said "we." But Kendall couldn't let one word inflate her meager hopes. She'd known he was married and wasn't so naive as to think that his wife's divorce threat in the heat of anger would be binding. She had to back off.

"Schoenfuss will have to let me work the case now. I'm staying here tonight, then maybe I'll go back and talk to him in the morning. Kahn's been fairly amenable. I think he'll let me in when Jordan's able to be questioned."

"Keep me in the loop. I'll pitch in again as soon as I'm back on my feet."

"Sure." She turned to leave, fighting back tears that threatened to fall as a giant lump blocked her throat.

36

Kendall woke up in her bed at the hotel and looked at the clock. It was nearly 7:00 a.m., too early to call the hospital and check on Nash and Jordan. Still moving cautiously, but at least on her own power, she got out of bed, showered and was getting dressed when her phone rang. It was Dawn Marshall, the caseworker from Chelsea's past.

Family Services had explained to Kendall that the records weren't computerized as far back as Chelsea Glausson's time, and it would take weeks to locate detailed records. The woman had been good enough to ask around and gave her the name and phone number of the woman who had been Chelsea's caseworker. Kendall arranged to meet her at the Mall of America, where Marshall was a member of an exercise group that walked there every morning.

At the mall, giant snow movers still worked at turning mountains of snow into an area resembling a parking lot. Kendall parked on the level where she was to meet Dawn Marshall and walked to the coffee stand Marshall had described. The only person near the stand was a woman in her fifties with snow white hair. She wore a blue jogging suit, dutifully performing stretching exercises while she waited. Kendall showed the woman her ID.

Marshall smiled and held out her hand.

Kendall gingerly lowered herself into a chair after shaking Marshall's hand.

"Family Services told me you might remember Chelsea Glausson. Her last name was Cochrane twenty-three years ago."

"I do remember Chelsea. I couldn't believe it when I saw the picture of her and her family on the news; I recognized her right away. She was such a beautiful girl."

"Why didn't you contact the police?" Kendall asked.

"There didn't seem to be any reason to, Detective. Chelsea had managed to rise above her past and have a wonderful family life. How could what happened to her family have anything to do with the past?"

"That's why I need to talk to you. What can you tell me about her? I know about the prostitution and the heroin, but that's about it."

Marshall took a seat opposite Kendall. "I was a rather over-zealous caseworker back then. I lasted a total of three years before I burnt out. I couldn't accept that I didn't have the ability to save everyone. It's an occupational hazard, I suppose." She chuckled. "I didn't get very far from it all, though. Now I'm the director of a shelter for young women. We take in runaways mostly. Nothing is as gratifying as turning a young life around."

"And were you able to do that for Chelsea?"

"No. I can't take any credit for Chelsea's epiphany."

"Tell me what you remember about her."

"It wasn't allowed, but I always carried a small notebook. I kept my own records and impressions of my clients, things that normally wouldn't be put in the files. After you called last night, I dug out the notebook with what I'd written about Chelsea Chocrane."

This could be the break Kendall needed. "So it stoked your memory."

"It did. Chelsea called me after she ran away from the last foster home, told me the husband had begun touching her inappropriately. She refused to come in, said she was nearly seventeen and could manage on her own. She got a job and waitressed for a few months. The next time I heard from her, she admitted the job hadn't lasted and she was working the streets. I told her I could help her, but it was too late. She already had a habit and refused to come in."

"Was that the last time you talked to her?"

Marshall sighed. "She called me one day and wanted me to meet her, said she had a problem. In my world that usually means drugs or an arrest. When I met her, Chelsea said she was pregnant. I told her I could help get her into a clinic where she'd get off the drugs and have the baby in a safe environment." She paused, rubbing her hands against her arms. "She claimed she'd already stopped using, that she didn't need rehab. She wanted to know about adoption and said she felt the child would be better off with people who could support it and give it a good home."

Kendall wondered where this was going. "But you didn't place her child, right?"

"No. I never saw her after that day. But she had a friend with her, a tough-looking girl who never said a word while Chelsea and I talked. Truthfully, I suspected maybe it was her friend who was pregnant and Chelsea was just trying to get the information for her."

"Why wouldn't she let you help her with the baby?"

Marshall met Kendall's eyes. "She asked me how much money she'd get from the agency that handled the adoption. When I explained to her the most they'd do would be to pay her living expenses and doctor's fees, she and her friend left."

"You never heard from her after that?"

"No. But two years later, when I began working at the shelter, the girl I'd seen with Chelsea that day started spending nights with us. I asked her about Chelsea. She told me Chelsea sold her baby for what she described as a 'shitload' of money."

Kendall didn't think the chill running through her body could be blamed on her weakened condition or the weather. Chelsea Glausson sold her baby. And now Philly could be meeting the same fate. Coincidence? It couldn't be.

"Do you have the girl's name?"

She handed Kendall a small slip of paper. "I knew you'd want it. Her name is Twyla Pratt; another girl who's succeeded in living an honest life. She takes in foster children and does some online work for a medical clinic. I'm pretty sure that's still her address. You'd better let me call her first and set it up for you.

"Twyla's a wonderful person, but she has horrid taste in men. If you're lucky, you'll catch her between the bastards."

Rather than drive back to the hotel, Kendall found an upholstered chair to park on while she waited to hear from Dawn Marshall. Caffeine and doughnuts kept her awake until her phone buzzed.

"I spoke to Twyla, Detective. She wants to talk to you, but she has this problem at home. Her latest bad boy moved in with her, uninvited. Sits in front of the TV all day drinking beer and smoking weed. She has these four foster kids and is worried about his influence on them, not to mention getting a visit from

Family Services before she can get rid of him."

"Are you saying she wants a quid pro quo? I oust the cockroach for her in exchange for what she can tell me about Chelsea?"

Marshall paused a moment. "I know it sounds bad, but believe me, she *is* great with those kids, and she takes in some of our girls to help out. Does them a world of good to work with the kids."

Nothing ever came easy. "No problem. I'll do what I can for her."

Twyla Pratt's neat, two-story bungalow was nicely fenced, the only house on the block that didn't look ready for a wrecking ball. A teenage girl answered the door wearing a smock smeared with paint. She led Kendall to the kitchen where a dark-skinned woman was stirring something in a kettle big enough to cook a small cow. She threw in a pile of sliced carrots, wiped her hands on her apron, and greeted Kendall with a friendly smile.

"Hi, I'm Twyla. You must be Kendall."

Kendall showed Pratt her ID. A small bedroom off the kitchen looked like it served as a TV room. Kendall could see a man's legs propped up on the foldout footrest of a large, leather recliner.

Twyla nodded in the direction of the recliner. "I'd really appreciate it, Detective," she said nervously.

"Can I assume you don't want to have any ties with this loser after today?" Kendall asked.

In a voice low enough not to be heard in the next room, she said, "Got that right. Lookit this." She pulled the collar of her blouse aside to show a bruise on her neck the size of an open hand. "Don't worry about the kid-gloves. Just don't want the girls or the younger kids to know what's going on. They're all downstairs now, finger-painting with the girls."

Kendall walked into the TV room, closing the door behind her. She announced herself and flashed her badge.

A heavily built, black man with a shaved head looked up at her, then back at the TV. She kicked the footrest with as much strength as she could still muster.

"Listen up, asshole. Get all your stuff together. You're going to vacate these premises—now!"

"An' why would I be wantin' to do that, bitch?"

Kendall was suddenly grateful for the knowledge she'd gleaned of her father's friends. "You've heard of Detective Jonathon Brady?"

Brady, who she hoped hadn't retired since the last time her father had told one of his famous stories about the man, was known as the worst hardass on the Minneapolis force. He and Jim Halsrud had gone through the police academy together and remained friends. Brought up on charges for excessive force more than once, he had the best solve rate on in the city.

At the name Brady, the man rose from the chair, his menacing gaze never leaving hers. Kendall picked up her phone. "I have him on speed dial in case you're thinking about doing something stupid."

Kendall followed him into an adjoining bedroom, where he pulled out a large duffel from a closet. She watched as he emptied the contents of one of the dresser-drawers into the bag and followed him to the bathroom where he added his toiletries. When he'd finished, she escorted him out the front door. As he walked out, she said, "I'd better not hear you gave Twyla any shit about this. If I do, Brady will have your ass in a cell so fast your head will swim."

Kendall watched as he drove away, then went back inside and joined Pratt on a worn, floral patterned sofa. "

"Thanks for the help," Twyla said. "So you wanna know about Chels?"

"We're trying to find her little girl. It's hard to know what might be helpful, so I need to know everything you remember about her."

The woman's eyes misted, and she pulled a used tissue from a pocket in her apron. "That girl was a blessin,' she was. Wouldn't be here today if it weren't for Chels. Don't know why anyone would do such a thing to her an' her family."

"Her caseworker told me you knew her when she was working the streets."

"Yeah, we were tight back then."

"You were with her when she went to ask the caseworker about adoption?"

Pratt sat back and folded her arms. "Yeah. I told her not to go there."

Kendall waited for an explanation.

"You had to know Chels," Pratt began. "When she got hooked on horse, she wasn't like the other girls who started usin', you know? Most of 'em, they get desperate, do anything for a fix, go downhill fast. But Chels got mad, kept talkin' about gettin' off the streets, gettin' clean and findin' a real job. Then when she got pregnant, she kicked it and done it all by herself except for a couple nights I sat with her. I told her if she went in, they'd jus' put her an' her kid back in the system."

"Did she know who the father was?"

"Nah. Chels didn't know how it happened. Jus' did."

"After suffering through withdrawal, she still wanted to give up her baby?"

"She tried to find a job, but when you're underage and been on the streets, not much out there. Chels was dead set on makin' a better life for herself an couldn't do it with a kid to worry about, too."

They were getting to what Kendall had come here for. "What did Chelsea do with the baby?"

She looked down and whispered, "She sold him. For ten thousand dollars."

Kendall watched as Twyla dabbed at her eyes. "Who gave her the money for the baby?"

"We heard about this broker; someone gave us a phone number to call. Chels never saw the person. But she promised Chels the people that wanted him was a professional couple that couldn't have kids of their own."

Chelsea's story was hitting Kendall too close to home. She had to get this over with. "Him? The baby was a boy?"

"A beautiful lil' boy, with a tiny face like a' angel. His skin was soft and the most beautiful color, coffee with cream. An' those eyes! Bright blue eyes, just like his momma."

The dates fit. Blue eyes and coffee-colored skin. Kendall's instincts were right; Chelsea's baby could have become Travis Jordan.

Kendall called Nash to tell him what she'd found out.

Before she began, he asked, "How did it go with the boyfriend?"

"He won't be back." Sometimes it was prudent not to give too many details. Kendall brought him up to speed on the day's progress.

"So, you're still thinking Jordan's her kid?"

"The timelines fit, so it's possible. I know is seems kind of out there, but it would explain a lot, don't you think?"

"It could. Do we know if Jordan was an adopted kid?"

"No. I have to call Kahn again and find out. I never got a copy of his file."

Kahn answered his phone on the first ring.

"Do you have any info on Travis Jordan's parents?" Kendall asked.

"No. He grew up on the streets. In and out of the system a couple times, but never in for more than a minute."

Kendall thought she might as well spring her theory on him rather than try to lead up to it. "There are indications he may have been Chelsea Glausson's son."

Kahn coughed loudly into the phone. "What did you say?"

37

Consciousness spiked Travis Jordan's mind long enough to make him aware he lay in a hospital bad. Too bad. He'd have preferred to be dead.

When he felt the cop's bullet hit his chest, he'd been sure it was all over. It didn't matter. He'd done what he needed to do—killed the bitch who'd sold him to men who used him as a sex object. He'd had no childhood. The few times he had a chance to sneak to the windows, he'd seen other kids laughing, walking to school, arguing with their parents. Over time, he became aware he was the one who was different. The others led normal lives, free of pain, torture, and humiliation.

Before she left him, his girlfriend Jen had begged him to forgive his mother, to consider she may have been forced to give him up or been promised he'd have a good home. But that wasn't what the men told Travis. He'd believed everything they said—he'd never questioned anything until he was too old to be of use to them and tossed out like so much garbage.

It had been too late to try to understand his mother's motives. Hate won out over forgiveness. She hadn't deserved a chance to explain, to lie to him.

Surrounded by machines and beginning to feel the pain of

the gunshot wound, he longed for Jen, the only woman he'd ever loved, the one he'd turned away when the blinding rage overcame him. Wishing for her was futile; she'd have nothing to do with him now, a man who'd murdered an entire family.

I need you Jen. He slid back into oblivion, hoping he'd never awaken.

38

Friday

Brynn had Kendall's computer set up along with the two Macs, when she noticed an email coming in. Kendall didn't use the email account on her laptop very often, and Brynn couldn't help but notice it was from someone in the Milwaukee PD. She tried Kendall's cell phone and got voice mail. Kendall was still in Stillwater. Maybe she should open the email and see if it was important. It was from a Detective Conlin.

Kendall,

This isn't anything urgent, so I'm just sending it to you in an email. If you have any further questions, give me a call. We interviewed Brittany Markowicz again. She told us there had been rumors suggesting another girl from EC took advantage of the virgin email solicitation. The girl's name is Ruby something or other. Not too many Rubys around, so she shouldn't be too hard to find if you need to locate her.

Richard Conlin

Why did the name Ruby sound familiar? Brynn hadn't heard much about the virgin emails, but remembered at one time Kendall thought they might have something to do with the Glausson case. She finished her computer search, the name Ruby still tweaking at her memory. It finally came to her. The psychic fair—the day she did Chelsea Glausson's reading—she'd taken people's names on a waiting list. One of them was a Ruby. Brynn couldn't recollect if she'd done a reading for her.

She'd been busy that day, and thought her unique appearance had given her an edge over the other psychics, Reiki healers, aura interpreters, and tarot readers. Her waiting list had been booked for the entire day. She'd asked the people to leave full names, but not everyone had.

She still had the list around somewhere; she'd kept it for follow-up contacts she'd never gotten around to doing. Brynn hated any form of marketing. It turned up still tucked into a bag with the cards and other things she'd taken with her to the fair and never unpacked. Ruby's name was second from the bottom. Brynn knew she hadn't done a reading for her, there had been too many to fit in one day, and Ruby's name wasn't checked off.

Her last name wasn't very legible, but with the help of the phone book, she finally figured out it had to be Rindsig. There were only three listings in the book for that name. One had two names, Carol and Jeffrey, so it probably wasn't that one. The other two just had initials, not first names. She called them both and established neither was the girl she was looking for.

It occurred to her Ruby might only have a cell phone, making it harder to find her number. She returned to her keyboard and suddenly remembered Kendall talking about Ruby; she was a student at UWEC. Brynn knew she shouldn't hack in, but Kendall might need the information. The student roster gave up the number. She wasn't sure what possessed her, but she punched in Ruby's number. After six rings, a woman answered and confirmed she was Ruby Rindsig.

"This is Callandra, the psychic interpreter. You signed up for a card reading with me at the psychic fair," Brynn said. "I'm calling to let you know I have a special running now. For December, private readings are half off."

What had she done? Brynn held her breath waiting for Ruby's answer. When she dialed the number, she'd had no intention of making her an offer for a discounted reading. It was a cool move, though. Maybe she could find out something for Kendall.

"When can you do it?"

Brynn's heart rate accelerated. "When do you want one?"

"Today."

Her mouth went dry. She told herself she could do this. Rindsig probably had nothing to do with anything. Kendall could cross her off the list of things she had to follow up on. "All right. How about one o'clock?" That would give Brynn enough time to get ready.

"I'll give you my address."

"You don't understand. I do the readings in my apartment."

"I can't get out. Can you come here?"

Brynn hesitated. She really wanted to do this for Kendall. "All right. What is it?"

Brynn had just gotten out the phone book to call a cab, when her phone rang.

"Hi. It's me, Ryan."

"Aren't you in school today?"

"No. There's a teacher's conference or something. I've been thinking. There's another ACT test in a few weeks for kids that missed the first one. I picked up a study guide and wondered if you'd help me get ready for it?"

"Why didn't you take it?"

"Uh, I'll tell you about that later."

Brynn hadn't expected to hear from him again, yet here he was, asking for her help. "I guess I could. But I have to leave now."

"Where you going?"

She remembered he already knew she did readings as Callandra. "I'm going out to do a reading for someone."

"Cool. Do you want a ride?"

At thirteen, when her mother took off and left her alone with the old man, Ruby quickly learned how to use her womanhood to manipulate him. Never certain if the guy was really her father, she convinced herself he was merely a joke foisted on her by her whore of a mother. Edward Rindsig ignored Ruby for the most part, but came sneaking into her bedroom the nights he drank, which began on Friday after he left work and ended when he passed out on Sunday night.

Years of alcohol abuse had left him with cirrhosis of the liver and erectile dysfunction, a term Ruby didn't understand until much later, but the condition enabled her to keep her virginity intact. His abuse hadn't included penetration. When the old man's cirrhosis got worse, he left her alone, and they exchanged places. Ruby delighted in making his life miserable.

She hated her life. By the time she was fifteen, her father was living on a monthly disability check that barely covered the rent on the piece of shit trailer they lived in. Even though she hated it, Ruby pushed herself to excel in school, recognizing the only way she'd get the hell out of the trailer would be through her education. Her grades rose, but money remained a problem. Money ruled everything. Without it, you were nothing; with it, life offered all kinds of possibilities.

No task was too small or too demeaning. Ruby did everything from babysitting to cleaning houses in order to inflate her bank account. She needed to save enough to pay for college. Her dream to work on Wall Street, where she'd learn to make her money work for her, drove her until she had more than seven thousand dollars saved, not nearly enough. By seventeen, she'd acquired the necessary skills to get a part-time job doing basic accounting for small businesses. Her bank account grew with her increasing business acumen when she picked the brains of a man whose children she babysat. An investment counselor, Ruby paid him special attention when he drove her back to the trailer late at night.

She thought little of her looks until she realized beautiful people were more apt to realize their dreams. She bought clothes at an upscale resale store, purchased a pair of contact lenses, and started experimenting with her hair and makeup. Transformed, she was satisfied she had one more weapon in her arsenal for achieving her goal—her looks.

Unfortunately, Ruby hadn't foreseen what would ultimately be the biggest hurdle to achieving her goals. She fell in love with Jeremy Dahgren.

After Brynn's call, Ruby closed the phone, her mind whirling. She had to figure out how to use the little twit to her advantage. She'd seen her with Detective Halsrud, knew they lived in the same building. The albino had to be up to something; otherwise, why would she have been using the university's computers when she wasn't a student? She'd seen Brynn there more than once, as recently as a few days ago. If she was a freaking hacker, she could get anything.

It was Ruby's own fault, she'd gotten greedy. So stupid, now that she had Jeremy and a secure nest egg. Her father was dead, and Sharky, her other stumbling block, was out of the way. Now she might have to remove another. And get rid of that screaming brat, too. How could she have known it would be so hard to sell a kid?

Ryan's mouth dropped open when Brynn got in the car, resplendent in her silky, white wig, makeup, and white dress. He gaped. "Who are you?"

"This is how I do my work."

He said, "Man. You should look like that all the time."

Brynn scowled. He must think she looked like a freak the rest of the time. She'd been told her scant hair and pale complexion made her look like a martian.

"Hey, I'm sorry. I like how you look either way, okay?"

They rode in silence until they neared the address she'd given him. He slowed down in front of a shabby, spottily populated trailer park, its narrow lanes buried under a foot of snow with deep ruts where a few vehicles had managed passage.

"You sure this is it?"

"Yeah. She said it was way in back and off to the right."

He parked at the curb. "This car won't make it in there. How are you gonna get in?"

She pulled a pair of rubber snow boots out of one of the bags she carried. "I've got boots."

"So how long do these things take?"

Brynn pulled on the boots. "Depends. They're all different."

"Do you want me to wait?"

"Sure." She couldn't figure out why he was being so nice to her. But she liked it. "I'm giving her a discount, so I'll keep it on the short side. Thanks for waiting. I'll be out in thirty minutes, forty tops."

Brynn plowed through the snow, uncertain she was doing the right thing. What could she really find out by doing a reading? She'd just do what she told Ryan; keep it short. Maybe they could stop somewhere for a burger on the way back.

The girl who opened the door had wild, red hair and didn't appear to be much older than Brynn. The minute the door closed behind her, Brynn felt uneasy. The trailer smelled bad and there was very little heat. A weird setting for a reading. Why couldn't Ruby have just come to her place? Forgoing small talk, Brynn took a seat in a built-in breakfast nook, and brought out her cards. Ruby wasn't acting all eager and friendly like people usually did when they had a reading.

Brynn had Ruby shuffle the cards and lay down the first row of four representing her past. Nervous, she'd forgotten to ask what Ruby wanted to know about.

"These cards represent your past," Brynn explained. It wasn't anything good. The girl must have had a hard life. A dark man, in the midst of two danger cards, sevens. "There's a man in your past; he was mean to you." She watched Ruby for a reaction. Rindsig didn't flinch, but Brynn noticed her mouth tighten. The cards were right.

It wasn't until the final row that Brynn became certain she never should have messed with something that should have been police business. The fourth row, like the two before it, held four warning cards. Was Ruby in danger? *Am I?*

Brynn pretended to be studying the cards while she formulated a lie to tell Ruby about what she saw in them. As she was about to tell Ruby she had a bright future, she heard a baby crying.

It was the last thing she heard.

When Brynn came to she was in a chair with her hands tied behind her and her legs bound to the chair legs. Her cheeks stung where Ruby had slapped her to wake her up. She felt a sore spot on her head throbbing in time with her rapid heartbeat.

Ruby's face twisted menacingly amidst a cloud of red hair. "Okay, tell me what that big cop knows."

"How would I know anything about the cops?"

"Don't play dumb. I know you two are tight. And I saw you working the computers at school."

"I only use those because I can't have my own. I'm on probation."

Ruby scoffed. "You, on probation? Yeah, right."

"I'm a hacker. They caught me."

Ruby's brow wrinkled. "Do they know about me?"

Confused, Brynn didn't answer. The police already had the guy that killed the Glaussons. What did this girl want to know? And why? Was she the accomplice Kendall was looking for? She remembered the baby crying. If it was the Glausson baby, Brynn was dead meat. Ruby would never let her out of the trailer alive.

She turned her head to glance around the room.

"Look at *me*, you little witch. What do they know?"

39

Driving home from Stillwater, Kendall neared Eau Claire, her mind on Nash. She'd gotten a call from Shari Nashlund. Nash was doing well, and she'd be taking him home soon with the aid of a pair of crutches. Shari even offered to pick up Kendall and give her a ride home with them if she didn't feel up to driving. Kendall made a decision to back off and not go back to the hospital. She didn't need any more drama in her life; Nash was back with his wife and there was nothing she could do about it.

The short text-message she'd gotten from Agent Kahn that morning reported Travis Jordan was still unconscious; it might be days before anyone could interview him, if ever, his prognosis still critical.

When her phone rang, she checked the screen. Ryan Nashlund. That was odd. She pulled over and clicked the phone on.

"Detective Halsrud, this is Ryan Nashlund. I'm with Brynn—or I was with her. I'm kinda worried."

"Why?"

"She had this appointment to do fortune-telling, you know? I gave her a ride over here and told her I'd wait till she was done. She said she'd be back out pretty quick and after she was in there an hour, I went and knocked. No one answered. I figured you'd know what to do."

What the hell? "She went to someone's house to do a reading?"

"Yeah. She said she'd keep it short.'

"Where are you now?"

"I'm still there. I couldn't drive in, so I left my car on the street. The place isn't plowed out."

It had been days since the snowstorm. "Where is this place?"

"It's a trailer park, the one north of town on the back road that comes out by Shopko."

Kendall recalled it was the trailer park where she'd gone looking for Ruby Rindsig before finding out the girl lived with three other students in a duplex near the university. She'd talked to Ruby's father there. Crap. Brynn and Ruby? Was it possible someone else in the trailer park was having a reading? Seemed like too big a coincidence; something wasn't right.

"I'm on my way," Kendall told Ryan. "Wait for me in your car. I'm about fifteen minutes from you. Maybe she'll be out by then. If she is, call me again."

Her concern surged to fear as she drove. Ruby Rindsig. Kendall had a bad feeling about her from the first day she'd met her at the Glausson house with Jeremy Dahlgren. Deciding to proceed with the utmost caution, she called Alverson and told him what was happening. "It may be nothing, but I'm having a hard time putting anything together that doesn't leave a bad taste in my mouth."

"Want us to meet you there?"

"Yeah, thanks. I'm still running at half-mast. Get there as soon as you can."

"We can be there in about twenty minutes."

Ruby's head felt like it was going to explode. She'd ruined every-thing because she snatched that damn kid. She could have had it all, but she'd fucked up. Now what? The cops knew too much.

She locked the door to the room holding Philly and Brynn. She had to get out of town fast, but what about her beloved Jer-emy? Her heart sank.

Then she realized she might not be able to have the man she loved, but she could still salvage her other plans. Before Jeremy she'd had everything arranged. The car and the money waited for her. Simple. She'd start over somewhere else, get the hell out of here and never look back.

When Kendall arrived at the trailer park, Ryan's car sat deserted on the street next to the entrance. Why hadn't he waited for her? Inside the trailer park, the foot of snow remaining from the storm had drifted in spots to more than three feet. The lane into the park held a mass of deep ruts where a few ambitious 4-wheel drive vehicles had moved in and out. She decided to walk in rather than chance ending up with her car stuck inside the park.

Kendall followed the ruts to the back lane. They ended where it branched right toward Rindsig's trailer. Except for what must have been Brynn and Ryan's footprints, the snow had not been disturbed by foot traffic. She was fighting her way through the snow when she saw it—curls of smoke coming from the edges of a window in the back of the trailer. She kept moving, an ugly premonition of what she'd find creeping through her head.

The other trailers in the lane appeared deserted and there wasn't enough smoke to be seen from a distance. Kendall dialed 911 as she trudged through a drift of snow as high as her crotch, her tender abdomen complaining about the exertion. She spotted Ryan in front of the trailer, slamming a tire iron against the door. As she approached, he stood back, panting. His young face twisted with anxiety as he took another futile swing at the door.

When he saw Kendall, he gasped, "I can't—it won't budge."

There had to be a deadbolt on the inside of the door. She scanned the trailer. The windows were too high and too tiny to attempt climbing in through them. Fire terrified Kendall, but she had to keep a clear head. She put her hand on Ryan's shoulder.

"Stand back, Ryan." Kendall pulled out her gun and screamed. "Brynn, can you hear me? If you can, move away from the door."

There was no response. Kendall couldn't blast the door open without being sure no one was near it. Kicking it in would be an option, but she was too damn weak. They had to get in before the fire escalated. At least the damn door opened inward. There was no time to worry about her painful midsection or show Ryan how it was done. She had to attempt kicking it in.

"Ryan, I'm going to try kicking it in. Stand behind me and I'll brace myself against you."

When they'd assumed the best stance, Kendall kicked at the door. Nothing happened. Two more tries and it finally cracked. One more, and she'd torn it from the deadbolt holding it in place. Like the door, her insides felt torn from their moorings, but she couldn't wait for backup or worry about her pain; Brynn's life depended on her. Kendall had to overcome her fear of fire and go into the trailer to get her out.

Warning Ryan to stay put, she rushed inside. The smoke, coming from somewhere in the rear, had begun to fill the trailer. Her eyes smarted, and began watering as she entered an open kitchen and living area. Twelve playing cards were spread out on a small kitchen table in rows of four, the rest of the deck scattered on the floor. Brynn had to be somewhere inside.

Kendall pulled the top of her turtleneck over her nose and turned left into a narrow corridor leading from the kitchen to a room at the opposite end of the trailer. Its door was closed, smoke seeping from its cracks pervaded the hallway. She hoped she wouldn't have to open it and placed a hand on it cautiously, pulling back as she felt the intensity of the heat. Coughing, she turned back to a room off the hallway that was locked on the outside with a keyless deadbolt that looked new. The door was barely warm to the touch.

Kendall quickly turned the lock, fear electrifying every nerve in her body. Inside the room, Brynn, hands tied behind her, lay on the floor in an overturned chair. Her legs were free, kicking at the latch of a large wire cage meant for a dog. A small child sat inside crying, curly hair in greasy tendrils. She looked nothing like the bright, sunny child Kendall had seen in the digital photos. But Kendall recognized her immediately despite the squalid conditions and her filthy clothing—Philly Glausson.

"Brynn, stop, I'm here! I'll get the baby out." Her words caused another fit of coughing. The smoke had thickened; Kendall had to get them all out—fast.

Brynn turned toward Kendall, revealing a ball of white material stuffed in her mouth, her face streaked with tears and makeup. Kendall lifted her up off the floor, pulled out the gag, and freed her hands. When she was sure the girl could walk, she pushed her toward the door and yelled, "Go!"

Philly's crying turned to screams as Kendall, her heart pounding and lungs bursting with smoke, worked the fasteners on the filthy cage. Her fingers fumbled from the heat and her fear, but she finally got it open. The baby crawled away from her and cowered in the far corner, coughing. As the air became impossible to breathe, Kendall's nostrils filled with smoke that travelled instantly to her lungs despite her shallow breaths and the shirt covering her nose. There was no time to cajole the frightened child. Or panic. Kendall reached into the crate and dragged the baby out.

She ran out of the trailer with the shrieking child and joined Brynn and Ryan as the sound of sirens filled the smoky air. Kendall took off her coat and wrapped Philly in it, holding her close to the warmth of her own body. Ryan covered Kendall with his, and the three of them huddled together as the fire department and the paramedics fought their way through the snow. The EMTs, first to arrive, wrapped them in blankets and insisted Brynn and Kendall go to a hospital to be checked out, along with Philly Glausson.

Before long, the trailer park filled with fire trucks and what looked like every cop from Eau Claire and Chippewa. Kendall's adrenaline high was fading, all she wanted was to go home and go to bed. She scanned the crowd for Gray Glausson. The first thing she'd done after the EMT's looked them over was let him know she'd found his niece. Then she'd put out an APB on Ruby Rindsig.

She spotted Glausson coming toward her. England, elegant in a cobalt blue coat with a dark, faux-mink hood, daintily tripped through the snow at his side. Knowing it would be only temporary, Kendall took Philly from the arms of a paramedic and handed her to Gray. His eyes glistened as he held the crying child. Kendall had to break the news that he wouldn't be able to take the baby home with him. She'd already been reminded that until the fire was out, the fire department was in charge of the scene, and they insisted the child be taken to the hospital.

"She's upset, but they think she's okay," Kendall said, dreading what she had to tell him. "They'll have to take her to a hospital to be examined, and probably keep her there overnight. It's also procedure in a case like this for the child to be held in custody until all the legal questions get sorted out. I've done everything I can to keep that from happening. The paramedics will let you ride along to the hospital, and I arranged for a social worker I know to meet you there."

Gray started to protest, but Kendall held up a hand to stop him. "While they're examining her, go home and get your copy of Chelsea's will. Since she awards you custody of her children, and you're the only surviving relative, it'll make it easier to cut through the red tape."

England started at the comment about family services. "They'd take her away from him? After all she's been through?" She stepped protectively toward Philly, who suddenly stopped crying. Philly twisted away from Gray's arms and reached out to England. Kendall hadn't thought the woman had a maternal bone in her body, but when she took the child in her arms, Philly clung to her. Astonished, Kendall realized after a moment it had nothing to do with maternal instincts—it was the perfume. England wore the same Joy perfume she'd seen on Chelsea Glausson's dresser. Its odor made Kendall nauseous; her mother had worn the sweet, lily-of-the-valley scent, which still reminded her of things she preferred to leave forgotten. But for Philly Glausson, the perfume's aroma had become a bridge to her mother.

"England," Gray said, "you ride with her in the ambulance. I'll meet you at the hospital."

Alverson appeared at Kendall's side. "I heard what you told them. Are you sure you can deliver?"

"I called Mary Ann Prusinski. She'll take care of it." Kendall knew if anyone could help, it would be Mary Ann, a 30-year veteran of family services.

Ignoring Alverson's continuing protests, Kendall left for the hospital with Brynn and Ryan.

After they were examined at the hospital, Kendall dropped Brynn and Ryan off on her way to the station. She had to convince Schoenfuss to put her back on duty. Sleep would have to wait.

Gray called to say that except for a bad case of diaper rash, Philly had been deemed in good health and hadn't been mistreated. She didn't appear to be suffering the after-effects of sedation, but they'd taken blood samples to be sure and were going to keep her overnight for observation. The girl still clung to England, who'd been encouraging the child to sleep. The social worker had advised Gray to hire a family practice attorney. He'd wasted no time hiring the best one in the area. The man was already attempting to find a judge willing to hold an emergency custody hearing so Philly could go home with Gray and England when she was released from the hospital.

Shoenfuss cornered Kendall as soon as she finished the call. "Hanging out there on your own again, Halsrud?"

He didn't give her a chance to speak. "My office, now."

Hoping to explain before he exploded, Kendall started talking the minute the door closed behind her. She told him how she'd happened to be at the trailer park after Ruby set fire to the trailer, leaving Brynn and Philly to die in the flames.

He grunted. "So you're trying to tell me you don't go looking for these things, they just call out to you. You're supposed to be on sick leave."

"I told you—I was on my way back from Stillwater, and I only went over there because a friend of Brynn's was worried about her." Kendall didn't pause to let him argue. "I want to work this case, sir. I have to be the one to interview Jeremy Dahlgren and the others who know Rindsig. I'm the only one who knows all the players."

"You're supposed to be recuperating. I can't have you going against doctor's orders, Halsrud."

"He said five days, and there are only two left. My only restrictions are no heavy lifting or long trips. I can do the interviews and desk duty for a few days. There'll be reports and calls to be made, too. I'd be busy."

He paused for a moment, studying the wall behind her. "How's the baby? No harm done?"

"Not unless you include losing her entire family." He hadn't said anything about desk-duty. She took the omission as agreement.

He grunted again. "Have you got anything connecting Rindsig to Travis Jordan?"

"Not yet. He'll be tried for the murders, but we don't have anything linking him to either Rindsig or Gerald Fostvedt. Either of them or both could have been accomplices. And if not, we need to figure out how Rindsig ended up with the Glausson child."

Schoenfuss fidgeted with a file folder. "You can work the case, but from the station only. The department won't be liable if you pull your stitches or something chasing leads. Any running around looking for this Rindsig woman will be delegated to the other officers. Understood?"

Kendall kept her expression emotionless, trying to hide her pleasure. She'd gotten what she wanted. "Yes, sir, understood."

As she turned to leave, he said, "Nice collar on Jordan."

40

Ruby Rindsig shared an apartment near the University with three other women who were immediately located and brought in for questioning, as was Jeremy Dahlgren, Sienna Glausson's boyfriend. Kendall had always suspected Ruby had her sights set on him and wished she'd gone with her instincts and taken a closer look at the girl after the Glausson murders.

Behind the trailer, they discovered a narrow path leading from the trailer to the next road over from the trailer park. Ruby's old K-car was parked on the side street, causing Kendall to wonder if someone had helped her flee. While her roommates were being questioned, a search warrant was being prepared for the apartment.

Jeremy Dahlgren had been waiting for nearly an hour while Rindsig's roommates were interviewed. They spilled what they knew about his involvement with Ruby since she'd moved in. He'd let the girl console him over Sienna's death, and not only with words. According to the roomies, he'd been there overnight on a regular basis since the Glausson home invasion.

Kendall entered the room where Dahlgren waited to be interrogated. She'd confirmed his alibi for the afternoon; he'd been in classes at the university.

"Jeremy, sorry you had to wait so long. Can I get you a drink? Soda? Water?"

He shook his head, avoiding her eyes.

"You're kind of quiet. Still grieving for Sienna?" *That shot should unsettle him.*

Dahlgren shifted in his seat.

"You know why you're here, don't you, Jeremy?"

"Yeah. That other cop told me about Ruby—that she had the baby.'

When Kendall had interviewed Dahlgren after the murders, he'd appeared genuinely torn up about his girlfriend Sienna's death. But only days later, he'd let another girl lead him to her bed. Kendall knew people reacted to grief in different ways, but sex with another woman before Sienna was even in the ground was just cold. *Men could be such pigs.*

"That's all you have to say? You were told about it?"

He sniped, "That's what happened—they told me about it." *He was giving her attitude.* He didn't even look like the all-American boy he'd been two weeks earlier. Gone were the high school letter jacket, neat haircut, and tidy jeans. Now his dark hair hung in his eyes, and his face sported a three-day beard. His jeans had holes at the knees. Had being with a witch like Rindsig corrupted him so quickly? Or had the sleazy version of Jeremy been lurking below the surface all along?

"So you're trying to tell me you had no idea Ruby had Philly? You didn't help her take the baby out of the Glausson house and bring her to the trailer?"

"Of course not!" he spat.

Kendall watched him squirm. "I'm thinking you and Sienna had a fight, you met Travis Jordan somehow, then you and Ruby decided to break into the house. Things got out of control—no one meant it to happen."

Dahlgren's face twisted with horror. "How could you think I had anything to do with that? I loved Sienna."

Kendall believed him. At least about the murders. Love, though? Hardly.

"You say you 'loved' her. Past tense. Now your allegiance is to Ruby—your new love. She *did* have something to do with the murders—she took Philly. Maybe she and Travis Jordan had a thing going, too."

His features stiffened, but he remained in control. " I don't know anything about that."

She didn't let up. "What? No pillow talk?" Dahlgren's face flushed. "Yes, Jeremy, we know how you grieved for Sienna—in Ruby's bed. Rather heartless, wouldn't you say?"

"Do I need a lawyer?"

Not words Kendall wanted to hear. "I don't know. Do you?"

Dahlgren shut down.

Worried she'd get no more from the boy, she said, "Jeremy, if you really had no part in the murders or the kidnapping, you need to tell me everything you know—now. Did Ruby know Travis Jordan?"

"No." He pushed his hair off his forehead. "She never said anything about Philly or that Jordan guy. She just . . ."

"Just what, Jeremy?"

He hung his head.

"Unless you want us to charge you as an accessory, you'd better tell me what you know."

Without looking up, he said, "She knew that other guy. Sharky."

"What about Sharky?"

"I saw her talking to him one time. It looked pretty intense."

"Did you ask her what it was about?"

Dahlgren sat up straight. "No. It wasn't any of my business who she talked to. And anyway, she didn't know I saw them."

Interesting.

Kendall questioned him until she'd reached a point he'd told her all he knew—or all he was ready to give up. She'd talk to him again when he'd had time to consider what he was risking by his silence.

Alverson was waiting for her when she came out of the interview room.

"Anything?" he asked.

"Yeah, but nothing that'll help us find Ruby. He saw her in a serious conversation with Gerald Fostvedt—Sharky."

"Wow. Think she was the one that offed him?"

"Probably. Did the roommates have anything to say?"

He snorted. "Two of them are nursing students. Hope they aren't on the job if I ever have a heart attack—couple of airheads. Claim they don't know squat about Rindsig. They took her in when another chick moved out. Said they don't hang with her. I tend to believe them, since the third one says they're never around, out partying all the time."

"And the third one?"

"She didn't tell me much, but I think she knows more than she's saying. Thought it'd be a good idea for you to have a go at her. "

Kendall's cell phone rang before she could join the third roommate, Leslie Frank.

"Kenny, I've been worried sick about you," her father said

hurriedly.

Kendall wondered where all his newfound parenting concerns were coming from. He hadn't been there for her as a kid and seemed determined to make up for it lately. For her, it never quite worked. The past was what it was; there was no going back.

"I'm fine, Dad. I thought Nash called you after my surgery."

"He did, but that was before everything else happened. Next thing I know, you're all over the news, catching criminals and getting treated for smoke inhalation."

"Dad, I really can't talk about it now. Didn't you notice we found the Glausson baby? How about a congrats on that instead of the phony mother-hen routine?" A few seconds of silence passed. "I'm proud as hell of you, Kenny. I'm sorry if I don't tell you often enough. I'll let you go, but how about coming here for dinner tomorrow? Finish your work, get some sleep and I'll cook you something that'll make you feel better."

"Can't promise anything, but I'll try, okay?"

Kendall entered the interrogation room. Leslie Frank sat in a metal chair, her wide girth spilling over its padded seat. Her dark hair, badly in need of a wash, rested on her full shoulders, and her complexion revealed the remnants of teenage acne.

Kendall took a seat across from her and introduced herself. "Leslie, I want to talk to you about Ruby. Are the two of you close?"

"No. I told that to the other cop."

"And you aren't friendly with the other girls?"

Leslie rolled her eyes. "Right. Like they'd be my BFF's. They don't have time for someone like me. But you wouldn't know what that's like."

Kendall quipped, "No? I was almost six feet tall by the time

I was in the eighth grade. I got called a lot of names. Want to hear a few?"

Leslie pouted. "Okay, fine. Kids were crappy to you, too. So what?"

"I was thinking Ruby wasn't your other roommates' type, either. They probably shunned her just like they do you. That would throw the two of you together to bitch about them. Did you and Ruby do that, Leslie?"

She shrugged her shoulders. "Maybe."

"Did she talk about Jeremy Dahlgren?"

The girl sneered. "She really has a thing for that guy. He's hot and all that, but everyone knew he and Sienna Glausson were tight. Ruby's a nerd, but she's way cute; she could have had lots of guys. She didn't need to go after someone who already had a girlfriend."

"Would you say she's fixated on him?"

Leslie nodded, squirming to center herself on the chair.

"Do you recall what time Ruby got home the night the Glaussons were murdered?"

"You think Ruby killed those people?"

"She had their baby, Leslie. If she didn't kill them, how do you think she happened to be hiding Philly Glausson?"

Frank's complexion paled, highlighting the red spots on her cheeks. A knock on the door interrupted them. Alverson beckoned Kendall out of the room.

"I'll be right back, Leslie." Kendall stood. "There's no reason for you to protect Ruby—she isn't your friend. Think about that while I'm gone."

Kendall followed Alverson to his desk. "They found a dead guy on a bed in the back bedroom of the trailer where the fire started—Rindsig's father. He must have had her late in life 'cause he was 64. Looked eighty, according to a neighbor. They're thinking he died of natural causes, but we won't know for sure until the autopsy."

He pulled a dog-eared notebook from his pocket. "We canvassed the trailer park and the neighborhood. A woman in the next trailer says Ruby kept her father in booze and suspects she was pocketing his disability checks. Her mother was a lot younger than the old man and took off when Ruby was about thirteen. After that it was just the two of them living in the trailer. There were never any complaints, but the neighborhood buzz was the old guy was molesting Ruby. She moved out last spring when she turned eighteen, which would coincide with the virgin email thing. Maybe she took advantage of it and made enough on her virginity to afford rent.

"The neighbors also said Rindsig didn't have many friends, so it looks like Dahlgren and the roommates are our best bets for info on her. But get this—a neighbor on the next street has a garage he rents out. Guess who rented it?"

"Rindsig? Why? She drives that crappy old car."

"Right. We found it on the street next to the trailer park."

"Get to the point. What about the garage?"

"Rindsig rented it—apparently she had another car. One she didn't drive around town."

"Make and model?"

"No idea. It wasn't in the garage and the old guy that owns the garage never saw it. He's housebound. The beater is registered to her father, and there's nothing registered in Ruby's name."

"Then she must have paid cash for a car and never got around to registering it." Kendall frowned. "That explains why we haven't found her. We were looking at the airport and bus station. We need the make of the car. Check out the kind of dealers that would be willing not to ask questions. And sales by owner. Oh, craigslist too."

"That could take weeks."

"Right now it's all we've got."

She returned to the interview room and found Leslie leaning on the table, her head in her hands. "Leslie, did Ruby ever talk about buying a car?"

"No, but I saw her looking at cars on her computer one time. She closed it when I came in the room."

"What did she say about it?"

"Nothing to me."

"We think Ruby might have been involved in Gerald Fostvedt's death, and we know she kidnapped the Glausson baby. If you have any information at all about Ruby, you have to tell us so we can find her. Don't you think she should be punished for what she did?"

"Yeah, but I don't know anything. She didn't tell me much," Leslie whined.

Kendall couldn't think of a reason the girl would be holding back, but maybe nerves explained any omissions. "We have a search warrant for the apartment. If there's anything there, we'll find it."

"They'll go through all our stuff?"

"Oh, yeah." There was something Leslie didn't want them to see. Personal? Or about Ruby?

"Ruby didn't have much," Leslie added. "She said she was saving up for new clothes."

"Did she talk to you about money? About those emails soliciting virgins?'

"I heard she did it; made some sweet cash for losing her cherry," Leslie scoffed. "She never talked about it, but one day I walked in when she had her laptop open and she was looking at one of those investment sites."

It was after midnight when Kendall got home. The canvasses of both neighborhoods turned up nothing further, and there were no leads on the car. Earlier in the day, Tarkowski called, offering their services in locating Rindsig. Kendall had accepted gladly. The Feds could cover the airports, trains, and bus terminals a lot easier than they could.

It was too late to talk to Brynn, so she made a sandwich and took it to the couch, enjoying being alone after the chaotic day she'd had. She looked at the message list on her phone. Two were from Nash. It might be childish, but she didn't want to talk to him. She'd found Philly; she didn't have to be around him anymore. Kendall couldn't get a picture of the two of them out of her mind—Shari and Nash—they'd be a handsome couple.

She had to stop thinking about him. Rummaging through the cupboard, she found some of Brynn's tea and let it steep while she showered. With Nash out of her mind, Ruby Rindsig popped up. Kendall had to talk to both the Dahlgren kid and the roommate again tomorrow. They both knew more than they'd told her.

41

Saturday

The next day cast no more answers to the mystery of Ruby Rindsig. It had only been two weeks since the Glausson murders. What was the connection between Rindsig, Fostvedt, and Travis Jordan? It drove Kendall crazy to think Ruby had gotten away without providing answers.

The fire department reported the fire in the trailer started in the back bedroom where a basket of clothing had been lit with lighter fluid. The body of a man identified as Ruby's father, Edward Rindsig, had been found on the bed. He'd probably died of natural causes, but they wouldn't know for sure until the autopsy had been completed. Could Ruby have caused his death? Kendall knew he'd been alive ten days ago when she'd been there looking for his daughter.

By the end of the day, the only new information was about the gun—the ballistics report confirmed the gun found in the trailer belonged to Ruby's father and had been the one that killed Fostvedt. If the fingerprints on it turned out to be Ruby's, they could add Sharky's murder to the other charges against her. Why hadn't Ruby taken the gun with her? But Kendall knew Ruby hadn't planned the events of that day. Ruby probably overlooked the gun in her hurry to flee the scene.

Kendall accepted her father's dinner invitation. She didn't really feel like socializing but home cooked food sounded more inviting than takeout or anything she could make herself. She arrived at the house to find that her uncle and Maggie Cottingham were joining them for dinner. Her father greeted her warmly, congratulating her on taking Jordan down and finding Philly Glausson.

"You have good instincts, Kenny. You knew all along the Glauson baby was still alive. How's she doing?"

"She's great. Glausson's fiancée and Philly really hit it off."

Glausson's attorney had succeeded in getting an emergency hearing to enable the hospital to turn Philly over to Glausson when she was released, but with Cottingham in the room, Kendall wasn't about to reveal any details.

"How's your partner doing? Is he still in the hospital?" Maggie asked.

Kendall turned away to fix herself a drink. "If you're talking about Adam Nashlund, he's not my partner. He's going to be fine. If you're asking about Hank Whitehouse, he's home now and doing well."

Cottingham didn't ask any more questions.

The meal had been delicious even if Maggie had prepared it. The Boston cream pie she served was Kendall's favorite. Obviously, the woman was still trying to suck up. Before leaving, Kendall went downstairs to talk to her uncle, who was getting ready to go out. He was pulling on a snowmobile suit and heavy, sheepskin-lined boots.

Looks like you're going out to the shack," she said.

Her uncle Al parked an ice fishing shanty on a cove of Lake

Wissota every winter. As a kid she'd enjoyed spending time with him in the shack, drinking cocoa, playing cards, and waiting for a fish to bite.

"Yeah, I just put it out last weekend. Not much happening yet." He stopped what he was doing. "Kenny, I'm glad you came over tonight. I wanted to talk to you about your dad. It's about time you give him a break, don't you think?"

It wasn't the first time he'd tried to bring Kendall and her father together. "Right," she said. "Like the one he gave me."

"Honey, all that happened a long time ago."

"But he stayed with my mother even after that. And he waited for her to come back for years. Now he's turned into a ladies' man and he can't get enough of all the divorcees and widows in Eau Claire."

"Kenny, he was obsessed with your mother; it took him time to get over her. It was like a disease, but he's over it now. I know you don't like Maggie, but she's good to him." He pulled a heavy coat out of a closet, and set it on the stairs.

Her uncle was right. Her father had been so focused on her mother and her needs, there had been little time left for Kendall when she was a child. She did harbor a grudge, one she'd never be able to leave behind. In her heart she blamed her father as much for ignoring what was going on as she did her mother for the things she allowed to happen. Kendall, an introverted teenager, had been ripe for seduction by her mother's salacious lover. Her father had ignored the signs of her mother's affair, and her mother had trusted her lover alone with her daughter. Forgiveness didn't come easily.

"I'm trying, Uncle Al."

"Good. You know, Maggie and your dad are planning on

going to the Bahamas over the holidays. I thought they'd tell you tonight. I know you don't like Christmas, but I'm going to be gone, too. I'm going to visit Gary and his family in Illinois. You're welcome to come with me; they'd love to have you."

"At least I won't have to make excuses this year. But thanks for the invite."

Her uncle shook his head. "I worry about you, Kenny."

Kendall tapped on Brynn's door when she got back to the apartment. Dressed in a robe and slippers, she invited Kendall in and offered her tea.

"Have you talked to Ryan today?" Kendall asked.

Brynn didn't turn from the stove. "He called me this morning."

"You're lucky he was with you yesterday when you went to see Ruby Rindsig." She'd decided not to ask Brynn what the hell she was thinking by going out to see a woman who was a possible murder suspect. Brynn had to have been asking herself the same question.

Brynn didn't respond. Was it going to be another one-sided conversation? "Ryan wasn't here tonight?"

"He had a date."

"That doesn't bother you?"

"Why would it? We're just friends."

"Sometimes feelings can change," Kendall hinted.

"I don't like him that way. He's a kid."

Brynn set out the tea and a plate of cookies. Kendall didn't point out that there was less than a two-year age difference between Brynn and Ryan.

Did you get that Ruby person?" Brynn asked.

"No, not yet. How are you feeling?"

"I'm fine. I just have some bruises." She showed Kendall the marks on her wrists and ankles. "Do you want me to look online for you? See what I can find out about her?"

"No, you won't need to work on it. The FBI is doing the transportation search. If I think of anything you can do, I'll let you know. I forgot to tell you, Schoenfuss has okayed an hourly wage for your help in the Glausson case. It'll be a week or so before you get it."

Kendall left when she finished her tea, trying to figure out what was nagging at her. It was something her uncle had said, but what?

It came to her as she laid in bed about to drift off. Obsession. He'd mentioned her father's obsession with her mother. Rindsig was obsessed with Jeremy Dahlgren. If Kendall was right about Ruby's obsession with Dahlgren, Ruby wouldn't be able to just cut him loose. Eventually, she'd be back for him. Kendall had to press the roommate again. The girl had to know *something* about Ruby's plans.

Kendall groped for her phone.

Alverson answered, his voice thick with sleep. "What?"

"We need to put a watch on the Dahlgren kid."

"It's one in the freakin' morning!"

"It's about Ruby. She's obsessed with Dahlgren. She'll be back to see him."

"No way. That chick's sunning herself on a beach in Mexico."

"When you talked to him, didn't you get the feeling he was reluctant to say anything bad about her?" Kendall asked.

Alverson fumbled the phone, and Kendall could have sworn she heard a woman's voice in the background.

"Well, yeah," he said, "but he wouldn't."

"Why wouldn't he?"

"He was poppin' her, wasn't he? He's a kid—fucking trumps everything."

"Are you saying he'd be so in lust that he'd defend her no matter what?" she asked.

"Sure. Don't forget, the Glausson girl's friends all said she and Dahlgren weren't getting it on. Ruby's putting out, that makes her golden in his eyes."

She had a lot to learn about men. "We have to put a tail on him 24/7."

In the early morning hours, Brynn crept back into her apartment, chilled from a walk along the river in the frigid air. The bruises from her skirmish with Ruby ached under her thin skin. Hate was a new emotion for Brynn, but it was easy to despise the person who'd done this to her and kidnapped Philly Glausson. After taking a hot shower, she moved toward the bedroom where Malkin waited, curled into a circle at the foot of the bed. She walked past the computers. And stopped. It wouldn't hurt to do a little searching before going to bed. She hadn't promised not to.

42

Sunday

Nash wasn't supposed to be on his feet even with crutches, except to go to the bathroom or to the kitchen for food. No driving or leaving the house; it sucked. At least the shot had missed his femoral artery or he might not be alive to bitch about his situation. He'd thought about leaving the house, but the temperature had risen, hovering around the freezing mark, and an ice storm had started to move through the area. He didn't dare try to travel in it.

If only Kendall would answer her phone. He wasn't surprised she was avoiding him, but she could at least let him explain. The pseudo-reunion with his wife had only come about because of his injury. He'd agreed to see a marriage counselor, something he'd never done before. He knew Shari had seen it for what it was—a last ditch effort to revive a dying relationship—an effort with little chance of success. She'd insisted the therapist would be right for them. Someone she knew had recommended the woman because of her no-nonsense approach. After an initial evaluation of a couple's situation, she preferred working with the ones whose relationships she believed stood a chance.

Nash didn't think they were one of those couples.

Schoenfuss turned down Kendall's request to put a watch on Dahlgren. The Feds had found a car at the Madison airport with stolen plates. The Eau Claire dealer who'd sold the car reported that the purchaser, a woman whose description he'd somehow forgotten, had paid cash for the vehicle. Checking manifests for flights out of Madison, they came across the name of a woman who had taken a late flight to Cancun the day before and whose passport turned out to be bogus. They hadn't found her yet, but the police in Cancun were trying to locate her in an effort to determine if she was Rindsig. She loosely fit Rindsig's description but without the red hair. The discovery of the suspicious woman waylaid any hope Kendall had for putting a 24/7 tail on Dahlgren.

As a favor to Kendall, Alverson and Joe Monson checked Dahlgren's whereabouts during the day, reporting nothing unusual in the boy's routine. He went to classes and was seen in the company of other students in between them. By three he'd checked in at his after school job, waiting tables at Olive Garden.

The ice storm hit Eau Claire in full force by four, causing power outages sprinkled around the area and enough accidents to employ every cop on the force. Kendall left the minute her shift was over, wishing she had better tires on the Highlander. She inched her way across town and parked in the back of the Olive Garden's lot after a quick trip into the bar where she could see Dahlgren still schlepping trays of food. She planned on watching him until he left work, then follow him to make sure he want right home.

Before Kendall left the station, Teed had called to let her know Fostvedt's print was a possible match to the one they'd found on Sienna Glausson's wrist. It wasn't a good enough match to be used at trial, but it didn't rule out the possibility that Fostvedt had been the one who'd attacked Seinna.

Adding to her problem list, Schoenfuss was still insisting she do the TV interview. Rianna Jackson from the TV station had left messages for Kendall—messages, like Nash's, Kendall hadn't answered.

Brynn hadn't found a thing on Ruby worth telling Kendall. Rather than subside, the pain from her injuries seemed to escalate with time. She rubbed her ankles, thinking a soak in a warm bath might help, when there was a knock at her door.

Ryan Nashlund carried in a brown, paper bag. "I brought us some Moose Tracks." He pulled a half-gallon container of ice cream from the bag.

She wrinkled her nose. "Kind of cold for ice-cream. What are you doing driving in this weather?"

"Never too cold for ice-cream. And I'm not driving. A friend dropped me off." He walked into the kitchen for spoons and bowls. "This stuff is great. You gotta try some." After he'd filled two bowls, he came over to where she sat in front of the iMac and handed her one. "What are you working on?"

"I'm trying to find something about Ruby Rindsig for Kendall."

"Like what?" He'd heard about the missing Ruby on TV.

"Something that'll help them locate her," Brynn explained. "Kendall thinks Ruby might come back to see Jeremy Dahlgren."

"Dahlgren? I thought he was tight with Sienna Glausson."

"He was, but after she died, he hooked up with Ruby. Kendall thinks because Ruby's got a big thing for him, she won't be able to stay away."

Ryan savored his ice cream, watching her search. "Hey, did you check out Facebook?"

"There wasn't anything there."

"Are you sure?"

"Pretty sure. I don't know too much about Facebook."

"Move over."

Brynn gave up her place in front of the computer. Ryan sat down and held up his hands, wriggling them as if readying them to play a piano concerto. "You'd be surprised what you can find on Facebook if you know how to look.

The pasta crowd at Olive Garden had begun thinning out when Kendall got the call from Brynn. "I found something for you."

"I thought I told you that wasn't necessary."

"She almost killed us," Brynn said. "I want you to get her."

Revenge could be sweet, even for Brynn. "All right, what have you got?"

"Ryan found it on Facebook."

"Ryan's working with you?" Getting another citizen involved was not a good idea; her luck with Schoenfuss could be running out.

"It's about Jeremy Dahlgren. His grandfather has an ice fishing place and Jeremy's been using it. He's been meeting someone there."

"Brynn, if it was posted on Facebook, it can't be Ruby. Too

public."

"Duh. It wasn't on his Wall; it was in private messages with no name on them."

Suddenly too excited to ask the obvious—how they had gotten hold of a private message—Kendall couldn't help thinking an ice fishing shanty in the middle of the night would be a ideal clandestine meeting place.

"Can you find me his grandfather's name? Or anything that would tell us where the shack is?"

Brynn ignored Kendall's question. "There's a weather emergency. You should come home now."

"I've driven in worse than this. Keep working on it."

Kendall dialed her Uncle Al. He might have heard of Dahlgren's grandfather. Luckily, cell service on the cove was surviving the storm. Her uncle picked up on the first ring.

"Hi, Kenny. What's up?"

She explained what she needed. "I thought you might have heard of him, but I'm not even sure if his last name is Dahlgren. It would help me a lot to know where his shack is."

"I don't recall a Dahlgren, at least not one that's a member of the Ice Anglers. I'll make some calls." Kendall knew The Ice Anglers was a local group of ice fishermen.

When she couldn't reach Alverson, Kendall called the station to see who was on duty. Shit. Paula Burnham. Kendall dialed her number.

"Burnham."

"Halsrud here."

"Thought you were on desk duty."

"I got the okay to put surveillance on the Dahgren kid." A small bending of the truth. "I got a tip he's been meeting Rindsig at his grandfather's ice shanty. I'm going to cover it tonight and thought it would be a good idea to have backup."

"She's probably laying on a beach drinking pineapple Daquiri's."

It seemed that's what everyone thought. "Maybe. But she was hung up on Dahlgren. I don't see her giving him up." But would Rindsig go to meet him on a night like this? There'd be an accident on every corner and cops attending them. Then, maybe all the better for Ruby; they'd be too busy to look for her.

Burnham expressed an irritated sigh. "No can do, Halsrud. We're up to our eyeballs here. Besides, if your chick is still sniffing after the boyfriend, she won't crawl out of her hole to meet him on a night like this."

At least Kendall could say she'd tried for backup.

Brynn came through with the grandfather's name, which was not the same as Dahlgren's. Thanks to her uncle, Kendall found out that Myron Wetzel's ice fishing shanty was one cove east of her uncle's on Lake Wissota. Now she wouldn't have to wait for Jeremy to leave; she could drive out to the lake and park near the shanty to watch for him or Ruby to show. Kendall checked her car to be sure she had what she'd need: a snowmobile suit, waterproof hat and a pair of Trekkers for the bottom of her boots. Even with the steel-tipped grippers, walking on the ice-topped snow would be a bitch.

She left the Olive Garden heading for Lake Wissota. The cove holding Myron Wetzel's shanty spouted at least a dozen of the tiny sanctuaries. A two-lane highway cut close to the frozen lakeshore. On the other side of the road was a supper club with only two cars still parked in the front lot. Kendall pulled in next to them with the Highlander pointed toward the cove. She'd barely parked the car when she got another call from Brynn and

Ryan; Dahlgren's visitor planned on meeting him tonight.

43

After a treacherous trip out on the cove making sure the shanty and its neighbors were uninhabited, Kendall returned to her car and settled in to wait for Dahlgren or Ruby to appear. She was parked within sight of the boat landing where Dahlgren would make his entrance onto the lake. Twenty minutes later, a car pulled in next to her, Paula Burnham in an unmarked.

Burnham got out of her car and settled herself next to Kendall.

"I thought you were up to your eyeballs," Kendall said.

"I was. Got tired of sorting out accidents caused by all the douche bags that can't drive on ice. What's the matter with people, they can't stay in on a night like this?"

"Didn't by any chance bring some food, did you?"

Burnham pulled a candy bar out of her pocket and handed half to Kendall. "So you think Rindsig's gonna show for a little nooky on the ice?"

"Dahlgren's meeting *someone* here."

"Hafta be her then; it's kinda late for fishing."

"Not really. The diehards are at it all night. My uncle sleeps in his; has a bell on his tip-up."

Burnham snorted. "Couldn't pay me enough to sit in one of

those things and wait for a fish to bite. Those damn heaters they use can cook your ass while you sleep. Or blow you up."

"Once we see Dahlgren drive up, one of us can follow him on foot."

"I'll man the car and watch for the visitor."

"Fine." Kendall didn't want to start a pissing match with the other woman by reminding her that she wasn't supposed to be doing anything physical. It had been nearly five days now since her surgery, and Kendall felt great.

Minutes later, a dark pickup entered the middle of the cove.

"Think that's the Dahlgren kid?" Burnham asked.

"No, he's driving the family SUV, and I think he'd use the boat ramp closest to the cove, the one just across the street. It's the fastest way here from where he works. We can see it from here. That truck's probably from one of the other shacks."

The pickup stopped in the middle of the cove, far from the area where most of the shacks were located. Kendall picked up her binoculars.

"Crap. I can't see much, but two men got out of the pickup and I think one of them is carrying an auger. Just what we need, some idiots setting up in the freezing rain. They could scare off Rindsig. I'm going out there and tell them to move on. Flash the headlights once if you see Dahlgren. He's driving a black Blazer."

In a dark snowmobile suit, with her Trekkers on her boots once more, Kendall edged through the trees surrounding the boat landing and out onto the lake. She moved cautiously across the icy snow, stopping behind each shack so she could keep an eye out for Dahlgren. She approached the two ice fishermen, knowing they hadn't heard her coming toward them above the whine of the auger.

Up close, she announced herself as a cop, the small lantern they had next to them just enough to illuminate her. The noise from the auger ceased.

She repeated, "Eau Claire police. I'm sorry, but I'm going to have to ask you guys to set up somewhere else. Move on to the next cove or go across the lake. Better yet, go home where you'll be warm."

When they turned to her, she saw her father and her uncle looking up from over the auger. Her uncle had ratted her out to her father.

"What the hell are you two doing here? Dad, you know better. You could blow this whole thing for me."

"Kenny," he argued, "I was a cop. I know what I'm doing. This is a hot spot. Guys come and go all the time. I've got a bottle of whiskey. We'll pass it back and forth just like anyone else would and no one will ever know we aren't what we look like."

Her mind raced with all the things that could go wrong. "No one's going to be coming and going on a night like this. And, please tell me you aren't carrying."

When he didn't answer, she fought to contain her anger. He'd brought a gun. "That's it. Pack up your stuff and get out of here."

She saw a flash of headlights from shore. "Goddamn it! Dahlgren's here. Like I said, leave!"

She edged her way off the ice and back to the shelter of the trees where she watched as Dahlgren's car moved slowly among the shacks and parked next to his grandfather's shanty, only about thirty yards from where she waited. She pulled a pair of night goggles out of her suit, watching as he entered the shanty carrying a bag of what looked like groceries. If he were expecting

Rindsig, he'd be prepared to offer her food and drink.

Ten minutes later, Kendall saw a dark figure slip out of the trees on the opposite side of the cove. She called Burnham and told her to stay put. Without ice grippers on her boots, she'd be more of a hindrance than help. Kendall would let Ruby get in first and get comfortable with her lover before rushing them. The element of surprise would work in her favor. The shack's only window faced out toward the lake so Dahlgren and Rindsig wouldn't see her as she approached.

Kendall deliberated. If it were Rindsig in there with Dahlgren, she didn't want to risk getting him killed. Ruby would certainly be armed. She'd had plenty of time to replace her father's gun with another model. They weren't going anywhere, and there was only one way out. Maybe she should wait it out. But then Kendall really didn't think Ruby would hurt Dahlgren; after all she was so fixated on him she risked her freedom to come back to see him when she could have been long gone.

For what seemed like hours but was probably only minutes, Kendall stood watching the shanty from the shelter of the trees, her extremities getting colder by the minute. Then she moved forward until she could watch from behind the neighboring shanty, about ten yards from the lovers. When she moved away from the shelter of the other shack, the ice pummeled her face like needles. At least she had the goggles protecting her eyes. Walking, even with the grippers on her boots, became nearly impossible on the ice-topped snow. Kendall second-guessed herself once more, thinking maybe Rindsig *hadn't* been able to get another gun. Her indecision overridden by the reality of the storm, she knew she couldn't tolerate its force much longer. She moved to the side of shanty and banged on the door.

"Police!" she shouted. "Open the door." She heard a rustling sound inside. Pulling clothes back on?

Kendall dodged back to the side of the other shanty.

"Ruby Rindsig," she shouted. "Come out. Now!" Kendall leapt further back just as a blast of gunfire exploded through the door of Dahlgren's shanty. Ruby had another gun.

"Ruby," she yelled, "there's nowhere to run. Toss the gun out and come out with your hands behind your head."

Her heart pounded in her chest. Had she done the right thing? Or would she end up with another ugly bullet-scar? Even worse, Ruby could escape, leaving Kendall's body behind, a lump frozen to the surface of the lake.

Jeremy Dahlgren emerged from the shattered doorway of the shack. Rindsig followed closely behind, holding a handgun aimed at his head.

"Ruby, please," he whimpered, "don't do this. It's time to give up. I'll be here for you, baby. Put the gun down."

Alverson had been right; Dahlgren couldn't see past his penis. Ruby Rindsig had total control over him. She kept the gun pointed at Jeremy's head.

"I'm sorry, Jeremy. I can't live in a cage." She turned toward Kendall, flinching as the tiny splinters of ice hit her bare face. "Drop your gun or he gets a bullet in the brain."

Jeremy's face registered shock at her words. "Ruby, please. I love you."

Suddenly, sirens screamed in the distance.

Panic filled Ruby's eyes as the sound of the sirens drew closer. Then Jeremy Dahlgren lost his footing, dropping clumsily to his knees. He reached for Ruby as he went down and she slid alongside him. A shot rang out as she crumpled to the ice, landing on her hip. Kendall felt a bolt of fear before she realized

Ruby's gun had only gone off as she slid on the icy snow. No one was hurt—yet.

Ruby sat up and raised the gun, aiming at Kendall, who fired back at the girl just as her own footing went awry. Her shot missed its mark, hitting Ruby in the shoulder. Ruby's gun flew out of her hand. Jeremy ran to her, and crouched at her side, putting pressure on her wound. He handed Kendall the gun as her father and her Uncle Al appeared next to them. She should have known they wouldn't leave her, no matter what she'd told them.

It was clear Jim Halsrud had jumped back into police officer mode. He helped her cuff Rindsig and Dahlgren while her uncle called for an ambulance.

"Sorry, Kenny," her father said. "I couldn't leave you out here alone."

Kendall looked down at Ruby who'd turned on the water works, probably to gain some sympathy. Jeremy, the fool, remained crouched next to her, whispering that she'd be all right. He'd stand by her.

"Dad, you should have left. I had the situation under control. You being here will have backlash on me. And Paula."

Paula had inched out onto the lake after hearing shots and calling for backup.

"Show a little respect, Halsrud. He might have saved your sorry ass."

Rindsig's shoulder wound, for all its bleeding, had only required stitches and bandaging. Three hours after the showdown at the ice-shanty, she was transported back to the station from the hospital in cuffs and leg chains, her face sullen. She'd been arrested, read her rights, and hadn't asked for a lawyer. Locked in an interview room with a bored expression, Ruby studied her fingernails as she waited. She'd dyed her red curls a dark, unflattering shade of brown and cropped them into a short, straight bob. Kendall watched her through the two-way glass, itching to start the questioning.

A celebratory mood reigned among the officers in the station. They had their kidnapper and possibly the person who'd murdered the Glaussons or at least acted as an accomplice. Schoenfuss entered the room without a word, parting the troops like the Red Sea. Without preamble, he ordered Kendall into his office and closed the door behind them.

"I'm not a happy man, Halsrud."

She fought to contain a shiver shooting through her body. Her time under the boss's radar had run out. Her only hope was that the capture of Philly's kidnapper had lessened his anger.

"You're on suspension."

Apparently it hadn't. She started to protest, but he interrupted her.

"Save it. I told you office duty only. You weren't supposed to be working out of the station. As soon as your surveillance of the Dahlgren kid turned up Rindsig, you should have handed it over to the detective on duty. You disobeyed a direct order."

"But—"

He raised a hand to quiet her. "Before you say another word, keep in mind that I could take your badge for involving a citizen. Your father and your uncle had no business anywhere near this collar. And you were out of your jurisdiction in Wissota."

She opened her mouth to explain.

"I said I don't want to hear it. You put lives in jeopardy while you approached a fucking ice-shack, for Christ's sake! Didn't it occur to you those things are made of cardboard and duct tape? A bullet could go through those walls like a cereal box. Consider yourself lucky you're alive and standing. The fact that no one but Rindsig got hurt was a fluke.'"

Kendall left the station knowing he was right about most of it. It wouldn't have been wise to point out to him how well the new shanties were built. Nevertheless, Rindsig could easily have sprayed bullets across all the walls of the shanty and Kendall wouldn't be alive to be standing here feeling sorry for herself. Why couldn't she just be grateful to be alive? Apparently, like Ruby, Kendall hadn't been thinking straight. But Ruby's obsession with Jeremy might have saved Kendall's life. And Jeremy—professing his love even with a gun at his head—how sick was that?

Love. How many times had Kendall seen deadly results in the name of that emotion? It was no wonder men and women in law enforcement had such mucked up relationships. For a fleeting moment, she wondered how it would have gone down tonight if Nash had been with her. Together, they might have had the good sense to watch the shack and get Ruby Rindsig on her way out.

Kendall arrived back at the apartment feeling like she'd been gone for days. She put a frozen pizza in the oven and poured a glass of wine. It felt good to have her own place to come home to. Why had she fought it for so long? Had her mother's obsession with appearances, the house in particular, jaded Kendall from desiring such things? It was time to let go of the past's hold on her.

44

Sunday

The next morning Kendall had breakfast in a small café. She ordered an omelet with a side of pancakes and was surprised how little of the huge portions she could eat. Must be the missing gall bladder. She supposed her body would adjust in time. Never one to obsess on her weight, Kendall nevertheless felt better without the pounds she'd shed after the shooting. But even the one pair of new slacks she'd bought had become too loose. It was time to find a balance with food. And everything else in her life.

After leaving the restaurant, she drove to visit Hank, who was recuperating at home. The Whitehouses lived in a small ranch-style home south of the city. Diane invited Kendall in and took her into the family room, where Hank sat in a leather recliner in front of a wide-screen TV tuned to a news show.

"Whoa. Here comes the big celebrity. About time."

She sat in a chair across from him. "Uh, I've been a little busy?"

"You did good, Halsrud. I'm proud of you." He flicked off the TV.

Hank didn't give out compliments freely; Kendall took a

moment to savor the praise. "Aren't you going to ask me why I'm here?"

"Sorry, kid. I already heard he suspended you."

"Everyone says it could have been worse."

"Right. How you doing since your surgery?"

"I should be asking you that question," Kendall said. "I'm great. No problems with the surgery at all. How about you? You're looking like your old self."

He turned to see if Diane was within hearing distance. "I can't stand this anymore. I love her, but being together twenty-four-seven? If this is what retirement is like, shoot me now."

"Then you'll be coming back?"

"The doc says not for a couple months, maybe sooner if I can get desk duty. I could take my retirement and do something else, haven't decided. Maybe I'll get a job at that buttwipe company where your boyfriend works. I heard they might have an opening."

"He's not my boyfriend. And if you're suggesting Nash's job will be open, Glausson wouldn't replace him just because he's injured."

"You're out of the loop. I heard he gave notice."

Trying not to appear too interested, she asked, "Is he coming back to the job?"

"Didn't hear what he's gonna do. Don't you talk to the guy?"

"We were working a case. It's over."

Kendall felt him studying her, knew he was trying to figure out just what Nash meant to her.

"I heard you guys worked good together," he said.

"You spend too much time gossiping. You need a hobby."

He shrugged. "I'm bored, people talk. Wanna hear what else I heard?"

"Go ahead. You'll tell me anyway."

"Heard him and Shari are getting a divorce."

Feeling her face flush, Kendal bent over and refilled her coffee from a carafe Diane had set in front of her. She straightened, her color returning to normal. "You sure about that? His wife came to the hospital in Stillwater when he got shot."

"Also heard it's amicable. Just saying—he's a good guy and he'll be available."

Right. Available to the next perky, petite woman he met. Not to Kendall. Her moment with Nash had passed.

Kendall's phone chimed after she left the Whitehouses.

"Kenny, how you doing?"

"How do you think I'm doing?" she snarled. "And it's still Halsrud to you."

Alverson ignored the reprimand. "What'd he suspend you for, a week?"

"Worse. 'To be determined.'"

"That blows. We kind of need you here, you know?"

"What's going on?"

"It's what's not going on—the Rindsig chick ain't talking."

"That's no surprise. Did she ask for an attorney?'

Alverson hesitated. "Not when I talked to her."

Kendall should have been the one interviewing Rindsig. Alverson wasn't the best interviewer. Ruby wouldn't be inclined to open up to him. "Anyone else have a go at her?"

"Yeah, Burnham. You know how that must have gone."

"What the matter with Schoenfuss? Couldn't he put someone in there who could do the job?" Kendall realized what she'd said. "Sorry. Nothing personal."

"No worries."

"Damn. Now is the time for her to talk. With all the evidence we have against her, it'll just be a matter of how many charges are thrown at her. Someone has to convince her to confess now and cut a deal, make her think it would get her sentence knocked down."

"I hear you," he said. "But there's no swaying the boss when he gets his mind made up, and he's the one that decides who goes in the box with Rindsig. We're working on finding a connection to Jordan, but so far, nada. We've got plenty to charge her with, but we can't get her for the Glussons with nothing to go on. And it looks like her old man died of natural causes."

"You have to work her, get her worried about getting the max, and convince her to tell us what she knows about the Glausson murders."

Kendall hung up, frustrated. She wanted to interview Ruby, but by the time her boss finally brought her back, it might be too late for her methods to be effective.

Wanting some connection with the case, she drove to Graham Glausson's house on Lake Wissota. Nothing wrong with an off-the-record visit to see how Philly was doing. England opened the door, clutching a wide-eyed Philly on one hip. The child had one hand grasping the sleeve of England's sweater, the other clutched the top of her white turtleneck.

Juggling the baby, England invited her into the spacious kitchen and poured her a cup of coffee. Philly, adorable in a yellow corduroy jumpsuit appliquéd with a bouquet of daisies, didn't appear frightened. She sat quietly on England's lap.

"How's she doing?" Kendall asked.

England grinned. "Good. I stayed with her in the hospital. She only woke up twice after I got her to sleep. She's been quiet, but other than that, pretty content. And hungry." Philly tucked her face into England's chest. "You must know about the hearing. Gray isn't here right now, but he won't be gone long. Once he got the right to bring her home, he had to get more things for her."

"I'm glad you got that settled," Kendall said. "I just stopped in to see how you guys were doing. She's really bonded with you."

"You know, I wasn't too happy when I found out we'd have to take her. I wanted kids, sure, but not yet. And I wanted them to be *our* children." England held Philly closer, struggling for words. "But she feels like my own child—already. I can't explain it. I love her as much as if I gave birth to her."

Kendall felt tears stinging her eyelids.

"Are you all right, Detective?" England asked.

It was all good. England's immediate love for Philly satisfied Kendall's concern that an adoptive parent could love a child as much as its natural mother.

"I'm fine. And you can call me Kenny." She smiled. "All my friends do."

45

Monday

Alverson called Kendall the next morning. "Schoenfuss wants you to talk to Rindsig."

Kendall hesitated. "When did you become his secretary?"

"I know you've been panting for this, so get your ass in here."

Obviously the boss didn't want to give her the satisfaction of asking her to come back. She made it to the station in record time and looked for him in his office, thinking she should at least check in. His secretary informed her he'd gone out and wouldn't be in until after lunch.

Not disappointed at his absence, Kendall immediately put in a call to have Rindsig brought down from holding. When they had her in an interrogation room, Kendall entered and offered her a cup of coffee. Ruby held it in both hands without raising it to her pale lips. Her dark bob had begun to fade, red streaks evident, the short tresses puffing out from her scalp.

Once again, Rindsig waived her right to have an attorney present. Kendall had planned just how she'd interview Ruby and began with a bitter accusation, hoping to unsettle the girl: "Tell me how you killed Sienna Glausson and her family."

She didn't really believe Ruby had been the one who'd murdered the Glaussons but hoped the shock value of her words would get Ruby talking.

"I don't have to tell you anything," Ruby sneered.

"That's true, you don't. But unless you change your mind, you could be charged with all of it. We know you murdered Gerald Fostvedt and kidnapped Philly Glausson. It doesn't take a big leap to think you killed all of them."

Ruby snapped to attention, her features devoid of their earlier attitude.

"But . . . Travis Jordan confessed."

Clearly, Ruby hadn't expected to be accused of murdering the Glaussons.

"Travis Jordan said a lot of things. Some of them were lies."

"Maybe I should get a lawyer." Ruby reached for her hair as if the long red tresses were still there to be twirled by her nervous fingers.

"Maybe you should. But then any leverage you have is off the table."

"What are you talking about?"

"If you didn't kill the Glaussons, and you tell me everything that happened that night, you'll only be tried for Fostvedt. And for taking Philly. Since no harm came to the child, you won't get the maximum. You might see the light of day before you're a wrinkled old crone. Go down for the Glaussons, too, and you can kiss your ass goodbye."

Rindsig eyed her through narrowed lids. Kendall knew she was sifting through her options. She hadn't mentioned the additional charges for the attempted murder of Philly and Brynn.

Added to the others, they would make a considerable impact on Ruby's sentence.

"I don't believe you."

"Suit yourself. If you don't want to talk about the Glaussons, then tell me about the emails that trolled for virgins. Is that how you got the big bank account?"

Rindsig's nostrils flared, but she said nothing.

"You didn't think we'd find out about the money? You must have invested it well to have more than fifty grand in such a short time. Tell me, Ruby. Did you sell you virginity to the highest bidder?"

"It was the only way I could go to college," she snapped. "My old man couldn't help, and my grades weren't that good, so I couldn't get a scholarship. I carried a 4.0 my first quarter at UWEC." She paused, as if to say she was proud of what she'd done to pay for college. "I answered the email ad and sent a picture. I got five grand when I got to the guy's hotel room and was supposed to get another five after the old fart popped my cherry. He was disgusting—fat, bald, and his back was loaded with hair—gross. After he did me, he asked me to stay. I told him no way, he'd gotten what he paid for and owed me the other five grand. He gave me the five and showed me another envelope. There was another twenty in it for me if I stayed the rest of the weekend."

She snorted. "Fool. Thirty grand to boink a virgin, and that doesn't even count the money he had to cough up for the guy with the website. He even trusted me to take the first ten out to my car and come back to earn the other twenty. Do you believe it?"

Teenage boys weren't the only fools. Kendall had checked the records; Jeremy had been a daily visitor. "And did you go back for the rest of the money?"

Ruby grinned. "For another twenty, I'd put up with his hairy back—and his stubby prick."

Thirty grand for sex with a virgin. Hard to believe. Kendall wanted to keep Rindsig talking, and steered her to the subject of Jeremy Dahlgren. "I'm surprised you didn't save your virginity for Jeremy."

Rindsig shrugged. "At the time I didn't think I'd ever get him away from Sienna. And besides, no one expects a girl to be a virgin anymore."

"Were you seeing him before Sienna was killed?"

"I got into his study group. Sometimes we'd get together alone. He told me he and Sienna weren't having sex, so he wasn't real hard to seduce."

"But he didn't leave Sienna."

Ruby glowered. Maybe Jeremy hadn't been the best subject. "What was Gerald Fostvedt to you?"

"Sharky?" Ruby sneered. "He was my puppet. A couple blow jobs and he'd do anything for me, you know?"

Progress. "What did he do for you the night the Glaussons died?"

Ruby sat back in her chair. Kendall was afraid she'd pushed too hard.

After a few seconds passed, Ruby cleared her throat and started talking again. "Jeremy picked me up for study group that night because my car wouldn't start. He gave me a ride home afterwards, but he wouldn't stay. I was afraid he was going back to see Sienna and was just lying to me about going home. So I called Sharky. He picked me up, and we drove over to the Glaussons' house to see if Jeremy's car was there. It wasn't, but we waited for a while to make sure he hadn't just stopped for gas or something. There was a strange car in their driveway. I thought maybe they had company that was staying over, or maybe Sienna was seeing another guy. I wanted to find out, so I got out of the car and snuck into the backyard. I saw a guy leave the house carrying a gym bag. After he drove off, I went to look inside the house. I saw Sienna's mom and dad in the kitchen. They looked dead."

"What did this guy look like?"

"I don't know. I didn't see his face."

"Didn't you think you should call the police?"

"I wanted to look around first."

The bitch was an opportunist. Of course she'd want to look around.

"I told him not to follow me, but Sharky came in anyway. We found Sienna and her brother after we saw the parents in the kitchen. They looked dead too. But Sienna started moaning. I told Sharky she was all his now. He'd always had a hard-on for cheerleaders, especially her. I went upstairs and found the kid in the playhouse. By the time I came back down with her, he was putting his pants back on."

Ruby's story, disgusting as it was, explained the evidence. She asked, "Why did you take the baby?"

Ruby took a moment, probably deciding whether to tell Kendall that last bit of the puzzle. "I saw on some crime show you could get a lot of money for a blonde baby. So I took her. I made a little cut on her arm so there would be some of her blood on the floor. That way the cops would think the intruder killed her."

"Sounds like you thought of everything."

Ruby reached for a lock of hair. "I didn't know it would be

so hard to get rid of the kid. I didn't think it mattered how long it took to get some money for her—everyone thought she was dead. Then I heard you talking about her at the station that day, telling them she was still alive. You screwed up everything."

Kendall stiffened. She should have remembered the day when Ruby had been there; Rindsig had known she wouldn't give up on finding Philly. "Then you were the one who shot at Gray and tossed Brynn's apartment?"

"You got your facts wrong. I kept an eye on things, sure, but nothing like that."

Ruby didn't appear to be lying. She'd given Kendall what she could, but there were still loose ends. The answers had to be with Travis Jordan—if he lived—and if he ever shared them.

46

Kahn called a week before Christmas. Kendall hadn't heard from the agent in days.

"Jordan's girlfriend showed up at the prison to visit him. We'd heard about her but were never able to get a name. I'm going to question her today in Stillwater. Jordan's refusing to see her, and to talk to us, but she's agreed to come in today. Thought you might want to sit in."

Kendall wondered at his generosity, annoyed that he hadn't called her as soon as Jordan became conscious, but quickly said she was on her way. She'd settle for what she could get now, and maybe he'd let her have a go at Jordan later.

When she arrived at the Stillwater station, she found Kahn pacing in the hallway. "About time, Halsrud. Ready to go in?"

Why did he look nervous? Kendall peeked through the two-way mirror of the interview room to get a look at Jordan's girlfriend. Unexpectedly gorgeous, she appeared to be a career woman, wearing a brown tweed jacket over well-cut slacks and an ivory, satin blouse. Hard to imagine her with the Travis Jordan Kendall knew.

"Sure that's the right woman?" Kendall asked.

"I know. Surprised me too."

Now Kendall understood his invitation. While maintaining their ogling rights, there were a few cops who demurred from interviewing attractive women—they were admittedly too easily distracted. She suspected it was more likely that beautiful women intimidated them. It was surprising for a Fed, however, despite Kahn's lack of social skills.

"Want me to go in first?" Kendall asked. "Maybe she'd open up more to another woman."

He hesitated, and then gestured toward the door to the interview room. "Sure. Go ahead. If you need me, I'll be out here watching."

Kendall entered the room; Jennifer Polanski stood on the other side of the table, her arms wrapped around her slender body as if she were cold. The room, however, was warm. In her late twenties, Jennifer's makeup was subtle and her dark hair expertly highlighted.

Kendall introduced herself and asked Polanski to take a seat across from her. She waited until they were both seated. "Jennifer, thank you for coming in. Can you tell me how long you've known Travis Jordan?"

"Almost two years."

"Where did you meet?"

Jennifer stifled a smile as if afraid it would be inappropriate. "At a club. I was with a date—someone I'd just met. It wasn't going well. Travis was sitting at the bar and he noticed I was miserable. He took pity on me and started talking to me when my date left for the men's room. He even offered me cab money."

"And did you leave?"

"Yes, but not in a cab. I had my own car. I'd met my date at a restaurant across the street. After I brushed him off, I met Travis there for coffee. He was so easy to talk to. Nothing like the men I usually dated—he listened like I was the most important person in his world. And for a long time, I believed I was."

"How would you describe your relationship?"

"We were planning on getting married. Until a few months ago, anyway." Jennifer sat back and crossed her arms.

"What changed?"

"He found out about his mother."

"You mean Chelsea Glausson. Do you know how he found her?"

"Yes. We were waiting in line to get into a club in St. Paul, when a man walked past. Travis saw him, did a double take, and just took off after him. I had no idea why. He left me there without a word and never came back." She slid off her jacket and took a drink from a bottle of water. "I waited for half an hour, then I took a cab back to my apartment. He showed up at my door two hours later looking like he'd been in a fight. He had a bruise on his cheek and I could tell his nose had been bleeding."

"Did he tell you what happened when he caught up with the man—or who he was?"

"I knew how Travis grew up—about everything they did to him," Jennifer said. "Sometimes he'd wake up in the middle of the night screaming. It was getting better, though. He said sleeping with me kept him grounded in the present, made the past seem more like a bad dream. I felt so bad for the little boy he used to be. Can you imagine growing up as a pedophile's plaything?"

Kahn had shared Jordan's medical history with Kendall. Jordan had been so badly abused as a child that he'd needed surgery in order to defecate naturally.

"Did he tell you how he happened to be with them?" Kendall asked.

"He didn't know," Jennifer responded. "They taunted him with different stories from time to time: his mother didn't want him and threw him into a dumpster; she sold him; or they broke into the house, killed his mother and father, and took him with them."

She sold him—one of the taunts true. Kendall repeated, "Did he tell you what happened the night he saw that man and ran off?"

"He told me the man he saw was one of the men who'd kept him as a child. He cornered the guy when he caught up to him, and they fought. When Travis threatened him, he admitted he bought Travis from his mother when he was a newborn, and told Travis she'd only cared about the money. She told them what they paid her for the baby didn't even cover her labor pains."

Kendall didn't want to feel sympathy for a murderer, but the thought of an innocent child living in such conditions was heartbreaking. "You felt sorry for him, Jennifer. Why leave him?"

"I didn't at first. He told me he made the man give him his mother's name. He said he'd find her and make her pay for everything they did to him. He threatened to kill her for what she'd done. I hate violence, Detective. I felt so much pain for what he'd been through, but I couldn't condone that kind of revenge. I tried to tell him he couldn't trust anything that animal told him. His mother could've had a good reason for giving him up and been conned into thinking he'd be placed in a good home.

"He wouldn't listen. After a few weeks I thought he'd calmed down and let it go. Then he admitted he'd hired a private detective to find her for him. When he got her married name and found out she had a family, it put him over the edge. His anger consumed him; I didn't recognize him anymore. I'd had enough. I asked him to move out."

"Did you hear from him after that?"

"Once. He called me in the middle of the night, sobbing. He'd been drinking and I couldn't understand most of what he said. He hung up on me when I started asking questions. That's the last contact I had with him and now he refuses to see me."

"Didn't you ever think about calling the police and letting them know what he planned to do?"

She sighed. "Of course, now I wish I would have turned him in. Don't think I haven't regretted that. But I knew they couldn't lock him up for something he only threatened to do. I'm sure he didn't even own a weapon at that time. And frankly, I really didn't believe he'd do it. I still thought he'd get over it eventually.

"What about the other two home invasions?" Kendall asked. "Do you know if he had anything to do with them?"

"Agent Kahn asked me that, too. The one in Green Bay was before we met, but my gut tells me he had nothing to do with it; he would have had no reason like he did with his mother and her family. The night of the murders in Stillwater, Travis was with me. I remember because it was the weekend of my birthday and we went away for a few days."

The story about the birthday weekend could be checked out. If Jordan hadn't done the others, how had he gotten the gun?

Two days later Kendall received an unexpected phone call before she'd even left for the station.

"Kendall? This is Gray Glausson. I need to talk to you."

"Is Philly all right?"

"She's fine. It's about Chelsea. We got access to the house a few weeks ago and we've been taking care of all their things. I found a key, a key to a safe deposit box Chelsea rented under her maiden name."

"Have you opened it?" Kendall asked.

He exhaled loudly. "Can we talk? If you can come out here, we'll have the coffee on."

"Sure, I can do that. But I'm curious now, what is it?"

"Chelsea left a video for her children in case anything ever happened to her."

"Some people do that. It isn't unusual."

"She left a letter, too—for the child she gave up."

47

Kendall drove to Stillwater carrying Chelsea Glausson's letter, memories of Nash invading her mind as she pulled up at the Stillwater hospital. Being there overwhelmed her with the pain of missing him. Pain seemed to be fitting for what she was doing, bringing Chelsea Glausson's letter to a man whose only contact with his mother had been at birth and on the night he killed her.

Gray Glausson told her he'd had a hard time deciding whether to open the letter; his first thought, was Jordan didn't deserve any consideration. He'd open it, read it, and throw it in the fire. After discussing it with England, he'd mellowed and agreed to send it to Jordan unopened, honoring Chelsea's wishes. In spite of everything, Travis Jordan was Chelsea's son. Once he read the letter, he'd have to live with its contents. If there were any justice, his mother's words would haunt him forever.

Kendall met Lucille Bellamy in the ICU outside of Jordan's room. "Thanks for meeting me here. I'm here in place of Mr. Glausson," Kendall explained. "I'm sure you can understand why he chose not to be here himself."

Bellamy smiled her wry half-smile. "Of course. It says quite a bit about the man that he was willing to send the letter at all."

"He loved Chelsea. He believes this is what she would have

wanted."

"Has anyone read it?"

Kendall had wanted to break the seal and read the letter ever since Gray had given her the envelope the day before. "No. Is Jordan talking yet?"

"Only to me." She told Kendall that Jordan still refused to talk to Kahn or any of the local police, and he still wouldn't meet with his ex-girlfriend.

He'd refused to talk to Kendall the day she'd met Jennifer Polanski. "We may never know if he's responsible for all three of the invasions."

Bellamy nodded. "I can't discuss any details, of course, but you know Jennifer Polanski alibied him for one of them."

"I'm not sure she's entirely credible." Kendall felt sure in her gut Polanski was legit but wasn't going to admit it to Bellamy. They'd verified the couple's hotel reservations the weekend of the Stillwater murders, but hadn't found a witness who could vouch for Jordan's presence.

Bellamy gestured to Jordan's room. "Let's get on with it." They passed the officer at the door and walked into the room. Jordan lay in the bed with the back cranked halfway up. He curled his lips at the sight of them. Being near death hadn't ruined his good looks or softened his sullen attitude, although his hair had grown in over the letters tattooed on his scalp.

"Travis, Detective Halsrud is here on behalf of Mr. Gray Glausson," Bellamy informed him. "Chelsea Glausson, your biological mother, left a letter for you in a safe deposit box. Mr. Glausson wants you to have it. He's sent it with Detective Halsrud."

Jordan stared blankly ahead.

Bellamy grabbed the TV remote from his left hand and turned off the set. "Travis, I told you before they've confirmed she's your mother. Your DNA matched hers."

Kendall offered him the letter. "I imagine you must be curious to see what your mother had to say to you."

His haunting sea green eyes met hers. "I don't give a crap what she had to say. The bitch sold me like a piece of meat. Keep the fucking letter—or burn it—doesn't mean jack to me."

Should she walk out? No, Chelsea Glausson wanted her words communicated to her child. Kendall slid a fingernail under the flap and pulled out a one-page letter. "Then you won't mind if I read it to your attorney."

Kendall's heart ached for Chelsea. There was only one similarity between Chelsea Glausson's situation and her own; they'd both given birth to a child they were unable to raise. Kendall had the advantage of knowing she'd placed her daughter in a good home.

She swallowed over the thickening in her throat and read aloud:

My beloved son,

I knew you for such a short, sweet time, yet if I saw you on the street, I know I'd recognize you. When I gave you up for adoption, I had no means to raise a child, and I believed giving you to people who would love you and provide a good home was in your best interest. The person who arranged the adoption introduced me to the couple who would be your new family. They appeared to be nice people; nevertheless, my heart broke when I handed you to them.

Years later, when I tried to find you, I discovered the agency I used was bogus. I found no trace of the person who arranged the adoption or the couple who took you. I tried to hire a private detective to locate you, but he told me with the little information I had to give him, it would be dishonest to take my money. I've prayed you had a loving home and the years were good to you. I want you to know, although I haven't been able to hold you in my arms, you've always been with me in my heart.

Please forgive me. I love you.

Your mother,

Chelsea Glausson

Kendall had a hard time reading the end of the letter. Jordan said nothing, his gaze remained on the far wall. Kendall folded the letter back into the envelope.

"Well, I guess that's it, then."

Bellamy left the room as Kendall returned the letter to her purse and moved to follow her. She walked to the door remembering the abused little boy Chelsea had searched for. Her sympathetic thoughts didn't last long as images of the Glausson family on the night of their deaths popped into her mind.

A voice sounded behind her. She turned to see Jordan propped up on one elbow, as far as his restraints allowed.

"Leave me my fuckin' letter."

Epilogue

Kendall, who'd never had any great love of the holidays, volunteered to work Christmas Eve and Christmas day so others with families could have those days off. Her dad and Maggie were in the Bahamas, and her uncle had left for Springfield to visit his son and daughter-in-law. Although she always complained about the family dinners on holidays, she felt oddly alone this year.

The night before Christmas Eve, Brynn met her in the hallway as she was coming home from work.

"What are you doing for Christmas?" Brynn asked.

"I'm working. I just got off shift now, and I'll be on for a twelve tomorrow and again on Christmas Day."

Brynn adjusted her tinted lenses. "Um, why don't you come to Morrie's party tomorrow tonight after you get off?"

Kendall hadn't heard about a party.

"There are a lot of people who don't have anything to do on Christmas Eve," Brynn explained. "So he's closing the place except for people who buy tickets to the buffet dinner he's serving. I'm going to help with the food. The tickets are only three dollars."

Because she still spent time with Ryan, Brynn had been Kendall's only connection to Nash these days. He'd finally stopped calling, and the day he'd shown up at the station on crutches, she'd made a rapid exit out the back after hearing his voice. Since Whitehouse had told her Nash was getting divorced, she'd never found the nerve to call him.

"Where's Ryan tonight?" Kendall couldn't help but ask.

"He has to get together with his grandparents tonight and the other relatives tomorrow night."

Kendall agreed to stop in at the party after work and offered to lend a hand if Morrie needed servers.

After she got home on Christmas Eve, Kendall sifted through her wardrobe, glad she'd given in to Nat's invitation for lunch and shopping on her last day off. After Nat told Kendall about the new woman in her life, Kendall had been more comfortable making an effort to regain their lost friendship. The red sweater she'd talked Kendall into buying, far from her usual sedate taste, would work for the evening. She put it on over a pair of dark gray slacks, added gold earrings, and let her freshly highlighted hair fall onto her shoulders.

There was a full house in the bar and sounds of Christmas music coming from the jukebox. She passed underneath a giant ball of mistletoe hanging conspicuously in the doorway, dodging an elderly man carrying a grandchild on his shoulders as she walked in. The scent of baked ham filled the air, and the buffet groaned with food. Latecomers loaded their plates with goodies.

Brynn, wearing her long, white hairpiece, had taken off her dark glasses and added a touch of makeup. She looked adorable in a soft, blue sweater and winter white slacks. Despite the look, to Kendall, Brynn still appeared vulnerable and younger than her years.

She and Kendall helped keep the buffet stocked until Morrie told them to take a break. They heaped food on their plates and found an empty booth.

"I sent in applications to five forensic science schools," Brynn announced between bites of food. "Ryan did too."

"Really?" Kendall hadn't thought the boy would maintain an interest in higher education. "What's happening with you guys? Still just platonic?" If she hadn't known Brynn as well as she did, she might have missed the soft flush that colored her pale neck.

"We're friends, that's all."

Kendall didn't push. Brynn was over the age of consent. A broken heart wouldn't kill her; it was something everyone experienced at some time or other. "Is he still dating a lot?"

"I don't ask him what he does when he's not around." Brynn slipped a forkful of mashed potatoes into her mouth. "It's none of my business."

Not forthcoming. This was the Brynn she was used to. They finished their meal entertained by Christmas music, laughter, and a steady stream of revelers meeting under the mistletoe. Kendall's favorite carol, "Oh Holy Night," played in the background as Ryan slid into the booth next to Brynn. He held a twig of mistletoe over her head and gave her a hasty kiss on her cheek.

"Merry Christmas," he said. Brynn flushed again. "My dad brought me here after the party," he added.

Ryan didn't say, "Dropped me off." Kendall looked hopefully toward the bar. Leaning on one of the stools, Nash sat facing her, barely recognizable in corduroy slacks, a beige sweater and a brown leather jacket. He was clean-shaven, his hair trimmed above his collar; she'd never seen him in anything other than his usual Army Surplus attire. Her pulse quickened. She couldn't avoid it any longer—she had to talk to him. She left the booth and stood in front of him, but words wouldn't come, the need to touch him so great that her brain disengaged and her tongue froze to the roof of her mouth.

Instead of complaining because she'd refused his calls and dashed away from him at the station, he grinned and pulled her to him.

"What are you doing New Year's Eve?"

Nash followed her up to her apartment after the party. She made them coffee, and they sat comfortably on the sofa. Kendall loved being close to him, his arm draped around her shoulders, her hand on his chest. Part of her wanted him to rip her clothes off and carry her into the bedroom, but her wiser half enjoyed the nearness, content to delay physical intimacy.

She filled him in on how things had come together in the Glausson case. "You may have heard some of it already, but the latest news is the FBI matched the prints found in Green Bay with one of Jordan's buddies; one of the two he was with when we found him at that bar."

"So it's looking like Jordan only did the Glausson invasion."

"Yes. Now they have to find the guys. They've been out of sight since the day they peeled out of that parking lot. Even their truck hasn't shown up."

"How's Philly doing?" he asked.

"Great. Gray and England have the whole family thing going now. They've scrapped the big, fancy ceremony and upped the wedding plans to February. Hasn't he told you all this?"

"Nah. He doesn't say much about his personal life."

"What about the threats he received? Did he ever find out who shot at him?" Kendall asked.

"The bullet was too mangled to be helpful, but he knows who was behind it—a disgruntled employee. Former employee, now. He decided not to complicate things by filing charges."

"Oh, one more thing," Kendall said. "Brynn's break-in turned out to be random after all. Two teenaged boys copped to it when they were brought in for another one in the area."

"Then I guess it's all wrapped up as much a it's going to be." Nash pulled back and faced her. "We need to talk about us."

Kendall was glad he'd been the one to bring it up, but hated to spoil the mood. "Go ahead."

"You must have heard Shari and I got a divorce. I want you to know it wasn't about you. Not all of it, anyway."

She turned to him. "You don't owe me an explanation. It isn't really my business."

He frowned. "It's going to be. Right?"

"I . . . I hope so." Her pulse fluttered.

"Shari and I, even though we love each other, it hasn't been working. We went to a therapist who finally cleared it up for us, made us realize the bottom line is we can't make each other happy." He drew a deep breath, exhaled. "I had to admit I have feelings for you. Saying it out loud made me realize I couldn't give you up. We decided to call it quits. But I have to tell you that Shari and I will always have a connection. I don't know if you can accept that."

Kendall rose from the couch. She had to be honest, as he'd been with her. "I want you in my life, Nash, but I can't promise it'll never bother me."

He stood and took her in his arms. "You don't have to promise me anything. We can take things one day at a time."

Holding him close, enjoying his male scent, she remembered what Whitehouse told her; Nash would be taking another job. It could mean he'd be leaving.

"Are you going to keep working for Glausson?"

"I will until I decide where to go from here. I'll be a cop again someday, but I want to do undercover. That might mean a bigger city. I'd have to leave Eau Claire."

Kendall wanted to believe his decision depended on her, but it was too soon to discuss their future. They should be deciding things like which movie to watch or whose apartment to spend weekends in.

He'd been upfront with her about everything. Kendall considered telling him about her daughter, then changed her mind. There'd be a better time to tell him.

Made in the USA
San Bernardino, CA
15 June 2015